THE WINTER KILLINGS

WES MARKIN

Boldwood

First published in Great Britain in 2024 by Boldwood Books Ltd.

Copyright © Wes Markin, 2024

Cover Design by Head Design Ltd

Cover Photography: iStock

A CIP catalogue record for this book is available from the British Library.

Paperback ISBN 978-1-80483-788-7

Large Print ISBN 978-1-80483-789-4

Hardback ISBN 978-1-80483-790-0

Ebook ISBN 978-1-80483-787-0

Kindle ISBN 978-1-80483-786-3

Audio CD ISBN 978-1-80483-795-5

MP3 CD ISBN 978-1-80483-794-8

Digital audio download ISBN 978-1-80483-791-7

Boldwood Books Ltd
23 Bowerdean Street
London SW6 3TN
www.boldwoodbooks.com

To Claire and Stuart

PROLOGUE

The vastness. Alive with snowfall.

Such sights!

She peels off her gloves. She reaches out. Cold stabs her fingertips.

Heavy ice crystals, growing heavier.

Spiralling.

White settles on dark.

Dead stars above. Light freed. It reaches her eyes.

Into her.

Around me.

She now belongs.

His noise does not compare to this freedom.

His pleas mean nothing.

The snow blankets him.

The dead of winter.

Snow. Stars. Bitter winds.

* * *

His corpse. Alive with hunger and need.

Watch them eat!
She observes. Sees the scavengers. Cold stabbing teeth.
Vultures pick. Rats gnaw.
She draws closer. Wants to share.
Scavengers depart. The appetites of nature do not care
    for her.
They are blameless.
Never has she felt like this.
Spiralled like this.
Shone like this.
Spring's renewal.
Warm red stone. Feeding insects. Awakening birds.

* * *

His remains. Alive with invisibility.
See the bacteria dissolve him!
She kneels. She surveys. Microorganisms are not for her
    eyes.
The insignificance of human wanting. Not nature's
    concern.
Who can blame it?
Happy in the vastness. Quarry stone beneath her feet.
    Forestry offering isolation.
Cold water down her throat. A shirt stuck to damp skin.
Energy and movement.
Everywhere.
For her, for nature.
Except for him.
His energy is back with the world. His return to nothing at
    an end.
The height of summer.
An overturned cart. Bones. Chains.

* * *

The fields and trees. Alive with colour.
Observe the world reborn!
She touches. She considers. A white shape of nothing on
*   red rocks.*
Dust on dust.
Shortening days. Softening lights.
Energy inside her.
I am reborn!
Evil stripped bare.
Autumn's harvest.
Separation.
A skull with no body. A body with no skull.
The fruits of my labour.

1

While finishing her pint, DCI Emma Gardner regarded the tapestry on the wall in front of her; carefully woven woollen and silken threads depicted Knaresborough Castle. Knights, readied for battle, occupied the scene's foreground.

When her empty pint glass was back down on the solid wood table, she panned her gaze to the bar where her colleague was ordering their next round and smiled. There was nothing Gardner enjoyed more than a mid-week pint or two in an olde-worlde pub.

Having been born and raised in the southern medieval city of Salisbury, rustic drinking holes were part of her *tapestry*. And Blind Jack's, with its beamed ceilings and flagstone floors, reminded her so dearly of home.

The only element that disappointed up here, in Yorkshire, was the ale.

There weren't many ales in the world that stood a chance against Summer Lightning, a golden ale produced locally by Hopback Brewery in Wiltshire. Since being seconded to North Yorkshire eighteen months ago, Gardner had contended with many new flavours before gravitating towards the local delicacy of Yankee – a pale ale brewed by Rooster's Brewing Company. Despite not even coming close to Summer Lightning, she wondered if, in time, she could grow to love it. In the same way she'd come to love Yorkshire itself.

Her thoughts on Salisbury gave her a momentary feeling of homesickness, and she realised then that maybe the choice of ale and décor wasn't the main reason for sudden nostalgia.

Maybe it was the freedom she'd enjoyed back then? To hit the local taverns after a day's graft and dissolve everything into a blur; or shoot ideas back and forth over a current case.

Such freedom, these days, was proving to be *way* out of her budget.

Recently divorced, Gardner was bringing up two young girls. Her eight-year-old daughter, Ana, and her nine-year-old niece, Rose. Although reasonably well-paid as a DCI, her often erratic hours, combined with a lack of any family in the area, made it necessary to employ Monika Kowalska, an au pair from Poland. Add to that, her grace period of accommodation provided for her with her secondment had expired, and rent was through the roof.

Yes, things were bleak, and getting bleaker.

So, five plus pints of beer several nights a week in a pub was an indulgent freedom that was out of the question. *For now,* she thought with a grin, *let's stick with once a week, and see how we go.*

She looked through the window at the monolithic, glamorous tree in the market square, and felt the bubbles of anxiety. The costs associated with entertaining two young children at Christmas were not to be sniffed at.

Really, I shouldn't be here at all, and I wouldn't be if not for—

Lucy O'Brien put the pint glass down in front of Gardner. 'Wonder if this one slips down as quickly as the last one?'

Gardner smiled. 'I'm happy to try it.'

Because there's nothing I enjoy more, Gardner thought, staring into O'Brien's eyes, *than your company right now.*

O'Brien held her gaze and returned the smile, causing Gardner to feel her usual spike of guilt and look away.

O'Brien was late twenties, and so considerably younger than her. She was also a detective constable, which made Gardner her superior.

Two red flags.

Two red flags that were ignored when O'Brien had asked her out for a drink three weeks back.

And had continued to be ignored every week since.

Gardner wasn't gay, had never *considered* herself gay, and still couldn't really believe that this possibility was on the table. But O'Brien's company was having a profound effect on her. It was undeniable. Intoxicating.

And, as for O'Brien, well, she *was* openly gay. She'd also dropped many hints that she'd had a crush on Gardner that she was convinced she wasn't misreading. Whereas flirtatious smiles, brief touches on the arm and long social conversations in her office *could* be passed off as an extremely close friendship, some of O'Brien's most recent moves had just been too telling.

She'd been there for Gardner at every turn.

Every rough turn.

Above and beyond.

Whether that be to provide her with a cereal bar for breakfast in an incident room when Gardner's nights had got late and fraught; or, after the breakdown of her marriage, providing herself as a shoulder to cry on; and, more recently, and far more significantly, taking her children to stay with her sister when Gardner worried that there may be some kind of threat at their own home.

Gardner took a large mouthful of her drink. Three weeks into this social arrangement, she realised Yankee was, in fact, tasting better. 'I could get used to this.'

'The beer?'

'Yes, I—' She broke off after catching O'Brien's raised eyebrow. *What're you implying?* 'But the company stands up too.'

'Glad to hear it.'

Christmas was always impossible to ignore. Whether it was the lit-up tree that dominated the market square, or the tinsel that adorned the old bar, it always found its way to you. Conversation invariably turned in that direction, and when O'Brien said she was spending it alone, Gardner spoke without thinking. 'Monika is going home to Poland. Come and have Christmas dinner with me and the girls.'

Wow... had she really just said that?

She picked up her pint and drank. Several mouthfuls in, she glanced at O'Brien, who was beaming.

What am I doing?

'It really is slipping down faster than the last one, isn't it?' O'Brien said and chuckled.

Gardner put the glass down and looked at it. 'Been a long week. What am I saying? It's always a bloody long—'

She felt O'Brien's fingers on her arm.

Another innocuous touch?

But if so, why am I tingling all over?

'The girls would love it if you came.'

'So would I.'

Shit, Gardner thought, tempted to finish her pint, but holding back, knowing how ridiculous it'd look to throw it back in so short a time.

She smiled at O'Brien.

Intoxication.

What the hell am I doing?

2

Henry Ackroyd had only been here for three days.

He wasn't yet used to the stench of piss, which had made him throw up more than once; or the rising damp, which seemed to reach out and clutch at him like a cold, clammy hand.

Still, Jay had given him some hope. 'If you trust Tommy, if you do as he says, he'll look after you. You'll get used to it all, and you'll enjoy the rewards.'

If anyone would know, then Jay would. He'd been here for a while. At least, he *acted* as if he'd been here a while. Working for Tommy Rose, taking the phone calls, welcoming in the junkies, serving up the product. The job fitted him like a glove.

So, despite his concerns, Henry had remained positive. He'd his brother Archie's advice to thank for that. 'I give them all the same advice first day,' Archie had said when he'd reached the lofty heights of store manager in a local McDonald's. 'You want to keep your job? Best to smile when you serve those burgers. Positivity always wins the race.'

Of course, Henry had known that this was all sanctimonious bullshit. His brother would never have the balls to say such things in the modern world, but the sentiment of what he'd said rang true. And it rang true in a cold house that stank of piss.

Positivity always wins the race.

And when Henry collected his first payment, it'd be more than Archie could ever imagine earning!

Talk about irony.

Henry paced the lounge, burner phone in hand, taking calls. The pacing helped to keep him warm.

He was too cold to sit still on the battered sofa. He regarded the television leaning against the yellowing wall, and the attached PlayStation, and realised he'd never seen them in operation. This job didn't throw up much free time. They worked through the night, serving addicts and rich yuppies.

Sleep when you're dead, not when you can make money.

Besides, 5 a.m. to midday was quiet. Plenty of time to snooze.

He caught a break between phone calls and stood over at the dusty old mantelpiece, observing his face in a cloudy mirror. He wasn't yet out of his twenties, and his hair was already thinning. His brother was five years older and hadn't yet lost a strand.

'Archie the arsehole,' he said and noticed, in the bottom right corner of the mirror, that someone had written their name in the dirt.

Dan.

My predecessor?

On the first evening, Henry had asked Jay what'd happened to his predecessor.

'Just do as Tommy says. Take what he gives you. Nothing more. If you do that, you'll be fine...'

Henry wondered if Dan had ignored Jay's advice. He also wondered, with a shiver running down his spine, whether writing his name in the dirt with his finger was Dan's last act on this earth.

He shrugged, turned and continued to pace. Dan had obviously not done what he'd been told.

He'd nothing to worry about. He'd been following Tommy's rules to the letter. Not that there were many. In fact, there'd only really been one. 'Just do what you've been doing small time, lad. Sell. Except, now, do it big time.'

Henry had been happy to oblige.

And, stinking as it may be, he had a roof over his head, and the promise of a first pay packet in four days. That it was illegal and immoral didn't bother him. His rules for living were simple.

If someone else is prepared to do it, then don't be a dickhead and opt out!

He once had a girlfriend who'd buzzed with morality. He'd watched her turn down well-paid jobs if they weren't ethical enough. That was a lot of jobs.

'Cutting your nose off to spite your face,' he'd told her.

'Get out of my life,' she'd eventually said.

Sod her, he'd thought. *Enjoy being a librarian for the rest of your life.*

And it now seemed like he'd made the right move. *I stand to win big, if I can keep my dinner down, and the hypothermia at bay...*

'Hey.' It was Jay, standing at the lounge door.

Jay came across as a man who'd been in this game a while. Which, according to Henry's calculations, should make him a big winner. Not that he looked, or sounded, like one. With a long, lank mop and uncontrolled facial hair, he cut a dishevelled figure.

In three days, Henry had yet to see him change his clothes.

It was genius, really. If anyone from the law came to the door, would they suspect this man of being a flush dealer? They certainly wouldn't want to get close enough to find out! He stank.

Another thing he'd noticed about Jay was that he drank like a fish. And not just beer, either, but spirits. Morning, noon and night, he'd seen him glugging from vodka bottles at regular intervals.

Henry was no stranger to alcoholics – his father had been one. Men like that couldn't function without high levels of alcohol in their bloodstream. And, with it in their bloodstream, they could give some appearance of normality.

Before you keeled over clutching your rotten stomach, of course. Which his own father had eventually done.

He wondered if Tommy knew about Jay's drinking.

And if he didn't, would he care that one of his most prolific dealers was a high-functioning alcoholic?

As Jay came into the lounge, swigging from a Coke bottle, clearly laced with vodka, Henry wondered if this was an angle he could exploit. Would Tommy *appreciate* the truth? Would Tommy *promote* him to the key man and replace Jay with a new apprentice?

Maybe that's what had happened regarding Dan?

Out with the old... in with the new.

'We're off the clock for one hour,' Jay said. 'Switch off. *Completely.*'

Henry killed his burner. 'Why?'

Jay sat on the battered sofa and sighed. 'Tommy's on his way.'

'Really?'

Jay rubbed his temples. 'He wants us to *do* something.'

Tommy's visit seemed rather sudden.

Shit! Have I cocked up? 'What does he want us to do?' Henry asked.

Jay didn't look up. 'Not sure. But just do as he says, like always, and everything will be fine.'

'Bit out of the blue, though, eh? What does he want?'

Jay looked up at him. His eyes looked tired and worn. Henry noted the sadness in them. Deep, fixed like a scar. 'For you to do your job. What he expects. You're at his beck and call.'

It sounded ominous. He watched Jay drink from his bottle while telling himself: *If someone else is prepared to do it, then don't be a dickhead and opt out!*

'Sounds *exciting.*'

Jay looked at him. He didn't answer, but simply shook his head and then lowered it again.

Maybe exciting was the wrong choice of word. Terrifying might be more appropriate.

Henry took a deep breath. No way was he backing out now.

I'm not cutting my nose off to spite my face.

3

Three pints of Yankee to the good, Gardner felt her worries and inhibitions dissolve.

Her thoughts regarding O'Brien were comforting rather than concerning.

She enjoyed looking into O'Brien's eyes and felt that she could tell her anything.

Which she did.

A traumatised childhood. A family at the mercy of Jack Moss, her younger brother.

'He's missing something.' Gardner pointed at her forehead. 'Something *here*. Something important.'

O'Brien nodded. She wasn't about to disagree. O'Brien had encountered Jack before while looking after his daughter, Rose, and had copped a blow to the head for her troubles.

'The best place for him right now is where he is,' Gardner said, 'in jail.'

So engrossed in her own tale of woe and those steady eyes that seemed to draw every morsel from her, she'd only now noticed that O'Brien was touching the back of her hand.

The front door of the pub burst open. Two middle-aged men,

complete with Santa hats and lopsided Christmas jumpers, stumbled in.

Gardner drew her hand back. 'I'm sorry.'

'Don't be,' O'Brien said. 'You can tell me anything.'

Gardner stared into her eyes again. *I know that. I really do.*

The door opened a second time in as many minutes. This time, a portly pirate strolled in, complete with eye patch.

If it wasn't for the large, wheeled suitcase he dragged, Gardner would've feared that she'd just slipped through a crack in time.

A woman, who was taller and, thankfully, dressed in more modern attire to bring Gardner back to reality, followed him in with another suitcase. They both went to the bar.

She flashed a look at O'Brien, who laughed.

'Your face!' O'Brien said.

'Have you not seen the pirate?'

'It's Robert Thwaites. He's local.'

'Is it not a bit late for a children's party?'

O'Brien laughed again. 'He's a storyteller. A very animated one, too.' She waved her arms. 'All grand gestures.' She patted her chest. 'And booming voices. Those suitcases are full of props.' She nodded at the couple at the foot of the stairs. 'That's his glamorous wife, Cassandra. Used to be the Avon lady around these parts.'

'An Avon lady! Bloody hell! I'm surprised you even know what an Avon lady is!'

'I'm not bloody Gen Z! The Avon ladies were still going door to door when I was a kid. These are the wilds of Yorkshire, remember? Took us a lot longer than you southerners to climb out of the Dark Ages and migrate to the joys of online purchasing.' O'Brien patted Gardner's arm and raised an eyebrow towards the stairs. 'Want to watch?'

'A retelling of *Treasure Island*?'

'One of my favourite books growing up...'

'Yes, even so, an adult pantomime or real ale and grown-up conversation?'

'Shouldn't knock it until you try it. Notice how busy it's getting.'

Gardner listened; the noise of conversations from the back room and the clinking of glasses was louder. Telling her *own* story, a very different story from *Treasure Island*, although potentially filled with as much drama, had distracted her from witnessing how quickly Blind Jack's could fill up. 'This Thwaites must be quite the draw.'

O'Brien laughed. 'Maybe. More likely, you're in Yorkshire. And here people are a sucker for free entertainment.'

Gardner was about to point out that there was nothing free about entertainment when the ale might as well be acid poured onto your disposable income, when her phone buzzed in her pocket.

'I'm sorry,' Gardner said, reaching for her phone. 'Might be about the kids.'

'No need to apologise.'

'When I was your age, hardly anyone looked at their phone while in conversation.'

'You sound like my mother.'

That's probably because I'm old enough to be her!

This thought concerned her, momentarily, but after reading the text message, it became the furthest thing from her mind.

She rose to her feet.

'Are you okay?' O'Brien asked.

No.

Gardner's heart thrashed in her chest. 'I've got to make a call... I'm sorry.'

As Gardner headed for the exit, she reread the message again:

I think I've found him. Phone me.

4

_____

If someone else is prepared to do it, then don't be a dickhead and opt out!

These words were now replaying on an endless loop in Henry's mind. But, for the first time in his life, they weren't helping.

Tommy Rose's instruction had knocked him sideways.

'Maybe someone else could do it? Someone who understands it better than me?' Henry pleaded.

Deaf ears.

Tommy was a beast of a man with a flattened nose and dead eyes. He didn't do conversations, and he certainly didn't answer questions.

Tommy simply repeated his instruction. 'I want you to do this.'

Beside him, Jay, who faced the same instruction, looked nonchalant. These instructions hadn't surprised him. Either all the piss he'd been drinking had numbed him, or he was simply used to performing such favours.

No... I can't... Henry stood. 'There's a line.'

Tommy moved aside and nodded at the door to show that it was just fine to use it and leave.

Shit! Did that mean he would be leaving empty-handed? 'I've been here three days.'

Tommy nodded.

'I've sold a lot.' Henry felt overwhelmed. Disappointed. There'd been so much hope in his current employment.

'A shame. You showed promise.' Tommy reached into his pocket and pulled out a large bundle of notes.

Henry's heart fluttered. That was probably more money than his sanctimonious brother would earn in a year! That could set him up good and proper...

Tommy slid off the elastic and peeled off some notes. He leaned over the coffee table and dropped a couple of fifty-pound notes in front of him. They nestled between two loaded syringes.

Is that it?

'Three days!' Dangerous to speak your mind when Tommy Rose was involved, but Henry couldn't keep it in. 'That's not even minimum wage.'

'That's your earnings minus my costs for finding you, for housing you, for training you.'

You found me in a nightclub dealing pills... you housed me in a rotten shithole... and what bloody training? He didn't speak his thoughts this time – they'd be too inflammatory.

Inwardly sighing, he glanced down and let his hand hover over the money and the needles...

Sterile needles.

Both Tommy and Jay had assured him of this.

If someone else is prepared to do it, then don't be a dickhead and opt out!

His hand initially descended towards the money, before changing trajectory towards one syringe... You can't get addicted just doing it the once, can you?

He flicked his eyes over to Jay. His drawn, emaciated face and hollow eyes acted as a warning.

But it won't be just the once, will it? Tommy will ask you to test it again and again.

Do you want to be a human guinea pig, Henry? The last line of defence between the production line and the disappointed punters?

No, this wasn't for him.

He opted for the money, brushed past Jay's legs and circled the left side of the coffee table, and did a full loop of the lounge in order to give Tommy a wide berth.

As he neared the door, he glanced at the paltry sum of cash in his hand, and the disappointment he felt was crushing.

Only earlier, he'd thought, he'd believed, that he'd one foot back up on the ladder of life. That he'd soon be looking down at his brother on a lower rung.

He glanced back at Jay, who'd already tied his upper arm, and was prepping a vein with two fingers.

If someone else is prepared to do it...

No... no...

He forced himself onwards, but inches from the door, he saw that smiling ex-girlfriend. The librarian for life. 'Now who's cutting their nose off?'

He lowered his head, shook it and sighed. Then he turned back in time to see Jay close his eyes and slump back on the sofa. The used needle hanging from his arm.

Henry recalled the bundle of notes that had just come out of Tommy's pocket. The bundle which had almost stopped his heart.

There was promise and hope in this room.

And money.

He turned and headed back to the sofa, determined to keep climbing this ladder. 'Okay,' he said. 'Just this once.'

As he returned to the sofa, he expected to catch a grin on Tommy's face. A smug reaction to his employee's lack of willpower.

But there was nothing. Just a stony expression, and then a swift nod when Henry picked up the needle and sat back down.

5

I think I've found him. Phone me.

I would if I could get through! Gardner thought, yanking up the hood on her ski jacket to cut off the sudden snowfall before hitting redial.

Voicemail again.

'Shit!'

Relentlessly, she continued to circle the Christmas tree in the market square, her face burning with cold, pounding her phone.

Voicemail. Voicemail. Voicemail.

A teenage couple with matching Christmas bobble hats who were only moments ago lost in each other's eyes looked up at her from a bench with concerned expressions.

Piss off. I know you think I'm a casualty of mulled wine, but that really isn't it.

She turned and paced back the other way, wiping snow from the phone screen with her sleeve.

Okay... one last try... I promise... come on... Cecile... pick up... pick—

'Emma, I'm sorry—' Cecile Metcalf's voice crackled. Her last words were cut off.

'Cecile?'

The line was dead. Gardner looked up at the stars. 'Could you give me a break?' Snow stung her eyes.

Breaking her promise, she tried again. Her frustration was intensifying. Her erratic stomping had scared the young lovers away, so she sat down on the bench beside a statue of Old Mother Shipton and stared at her phone screen.

She opened her mouth to swear, but then her screen lit up with a message.

Cecile!

> I'm sitting on a house in the arsehole of nowhere. Reception is crap. Hope this finds a way through. I didn't want to give you half a story...

Having exceeded its characters, the message had broken. The other element was awaiting reception and a tower to bounce off. 'Give me strength!'

Cecile Metcalf was a former detective inspector, who'd been one of Gardner's mentors during the earlier stages of her career in Wiltshire. After a heart attack in her forties, she'd decided life was just too short for what she called 'the excessive male-dominated bureaucracy' and had taken early retirement. This was over ten years ago. Since then, Cecile had built a successful business offering investigation services for finding people. It was popular with estranged siblings who'd lost one another, or families torn apart by overseas conflict.

Her results spoke for themselves; she was highly skilled.

And, to Gardner, her services were free.

They'd remained close friends, and in constant contact since Cecile retired, and when she'd heard Gardner's tale of woe of a lost colleague, she'd offered her help.

At first, Gardner had refused because she wanted to keep it off the books. But Cecile had offered to keep it discreet and take the case herself rather than use any of her many staff. Gardner had still refused because Cecile was getting too old for long trips and surveillance. But Gardner was also desperate and, eventually, Cecile's insistence broke through what was, ultimately, a very fragile resistance.

Her phone beeped. The message was complete. She read on:

> ...and get your hopes up. I'm sending an image of the man I found. He's in this house. I'll give it one more hour and then I'll drive home and phone you. C x

She double checked her messages, but knew already that no photo had come through, or was likely to – not until Cecile got some better reception.

One hour.

How the hell do I stay calm for one more hour?

Well, she could start with the alcoholic beverages behind the bar in Blind Jack's.

And, if she suddenly had to go anywhere, she could get a taxi.

Inside, O'Brien smiled up at her while simultaneously pointing at a fresh pint that awaited her.

Gardner smiled back, and their eyes locked. But now the eye contact quickly became awkward.

She averted her eyes, wondering if she was just being emotional because of Cecile's discoveries. But that wasn't the entire story, was it?

A wave of sadness washed over her because she knew, at this very moment, that she could no longer allow this to develop into something inappropriate and unprofessional.

No more playing, Emma. She wants more, and you can't give it to her.

It had to end tonight.

'Everything okay? You looked stressed out before.'

'Yes... Rose had a temperature,' Gardner lied. 'Monika just thought it best to clear the Calpol with me first.'

'I see.'

Then she sat down and drank deeply, trying to shift away the emotions clouding her, but it was probably useless.

Other than her children, there were two people she cared for deeply in this world.

A young woman, with warm eyes, and a beautiful heart that she'd have to break.

And an impetuous ex-alcoholic who'd vanished without a trace.

The only way out of this was a complete distraction. 'Actually, I think I'd like to check out the storyteller.'

6

Before the needle, he'd felt cold.

Not just from the lack of warmth in the room, but also from the events playing out in front of him.

Watching the new boy, Henry Ackroyd, flounder at Tommy's request, was a hard watch. Henry was only in his twenties. He'd every right to flounder. Listen to his gut and run.

However, after the needle, a warm flush washed away the cold, and the sinking began. Henry and Tommy's standoff dissolved into atoms. He made a deep descent away from the brightness, away from a frantic place of worry, doubt and crushing pain, into a slower place. A shallow, smooth and silent void in which he could float.

Time had lost relevance.

Moments he loved had no longer ended.

And yet, even in this void, it felt tangible.

His daughters, Molly and Lucy.

His wife, Rachel.

His mentor, Anders.

His young friend, Arthur.

Tangible.

Maybe it wasn't a void after all?

Maybe DI Paul Riddick had returned to a world he no longer had.

And right at this moment, he didn't have to worry about staying or going.

Because it simply was.

7

To his credit, the storyteller's skills extended beyond fancy dress.

However, Gardner's mind was too plagued for focus, and Robert Thwaites, despite his athletic prancing, repertoire of facial expressions and a booming voice threatening to make the wooden beams in the ceiling drop, failed to entertain her.

Robert had commandeered the corner of the upstairs back room. It limited his show to a small treasure chest perched on a table, that he circled as he told his tale, pausing every now and again to jab and sweep at the air with a fake cutlass.

There were two filled tables and the remaining spectators stood. Fifteen patrons, including Robert's wife, ex-Avon lady, Cassandra, who stood directly to the left of Gardner and O'Brien.

And what a time she was having!

She stared doe-eyed at her husband as he performed, her mouth moving in sync with the words he used. She looked like a teenage girl at a boy band concert!

'Around me, around the cove,' Robert stage whispered, moving closer to his small crowd. 'Lay the bones of the greedy. Stark warnings to the likes of' – he narrowed his unpatched eye and moved it closer to a middle-aged man as if to examine him – 'the foolhardy.'

The audience laughed. So did the middle-aged man, although the sudden glow in his cheeks betrayed his embarrassment.

What a bloody pantomime.

Gardner looked at O'Brien who was laughing – surely she was faking amusement?

When she turned her attention back to the eccentric thespian, she felt O'Brien's fingers stroking her own.

And then the dam that had kept her concerns and doubts penned back for the last couple of months finally collapsed.

She closed her hand into her fist and pulled it away. She then looked at her colleague apologetically. 'We can't do this.'

O'Brien's face dropped.

Gardner opened her mouth to apologise, only for the storyteller to pick up volume. 'Remember, patrons, this is an isle forsaken by men and maps. Many suspected, but never really knew, if Valentina's curse was indeed a great bounty, or a trap ready to claim their lives. Do you not recall, mates, the warnings that it was her enduring love and passion for someone she could never have that led to her downfall? How could anyone trust such a great treasure?'

Gardner was glad she'd been interrupted by the thespian; her apology would surely have been pathetic.

She took a deep breath to stem the inner turmoil she was feeling while the tale of this old seadog's adventures continued in a swashbuckling, grandiose fashion. And, although the surrounding punters were lapping it up, expressing themselves with guffaws and the occasional cheer, Gardner become more and more tempted to remove herself from the pub.

But when she glanced at the sadness in O'Brien's face again, she decided that leaving now would only intensify her disappointment and the embarrassment. So, she drank from her pint glass, hoping that more alcohol would steady her need to flee.

'...and it was this dream that told me that the treasure... the vast treasure... had been tucked within a chapel ruin.' He swigged ale from another of his props – a tarnished metal tankard. He purposefully let the ale run down over his chin and down his front.

Cue more raucous guffaws.

'And naught but silence and spiders guarded it.'

While Robert mimicked the creak of the chapel doors, the skitter of the spiders and the sound of his own steps, Gardner leaned over to O'Brien's ear and whispered, 'Let's go down; we need to talk.'

'I want to watch the show,' O'Brien whispered. She didn't turn to look at Gardner.

I've hurt her. 'Okay... after?'

'I thought you might have somewhere to be.' O'Brien didn't bother whispering this time.

There was a woman's voice behind Gardner. 'Shhh... I'm trying to listen.'

'Sorry,' Gardner whispered over her shoulder, without looking back to see the offended party.

'My hands,' the storyteller continued, holding them up to his audience. 'My hands, gnarled as the ancient driftwood that lines the shores of this isle.' He turned from the audience and went around the side of the table, and to another prop: a wooden treasure chest. 'My hands hovered above the bounty, the curse...' He raised an eyebrow and turned to smirk at the small crowd. 'The mystery.'

There were murmurs of excitement from several of the listeners. Gardner was desperate to move to O'Brien's ear again and whisper more apologies. But not only would she incur more wrath from O'Brien, but she now had a frustrated patron just behind her too.

Gardner felt her stomach cramp. She dealt with the discomfort with two mouthfuls of ale.

Robert still had his hands over his fake treasure chest, and was letting them quiver dramatically, as if it was a source of supernatural energy. Gardner suddenly felt irritated by him.

She closed her eyes and took another deep breath. *Give him a break, Emma.* Yes, this wasn't her bag, but her irritation was because of her own conduct this evening and not this well-meaning showman.

She opened her eyes and cast another glance at O'Brien, who still looked annoyed, and then over to Cassandra. Her hand was to her mouth as if the tension over what was in the chest was tearing her in two. Ridiculous really from someone who must have seen this performance a thousand times.

Again, harsh, Emma!

This was a family business – Cassandra probably considered it a job to help with the atmosphere. If she was kicking back at the bar, drinking the profits and rolling her eyes, wouldn't that be more ridiculous?

Finally, Robert moved his bloody hands down to the treasure chest and traced the cheap stainless-steel latches. He suddenly looked up, wide-eyed. 'Hear that thunder! Believe me all – the curse is real! A storm had arrived that could sink a thousand ships.' He held a finger in the air. 'Never again would I underestimate the power of unrequited love, and neither should you.' He lowered his finger, took a loud deep breath and closed his eyes. 'And then, I doubted whether I could go on. Something was not as it should be. My memories of that story. Of Captain Raphael Duarte's head being torn from his shoulders. All semblance of God was gone from Valentina's world. What was I doing here? At the bounty of evil?' He flicked back one of two latches. 'And yet I couldn't stop myself. The mystery was too great. What had the wretched pirate queen placed in here before her final breath?' His hand hovered over the second latch. He looked at the audience. 'You...' He pointed at the man he'd embarrassed earlier. 'Would you've opened it?'

'No,' the man said, laughing nervously, and looking at his partner.

'Not even for riches and rewards? I think the chance of the abyss may be a risk worth taking. I opened it... Do you wish to know what I found?'

'Yes,' the man said meekly, looking awkward. Gardner saw his partner nudge him. 'I do. Yes, I do!' the man said, loudly, forced to enter into the spirit of the thing before shaming him and his wife.

Gardner's phone buzzed in her pocket.

'Now... we must all be silent,' Robert boomed.

Gardner took her phone from her pocket. The image from Cecile had arrived.

'So, I flicked the second latch.' He gasped. 'All the while contemplating what awaited me. Jewels... gold... coins?'

Gardner had to force back a gasp of her own as she stared at the photograph of a dishevelled, emaciated man sitting on a garden wall of a decrepit terrace house, swigging from a Coke bottle. His hair was long, and he was unshaven, but it was unmistakably him.

'Or would this lost soul, consumed by her own darkness, have left a void?' A thumping sound made Gardner flinch and she looked up. Robert bashed his own chest. 'My heart was thrashing.'

Exactly how I feel.

It was him. Riddick.

Her mind whirred. She didn't know what she felt.

Relief that she'd found him?

Despair over the fact that he looked more broken than ever?

Robert threw back the lid of the chest.

Riddick was alive... he was *alive... alive*!

'It was the head!' Robert shouted, reaching into the chest. 'The missing head... Captain Raphael Duarte's head!'

There were murmurs of astonishment from the crowd.

Gardner leaned over to O'Brien, who looked as far removed from the tension and drama in the performance as anyone could be. 'I've got to go... Sorry, something incredibly urgent—'

'Shit... Christ,' Robert hissed. 'Shit!'

Gardner turned in time to see Robert pulling a skull from the chest before recoiling, releasing the grip on his prop. It fell back into the chest with a clatter.

There were more gasps and guffaws from the crowd over Robert's revelation.

However, the image of her wasted former colleague hunched over on a garden wall completely distracted Gardner. She desperately needed to get out of here. 'I'm sorry, Lucy.' She turned to leave.

Robert's voice was growing in volume. As were the number of obscenities used. 'What the hell? What the hell is that doing in there?'

Realising Robert had clearly slipped out of character, Gardner swung back in time to see him throw himself back against the wall, staring wide-eyed at the treasure chest.

Gardner felt her instincts kicking in.

Something's very wrong here.

But the crowd didn't think so. They were enjoying his performance of shock and horror, clapping and guffawing.

The drama hadn't been this good before; nowhere near. To go up so many notches in quality could mean only one thing...

She confirmed it by looking over at Cassandra. Gone were the doe-eyes and the fangirl response. She, too, was stunned.

'That's a real sodding skull!' Robert shouted.

Confirmation...

Gardner marched over to the treasure chest and stared down.

Indeed, the skull was no cheap prop.

She turned and watched Robert edging around the wall, past the window, which showed the market square Christmas tree in all its glory, to Cassandra's side. 'That's not mine... I didn't put that in there...' he shouted over to Gardner.

The noise from the crowd quietened. The penny was dropping.

She turned and saw one old couple still clapping at the table. Robert Thwaites looked like he was going to keel over from a heart attack, for pity's sake!

And Gardner, herself, had just broken the fourth wall.

Gardner, who still had her phone in her hand, exchanged it for her badge in her pocket. She held it up. 'DCI Emma Gardner.'

Silence descended, but people still glanced at one another, perhaps confused over whether this was part of the show.

It'd be a very random show, Gardner thought. 'I'd like everybody to go downstairs please, quietly, and slowly. Nobody is to leave.'

'It's not mine!' Robert said, plucking off his eye patch.

Gardner looked at O'Brien. 'Detective Constable, can you stay with the remains while I make the calls?'

'Remains?' Cassandra gasped.

O'Brien nodded. 'Yes, boss.'

8

Henry Ackroyd made a horrendous groaning noise.

It pulled Riddick from his semi-conscious state and he turned his head.

Beside him, Henry thrashed about.

Riddick tried to reach out, but his arm was slow to respond. By the time he was close enough, Henry's convulsions had pitched him forward from the sofa.

There was a loud cracking sound.

He'd hit the edge of the coffee table before rolling off it onto his back.

'Shit,' Riddick murmured as the world spun around him. He leaned forward, but coordination was an issue, and he didn't want to end up the same way as Henry, so he eased himself down to his knees between the sofa and the table.

He took a deep breath. *Steady yourself, Paul.* He exhaled and took another breath. The world was spinning, and he could so easily let himself fall back into that void, but he had to keep going. Henry was young. *And I allowed this to happen.*

He reached out again. This time his hand fell to one of the lad's legs. Henry, who was lying on his back, didn't respond.

Riddick tried shaking him but wasn't sure if he'd put enough energy into it to register.

Damn it, you old dickhead. Move yourself.

Feeling close to vomiting now, Riddick worked his way between the sofa and the edge of the coffee table, until he had more space. He couldn't measure the time it'd taken to achieve this, but he eventually made it to Henry's side.

Oh God.

The gash in the centre of Henry's forehead looked severe. Blood ran over his pale face, mingling with the white froth that oozed from the sides of his mouth.

He knew Tommy was there, watching. 'He needs... help... quickly.' It surprised him he got the words out. 'Please.'

Riddick slumped to his side now beside the motionless man. He wanted to lift himself up, feel for Henry's pulse, maybe get a phone call off to the emergency services, but the floor seemed to suck him down, not allowing him to move.

He glanced towards Tommy standing above them now, looking down.

'He... needs... help,' Riddick managed.

'He's past that,' Tommy said.

'Phone...'

'Who?'

'Help.'

'You're out of your mind! You've forgotten what's in this house?'

Riddick couldn't find the energy to respond. A good thing. Right now, his world may have been fragmented, but one thing was still clear. Demanding that Tommy invited emergency services to one of his main cribs was suicidal. Watching Henry lose his life was soul-destroying, but it'd surely cost both their lives if he pressed this issue.

Riddick closed his eyes, shutting out the swirl.

Tommy said, 'Seems I was right to be concerned about this

batch. It's fried the both of you. I'll maybe cut it some more and let Taz and Sonia give it a whirl. But you've worried me, Jay, with your sentiment. You know what we've got coming in this week.'

Riddick tried to say, 'Sorry... everything lost focus,' but he wasn't sure if he got the words out. He hoped he had done. This was all he had left, and he needed it.

He closed his eyes and fell back into nothing.

9

Blind Jack's attracted attention. Mainly from drunken locals staggering home from other pubs. Despite being below his paygrade, DI Phil Rice took on the task of waving on the rubberneckers with relish; he always enjoyed the opportunity to demonstrate his power.

The residents of Knaresborough knew Rice as a no-nonsense copper. He genuinely believed that being part of law enforcement meant that you were on one side of a great war. Although Rice would never admit to it, he believed war needed a healthy dose of testosterone, and a complete absence of modern-day bureaucracy and political correctness.

As a result, Gardner worked hard to keep him in check. She could chalk it up as a success to date. Frequently, he'd proven his hidden efficiencies.

And to be fair, the way he waved on the rubberneckers with perfect ease was commendable.

There was, of course, a notable exception. A group of off-the-rails local kids watching intently from the sides of the Christmas tree. Rice's evil eye had no impact on the new gen, of course. They knew a more rigorous system protected them than their predecessors and didn't know what Rice's desired 1970s approach to policing looked like.

As Rice wielded his axe, Gardner hopped from foot to foot to keep warm, while forensics went about their business indoors. It was a small public house, after all. The fewer trampling around in there, the better.

They'd already confirmed and recorded the identity of every person in the public house this evening, and after being warned that they may be contacted over the next couple of days, they'd long since made their journeys home.

'Are you pissed, boss?' Rice asked, approaching Gardner.

'I'm certainly pissed off that you just asked me that.'

'Fair question; you were in the pub...'

She held up three fingers. 'Three pints of ale, Phil.' It was four, but she preferred to keep ammunition from a cut-throat soldier like Rice.

'Ale? Really?' He looked intrigued.

She scowled. 'You really are from the Dark Ages.'

'You just didn't strike me as the ale type.'

'This is 2024. It's a fact that women can acquire the taste for hops too.'

He held up his hands. 'Don't know where you get these ideas from, boss. I just saw you as sophisticated, more of a prosecco drinker.'

'Prosecco... sophisticated... Jesus wept. The kids bloody drink it these days!'

'Did someone say prosecco?' Ray Barnett said, coming up alongside his two colleagues.

'You like prosecco?' Rice asked.

Barnett, a tall, black DS, was a fourth dan in jujitsu, who threw weights around for fun; she imagined protein shakes were more his thing.

'Partial to a glass... or two on a Friday,' Barnett said and winked. 'Why?'

Rice shook his head, looking disgusted.

Gardner snorted. 'You've just shattered one of his many stereotypes. Sophisticated middle-aged women drink prosecco. Not men. And certainly not strong ones.'

'Bollocks,' Rice said, frowning. 'I don't think that. And I never said Ray was strong.'

'Let's not forget Phil also thinks three pints of ale is a lot for a wee lassie,' Gardner continued, glancing at Ray.

'Did I say that?' Rice asked. 'How did you work all this out? By the way I walk? Sherlock Holmes you aren't, boss.'

Gardner kept her eyes on Barnett and raised her eyebrow.

'No comment,' Barnett said. 'But I've requested the CCTV footage from behind the library.'

Robert and Cassandra had already informed them that someone had broken into their car behind the library while they'd been indulging in pre-show drinks at another local pub called Six Poor Folk. This, Robert believed, was the only way the skull could have ended up inside the fake treasure chest. 'When I packed earlier,' Robert had said to Gardner, 'it was a plastic skull in there. Someone must have planted it after smashing the car window.'

Barnett looked at his notes. 'And I've got more information on Robert and Cassandra Thwaites.'

Gardner listened as Barnett went through the extra information on Robert, who she'd only briefly questioned. He'd been rather stunned by the experience, so Gardner was planning to follow up back at his house in a short while.

Rice stopped him mid-flow. 'He's a commercial solicitor?'

Barnett nodded. 'Was... yes... retired a good while back, when he was fifty-five. He's been doing this show lark for over ten years!'

'The man is a bloody ageing hippy!' Rice said.

Gardner rolled her eyes. 'He's a storyteller.'

'Storyteller, thespian, hippy...'

'Being arty doesn't make you a hippy.'

'Maybe not,' Rice conceded. 'But it doesn't really make you a commercial solicitor either. How many artistic lawyers do you know?'

'None that I know of,' Gardner said. 'But I don't have a large sample of lawyers in my friendship group, and those I have, have never disclosed their artistic interests to me.'

Rice grinned. 'Because they don't have any.'

'Hmm,' Barnett said, 'I've met several lawyers who could spin a good yarn to be fair.'

'True enough,' Gardner said.

Ignoring the irritation on Rice's face, Gardner requested Barnett continue.

'Sixty-five, and Robert shows no sign of slowing down. He's built himself up quite a name as a storyteller, employed by festivals and events. He's branched out into making audiobooks for authors.'

'These artistic types keep themselves busy,' Gardner said, unable to resist baiting Rice a little. This was out of character for her; maybe, she was spreading irritation around because of how she currently felt regarding the Riddick and O'Brien situations.

She wouldn't be sharing the revelation that Riddick was alive with these two men around her. Rice, for a start, despised Riddick. And that feeling was very mutual. Rice and Riddick had come to blows on the roof of Harrogate hospital shortly before Riddick's disappearance. Rice was adamant he'd been there to help Riddick, who was reasoning with a murderer and flirting with danger. Riddick had held Rice responsible for the murderer's subsequent suicide and had rained fury down on him. The murderer had been a vulnerable young man with learning difficulties who Riddick had befriended and been trying desperately to save.

Barnett had always liked Riddick, more so than Rice, anyway, although that really said little. Most people liked Chief Constable

Rebecca 'Harsh' Marsh more than Rice and that was bloody saying something! Rumour had it that Marsh kept a box hidden in her office, which contained countless police IDs – memorabilia from all the careers she'd ended.

'Like a serial killer's trophy cabinet,' Riddick had said to her when they'd first met.

Utter bullshit, of course, but it gave you the flavour of her popularity.

So, even though Rice was less popular than Marsh, which beggared belief, Gardner persisted. She just couldn't let go of the feeling that there was a decent officer in there waiting to break free from the chains of his masculinity and shackles of narrow-mindedness.

There'd been glimpses.

Although, when it was cold, and the snow was coming down hard, as it was doing now, positivity and optimism often took a back seat...

After Barnett had given a potted background on Cassandra Thwaites, which included the illustrious career path with Avon, Gardner heard her name being called. She turned to see Robin Morton, the forensic pathologist, coming towards her from the front of Blind Jack's. The swirling snow immediately went to work on her paper suit, and she was shivering by the time she got to them. She'd obviously peeled off her outdoor jacket and left it indoors.

Gardner unzipped her jacket, intending to offer it, but Barnett had already beaten her to it and was draping his own over Robin's shoulders. Robin smiled up at Barnett. 'Thanks.'

Gardner glanced at Rice, who'd certainly not unzipped his own jacket. He'd a sneer on his face. No doubt considering Barnett's act of kindness an act of flirtation.

It was rather concerning to Gardner how well she could read him now, and yet, even though she knew what she was up against, she persisted in trying to chisel something out of him.

'Good news, Robin?' Gardner asked, knowing already that there wouldn't be. Earlier, Robin had informed her about this. Old remains were fiddly and often took a long time.

'I can't confirm much without a forensic anthropologist,' Robin said. 'Only that it's adult.'

'We work well with gut feelings,' Barnett said and smiled.

She grinned up at Barnett.

God... they *were* bloody flirting!

Well, at least it may loosen her lips...

'Probably male,' Robin said, and touched the back of her head. 'The external occipital protuberance is very large.'

'The *what*?' Rice asked.

'That bump at the lower rear of your head. It tends to be more prominent in males. There are other markers like that – the angled forehead, the lower cheekbones... but please... I can't offer a guarantee.'

'Age?' Rice asked.

Barnett flashed Rice a look which clearly said: did you not just hear what she said?

Don't start defending her, Ray... Gardner thought. *You must know that Rice wouldn't have any hesitation in calling you out on a crush. Could be very embarrassing.*

'Not old, but I'm guessing some way past middle age. There's been some teeth loss, and some resorption of the jawbone, but again, this is purely conjecture right now. You're only likely to get an age range from the forensic anthropologist. Best guess on my limited expertise would be fifty-plus, male. The post-mortem interval is a nightmare from skulls, though. It's better with the rest of the body. Even with the best in the business, this one is going to be frustrating.'

Gardner nodded.

'Fiona would like to speak to you,' Robin said, smiling.

Gardner looked up at the entrance to Blind Jack's. She'd already greeted Chief Forensic Officer Fiona Lane tonight, but their last meeting two weeks ago had been awkward.

Fiona and Gardner had become friends in the eighteen months following Gardner's secondment up north. Gardner had, under the influence of red wine, confided in Fiona about her growing affection towards O'Brien, hoping for some light advice. What she'd received had verged on outrage and a firm warning that this couldn't possibly end well for Gardner.

Over the weeks since, Gardner, feeling irritated, had avoided Fiona like the plague. She was only now realising that she was being grossly unfair. Fiona had been right and had simply fallen victim to a projection of Gardner's own messed-up emotions.

Still, Gardner was in no mood for it right now. 'What's it about?' Gardner asked, hoping she could bypass the awkwardness.

'I found a folded note in the skull's jaw...'

'A what?' Gardner said, stunned she was only just learning about this. This wasn't something that was going to be bypassed. 'What did it say?'

Robin shrugged; Barnett's large coat slipped from one shoulder. Barnett, himself, reached over to slip it back up for her. 'I don't know. I didn't open it. Fiona took it and told me to get you.'

Bloody hell. In I go then.

Gardner looked between her colleagues' intrigued faces. 'Wait here.'

Rice groaned in disappointment.

'Phil, I need you to get the car ready to drive us to the Thwaites'. Robert has had enough time to settle his nerves.'

She looked back at Barnett who, despite looking disappointed, at least didn't groan. 'Ray, please press on with the CCTV.'

She went back into Blind Jack's and over to O'Brien. She'd volunteered to log everyone in. Unnecessary, because someone of lower rank could have taken the job, but she'd been first on the scene, literally, and felt some responsibility for it. Professionally, but coldly, O'Brien logged Gardner in and handed her a suit.

'Are you okay?' Gardner asked.

'Yes, boss, of course,' O'Brien said, without looking up from the logbook and meeting her eyes.

Gardner looked both ways, checking she could whisper without it entering someone's earshot. She leaned in. 'We need to talk. Properly. I think there have been... some... well... some misunderstandings?'

'Everything seems clear enough,' O'Brien said, looking up now.

Shit. If this was a bowling alley, she'd just missed the pins for the umpteenth time.

It always surprised Gardner that for someone who ran an incident room so effectively, she could turn her own personal life into such a circus.

Maybe she should try to be open and honest for a change. 'I was shocked before, when I got that message because... he's been found.' Gardner shook her head.

'Who?'

'Paul.'

O'Brien's eyes widened. 'Alive?'

'Yes.'

O'Brien reached out and took Gardner's arm. 'Why didn't you say?'

The physical contact immediately brought a tear to the DCI's eye. 'I still don't know enough about it.'

'Are you okay, Emma?' O'Brien said, all attitude gone. 'Do you need me—'

'DCI Gardner?'

Gardner slipped her arm away from O'Brien who, fortunately, had already loosened her grip. She turned to look at her estranged close friend, Fiona Lane. She could tell from her darkened expression that the intimate moment between a superior and a younger officer hadn't gone unnoticed. 'Yes... sorry, Fiona. I believe there's a note?'

Fiona looked at O'Brien and then back at Gardner. Gardner wasn't sure if she was making a point that she needed some privacy or was simply reinforcing her view that this whole scenario was ludicrous and a train about to go off the rails.

'Lucy is okay to hear. What did the note say, please?'

'It was a printed note. It said: *Why don't you tell a true story, Robert?*'

Gardner took a deep breath.

'We'll get the note tested for DNA,' Fiona added.

'Thanks.'

'What do you think it means, boss?' O'Brien asked.

Gardner looked between her two colleagues, thinking. 'Well, the true story is not Valentina's curse... so, we'd best ask the great storyteller himself, hadn't we?'

10

'Staring at a phone screen doesn't make it ring,' Rice said from the driver's seat.

Gardner, who was desperate to hear from Cecile regarding Riddick, ignored her assistant SIO's sarcasm, and slipped her phone back into her jacket pocket. 'Don't want to miss a beat,' she lied. 'You know how fast Ray can be. He'll have that CCTV before we know it.'

'Yes... about that...'

'Go on.'

'Doesn't it sound far-fetched to you?' Rice indicated to turn off Bond End onto the Waterside. 'Someone smashing a car window and then replacing a plastic skull with a real one?'

She stared out of the window at the River Nidd, the mystical ribbon which wound its way through medieval Knaresborough. During the day, a scenic destination as it flowed serenely beneath the arches of the venerable viaduct; late at night, in the nocturnal stillness, a timeless guardian of Knaresborough's centuries of secrets.

'What's your working theory?' Gardner asked, eyes hypnotised by the moonlit river. 'That Robert did this to himself? Pulled out the skull of his victim for everyone to see?'

Doesn't sound plausible either, does it?

'Maybe his wife put it there? The remains of the person he was having an affair with?'

Gardner snorted. 'You writing a book now, Phil? Besides, you heard Robin, it was probably a male.'

'So,' Rice said. 'Why can't he be having an affair with a man?' Rice looked at her with a raised eyebrow.

Fair point. 'I'm glad you called me out on that assumption. Shows I'm getting somewhere with you at last.'

It was his turn to snort.

'But, no, she didn't know either. I saw her eyes... her expression... Cassandra Thwaites was as stunned as her husband was.'

Rice swore and suddenly slowed. He moved to one side for two staggering idiots. 'Get some bloody hi-vis jackets, you dickheads.'

Gardner enquired about the reason behind his constant anger.

He grunted indignantly, turned left up a steep driveway and parked alongside the police vehicle that had brought the couple home.

'Always wondered who lived here,' Rice said, eyeing the large house, perching high on the Waterside. 'Never guessed it'd be an oral storyteller and the Avon lady.'

Gardner gazed over the fusion of modern and traditional, impressed with the multi-paned sash windows, and the staggering views it must surely offer. She pulled out her notebook and scribbled in a reminder to get a comprehensive list of all the businesses Robert had acted on behalf of during his days as a commercial solicitor.

Gardner caught Rice smiling at her out of the corner of her eye. It was unusual to see him smile and she felt momentarily uncomfortable. 'What?'

'Just that you brush up nice...'

She raised an eyebrow.

'Can I say that?' His smile waned slightly.

'No, you can't. Piss off.' She cracked the door and stepped out.

'Jesus. Can't win. Just trying to be nice,' he mumbled. 'You told me to stop being so angry all the time.'

'Yes,' she said to him over the roof of the car. 'But I never told you to be creepy.'

He looked irritated. 'You know, there was a time when saying someone brushed up—'

'Not now, Phil. There's only one story I want to hear from a bygone era...' She pointed at the house. 'The one referred to in that note.'

Problem is with any good storyteller, Gardner thought, approaching the house. *They're bloody great at spinning a yarn.*

11

DC Doug Banks welcomed Gardner and Rice into an entrance hall framed with potted topiaries. After he'd shown them into a living area, warmed by a blazing fire, Gardner told him he could get off home.

Cassandra Thwaites, who still hadn't changed from her glamourous attire, was nursing a glass of red wine on the sofa closest to the fire. A half-empty bottle was standing on the rug at her feet.

The storyteller himself, sat on the sofa opposite her, head lowered. He'd put an end to the earlier pantomime by changing out of his pirate costume into loungewear and had relinquished the ridiculous tarnished tankard for a crystal whisky glass, which he sipped from regularly.

'Can I get you anything to drink, DCI Gardner?' Cassandra asked.

'No thank you, Mrs Thwaites.' Gardner moved closer, so she could see Robert in profile. The transformation from the man she'd watched perform earlier was rather startling.

Gone was the bluster, the grandiose gestures, the ruddy skin and booming voice, replaced instead with a pale complexion, and a jittery demeanour.

Maybe this storyteller would be more transparent than she'd initially feared? After all, he didn't look like he was capable of much right now, never mind crafting another fanciful fable like Valentina's curse.

Cassandra stood. 'Please sit here.' She moved to the sofa opposite and sat alongside her agitated husband.

They hadn't met Rice earlier, so Gardner introduced him before they sat. 'How are you feeling now, Mr Thwaites?'

He took another mouthful of whisky, swallowed, looked up and gestured down at his glass. 'Better now, I guess.'

It's a bad guess, Gardner thought. *You look worse.*

'It was the weight of it,' Robert said. 'That's what I can't get out of my head.'

'The skull?' Rice said.

Robert nodded. 'Yes. It's heavier than my fake one. It felt more dense... more solid. Not as smooth as the other either.' While holding the whisky glass with one hand, he made a curving gesture with the other as if stroking the skull. 'Rough. The cold, too. I'll never forget the cold.' He wasn't making eye contact with anyone and looked deep in thought. 'Within seconds, I knew I was clutching on to someone who was dead.' He shook his head, dropped his empty hand and took another drink. 'I'm sorry for the state of me.'

'Don't apologise,' Gardner said. 'Anyone would feel the same.'

He looked up at her with a raised eyebrow and his top lip quivering. 'A skull is going to be bloody old, right? So, I guess that this isn't a murder victim, is it? Maybe it's from a science lab, or someone dug it up as a prank?'

'There are a lot of questions right now,' Gardner said, thinking, *You're the storyteller, you tell me!* 'And we know very little.' *Apart from that very incriminating message in the jaw, but I'll get to that momentarily.* 'But a skull doesn't have to be old... no. Decomposition can be fast, quick, dependent on certain factors.'

'Still, it must take years and years, surely?'

'Not necessarily. Dependent on humidity and insects, it can be surprisingly rapid.' Robin had said that in optimal conditions, the bone could be exposed in a matter of weeks. Not discounting the possibility of someone treating the remains with chemicals. 'We really can't say yet.'

Robert looked at Cassandra, who was making quick work of her wine. She didn't return his gaze. 'So, I'm under suspicion for murder?' He looked back at Gardner.

'No one has said that. We—'

'But if he's been murdered *recently*... well, how does that look?'

'Yes,' Cassandra said, nodding. 'I mean, what's everyone going to think?'

Their responses felt nonsensical, almost farcical, but shock was known to have such an effect.

Guilt, too, occasionally, Gardner thought.

Rice sighed.

She was stunned he'd lasted this long, and his following comments came as no surprise. 'People are going to think exactly the same thing as if they'd been murdered ten years ago... one year, ten years, twenty years... one bloody day... why do you consider time so relevant a factor if someone is murdered?'

Robert and Cassandra stared at Rice wide-eyed as if he'd just delivered an unthinkable revelation, rather than the plain obvious.

'And what makes you think it was a man, anyway?' Rice pressed.

Robert shook his head. 'Sorry... I didn't—'

'You just said *he*.'

Well-spotted, Phil, Gardner thought, *glad you're on the ball. My head has still not settled from the beer and the emotion of the evening.*

'Did I?' Robert's face melted into panic. 'I meant nothing... I just thought... assumed that...'

'Assumed that he was a man. But why?' Rice pressed. 'Our pathologist can't even bloody confirm that.'

'Do you have to swear so much?' Cassandra asked.

Gardner touched Rice's leg to suggest that he cool it. She saw the frustration on his face, but he parked the verbalisation.

'We're as passionate about getting to the bottom of this as you are,' Gardner said, regarding Cassandra. 'My colleague's questions are fair. He'll moderate his choice of words though.'

She didn't need to look at Rice to know his blood would now boil. Instead, she regarded the woman who'd just called out Rice.

Cassandra Thwaites didn't seem as flustered and anxious as she'd done earlier when her husband had discovered the skull. Her eyes were narrower, and she looked deep in thought.

Calculating?

Maybe Rice had been onto something earlier in the car when he suggested her involvement?

'It's obvious why my husband thought it was a male skull,' Cassandra said, her confidence growing by the second. 'In the narrative of Valentina's curse, he's pulling out the captain's head. I guess, in my husband's mind, the skull remains male.'

Robert nodded. 'Yes.'

Good answer, Gardner thought, and jumped into her next question before her irritated partner could flare again. 'You mentioned the possibility of it being a prank before? What makes you think that?'

Robert shrugged. 'Nothing in particular. In retrospect, it was a stupid suggestion. Hardly a prank smashing my car window, eh?'

'Still, could you think of anyone that would do this? Someone you've offended, perhaps?' Gardner asked.

Robert shook his head and looked at his wife. 'No... can you, love?'

Cassandra shrugged. 'We don't have enemies. In fact, we're the opposite. We're churchgoing and are part of several social groups.'

'Maisie?' Robert sat up straight.

'Don't be ridiculous, Robert,' Cassandra glanced at her husband and gave a dismissive shake of her head.

'Who's Maisie?' Gardner asked.

'Maisie Bright,' Robert continued. 'Our neighbour. She came round the other week. We had a fall out about our tree overhanging her garden. She always jumps nought to a hundred in two seconds flat, and I'd got a headache. I didn't mince my words when I told her she needed to sling her hook. She's a widow. You know we've bent over backwards over the years to help that woman out. Taking food around, bins out, but you know, enough was enough—'

Cassandra cut her husband off by putting a hand on his leg. She looked at him with concern. 'Maisie didn't smash our car window and plant an actual skull in your car.'

'I guess,' Robert said, now looking rather embarrassed. 'I was just trying to think of someone we fell out with.'

'What's her full name?' Gardner asked. 'We'll check it out—'

Cassandra fixed Gardner with a stare. 'She's eighty-five.'

Gardner moved her eyes to Robert, trying to fathom if his bumbling fool behaviour was down to shock, alcohol, or well-honed acting skills.

Robert noticed the stare and looked embarrassed. 'My wife's right. Sorry. Looking back, I was probably rather too harsh on Maisie.'

'I'd say. Eighty-five is quite an age, sir,' Rice said.

Gardner stared at Rice. *Don't.* When she looked back at the couple, she saw Cassandra was glaring at Rice, too.

Still not quite feeling ready for her big reveal on the note, Gardner turned her attention to Cassandra – she was yet to be questioned at any length over the events at Blind Jack's. 'Mrs Thwaites, could you please recount the events of the evening in case any important details were missed?'

'Of course.'

Gardner and Rice made notes. In due course, Gardner would compare back to her earlier interview with Robert, but no discrepancies stood out at her now. They described how they parked in a space behind the library and went for a pre-performance drink in Six Poor Folk. Robert had explained earlier that they knew the landlord well, and he'd be happy to confirm their presence there. When they returned to the vehicle to retrieve their props, someone had smashed the rear left passenger seat window with a brick, and the alarm was blaring.

'Glass all over the back seat,' Cassandra said.

'So, why exactly do you think your car window was smashed?' Rice asked.

Cassandra finished her wine and put the glass down at her feet. 'The main case was on the back seat. It was too big to be dragged out of the passenger window. We assumed the thief only realised this after they smashed the glass. Obviously, we now know different. Someone put that skull in there.'

'Did you not think to check the contents of the case before the performance?' Rice asked.

'We did,' Cassandra said. 'There was nothing missing. Or at least, we *thought* nothing had been taken. We checked inside our cases but, we didn't go as far as to look inside the treasure chest.'

Robert groaned. 'Wish we had done.' He rubbed at his temples, mumbling, 'Bloody hell. No one is ever going to book me for an event again.'

Potentially the least of your problems right now, Robert, Gardner thought. *Anyone who saw fit to do this to you might take a bolder approach next time.*

'Maybe it'd have been best to call the police at this point,' Gardner said.

Cassandra sighed. 'In fairness to Robert, he *wanted* to. He said it may affect the insurance claim if we didn't. When I pointed out that the excess made this pointless anyway, at least compared to what he'd be earning for his show, we both decided to press on with going to Blind Jack's.'

'And you were happy to leave your car open?' Rice asked.

'Well, it wasn't open. Not as such. Nobody would've been able to open the door. We covered the back seat with a stash of shopping bags to protect it as best we could from the snow. But, yes, I get your point. It was risky, but my husband's shows are very important to him.' Cassandra looked at him. 'And me.' Gardner saw the admiration in her eyes that she'd witnessed earlier in the evening when she'd been mouthing the words he was speaking like a superfan at a concert.

Robert looked at his wife apologetically.

Cassandra looked down at the bottle and glass at her feet, sighed and reached down to refill.

The vigorous fire alongside Gardner crackled. She looked over in time to see the cascade of sparks burst from a split log. Her eyes rose to the mantelpiece where a picture of a woman with windswept red hair and sunglasses stood in the foreground on the Sydney Harbour Bridge with the elegant, sail-like Opera House in the background. It was a destination that had always appealed to Gardner.

A destination that had never felt so far away, considering her current financial situation and family circumstances.

'Our daughter,' Cassandra said, clearly noticing Gardner staring at the photograph. 'Ruby May. She lives in Sydney. Has done for nearly ten years.'

'Must be nice for holidays.'

Robert nodded. 'Yes. We'd like to get there more often, but the shows are doing so well of late.'

Gardner noticed Cassandra lowering her head. *A source of disagreement, perhaps? Work commitments keeping them away from their daughter?*

'It seems everyone wants to book a show in winter, which is when we most want to go,' Cassandra said. 'Storytellers by a crackling fire on a cold eve, I guess.'

How romantic... Her thought reminded her of how unromantic her own evening had been.

'Mind you, the summers are no better. Awash with festivals,' Cassandra added, taking another mouthful of wine without raising her head.

Robert put a hand on Cassandra's leg and looked at her apologetically again. 'But Ruby is yet to have children,' Robert said, momentarily coming from his morose stupor, 'but as soon as she does, wild horses won't stop us. She's thirty-three, and happily married – won't be long now.'

Gardner made a note to contact Ruby in Australia.

'You clearly love your job,' Gardner said to Robert. 'To still be working so hard in retirement.' She didn't think it necessary to add, *while possessing such wealth.* After all, the house had made that obvious.

Robert beamed. 'Yes. I've always wanted to tell stories. *Always.*'

'You've a lot of talent, Mr Thwaites,' Gardner said. 'I watched you tonight.'

'I know... I saw. It's kind of you to say so. I'm sorry it had to end... so... unexpectedly.'

Me too. I was in the middle of a rather significant situation with Lucy.

'I've never been so happy, professionally. I retired from law in 2013 when I was fifty-five. I just couldn't handle the day job any more. The creative calling was too much.'

Great option if you've got it, Gardner thought. *Some of us have bills to pay. You clearly didn't have that concern.*

'Not that I'm ungrateful for the opportunities I had as a solicitor. I've been able to provide well for Cassandra and Ruby. But still, it's only now I feel truly blessed to be able to do this, day in, day out.'

Gardner noticed now that Robert was coming more and more alive. It seemed the earlier shock was starting to settle, and the whisky had finally delivered its medicinal kick.

'Are you still involved with your old company?' She looked down at her notes. 'Long, Oakes and Thwaites Ltd. Is that correct?' Gardner asked.

'Yes,' Robert said and smiled. 'I still have some shares. I'm still good friends with Arthur and Reg. They thought I was bonkers walking away at fifty-five, but they get it now. Age is sobering. You realise how little time remains. They, too, have found more things they enjoy, and I'm glad for them.'

'You must have worked on behalf of lots of businesses during your time as a commercial solicitor?' Rice said.

'More than I can remember. And many of the big ones too. Three years before I left, we were the most in-demand company in the country. As you can imagine, the work-life balance was a disaster zone. I barely came up for air. I wanted to spend more time with Cassandra.' He reached over and took her hand. 'And I wanted to tell stories. A lot of stories.' He smiled.

Again, Gardner thought, *a simple move to make when you were rolling in money, as you most certainly were.*

'I don't mean disrespect, but I guess that over the years, working with a lot of companies, and against companies and individuals, you may have upset people?' Rice looked at his own notes. 'Some more powerful than your elderly neighbour, Maisie Bright?'

Robert sneered at Rice's sarcasm. 'Yes. But it was a job. People on all sides of that fence understand that. Business is business.'

'They say that in the mafia too,' Rice added.

Gardner glared at Rice and then glanced back at Robert. 'Do you think there's any possibility that what happened tonight is linked to your old life?'

'I doubt it very much.'

'It may help us if you had a think on it,' Gardner added.

'I will,' Robert said and smiled.

Gardner fixed him with a stare. 'You see... there was a note, Mr Thwaites. Left for you. In the jaw of the skull. I guess whoever staged this intended for it to fall out when you picked it up. I'm sure they wanted you to see it.'

'A note? I don't understand... I saw nothing...' He leaned forward on the sofa, throwing a quick glance into his tumbler, perhaps to check if there was enough of the good stuff left for what was about to be unleashed on him. 'What did it say?'

Gardner flicked her eyes between Cassandra and Robert, wishing to gauge both reactions. 'It said: why don't you tell a true story, Robert?'

Gardner held her breath and waited, hoping for a sudden realisation from either of the two individuals on the sofa in front of her.

But there wasn't one.

Just silence.

And the more and more Gardner watched them, the more and more obvious their emotional state became.

Dread. Cold dread.

The splitting of a burning log punctuated the silence. Gardner breathed in the sudden scent of pine and asked, 'Does the note mean anything to you?'

Cassandra drank her wine and slumped back on the sofa. Robert looked down into his glass, swirled the amber liquid and then looked up, fixing Gardner in his stare. He shook his head.

'Nothing?' Gardner asked.

'No,' Robert said. 'I can't think what it could mean. It sounds... ridiculous...'

Cassandra nodded beside him.

Gardner made a note and then glanced at Rice, who was clearly thinking the same thing.

A lie.

The great storyteller had returned.

12

After they were back in the car, Gardner looked at Rice, and opened her mouth to voice her concerns.

'I know,' he said, getting there first. 'He's a right wolf in grandma's clothing.'

'I've never heard that before.'

'I think I just made it up,' Rice said, proudly, brushing snow from his hair.

'Well, my mother always said, never trust a pirate,' Gardner replied, smiling.

'Really? She said that?'

'No.' Gardner laughed. 'When did she ever know a pirate? When does anyone?'

He laughed. 'So, we agree that Robert Thwaites knows why that skull is there?'

'Yes, for once we're agreeing,' Gardner said. 'And it's connected to something in his past.'

'They're in their sixties. That's a lot of past. Murky, too. Capitalism. Full of big business and the rats that thrive there.'

'Your favourite topic.' She gazed out over the black and inky

Nidd. 'But somewhere in the murk lies that true story, and we'll get to it.'

'Well, we best crack on. That rich, secretive couple is in danger... it's clear to see. I dread to think what anyone who's got the gumption to stitch someone up with an actual human skull is capable of.'

'I'll ask Marsh to have him watched.'

'Good luck with that.'

'Yes, she likes to make it clear that manpower is at an all-time low.'

'Just add some spice. Tell her that the next skull recovered could very well belong to Charles Dickens in there.' He pointed at the house. 'She won't want to risk that.'

Rice had made a fair point. Robert may have been lying out of desperation. To protect himself. However, what if the person who left him that skull wasn't threatening him, but merely teasing him, before their next move? Which was, as Rice said, to take his head.

'Okay.' She took her phone out. 'First, Marsh, and then, we need to get in touch with this Ruby May Thwaites. Find out if everything is hunky dory in Oz.'

Maybe there was a reason she'd opted to live on the opposite side of the world to Mummy and Daddy. A reason concerning *them*.

Rice smiled. 'You know, boss, I think we're moving in sync.'

'Yes, this is much better than usual.'

'What do you mean?'

He looked genuinely offended. She decided to add humour to the situation, best to keep him onside. 'Have you forgotten about your earlier inappropriate comment regarding my appearance?'

'Boss, it was bloody positive!'

'Using my beauty to give me worth?'

'So modest!' He guffawed. 'You can't call yourself beautiful!'

'I didn't.' She pointed at him and gave him a wink. 'You did.'

He was red-faced. She *did* enjoy winding him up!

'You can't take my compliment after bloody berating me for it!' he hissed.

'And stop swearing, too.' Gardner smiled. 'Cassandra almost choked on her wine.'

Her phone rang. It was Barnett.

'Ray?'

'I know I'm quick, but this was ridiculous,' Barnett said.

Gardner sat up straight. 'You know who switched the skulls in the back of the car, don't you?'

As he told her, she watched the moonlight dance on the murky Nidd.

13

The crumbling terraced house in Starbeck stood in stark contrast to the Thwaites' residency on the Waterside.

ID ready, Gardner knocked on the door. While they waited, she glanced at the patched-up cracked front window. It reminded her of her own home as a child.

A woman in her mid to late thirties opened the door, smoking. Her hair glowed a bold purple, a stark contrast to her drab habitation. Despite being clean, her clothes had clearly faded with age, and clung to her curves in a way which suggested that they may have fitted better in her leaner younger years.

'Mrs Ann Midgely?'

'God... not again.' She blew out a stream of smoke. 'How many sodding times?'

'DCI Emma Gardner and DI Phil Rice. Are you Mrs Midgely?'

'Yes... what's *he* done?'

Gardner suspected she was referring to her son. The only other known occupant of the house. 'Is it possible we could come in and talk? It's freezing out here.'

'Only when you tell me what my little shite has gone and bloody done this time... he doesn't mean it, you know. He's sodding impulsive. I've told you lot this. I've got the documents upstairs. He can't always help it. ADHD. Is it a bike? Has he nicked another sodding bike?'

'Ma'am,' Rice said. 'You wouldn't have police inspectors on the doorstep for that.'

Her face, which until now had been firm, paled slightly. She took a hard drag on her cigarette.

Okay, soften your tone, Rice. This isn't uppity Cassandra Thwaites. Adapt to your bloody audience and don't start a bonfire.

'Is Sam in at the moment?' Gardner asked.

Ann turned and shouted into the house. 'Get here you little shite...' Then, she looked back at Rice. 'Met a few like you before.' She exhaled and sneered. 'Smug bastards, like... Lord of the Manor... until they're pissed in the corner of a pub, lonely, desperate for some attention.' She winked.

Well, can't say you don't deserve it, Phil...

Gardner knew Rice wouldn't let that stand, so she spoke first, hoping to cut him off. 'Still best we come in and chat to you both, Ann.' She used her first name now, attempting to break the ice. 'It may be a misunderstanding. We just want to clear this matter up and leave you to it.'

'Might as well,' grunted Ann. 'He ain't going to come to the door. He's only just rolled in through it thirty minutes back and plonked himself in front of the TV. He ain't moving for love nor money.'

Puffing on her cigarette, she led them through a hallway that was clean. The carpets weren't new, but they looked freshly hoovered. There was also a pleasant scent in the air. Gardner felt reminded of her childhood once again. Her parents had often struggled, but they'd remained house-proud. Always stoic in the face of adversity.

And they'd been forced to face a lot of adversity over the years with her brother, Jack, as he became more and more withdrawn, deviant and at times, dangerous.

It seemed like Ann Midgely had her fair share of challenges, too.

Fourteen-year-old Sam Midgely was sitting on a sofa, feet up on a coffee table, smoking.

'Oi, you cheeky little shite,' she said, snatching the cigarette from his mouth. She reached down to the ashtray to put it out but opted to put the end of hers out and continue with the one Sam had nicked instead.

'Sorry, Mum,' he said, blowing out smoke. 'When I see them, I just can't help it.'

Ann turned to Gardner with an exasperated look on her face. 'Impulsive. You see?'

Gardner nodded, so did Sam. She wondered how many times a day this excuse for his behaviour was made. She imagined his teachers at school would be sick of hearing it; if he attended, that was.

She felt Rice's eyes on her and they exchanged a look.

It wasn't hard to read him as per. There was a wry grin twitching at the corners of his mouth. He'd already made it clear several investigations before that he was firmly in the camp of ADHD being an artificial construct. He might as well shout: *It's bullshit! The kid is taking the piss.*

Gardner wasn't that narrow-minded. She was no doctor and didn't pretend to be one. Maybe the fact that she'd been brought up with a brother who was sociopathic had made her keenly aware of neurodivergent minds. She was happy to listen to the professionals.

She looked at the boy. He was focusing on the ashtray, watching his mother's stubbed cigarette spew off its last trail of smoke. Addiction turning his eyes to giant spotlights. Even so, nicotine addiction was the least of this boy's problems just now.

Gardner introduced herself to Sam. He grunted his greeting.

'What you been up to tonight?' she asked.

'Nowt.'

'Where have you been?' Rice pressed.

'Nowhere.'

Gardner looked at his mother as she delivered the next line. 'We know that isn't true, I'm afraid.'

'Besides,' Rice said, 'your mum said you only got in thirty minutes back.'

'Bloody hell,' Sam said, glaring at his mum.

Rice pointed down at a damp hoodie on the sofa. 'Is that yours, Sam?'

Sam still didn't look up at Rice. 'Eh? Yeah, why?'

'Just thought it looked rather distinctive. The logo on the chest. Is that an eagle?'

Sam glanced at it. 'Guess so.'

'Don't see many of them about, do you?'

'So?' Sam shrugged, reaching out and touching the hoodie. 'It was my dead dad's. Got it from another country – God knows where.'

'He was away with the army a lot,' Ann said. She lowered her eyes. 'Before.'

'I'm sorry,' Gardner said.

'Don't be. He wasn't shot,' Sam grunted. 'Heart attack. Boring, eh?' He snorted.

Ann flinched, turned slightly and put the cigarette to her mouth.

Gardner wanted to reach out and touch her reassuringly on the arm. The pain on her face was clear to see. She held back. Touching anyone in this volatile situation wasn't a great idea.

'What's this about, anyway?' Ann asked, blowing out smoke and suddenly turning back.

'Shall we all sit?' Gardner asked, wanting to try to soften the atmosphere first.

'No,' Ann said, folding her arms. 'Get to the point. Sam has school in the morning. He needs his rest.'

It was one in the morning! If she wasn't already feeling great sympathy for Ann, she may just have said something.

Turns out she didn't need to. Rice was making a big show of looking at his watch beside her.

'You try to get the little shite to bed,' Ann said, her cheeks glowing red.

Gardner looked down at the youngster. *Best to just get on with it.* 'Okay. Sam, where were you at around eight tonight?'

'Here... hadn't made it out yet. Mum? You tell them.'

Ann betrayed herself with the slightest hesitation. 'Yes... he was here...'

'Until?' Rice asked.

Ann opened her mouth, but Sam responded, 'Nine-ish.'

'Funny that,' Rice said, who pulled his phone out and tapped the screen. He then turned it around and showed the still image of Sam at the front of a queue in McDonald's. He'd the hood of his distinctive eagle top raised, but it was clearly him. Their burgers weren't of good quality, but their cameras certainly were. Robbing Mr McDonald was a very serious offence. It was a shame that the council didn't feel the same way... the library CCTV of the car vandalism had been a shit show. 'Is that you?'

Sam glanced at it but didn't respond. He continued to fiddle with his hoodie.

'Looks like you,' Rice said. 'And look, there's the eagle on the hoodie, too. And the time stamp says six minutes past eight.'

'So, I went for a Maccas,' Sam grunted. 'Then I came back here, ate it and went out again. Ain't that right, Mum?'

Ann nodded, but she was looking less and less sure of herself as the conversation unfolded.

'The thing is, Sam, while you were there, you assaulted a female member of staff,' Rice said. 'I won't show the footage of that.' He looked up at Ann. 'Unless your mum wants to see it?'

She glowered at Rice, no doubt thinking the same thing she'd articulated on the doorstep. *There's that smug bastard again! Full of himself, but lonely and miserable.*

'She refused to serve me!' Sam said, looking up at Gardner, rather than Rice.

The child looked pale and undernourished.

'Because you gave them a mouthful of obscenities,' Rice said.

'She wouldn't give me a bastard Big Mac!' Sam said, still aiming his responses at Gardner.

Gardner had seen this before. A child used to arguing with his loving mother but fearful of the aggressive father. Rice and Gardner had taken on those roles.

'Because there was no cheese left,' Rice continued.

'She could've given it me without cheese – wouldn't have bothered me too much!' Sam continued to fight his corner while keeping his eyes off his outspoken foe. 'I Just told 'em to put more of that nice sauce on.'

'Problem is their policy doesn't allow this,' Rice continued. 'They're instructed to sell only as marketed.'

'Eh?'

'They've to sell it how it looks in the picture.'

'It never looks how it does in the picture!'

'Well, it definitely has cheese in the picture.'

Ann was now staring at Sam in disgust. 'Did you hurt a *woman*?'

Her emphasis made Gardner wonder if she'd be okay with it if it'd been a man.

'I only pushed her!'

'Your father would—'

'Piss off with that,' Sam said, kicking the table. The ashtray skidded, but fortunately, didn't go over the side.

Gardner looked between mother and son. Both looked furious, and set to explode, and they were still to get to the main reason they were here.

She nodded at Rice to inform him he'd done his part, and it needed reining in.

'You hurt her, Sam,' Gardner said. 'It's serious, and needs to be followed up on, but that isn't the main reason we're here tonight.'

'Eh?' Ann said. Her voice was getting louder. 'It gets worse than *that*?'

Gardner took a deep breath. 'Your behaviour in McDonald's put you in the system, Sam. There was another offence not soon after.'

'Wasn't me... I came straight home. Just told you that.'

Gardner plucked out her phone and showed Sam a short video. Gardner had watched it several times. It was distant and grainy. It showed someone with a hoodie drawn up, approaching the other side of a BMW, brick in one hand and a plastic bag in the other. There was no sound. The lens pointed at the wrong side of the car, so the actual smashing and manipulation of Robert's props – if that'd indeed happened – wasn't picked up.

Sam snorted. 'Could be anyone that!'

'So, you're saying that it wasn't you?' Gardner asked.

'Yes. Exactly what I'm saying,' Sam said, glaring at Gardner.

'You heard him,' Ann said. 'He's telling the truth. Hard to tell who that is on there!'

'I agree,' Gardner said. 'At first glance, the footage isn't good enough to identify Sam.'

'Nowt to do with the footage! It just wasn't me!'

'Except,' Gardner said, fiddling with the phone. 'We zoomed in and...' She turned the phone back. 'That's definitely you.'

'You can't see any face under that hood,' Ann protested.

Rice nodded. 'No, you can't... but we can see the eagle on the hoodie.'

The room went quiet.

Gardner would agree with Ann that Rice was a smug bastard, but Jesus, did he know how to silence a room.

Sam was shaking his head, panic on his face now. 'I wasn't wearing that tonight...'

Rice feigned a confused expression. 'But we just saw an image of you wearing it at McDonald's.'

'Yes... but... someone else must have had the same hoodie. I left it here when I came home.'

Rice nodded. 'You sure about that? As I said before I've never seen one like that. And you said it was unique.'

'I didn't. I just said my dad got it from another country.'

'Making it unique,' Rice said.

Ann was shaking her head. She knew the game was up. She mumbled something under her breath. Gardner couldn't make it out. However, she then repeated herself at a higher volume. 'What've you done now?' She moved towards her son and raised her voice even louder. 'What've you done now, you little shite?' She leaned over and whacked him across the head.

'Piss off,' he cried, swerving the next blow.

'Everything I do... Everything...' She leaned further in, whacking him again, just before Gardner got to her and restrained her.

Surprisingly, considering her size, it wasn't too difficult to pull Ann back. Gardner suspected she was allowing her to do it. Sam rubbed at his head. 'You mad bitch. Piss off!'

'It's not my fault, you little bastard. It's not my fault about your father.'

Sam stood up, shouting, 'I never said it was!'

Gardner saw Rice edging forward, ready to restrain too.

'Then why do you treat me like this?' She sagged back into Gardner's arms. 'I'm trying... I'm sodding well trying.'

'I *gave* you some of that money, didn't I?' Sam shouted. 'I didn't just do it for myself.'

What money?

Ann lowered her head. Sam did, as well, realising he'd said too much.

'That car window was smashed, Sam, and something very serious occurred tonight after that event. What was in that plastic bag?' Gardner asked.

'I dunno! It wasn't me.'

'If you know what was in that bag, Sam, then you realise how serious this all is. That wasn't a fake object that was placed inside the car.'

Sam had tears in his eyes now and was shaking his head. 'Honestly, I don't know. Mum, I don't know what they're on about.'

Ann's tone softened. 'You told me that thirty quid was for helping Dex's dad out at his garage last weekend?'

Sam sat down, shaking his head, tears still running down his face. 'Mum... tell me what to say. I don't know what to say.'

Ann glanced over her shoulder at Gardner. 'Let me go... please.'

Gardner nodded and released her so she could sit next to her son. She looped an arm around him and pulled him in tight. She kissed his head. 'The truth, Sam.'

'I'm sorry. I'm an idiot.'

She kissed his head again. 'What happened?'

'I'm going to be in serious trouble.'

Ann looked up at Gardner.

'What was in the bag, Sam?' Gardner asked.

Sam looked up at Gardner with red eyes. 'A skull. A bloody skull. She told me not to look in the bag until I got there, and then to replace whatever was in the fake bloody treasure box with it. I didn't know... you think I'd have walked from Macca's to town with a bloody skull in a bag!'

'You were seen, on that CCTV footage behind the library, walking away with the same plastic bag,' Rice asked. 'What did you walk away with?'

'The fake skull.'

'And where's that?'

'I chucked it in the bin at the front of the library.' He looked between Gardner's and Rice's faces, then up at his mother again. She, too, had tears in her eyes. He then curled up in her arms and sobbed. 'I didn't know, I didn't know...'

'Sam, this is important, and if you help me with this right now,'

Gardner said, 'I'll help you as much as I can. Who asked you to put that skull in the treasure chest?'

14

The snowfall had intensified.

'Bloody hell,' Rice said, firing up his car. 'It's practically a blur.'

'Go slow,' Gardner said.

He edged the vehicle out. 'And having just considered breaking my land speed record. Excellent advice!'

Watching Rice as he gripped the steering wheel and focused intently through the windscreen, Gardner delivered Sam Midgely's story to Barnett by phone.

After the call, Rice asked, 'Are we planning on getting some sleep this evening, boss?'

'Depends on what Ray finds out, I guess.'

'Jesus, would you look at this!'

'Look is probably not the right word.'

Rice's wipers were flailing against the thickening blanket on the windscreen, obscuring most of the outside world, including, most concerningly, other vehicles and road markings.

Rice slowed to a crawl. And yet, despite this, each turn and press on the brakes were still a cautious dance.

Gardner's phone glowed and vibrated.

'Nah, not Ray,' Rice said. 'RoboCop wouldn't even be that fast.'

Her pulse quickened when she saw the name on the screen.

Cecile Metcalf.

The promised returned call.

She glanced at Rice. Letting him on to what was going on here was a complete non-starter. No good could come from him discovering she was trying to locate one of his sworn enemies.

Still, no chance she was ignoring this call, and she wouldn't be stepping out into this blizzard... so, she'd just have to be discreet. She answered. 'Cecile.'

'I'm sorry about earlier. It seems the northern infrastructure doesn't cater for telecommunication. What happened to "levelling up"?'

'Cecile... it's a yes from me.'

'Sorry?'

'Earlier... the image?'

'Ah, okay... I sense you're busy right now...'

She glanced at Rice. He appeared to have all his attention on the deathtrap of a road, but he'd be listening. Of that, she was certain.

'Yes, but I need it in a nutshell.'

'You won't like the nutshell... Look, I'll call as soon as it's convenient—'

'*No!*' She took a deep breath, realising she'd raised her voice slightly. She glanced over at Rice who quickly threw her a concerned look before being forced to return his attention to the road. 'I'm snowed under, but please fill me in.'

'Snowed under,' Rice murmured, sniggering to himself. *The bastard was certainly paying close attention.*

Cecile sighed. 'He's fallen in with a bad crowd.'

Gardner shook her head. She made it sound as if Riddick was her wayward son or something. 'Who?'

Cecile sighed again. 'A very bad crowd. A dangerous one. The place he's staying at... well... Emma, you're really not going to like it.'

She wanted to scream, *'Get to the bloody point,'* but she was already failing miserably at being discreet before throwing that into the mix.

'A squat. You saw on the picture. A run-down one. Shit. There's drug dealing going on. I've watched several junkies going in and out. Brief visits. It's clear they're scoring... I'm sorry, Emma.'

Doesn't mean it's him! 'How sure?'

'Crystal clear. Like I said. I haven't seen Paul dealing, specifically, but he's *definitely* in there.'

Not good. 'There'll be a reason.'

Gardner glanced at Rice, who threw her another inquisitive look. She glared at him and mouthed, 'Piss off! It's personal.'

He shrugged.

Gardner said to Cecile, 'This won't be what you think.'

'I want to believe you, but... I don't know...'

I need to speak with him. Gardner opened her mouth to make the request. 'I'll—'

'I'll speak to him... tomorrow,' Cecile interrupted.

No. This is my problem. 'Let me.'

'Too dangerous.'

'And it isn't the same for you?' She took a deep breath. She could sense Rice's wandering eyes again. 'Look, it's me or nothing. I'll text you later, okay?'

'Relax, I know what I'm doing, and I can take all emotion out of the equation. I promised I'd get to the bottom of this, and I will.'

'I said I'll speak to you later—'

'Of course. Look, I'm going home to rest. Let's speak first thing. Good night.'

The phone cut off. *Shit.*

Feeling irritated, she willed Rice not to ask the inevitable question.

'You sure everything's okay?'

'What didn't you understand about *piss off*, Phil?'

Rice widened his eyes. 'Woah. Sorry, boss. Just worried about—'

'You're one of the most thoughtful nosey bastards I've ever met. It's about ex-husbands, and marital issues... things you'd prefer to know nothing about,' Gardner said. 'Now, keep your eyes on the second ice age.'

She shook her head, suddenly feeling like she was going out of her mind.

Riddick... drug den... dealing...

What was she supposed to do with all of that?

She took a deep breath, closed her eyes and focused.

This was up to her. Not Cecile.

She opened her phone and texted Cecile, keeping a lookout for Rice's wandering eyes.

> Can I have the address, please? I appreciate everything, but I want to handle it from here.

She waited for a reply. None came. Maybe she was driving.

Later, she'd get that address and, tomorrow, at some point, she'd go and drag him out of this squat.

As they drove back into Knaresborough, Gardner's phone kicked up again.

'Ray,' she said, looking at the screen.

'Just when I thought there might be an outside chance of getting to bed,' Rice muttered.

Gardner answered the phone.

Barnett went straight into it. 'Okay, I got the CCTV footage from St James retail park and the industrial sites on Grimbald Crag.'

Gardner and Rice listened as Barnett confirmed the first part of Sam's story. Ten past eight. Sam, hood up on his eagle hoodie, bolted out of the McDonald's, having just assaulted the server. He sprinted right across the wide car park, until he reached the raised cut-through that zig-zagged once before breaking out on to Grimbald Crag Close. Kids often gathered in that cut-through at night. It was a blind spot for CCTV, and so a suitable place for smoking and underage drinking.

'The camera on the industrial estate picks up the Mercedes that Sam described, turning left off Grimbald Crag Way onto the Close. The car, as claimed, slides up alongside the cut-through.'

Gardner recalled Sam's confession. 'At first, we thought it was someone's mother, but then she just wound down the window. She wasn't young or old. Around your age. She asked if anyone wanted to earn some money. Easy money. One hundred quid. Obviously, everyone wanted in, but I wasn't letting that one slide. Jim started arguing with me, but changed his mind when he saw how definite I was. It was mine. And he knew. She told me to get in the back of the car.'

Barnett continued his report. 'Sam jumps into the back of the Merc. The driver spins the car and turns right back out onto Grimbald Crag Way. I'm still waiting on ANPR to see if we can track the vehicle's movements.'

If Sam was to be believed, and, so far, she saw no reason to doubt these events, he was driven up York Road, into town, and dropped off at the top of Jockey Lane. There, he'd go on to fulfil his task.

'She just said, grab the tied plastic bag, and head down to a black BMW parked behind the library. She gave me the registration too, but I only remembered the first half when I got to it. YT24. It was enough. When she started telling me about the treasure chest, I thought she was completely mad, but she'd been waving a hundred quid at me for a while now. So, I thought, why not? She told me to get into the car, find the treasure chest and empty the contents of the bag into it. She only had two other clear instructions. First, I should remove whatever was already inside the treasure chest and chuck it. Second, I shouldn't look in the plastic bag until the last moment because getting it out in public would be dangerous.'

'So,' Barnett continued. 'I've sent someone to retrieve the plastic skull from the bin outside the library, and I also found out who this Mercedes belongs to.'

Gardner looked at Rice who was desperate to know what Barnett was telling her.

One thing was for certain: they weren't getting home and out of the weather that easily.

15

Rice tried to reverse park in treacherous conditions. It didn't look like it was going well.

'I'll get out and help,' Gardner said.

'Behave. I got this.'

'No need to be a hero on my account. I won't tell everybody back at the station that Phil needed help with—'

Gardner's phone vibrated, indicating a message.

Cecile?

She slipped her phone from the inside pocket of her ski jacket.

Lucy.

Her heart sank as she read the message.

> I'm sorry for my behaviour tonight. This was all my fault. L x

Gardner inwardly sighed. *It's not your fault, Lucy. I wanted your company. Desperately. Still do. But I'm your boss and older...*

She read the message again.

She seemed so young.

Gardner gulped. She typed out a message:

> Not your fault... I jumped on your advances like a damn ravenous wolf.

Fortunately, Rice's cheer at his successful reverse park interrupted her flow, so she didn't impulsively hit send.

She deleted the message.

'Everything okay on Planet Boss?' Rice asked.

'Just tired.'

'Alcohol wearing off?' he asked, smiling.

'You're becoming progressively more irritating, so I suspect that's possible.'

She quickly typed out a less controversial message as Rice exited the car.

> Nothing to apologise for. Phone you later. E x

Outside the vehicle, the snowfall remained fierce. Fortunately, both officers threw up their hoods as they closed the short distance to the front door.

They were in Aspin, outside a semi-detached home, which, on appearance anyway, acted as a happy medium between the two residencies they'd visited tonight. Not too garish and spectacular, like the wealthy Thwaites' residence, but neither was it a run-down scar on an already bleak area like the troubled Midgely home.

The door opened and a woman wearing a *Star Wars* T-shirt and baggy, comfortable joggers stood there. Her tangled hair was loosely tied back. She wore thick, black-framed glasses. At first, her eyes darted between her two visitors as if filled with panic, before averting themselves downward.

Showing their IDs, Gardner introduced themselves. 'Are you Ms Jessica Beaumont?'

'Uh-huh, yeah... that's right.' Gardner already knew her to be thirty-five, but she looked much younger.

'Have you got a minute?'

'Yes... sure...' She kept her eyes downward. 'About the car? I'm sorry about that.'

'What're you sorry about?' Rice asked.

He wasn't being his usual aggressive self; the question was genuine. Why was she blaming herself for having her car stolen?

'It's my fault,' Jessica said, still not making eye contact. 'Sometimes I just lose concentration. Lose focus. Mum used to say I'd gone off into the Twilight Zone.' She blinked and wrung her hands together. 'I must have gone there. And the car was stolen. It's the only thing that must have happened. But it hasn't happened for a good while. So, I'm sorry.'

Gardner and Rice exchanged a confused glance.

'Yes, it's about the stolen car, Ms Beaumont. It was taken yesterday, I believe.'

'Yes.' Her eyes flicked up and down again. Just once. 'But as Joe says at work, I practically gift-wrapped it! I cried a bit when he said it. He felt bad, but he shouldn't sweat it. Told him that. I cry a lot.'

'What do you mean gift-wrapped it, Jessica?' She nearly always used their surnames unless requested to do otherwise, or unless the person she was talking to seemed in great need of reassurance. Ann Midgely had, earlier. And now, it seemed, Jessica was the same. She believed you could never inject enough warmth into a cold context.

There was the sound of someone shouting upstairs.

Gardner looked upwards. *Is that why you're on edge?* 'Who's here with you, Jessica?'

'Jess. Just Jess. My father calls me Jessica. It makes me feel that I'm getting things wrong, you know.'

'Jess, please, tell me who that was... upstairs?'

'My father.' She offered another quick glance up, but then quickly returned to default eyes down.

'We didn't know he lived here... with you,' Gardner said.

'He doesn't. Or, at least, he didn't. But he does now. His

Alzheimer's is bad. He refuses to go into a home. He told me straight out. It's there with you, in the house I paid for, or I go out by falling down the stairs in this one. That house is four floors, there are a lot of stairs... I thought this for the best.'

'But are you in any danger?' Rice asked.

'Oh no...' She chanced another look and a smile. 'No... nothing like that. He's nice. Usually. He used to be nice all the time. Now, he kind of forgets a lot of things. Sometimes he forgets he's nice, I guess... Sometimes he swears, and sometimes he drops things, but he'd never hurt me.'

'You look tired?' Gardner asked.

'Oh no, I'm fine... sometimes I come across as a little awkward, you know?'

'Can we please come in, Jess?' Gardner said.

Jess nodded. 'Please take your shoes and coats off.'

'Of course.'

Gardner noticed the sunflower lanyard hanging from the coat pegs as she hung her jacket up. It certainly explained her anxiety and reluctance to make eye contact.

While Jess was walking into her lounge, Gardner caught Rice's eyes and pointed at the lanyard. She tried not to stifle her assistant SIO too much, as sometimes his abrupt nature came in useful, but in this instance, she expected him to remain well and truly stifled.

Rice and Gardner followed Jess into the lounge. It was immaculately tidy and comfortably furnished. It was also boiling hot.

Jess was over at the sofa, righting the cushions. 'Sorry it's so hot. My father. He can't handle the chill any more. I know it's expensive... I told him that. Countless times. But he doesn't care about paying. He pays for everything. Always has. He paid for this house. I think I told you that.' She pointed at a two-seater sofa. 'Please sit. He's always cared for me and now I care for him. Does that make sense?'

'Yes,' Gardner said, sitting.

Rice didn't sit. With it being a two-seater, he was doing the gracious thing for once and leaving it unoccupied for Jess.

Jess didn't take the option, though, and simply hovered in front of Gardner.

'Again, I'm sorry about the car,' Jess said.

'Yes, maybe, you could... aren't you going to sit too, Jess?' Gardner asked.

'I'm fine,' she said. 'Sitting still can be harder work. Always had a lot of energy.' She pointed at Rice. 'You can sit down if you like.'

'No... I'm fine,' Rice said. 'Please sit, Jess, we've some questions.'

She nodded and perched on the edge of the sofa awkwardly. 'I should have known a small sofa was probably a bad idea but it looked nice, and no one ever seemed to visit... only my father, every now and again, before the Alzheimer's got bad and he moved in. I'd buy a one-seater, or even a two-seater, to match this two-seater, but they don't make them any more, and I just can't handle a mismatch.' She looked down as if addressing the floor.

'I know exactly what you mean,' Gardner said. 'And thank you for having us in, Jess. I understand it's past two, and I hope we haven't woken your father. Can I ask you what happened regarding your Mercedes?'

'It's not mine. It's my father's.'

'I see,' Gardner said, taking her notebook out. 'But it's in your name?'

'Yes... he doesn't drive any more.'

'Okay. Technically, it's registered to you, even though your father paid.'

'Ah... yes... I understand.'

'Now, you said it was your fault it was stolen?'

'Yes, I left the key in there. At least, I must have done. These new cars are hard to steal... apparently. You *need* the key, really. So, I *must* have left the key in there. Sugar. I'm sorry.' She tapped her forehead. 'Idiot.' She kept on tapping it. 'Idiot... idiot...'

Gardner looked up at Rice, concerned he might step in and restrain her. Jess was stimming and it wouldn't be appropriate to stop her. Fortunately, Rice didn't make a move.

After Jess had stopped tapping her forehead, Rice said, 'It's hard to steal without the key... but not impossible... could you talk us through how you think you left the key in there?'

'Idiocy. The day before yesterday, I drove to work, because it was raining heavily and wasn't snowing for once. Yesterday, I didn't drive to work because it was snowing again. I walked and when I walked home at the end of the day, then, well, my car was gone. So, I must have left the key in the ignition, and the door to the car unlocked. Gift-wrapped, Joe said... and, now I see how he was just trying to be funny. But I don't always get that. And at the time, I was anxious... and felt like a fool... but I *am* a fool. I guess, it's true. Gift-wrapped. I practically gave it away.'

Jess was a car insurer's best friend.

She imagined them rubbing their hands as she made a report; it made Gardner feel sick to the stomach.

'But can you remember, for absolute certain, that you left the key in the vehicle?' Rice asked.

'It's not in my bag or on the key rack.'

'Where's the key rack?' Gardner asked.

'By the front door.'

'Were there any signs of forced entry when you returned home from work?'

Jess shook her head. 'The door was locked.'

'Are you certain?'

'Definitely... I think...'

'You don't sound too convinced, Jess,' Gardner said.

'Unless I went into the Twilight Zone... but... no... I'm convinced. My front door was locked. I locked it when I went out and unlocked it when I came back.'

'The back door?' Rice suggested.

'No... same... I check the back door every night before I go to bed. It was locked last night. And is still locked, because I've already been to bed tonight, you see, before you phoned ahead to say you were coming. That door hasn't been used.'

'How about your father?' Gardner asked. 'He must have been in. Could he have popped out and left the door unlocked?'

'He doesn't go out. He's past that stage.'

'Could he have opened the door for someone?'

'He doesn't get out of bed.'

'Do you have a nurse?'

'No... no... he...' She dropped her head. 'He won't have one.'

'So, if the key hasn't been taken from the house,' Rice said, 'then, maybe you took it out with you.'

'Yes... it's possible. But it would've been in my bag. And it certainly isn't in my bag right now.'

'Can you think of a time that you left your bag unattended?' Gardner asked.

'No... no... I just went to work. I work at Oxfam in town. The bag is in the room where we store donations. No one has access to that room apart from me and Joe.'

'Joe?'

'Yes, Joe Harris.'

Gardner wrote his name down.

'But he's over seventy and doesn't drive. He has epilepsy.'

Gardner circled his name. If he'd access to those keys, he'd need to be ruled out.

'So, as you can see,' Jess said, looking at Gardner for the first time in a long while. 'I had to have left them in the car. I'm an idiot. What if it's one of those joyriders? What if someone gets hurt?'

'We don't know that for certain,' Gardner said. 'Jess, where were you earlier tonight between eight and nine?'

'Here, of course.'

'What were you doing? Can anyone verify that?'

'Of course... I was online with Madeline Sharp. On Zoom. She's my best friend. In fact, we were on there for a good couple of hours tonight.' Gardner wrote this down, too, hoping the alibi checked out. She didn't want to go in any harder on this vulnerable woman.

There was another loud, incomprehensible shout from upstairs.

'I'm sorry,' she said, leaning forward onto her knees. 'I'm sorry... I'm sorry...' She bounced her heels up and down.

Another shout.

'He's a good man... He *was* a good man.'

'Are you safe here, Jess?' Gardner asked.

'Yes... I'm sure... he's never hurt me. Never will.'

'Has he ever hurt anyone?' Rice asked.

'No... no...' She continued to bounce, looking down at the floor. 'He says nasty things sometimes, but not so much to me. To people that come around. Nurses and doctors. Unfamiliar faces. That's why I can't have a nurse. I couldn't risk it.'

'Who've you spoken to about all of this?' Gardner asked.

'I've spoken to people. I've been warned that he'll stop recognising me... and, well, then, he should go into a home. For my safety. But he's still okay... I promise. And my job has been kind. Oxfam are understanding. There are always people to take my shift if he has a dreadful night. I don't need money. I've access to my father's money for living expenses.'

Gardner heard more shouting.

'Is he shouting for Daisy?' Gardner asked.

'Yes... he's confused,' Jess said, rising to her feet.

'*Daisy!*'

'Who's Daisy?' Rice asked.

'Daisy was my mother. She died a long time ago... he's *so* confused.'

Gardner followed Jess out of the lounge door and to the foot of the stairs. She could sense Rice following just behind her.

'*Daisy... I need you now!*' Her father shouted.

Jess turned to Gardner and Rice. 'Please... you can't come up. If he sees you, it'll make him worse. If he sees me, it'll calm him down—'

If he still recognises you, Gardner thought.

'Best we come,' Rice said.

'Please,' Jess said. She had tears in her eyes. She looked at Gardner and Rice for the longest period she'd managed since they'd arrived.

'We'll stay here until you give us a signal that he's calm,' Gardner said.

'Okay... thanks...' Jess disappeared up the stairs.

Rice came around Gardner and looked at her with an eyebrow raised. 'And when he hits her?'

'It's on me,' she snapped back.

From the foot of the stairs, they watched Jess disappear into a bedroom.

There was no more shouting, just hushed whispers. What was actually said was difficult to hear. A minute later, she appeared at the top of the stairs again and looked down. 'He's calm... I need to stay with him for a while... until he's resting again...'

Gardner held her hand up. 'Okay, Jess, we'll be in touch.'

Outside, the snow was such that they didn't communicate until they were back in Rice's car.

'My father was a bastard when he had his mind; thank God, he didn't hang around long enough to lose it,' Rice said.

Gardner didn't really have a response. It sounded cold, but Rice's relationship with his father, who'd once been a DCI, was a sensitive area, and not one she'd like to get into right now.

'She's got it tough,' Gardner said.

'She needs to send him packing to a home. Especially when she has her own needs.'

'So, what do you think of her leaving the keys in the ignition?'

Rice shrugged. 'Who knows? That house was immaculate. I find it hard to believe that someone with that much attention to detail leaves the keys in the car.'

'Me too. But I don't think that girl is involved, do you?'

'She'd have to be a spectacular actress.'

'Still, it was stolen from around here. So, first thing tomorrow, we need to get some officers pounding these doors to see if someone witnessed something. And we need to speak to Joe Harris, the colleague, and Madeline Sharp, the alibi.'

Rice nodded. 'Yes, unless ANPR hooks us our fish first. Shall we try for some sleep then?'

'No harm in trying, I guess.'

16

————

Irritated, Gardner sat in the kitchen staring at the message she'd sent Cecile Metcalf over an hour ago.

> Can I have the address, please? I appreciate everything, but I want to handle it from here.

Then the next one twenty minutes ago:

> ??

Cecile had done her a massive favour, and she didn't want to badger her at almost three in the morning, but not responding to her request had her convinced of one thing: this situation regarding Paul was incredibly serious.

Eventually, she caved and phoned Cecile.

Voicemail sent her frustration into overdrive. She took a deep breath and collected herself. 'Please, Cecile, if you're still up, get back to me. I need more details. No one knows him like I do. If I can get to him, I *can* help him.'

She put the phone down on the table and massaged her forehead.

What bloody spell do you have over me, man?

Surely, most people would've turned their back by now.

She looked up and caught sight of the wine rack, freshly stocked in anticipation of Christmas, and resisted the urge. She'd already had four pints – albeit around five hours ago – but drinking now would make her unfit to drive to the morning briefing.

She finished her cup of decaffeinated tea and headed up to bed via the children's bedrooms, to kiss their foreheads. They'd be paying her a visit sometime soon, but for now, they were asleep.

In her room, lying in bed, she realised how fortunate she was.

She loved and felt loved.

With sadness, she thought of Sam Midgely. A boy who'd lost his father. A mother who loved him but didn't know how to show it. An anger towards the world propelling him deeper and deeper into trouble. It was a familiar story. Told thousands of times. A happy ending was a rarity.

Then she thought of Jess Beaumont. A woman who didn't quite fit in society. Feeling duty-bound in every decision. Beholden to a dying man who could be angry and abusive. Tapping her head, calling herself an idiot.

Where was her love? Who had her back?

Cassandra and Robert Thwaites. A couple with everything. Money, and a deep affection for one another. The envy of all. A beautiful daughter following her dreams. *What a story!*

Except...

Was it a true story?

Why don't you tell a true story, Robert?

And the woman driving the car... who are you? How much pain must you be in to introduce a scenario that will bring the lives of others crashing down?

In bed, she touched her lips, which, moments before, had pressed against the skin of her children.

Ana and Rose.

Her friend, Paul Riddick, had once had two beautiful daughters.

Was I too hard on him?

For everything that'd happened to him, his passion and desire to help others had burned strong. And yet, she'd turned her back on him in the past.

Alcoholism, aggression, even murder... yes, it wasn't a pretty picture, but neither was losing everything that you loved in such horrendous circumstances... and now, where was he?

Neck deep in drugs and crime.

Could I have stopped this?

Should I have put my morals and sense of personal betrayal aside?

Tearful, and unable to sleep, she texted O'Brien to see if she was awake. She responded almost immediately, and so called her.

'Boss... sorry, Emma...'

'I thought you'd be asleep by now.'

'I can't. You can't either?'

Haven't even tried yet... jury's still out on whether I will.

'I'm sorry,' O'Brien continued.

'For what?'

'For... you know...' She broke off.

'Listen, none of this is on you.'

'Yes, but—'

'None of it, Lucy. Still, that's not why I'm phoning now. To talk about us.'

'*Us.* Okay...' Gardner could only imagine how stunned O'Brien must have been by her using that word.

And why had she used it? Was it something she really wanted?

'Is it about Paul?'

'No,' Gardner said.

'What happened tonight with Robert Thwaites?'

'Definitely not... no... I'd just like to talk to you about my children, if that's okay?'

'Of course it is,' O'Brien said.

So, Gardner spoke at length about Ana and Rose, and how fortunate she was to have two loving children in her life.

17

For John Atkinson, the morning was as cold as they come.

Yes, the flimsy farmhouse walls, and the draughty, cavernous bedroom, played a part in that, but it wasn't the entire story.

The freeze was mainly because of Jen, who was lying in the same position she'd fallen asleep in.

With her back to him.

'Enough,' he said.

His demand got no response.

'Please?' He softened his tone.

Nothing.

With neither option working, he vacated the marital bed and gazed out of his window over the white wilderness...

His eyes widened. 'Bloody hell!'

Ahead, on the outskirts of his property, smoke was rising from behind a patch of trees.

At sixty-seven, John had been trying, of late, under the doctor's advice, to avoid too much exertion first thing in the morning, for fear of writing off the rest of the day to exhaustion or injury.

Trekking the length of his farmyard in deep snow, with a shotgun hung over one shoulder, was exertion and then some.

But a wispy trail of smoke marring the otherwise pristine blue sky above his property was a cause for concern. So, he allowed curiosity and purpose to drive him on, while his fast breaths pumped mist into the cold air.

Heavy boots crunching in the snow, he regarded the surrounding trees and bushes, which often soothed him when so delicately frosted. Today, he couldn't find any comfort in the sight.

Because something was very wrong.

His path led him past several barns. Their red paint striking against the white landscape. His animals seemed quieter than usual. He considered checking, but the smoke was the biggest priority.

Over halfway, he swept his eyes over the distant trees, fences and barns, their outlines softened by snow. Then he let his eyes fall to the ground again, scouring for footprints and other signs of intruders.

Nothing.

Twice he stopped to catch his breath. Then, he'd remain still and listen, but only ever heard the eerie, soft whistle of wind, punctuated by the noises of his animals.

When he was close enough to the smoke for it to interfere with his vision, his heart raced.

There had been a visitor!

Up ahead, a fence marked the boundary of his farmland. A trail of footprints led from the fence towards a small derelict red barn ten metres off to his left. When John was close enough to the footprints to tell that whoever had trekked one way had headed back again, he raised his eyes to the patch of trees just beyond the fence which hid the source of the smoke.

Technically, whatever had been vandalised was not on his property.

He looked left. However, the derelict barn the visitor had visited most certainly was on his land.

He took his shotgun from his shoulder. He'd already checked it was loaded, earlier, but as was his habit, he cracked it to double check again.

Good to go.

He turned the shotgun between the barn and the patch of trees. The barn had been out of use for many years, so he opted to check out the smoke first.

After catching his breath again, he climbed over his fence, and followed alongside the two sets of footprints and approached the trees.

The road into town lay beyond. An unlit road that allowed a national speed limit of sixty.

So, it didn't really come as a major surprise when John Atkinson saw that the source of the smoke was a vehicle.

In a frame of spiralling snowflakes, the smouldering Mercedes looked rather surreal.

John didn't get too close. He'd only just fought off a bout of pneumonia and wasn't about to let those fumes antagonise his lungs.

Still, he didn't need to get any closer to know that this had been no accident.

The wreckage was some way back from the trees and the bonnet didn't look dented.

There'd been collisions in the past up here, silly kids, hitting ridiculous speeds. There'd been some nasty ones, all right, but never had he seen such a shell of a vehicle left behind before.

Blackened patches and blistered paint marred the once sleek exterior. The soft light revealed the glinting jagged edges of the shattered windows.

Keeping his grip on the shotgun tight, he called out, 'Hello?'

He turned full circle, scanning the surrounding trees and road that wound off into the distance for signs of movement. 'Is anyone here?'

Nothing.

He tried to weigh up where the person who'd intruded on his

property and headed to the barn had gone. If they'd set fire to this vehicle, which appeared to be the only plausible explanation, then they either walked down that road, someone else picked them up, or—

He caught movement off to his left.

Finger on the trigger, he swung his weapon at the source.

With his heart hammering in his chest, and his eye against the sight, he watched a red squirrel scurry up a tree.

He lowered the weapon and sighed. 'Almost made a mess of you, little man.' He'd be happy to kill a grey one – they were vermin. But a red one... no... that'd have put even more of a downer on the day.

Maintaining some distance from the wreck, he circled to the other side. He looked down and saw the footprints moving off to the road several metres away. There was a long indent in the snow that moved in a line alongside the footprints.

A bike.

He looked back at the vehicle. Not a roof rack.

A fold-up bike, perhaps?

Ahead, beyond the trees and the fence, he sighted his derelict red barn again.

His mouth ran dry.

But why did you go in there?

Approaching the derelict barn, John wondered how long it'd been since he'd last been in there.

A fair number of years. He'd closed it down after the roof had rotted beyond repair and had earmarked it for flattening. If his daughter had still been a child, and not a grown woman, he'd have done it the very next day, but as no one would be silly enough to venture in, it'd hit the back burner, as did most things these days. What with his age, and the doctor's advice to avoid too much exertion.

Knowing that whoever had paid it a visit the previous evening had probably already cycled off didn't seem to help with his anxiety, so again, for the third time, he cracked and checked his shotgun cartridges.

He expected to find the barn broken into but was surprised to see that it hadn't been. It seemed he'd forgotten to put a padlock on; an oversight on his part. A rickety old structure like this one really should have been closed off.

John pushed the door open, and the hinges groaned in protest.

He leaned in. 'Anyone in there?'

Of course, there was no response, because deep down, he already knew it was unoccupied.

Still, you could never be too careful.

So, as he stepped inside, he led with his weapon. 'I've a shotgun, so any sudden surprises will end badly...' His voice echoed through the empty space.

Feeling more confident that he was alone, he moved further into the barn, breaking through each sliver of light piercing the weathered wooden wall.

He turned the gun side to side as he advanced, ready for an intruder, but he only saw dust motes dancing in the slivers.

'Nothing here, John,' he mumbled to himself.

He took a deep breath through his nostrils. The place was a pungent mix of musty hay and rusting metal.

Sighing, he paused halfway into the barn, realising it was time to trek back. However, just before turning, his eyes finally adjusted completely to the limited light, and he caught sight of something in the far corner of the barn.

His breath caught in his throat. 'Good lord.'

He sighted the shape with his shotgun and continued.

Several steps later, and after confirming that the shape was of a figure, he felt his stomach turn, and tasted the acid rising at the back of his throat. 'Stand up... *now*... I see you. *Now*.'

He waited.

The figure remained completely still.

'Do as you're told, man, or I'll shoot you. Don't be in any doubt.'

John took another step, hands tight on the shotgun, eye pressed to the sight, the figure growing larger and larger. 'This is my land... stand and—'

He flinched and darted backwards. 'Jesus wept.'

He shook his head. 'It can't be.'

Retreating to the exit, he chanced one last look in the gloom at the gift left by last night's visitor.

He recalled his cat, Tara, who'd died earlier in the year. Her gifts of dead rats and the like. Not pleasant. But never had he received a gift like this.

A human skeleton.

A *headless* one at that.

Outside, he returned to his farmhouse as quickly as his ageing legs would allow him.

He needed to talk to Jen about the next steps.

It'd be a brief conversation. What choice did he have but to call the police?

If it'd just been the burned-out car, he'd have left it, and let someone else call it in. After all, it'd been outside his boundaries.

But now, if he left it, and the police widened their search net, they'd discover the skeleton anyway, and put him firmly in their crosshairs.

No. It was best to be open and honest about the event. Avoid suspicion. Point the skeleton out to them. Hope their scrutiny of his farmyard went no further than that red barn and that patch of trees.

Jen would have to understand that this was the lesser of two risks.

At least one thing was for absolute certain, now. Jen would have to knock off the silent treatment.

18

After viewing the remains in the red barn, Gardner joined Rice back outside.

Mercifully, the snow had taken a break, although today's forecast was rather bleak. The snow was causing all kinds of disruption. Travel, usually the first casualty of bad weather, was a write-off, but most significantly, for Gardner, was that the forensic team were working with the burned-out vehicle and the decapitated skeleton in the barn in horrendous conditions.

At Marsh's request, the authorities had gritted the roads leading from town to the farmyards earlier than scheduled. At least her people had the safest possible access.

They'd already confirmed the wrecked Mercedes as Jess Beaumont's. Presumably, the same woman who'd transported Sam Midgely to the library yesterday to plant the skull, had deposited the skeleton in the barn, doused the vehicle in some kind of accelerant and then used a fold-up bike to exit the scene.

It seemed their perpetrator had considered the Mercedes past its sell-by date. She'd been right. Every police officer in the area was aware of it.

Still, Gardner thought, looking at the white expanse, *cycling back in the snow?*

This was one driven individual.

Gardner was half-expecting a report of someone in a ditch, lying frozen alongside the bike, but no such news yet.

Or no such *luck* as Rice had commented earlier.

'And?' Rice asked her, approaching her at the taped entrance to the barn. He was rubbing his hands together after forgetting his gloves. That had been a grave error. 'Well, is it worth me suiting up too, boss?'

Gardner peeled off her own white oversuit. 'No. I don't think you're likely to recognise him.'

Rice raised an eyebrow. 'Him?'

'Robin thought the skull was male, remember?'

'So, you're assuming it's the same victim?'

Gardner screwed the suit into a ball. 'I guess I am. There's another note. In the ribcage this time.'

Gardner marched over to a bin liner readied for suits and dropped hers inside. She paused and stared out over the burned-out vehicle, and the SOCOs investigating it.

She heard Rice crunching in the snow behind her to keep up.

When he was back alongside her, she said, 'Ever feel like everything is just one big game?'

'You serious?' Rice said. 'Every day! Come on, what did the note say?'

'The note said: *Even in the middle of nowhere, John, the truth exists.*'

Rice stepped in front of her and turned full circle with his hands outstretched. 'Guess we can class this as the arsehole of nowhere.'

'Those weren't the words.'

'Same thing. So where exactly, in this *arsehole*, is the truth, do you think?'

Gardner pointed in the distance at the farmhouse. 'In there.'

'You sound confident.'

Gardner trudged away in the snow, saying over her shoulder, 'No point in playing a game if you're not confident.'

* * *

Clouded with deep-set wrinkles all over his face, the farmer, John Atkinson, looked every second of his sixty-seven years. With calloused hands, he fidgeted with a plaid cushion on the sofa on which he sat. Jen Atkinson, who sat alongside, also possessed many wrinkles, but the majority congregated around her eyes.

Both their gazes flitted restlessly around the room. Gardner tried to follow their eyes around the lounge. A cold fireplace, heaped with the ashes from the previous day; antique farm tools decorating the walls and a wooden table holding a vase of wildflowers.

So far, Rice and Gardner's questions had yielded little beyond what they already knew.

John's sighting of the smoke, his slow lumbering walk, his encounter with the burned-out vehicle and his final, grisly discovery.

She could understand John being completely shaken up following that experience, but his wife, Jen, appeared a lot worse.

'Just keep ourselves to ourselves, as you can see,' John continued. 'No reason for anyone to bother us like this.'

The note, which Gardner was yet to get to, seemed to suggest someone felt they had a reason.

Rice was pacing alongside the mantelpiece, looking at some family photographs when he spoke. 'Still rather peculiar, isn't it?'

Gardner watched John's eyes dart nervously and fall. His wife chewed aggressively at her bottom lip.

'Don't you think?' Rice continued.

'I suppose,' John said.

'I *mean*, why your property, Mr Atkinson?' Gardner asked. 'Why *your* barn?'

'*Derelict* barn,' John said, his eyes darting up to her face. 'I'd nothing to do with it.'

'I appreciate that, but it still belongs—'

'It was due to be demolished.'

'When?' Rice asked.

'A couple of years back,' John said, shrugging. 'My legs aren't what they once were. Or my back. Things get put back these days. Doctor's orders.'

'I see. Just you two here, is it?' Rice said.

'Yes, why?'

'Who's this?' Rice asked, pointing at a framed picture.

'Clara. Our daughter.'

'You all look happy,' Rice continued.

'And younger,' John said and laughed, but he'd clearly forced his light-hearted response.

'Family holiday?' Gardner asked.

'A long time ago. Fifteen years,' John said. 'Lanzarote. She's in her mid-thirties now.'

Rice nodded. 'And what does she do?'

'She works over in Thailand, Southeast Asia. Teaching. Has done for many years now.'

The link was like a spark of electricity jolting through Gardner. She exchanged eye contact with Rice and caught the same response in his expression.

Ruby May Thwaites. Mid-thirties. Lived overseas. Sydney.

Clara Atkinson. Mid-thirties. Lived overseas. Thailand.

'Beautiful country,' Gardner said, controlling her surging adrenaline. Links were everywhere. Many would be coincidences. 'Does she come home often?'

'Not as much as we like,' John said. 'She's back in England right now. Staying with her boyfriend, Doug, in Coventry. She'll be over here for Christmas Day. Weather permitting.' He sighed.

Gardner looked at Jen, who, apart from a brief greeting before, was still yet to speak. She did glance up and make eye contact, every now and again, more times than Jess Beaumont had yesterday anyway, and seemed engaged in the dialogue. But she was clearly too nervous to speak. 'Mrs Atkinson, what's your take on these events?'

Her brow creased, and she gave a quick shake of her head, clearly unsettled by being suddenly dragged into the dialogue.

'I don't know...' She looked up and made eye contact for the first time in a while. 'Someone disposing of a body, perhaps? Best place, I guess. The middle of nowhere.'

Gardner recalled the note. *Funny you should say that.*

'Strange though,' Rice said, coming away from the mantelpiece. 'That a murderer would wait until the victim had rotted to a skeleton?'

John put the plaid cushion down on the sofa beside him. He looked up with narrowing eyes. 'You're the police... what's your take?'

How quick was that descent into aggression?

'That if it wasn't for the burning car,' Rice said. 'Those remains would probably have gone undiscovered.'

'So, what's your point?'

'The car was just a means to draw your attention to your barn. I think someone wanted you to discover the body.'

'Nonsense.'

'You asked for our take,' Rice continued.

'Wish I hadn't. This whole thing is surely opportunistic. Someone grabbing a chance to dispose of a body, and then burning the car to cover tracks and get rid of the DNA and other evidence.'

'Hardly covering tracks by setting fire to a vehicle not twenty metres from the body,' Rice said.

'Enough,' John said, standing up. 'I don't really get the point of this questioning. I've told you everything that happened... the car and the *skeleton*. This has nothing to do with me. No one has targeted me. My money is on opportunity. As I just said. So, until you have otherwise, then I've animals to feed.'

Gardner fixed him with a stare. 'It wasn't an opportunity, John. There was a note left in the ribcage. A note with your name on it.'

John paled. 'Jesus.'

Jen stiffened. Gardner was concerned that she might just bite through that bottom lip.

'That makes little sense.'

Gardner took out her notebook and read from it. '*Even in the middle of nowhere, John, the truth exists.*'

Gardner watched him take deep breaths as he processed it. He sat down again.

Rice drew alongside Gardner. 'Middle of nowhere, Mrs Atkinson. Like you said before. This person had the same thought.'

She opened her mouth to reply. No words came out. Gardner saw the blood on her bottom lip.

'John is a common name,' John said.

'It is,' Gardner said. 'But these occurrences aren't common. Someone has worked to make them happen. Seems they knew the name of the person who'd make the discovery.'

John shook his head. 'Do I need a lawyer?'

Gardner did her best to look surprised. 'Of course, that's up to you... if you feel you need one, then, by all means, let's get that arranged.'

'Well, I *don't* feel I need one,' John said, looking more and more flustered.

'It's up to you,' Gardner continued. 'Maybe, then we can continue everything at the station and—'

'Listen,' John said, raising his hands. 'I don't know what this is about!'

'Well, let's start with the truth,' Rice said.

'That is the bloody truth.'

'No, sorry, I meant the note. What do you think the truth on the note is referring to?'

'I've no bloody idea!'

'Is it regarding a lie, perhaps?' Rice said. 'Can you recall any lies you've told?'

'Ridiculous,' John hissed. 'I convinced my daughter that Santa Claus existed until she was ten. Does that count?'

He looked at his wife for support, but she was too busy wringing her hands together and drawing blood from her bottom lip.

Gardner pressed on by asking John whether he knew Robert Thwaites, or Jess Beaumont. Neither name seemed to trigger a response in him. She held back on telling him about the skull recovered last night, which may or may not be from the skeleton in the barn. It was a card she may need later.

Both detectives made extensive efforts to delve into John's past, but he responded with monosyllabic answers and provided very brief biographical details. Farming this land had been his entire life, and before that, his father's. He'd been an only child and, after he and his wife had passed, the property would go to Clara. She and her boyfriend, Doug, had already expressed an interest in taking over one day. Leaving behind the excitement and sun in Thailand to build a family and a business on this land.

Gardner wrapped up the conversation by getting consent from John and Jen for DNA samples. They'd get cleaned up and head into the station, where they'd also record more detailed statements.

Afterwards, trudging back through the snow, Rice said, 'Not sure what this crazy lass had in mind, but delivering bones and notes to these two old men isn't convincing anyone to give up the truth.'

'No,' Gardner said. 'But I expect she knew that already. Whoever is orchestrating this knows what they're dealing with. She sees the truth buried deep. I think you give her very little credit by calling her crazy, Phil. I also think we need to up our game.'

'Up our game?' Rice said, and guffawed. 'How?'

'I don't know yet. But I fear unless we dig up this truth before she finally exposes it, things are going to get messier.'

A red squirrel watching her from the branch of a tree she was passing surprised her. Usually, they ran a mile.

This one clearly felt invincible.

Gardner wished she felt this way, but with no idea where this woman was going to land her next blow, she felt anything but.

19

Cecile Metcalf had been finding people for a long time, and it wasn't unusual for them to turn up in the most unexpected of situations.

But finding a detective inspector dealing drugs from a squat had to be her most unusual yet.

And yet maybe she should have seen something like this coming?

Gardner had warned her that Riddick was an alcoholic who'd lost his wife and two children in horrendous circumstances.

It was hardly a surprise that he was *this* broken.

Still, Gardner had remained adamant that his heart was a good one – so the fact that he was now dealing drugs, and *destroying* lives, was rather out of the blue.

Finding Riddick propping up a bar in the middle of nowhere, or beneath a bridge by a burning drum, or in a sleeping bag in a shop doorway would've felt more fitting to Cecile.

What worried her most was that Gardner had Riddick all wrong.

A passionate man driven for justice regardless of risks? *Really?* A sympathetic individual who'd support the vulnerable no matter the costs? *Are you sure?*

There was no justice, or support for the vulnerable, in the selling of drugs.

No, drug dealing was as far from, 'he holds himself to high standards, Cecile. I don't think I've ever seen a moral compass like it,' as it came.

Cecile, having decided that Gardner's judgement must have been clouded over Riddick, had already made the decision to see this one through on her own.

She'd take all emotion out of the equation.

And if there was one thing that could escalate this whole situation into something dangerous, it was emotion. So, having left her car far down the street, Cecile approached the crumbling terrace on foot.

She felt bad shutting her close friend out and ignoring her calls, but there were conclusions to make. Cleanly, objectively and swiftly. Gardner would bound into that house like a bull in a china shop!

As she passed an old Toyota with flat tyres, she caught her reflection in the glass.

Even though she'd spent the morning prepping herself, seeing the stained and tattered clothes still stunned her. As did her unkempt hair, which she'd deliberately worked into tangles. She'd considered smudges of dirt on her face and hands to really mimic the harshness of street life, but was concerned about hamming it up too much. She had, however, used make-up to paint dark circles beneath her eyes. This hadn't been the first time she'd donned such a disguise, but it'd been a fair number of years since last time, so she believed her age had helped her pull it off more successfully. It'd added to the weary and worn-out look of someone battling addiction.

Although her heart was thrashing in her chest, and the danger before her had her mind playing with serious consequences, she had to admit to thriving off the task.

She glanced right at the crumbling garden wall on which she'd snapped Riddick the previous day and approached the blistered front door.

She lived for moments like this.

Moments of truth and discovery.

Time to find out what you're really up to, Paul.

The downstairs windows were boarded over, so she could hear muffled music creeping free of the property. After knocking on the front door, she took a step back and hopped from foot to foot, desperate to look agitated, and in need of a fix.

For most of the night, she'd considered the scenario in her head. Riddick, or the other bloke he was working with, would answer the door. Cecile would apologise for not phoning ahead, but she'd show that she had good money for a score.

She was confident.

But then, Cecile always felt confident.

Over the years, she'd known a lot of success.

She'd been a bloody good DI, and an even better private investigator—

The door opened.

Still hopping from foot to foot, rubbing her hands together and blowing plumes of white into the chilly morning air, she readied herself.

Unfortunately, neither Riddick nor his companion had opened the door.

Instead, she came face to face with someone she'd not expected to see. Tommy Rose.

And the big, evil bastard looked pissed off.

20

Marsh was playing hardball and, as a result, Gardner's incident room was ridiculously quiet.

The boss stated that this wasn't a murder investigation until they identified a victim. These could be old remains, dug up from a grave-yard, and dropped on a couple of elderly men as some kind of sick prank.

Budgets were tight as it was. Marsh wanted far more before she'd consider lifting and throwing that kitchen sink. Gardner had tried to explain that without a kitchen sink on a collision course, 'more' would remain elusive, but Marsh was not one for moving when her decisions had been made.

To argue otherwise was as pointless as trying to teach an owl to enjoy sunrise.

At least Marsh had consented to Rice and Barnett, which gave her some necessary experience. DC Cameron Suggs and DC Brad Ross made up five.

Rather man heavy.

But then, wasn't it always up here in Yorkshire?

She felt disappointed that she didn't have O'Brien. Not because of her feelings towards her, but because she was so bloody effective.

She smiled when she looked down at the desk at the front of the incident room. O'Brien had ensured her presence remained felt by leaving two cereal bars there.

She bit into one. Yoghurt coated. Her favourite.

And didn't Lucy just know it...

During the last couple of investigations they'd shared, O'Brien had always brought a spare cereal bar in for her. It was what had first caught Gardner's attention. The kind gestures. The second thing that had caught Gardner's attention was those eyes.

Suggs, Ross and Barnett were on time.

Predictably, Rice wasn't.

'Coffee machine,' he gave as an excuse, shrugging. 'I always seem to get stitched up with emptying that bugger.' He put a coffee in front of Gardner. 'Large cappuccino as requested, boss.'

Nice, Gardner thought. *Wriggling your way out of a bollocking because you were doing me a favour.* He sipped his own coffee and went to sit.

All four men sat in bulky, zipped-up winter jackets, rubbing their hands.

It wasn't freezing in here, but it was taking them time to warm up after coming in from the cold.

The infamous budget cuts and spiralling energy costs had resulted in a lukewarm HQ.

Still...

She looked at their faces.

'Before you wave your scarves, can I remind you that this isn't a football stadium? Take your bloody jackets off.'

They complied, half grumbling, half sniggering.

'Now, Cam, I haven't asked you on board because of your sense of humour—'

'Good job,' quipped Ross.

'You're not funny either, Brad,' Gardner said, flashing Ross a look. 'But I'll get to you in a minute. Cam, you're here because of your IT skills. You can handle HOLMES now as I haven't got access to my usual gap-year student, Matt Blanks.' Matt Blanks wasn't really a gap-year student; he just looked rather young for his already young age. 'You can back up Ray as he does what he does best – negotiates the data.'

'Data!' Barnett snorted. 'All that time I spend in the gym, and you confine me to a desk.'

Gardner regarded him. 'Take it as a compliment that your intelligence trumps the size of your guns... and back to you, Brad. You're not funny, but you've one of those gentle faces that people just love. First, I need you to stop by on Madeline Sharp, confirm she was online with Jess Beaumont between eight and nine last night. Then, I need you to speak to her colleague at Oxfam, Joe Harris – let me know if you think he has it in him to swipe her keys from her bag. He's seventy and doesn't drive, but be diligent. After that you can start knocking on doors. You can begin on Jess's road. Someone may have seen this suspect stealing the Merc the day before yesterday.'

'No reports were made,' Ross said.

'True,' Gardner said. 'But people can be deliberately ignorant if it saves them bother. If Jess left her key in the vehicle, and this woman simply climbed in and drove off, they may have thought she was borrowing the car – friend of the family, perhaps. Yeah... I know... long shot... but I've lost count of the number of times it's come down to long shots.'

'Now,' Gardner said, turning to the board and pointing out a photograph. 'The skull that Robert Thwaites pulled out of the treasure chest and...' She moved her finger to the skeleton discovered that morning. 'And the skeleton discovered at the back of John Atkinson's barn. The presence of the burned-out car our suspect was driving, and the written notes left with each part of the remains' – she turned and pointed downwards to the photocopied sheets already laid out for them – 'leave us suspecting that the parts could be the same body. Until that's confirmed by forensics, this isn't a conclusion. Neither is it a conclusion that this body is complete.'

'Be a pleasant set of conclusions,' Barnett offered. 'It'd suggest that there're no more grisly discoveries to come.'

'I agree,' Gardner said. 'But for now, it stays as hope. As I tried to stress a moment ago, our fingers are still in the wind. We don't know where this is blowing. Hopefully, forensics will tell us how this person died, but Robin couldn't identify any telltale signs at the barn or pub. No wounds, or trauma to the bones.

'Identifying the body, or *bodies*, is our absolute priority. If this is an old body, dug up as some kind of prank, then we're not the team for it. If this is a murder investigation, then I need more boots on the ground. Right now, we're in flux.' Even though she knew the door was shut, she checked anyway. 'Nothing worse than being in a state of flux with *her indoors* looking over your shoulder.'

Her indoors was an old-fashioned term for wife at home and had been used by Rice recently. Of course, it was old-fashioned and sexist, but drew a laugh now due to its ironic use. Marsh never left the place, and she micromanaged it to within an inch of its life. It often proved to be a bloody nightmare.

'So, let's find out whether this is a murder. Once and for all. Now, we know decomposition could have occurred in only a matter of weeks if conditions were right, so that leaves our window wide. The best bet is to scour archives for missing people in North Yorkshire over the past number of years. Ray, you good with that?'

He nodded and Gardner continued, 'Obviously, we will look for links between these missing individuals, the Atkinson family and the Thwaites family. Forensics remains our best bet, so we've facial composites being computerised from the skull. Obviously, there'll be a tonne of variation with skin colour and hair, but it might hit on someone reported missing.

'I've also got Marsh's permission to use a couple of officers to re-interview Sam Midgely. I'm going to bring the forensic artist in too, so Sam can describe the woman who bribed him to plant the skull. Also, this suspect spent a reasonable amount of time behind the wheel of that car, so let's see if ANPR clocked her anywhere else. We may get an image of her behind the wheel.

'Back to the Thwaites and the Atkinsons. If their evasive interviews weren't enough to convince you they were hiding something, then have another read of those notes. What interests me is that they both have daughters, mid-thirties, and both living and working overseas. Phil is speaking to them later today. Clara Atkinson is currently back over in Coventry, whereas, as far as I know, Ruby May Thwaites is still in Sydney, Australia.

'Meanwhile, I'll lead when the Atkinsons and Thwaites give their detailed recorded statements this morning. Hopefully, the pressure of being in an interview room will crack their veneer, and they can give us a clearer idea of why they've been targeted with either a prank or a real murder victim.'

'Judging by their attitudes so far, I wouldn't hold your breath,' Rice said.

'No, Phil, you're probably right. I suspect they've been lying about something for a long time. And, as we all know, the longer you lie, the better you become at it.'

* * *

After everyone had left the incident room, Gardner took a deep breath and tried to rid herself of a toxic anxiousness with a slow exhalation. Throughout the entire briefing, she'd been forcing herself to stay focused when all she could think about was Riddick.

She knew now that she was being deliberately ignored by Cecile, and her five phone calls earlier hadn't been responded to. After trying again and being sent straight through to voicemail for the umpteenth time, she flirted with different reasons for Cecile's unexpected behaviour.

Was she concerned for Gardner? Scared that the shock of seeing Riddick in this state would be too much for her?

Or did Cecile simply fear that Gardner would storm on in there and put the lot of them in danger?

Maybe Cecile felt ownership over the case that she'd spent a long time working on gratis, and now wished to close it down herself and bring Riddick home?

Unfortunately, there was another explanation, and the more Gardner thought about it, the more concerning it became...

You haven't gone and got yourself into trouble, have you, Cecile?

21

The concern that maybe she'd bitten off more than she could chew was a rare feeling for Cecile.

It wasn't so much Tommy's size; she'd encountered her fair share of towering, stern, muscular men before. It was his reputation as a violent drug dealer that sent a shiver down her spine.

Her old contacts with the force had divulged that he was responsible for countless murders and disappearances. He was also Teflon; nothing ever stuck. She also knew he had links to prostitution, weapons and, more recently, human trafficking.

He was bad news.

Cecile had watched him leave at ten o'clock last night; she'd certainly not expected him on the doorstep this morning. This wasn't his home, so why had he come back here?

She inwardly cursed herself. She should have come earlier, scoped the house some more, checked for unwanted guests. But that was all irrelevant now.

What was relevant was that *this* junkie act of hers had to be beyond perfect, because if he saw through her, she wouldn't be walking away.

So, Cecile, right now, you're a druggie in need of a fix, nothing more, nothing less.

She wrung her hands together, bounced from foot to foot and fidgeted for a score.

'You didn't call,' Tommy said.

'I know people,' she said. 'They come *here* for me... usually.'

It was the start of her lie. The one she'd prepared for Riddick, the man who supposedly had a heart of gold, and was *not* a homicidal monster.

'Doesn't mean you don't phone ahead,' Tommy grunted. 'And why aren't these people coming for you today? Look at the state of you.'

'Because...' She pulled out a bundle of notes with a trembling hand. 'They rip me off—'

'*Put* that away.' He smacked his head. 'What's up with you?'

'Sorry,' she said, slamming the money back in her pocket and lowering her eyes. Standing up to him and being assertive would be a bad idea. He was used to subservience and fear. It was better he was in his comfort zone, rather than giving him any more adrenaline to play with. 'I can go.'

And God, did she want to leave right now!

Her plan to speak to Riddick had clearly failed. Was he even still here? For all she knew, Tommy could have returned and slung him out at the crack of dawn while she was still getting herself ready. Worse still, maybe this monster had put him down?

No, it was best to make a sharp exit. 'You're right...' She turned. 'I'll pay them—'

'*No*. You're here now. I admire your balls. You want to save a few quid. Who doesn't? Get in here.'

Not the words she wanted to hear.

Going into a confined space with Tommy Rose. There was biting off more than you could chew... and then there was choking to death on it.

She took a step away. 'No, I can't—'

'Now.' She felt his large hand on her shoulder. 'I insist.'

She no longer needed to act like the anxious junkie on the outside, as her insides felt like they were melting.

Get a grip Cecile. To survive now, you need to get a sodding grip.

If she attempted to run, and he caught her, she'd be dead before she could talk him round. She turned back. He'd already stood to one side, lifted his arm high and gestured she walk beneath the tower he'd made.

She complied, bobbing beneath his arm, catching the scent of body odour.

Behind her, she heard the door close, and her heart fell.

She turned to look at him. He was smiling. 'Now let's see what we can do for you.'

Her breath caught in her throat, and her mind went into a spin. *He knows*, she thought.

The man wasn't just a mass of muscle. His senses were just as robust.

He's seen right through me.

22

In her office, smiling, Gardner typed O'Brien a text message thanking her for breakfast. After sending it, her phone rang.

Fiona Lane.

Her smile fell away as she recalled their recent frosty encounters.

'Morning, Fiona.'

'I wanted to put you in the loop immediately regarding a line of enquiry that's been thrown up.'

Straight to the point... Not even a good morning!

'We've recovered traces of a reddish quarry dust from the skull, the remains at the Atkinson farm and even the handwritten notes. We're testing it now. If this quarry dust has a unique mineral composition that differs from other sources, then, well, we've something significant. Historically, we've had results from similar findings in other cases.'

Gardner felt a surge of excitement. She'd encountered this before during a case in Salisbury. In that instance, it'd been soil acting like a fingerprint due to the specific combinations of minerals. It'd taken a while to source local farmyards to identify the location, but it'd proven itself to be a breaking lead.

'Brilliant,' Gardner said. 'How confident are we?'

'Still early, but we've the right people on it. They'll be examining the shape and size of the particles, and there are some powerful techniques like X-ray fluorescence which could throw up a distinct chemical signature. We need to be collecting samples from your local quarries, so we're ready for a match. That's where you come in.'

Except manpower right now is at a premium...

Still, this process had worked before, so she'd need to approach Marsh, guns blazing.

After the call, which fortunately didn't involve any reference to Gardner's inappropriate relationship with a younger officer, Gardner made her approach by phone.

Marsh provided a single officer to collect samples.

Better than nothing.

Despite her never-ending anxiety over Riddick and Cecile, she felt somewhat buoyed by the significant step in this investigation and moved with purpose towards her next interview with Robert Thwaites.

23

Riddick was suffering this morning.

Raising his blood alcohol levels again usually did the trick. But, today, it barely touched the sides.

A heroin comedown was partly to blame, as was the image of Henry's lifeless face which refused to vacate his mind. And, to make matters worse, Tommy had returned at the crack of dawn.

Riddick had to be on the top of his game when Tommy was around. Even though Tommy looked like a stupid psychotic meathead who could be easily duped, the truth was very different. He was smart and vigilant. He wouldn't have climbed this high up the food chain if he wasn't.

If Tommy got a sniff of Riddick's former life, there wouldn't even be time for a discussion. Likewise, if Tommy found out about Riddick's drinking, the outcome may very well be the same.

Admittedly, Tommy may have been turning Riddick into a junkie by using him as a guinea pig, but it was, at least, an addiction the bastard could control. He'd probably consider Riddick's alcoholism more trouble than it was worth. Riddick, therefore, was very careful to excuse himself to the toilet whenever he needed a swig of vodka.

On the plus side, one of Tommy's men had taken away Henry's

body in the dead of night. The sight of the lifeless youngster on the floor had been devastating, and if he'd remained, Riddick doubted he'd have been able to free up enough cognitive space to negotiate his tricky situation.

His phone being switched off was an additional bonus. Tommy didn't want Riddick dealing this morning because he was awaiting confirmation of something else that was in the works. Something that would involve this property.

That *something* was what'd drawn Riddick into this whole sorry mess to begin with.

After taking another swig of vodka and depositing the bottle back with two empty ones behind the panel of the old bath, Riddick looked at his emaciated, unshaven face in the mirror and sighed.

He wondered, briefly, if his family, had they still been alive, would recognise him any more.

After shaking his head and admonishing himself for such ridiculous thoughts, he took himself back off to the living room. When he reached the doorway, he froze. His eyes darted between Tommy and an unexpected visitor. The woman looked nervous and sickly. Bearing, Riddick believed, all the hallmarks of a junkie experiencing withdrawal.

But Riddick's phone was off, so why would there be a punter in the lounge?

And why would Tommy even let her in? Dealing with waifs and strays was way below his paygrade... unless...

Was something else at play here?

He observed her, looking for something out of the ordinary in this fidgety woman. Late fifties perhaps? She was older than usual, that was for sure... Few junkies made it to this age unless they started late in life.

The woman met Riddick's eyes, and his adrenaline surged.

The exterior may have been a perfect match for other individuals of her ilk, but there was a glow in the eyes, a vitality that really shouldn't have been there.

Something was wrong.

He looked over at Tommy, who stood at the door to the hallway, clutching the frame, leaning in, *looking* at him directly.

The guest was now *Riddick's* problem.

God! Did everything always have to be a sodding test in this world?

'Phone was off,' Riddick said, addressing the woman. 'How come you're here?'

The woman, who still had her eyes on Riddick, said, 'I didn't have a number. I *know* others who—'

'There's only one way in,' Riddick said. 'There's a process.'

Which begs the question, Tommy, why the hell have you let her in?

He could hear Tommy tapping the doorframe as he scrutinised.

Riddick needed to play it safe. 'You're going to have to leave and—'

'Too late for all that now,' Tommy interrupted. 'She's in.'

Did you see the same glow in her eyes, Tommy? Did you, too, detect something was off with her? Is that why you let her in?

Of course, you did, because the rumours are true, aren't they?

You're one smart cookie.

You want to put her down, or...

He inwardly sighed.

Do you want me to put her down?

'Okay,' Riddick said, looking at Tommy. 'So...?' He broke off.

Tommy dropped his hands from the doorframe. 'Just do your thing... attend to her needs.' He smiled at her. 'Sometimes I bend my own rules. Must be something about you' – he waved his finger at her – 'that caught my attention.' He looked back at Riddick. 'I'm going to make a phone call. Quick as you can now.'

He disappeared out of sight.

Riddick paused, listening for Tommy's first steps on the stairs. Then he approached. Again, he met her eyes, and again he saw a vitality he shouldn't be seeing. Suddenly, the nerves she must have been feeling with Tommy casting a shadow over the room suddenly seemed to lift, and she sat up straight.

He took several steps back.

Most junkies that visited here would be up and down like yo-yos, pacing. Not sitting up ramrod straight.

He waited until he could hear Tommy's footsteps on the floor above his head before talking. 'I'll have to search you for bugs.'

She looked at the empty doorway, and then looked back at him, more determined than ever. 'I'm not bugged.'

This was *so* wrong.

'Sorry if I don't take your word for it. Stand up, please.'

She reached into her pocket and put a bundle of notes on the same coffee table from which Henry Ackroyd had picked up last night's fatal dose.

He strode forwards and looked at the pile. This was a large amount of money for a low-level junkie, suggesting it was either stolen, or this was a police set-up – although, he knew from experience that they'd be more clued up.

Had Tommy seen this money?

If he had, he'd have thought exactly the same thing as Riddick was thinking...

'Last time. Stand, so I can check you.'

She shook her head. 'I'm not police. I'm ex-police... like you.'

Riddick felt his stomach turn over. He sucked in a deep breath and took a step backwards.

He opened his mouth to speak, but she put a finger to her lips.

He listened to footsteps on the floor above them, and Tommy's voice booming as he spoke into his phone.

'We don't have long,' she said, standing. 'We need to go.'

'Who the hell are you?'

'I'm here to get you out.'

'It's you that needs to get out. You're about to get me killed. And yourself.' He looked at the money. 'And leave that... he'll expect it now.'

'Come with me now, Paul.'

Jesus... she knows who I am... what the hell is happening?

The world spun. He backed away and steadied himself against the mantelpiece. He focused on trying to slow his breathing down.

'I'll walk straight out now, but only if you walk out with me.' The woman approached.

'I can't... I'm not done here.'

'You've no choice. My name's Cecile Metcalf. Emma sent me.'

Emma? He closed his eyes as he leaned against the mantelpiece, desperate to get his breathing under control.

'Listen to what I'm saying to you, Paul. *Emma sent me.*'

This wasn't happening. Couldn't be happening. Not now.

'Emma sent—'

'I bloody heard you the first time,' he said, opening his eyes. 'Now, get out before I drag you out.'

'If I leave without you now, then you know Emma will come back here.'

Riddick looked up. 'No. She can't...'

It was over. He'd tried, but he'd failed, and now, to protect Emma, he had to leave. He was about to ask Cecile if Gardner knew where he was, but then realised it was a pointless question. If Gardner knew, she'd be here already.

But even the fact that she didn't yet know was irrelevant. What was he going to do? Knock Cecile over the head and tie her up?

No.

It was over.

'Okay, I—'

Cecile cut him off with a finger to her lips.

Tommy's voice from the floor above had stopped.

'Come on,' she whispered.

But it was too late.

Riddick could hear Tommy coming downstairs.

24

Expensive solicitor in tow, Robert Thwaites delivered his detailed statement.

Now he'd come to terms with the shock, and sobered up, his recount was coherent, and more in keeping with what you'd expect from an experienced storyteller.

Unfortunately, the improved clarity in the sequence of events brought nothing new to the table, and if anything, made the elusive truth hinted at in the note feel even more elusive to Gardner.

Midway through the interview, she'd concluded that she'd need something from his past to approach him with. Something that would send him into a spin. Crack his articulate veneer.

Gardner also re-interviewed his wife, Cassandra. She remained as robust as ever. Her story didn't vary from her account last night and offered no differences from Robert's version either.

While John Atkinson was being readied for the interview, Gardner made another series of futile attempts to contact Cecile before catching up with Brad Ross. Ross had spoken to Madeline Sharp to confirm that she'd been online with Jess Beaumont the previous evening, ruling her out of the crime. Ross was now off to speak to Joe Harris, her Oxfam colleague.

Gardner then contacted Rice, who'd spoken to the Atkinsons' daughter, Clara, by phone. Clara had been left completely in the dark regarding the morning's events at her parents' farm. It was something she'd be flagging up in her upcoming interview with John. No doubt his excuse would be that they didn't wish to worry her, wanting to protect her from upsetting news. But Clara was thirty-five. And eventually, she'd find out that there'd been a body recovered from her parents' barn – wouldn't it have been better for her to hear it from them rather than Rice? Rice had been pressuring her for more information on her parents, but Clara remained guarded, just like her mother and father. She agreed to discuss things further with Rice when she came back to the farmhouse in a couple of days. Rice was yet to contact Ruby May Thwaites. The time difference with Australia made that quite awkward right now.

As she headed back to the interview room, Gardner tried to keep herself focused and positive by reminding herself of the quarry dust, but she couldn't help but feel she was no closer to discovering whether this was an actual murder. Metres from the door of the interview room, her phone rang. It was Robin Morton, the pathologist. She felt a tingle of excitement, but tempered it slightly, because it was probably just the confirmation that some composite images built from computer software using the skull were on their way.

But it was so much more than that.

Enough, in fact, for her to delegate the interview with Atkinson to someone else, while she contacted Rice and Barnett to tell them they'd just moved up a gear.

25

Sweating and agitated, Riddick was on his knees, rooting through the safe hidden beneath the kitchen sink. He counted out five baggies, threw Cecile's money into the safe and locked it.

Back in the lounge, he found Tommy now sitting alongside Cecile.

Understandably, she was as white as a sheet.

The size difference between them was significant. If Tommy so chose, he could draw that arm tight and throttle her.

Riddick dropped the baggies on the table in front of her.

Tommy prodded them. 'Enough to kill several horses there.' He stared left at Cecile. 'You're hungry, aren't you, lass?'

'There're a few of us... not just me,' Cecile said.

Tommy nodded. 'That's good news. It pays to keep our customers breathing.' He nodded at Riddick. 'And you're happy?'

'Yes. No bug. All done.'

Tommy glanced sideways at Cecile again as she slipped the baggies into her pocket.

'All good then.' He stood, keeping his eyes on Cecile.

Cecile glanced up at him, smiled and stood too. 'I'll be off, then.'

Tommy clicked his fingers. 'But wait... where are my manners?'

He regarded his watch. 'Stay a while. We've got some time to kill.' He nodded at Riddick again. 'Fetch the equipment from the kitchen. It'd be rude not to let... sorry...' He looked back at Cecile. 'What's your name?'

'Pat,' she said.

'Well, Pat... it'd be courteous to let you sample the goods.' He raised an eyebrow at Riddick. 'I assume that this is the *new* stuff you tried last night?'

Riddick nodded, his stomach doing somersaults.

'Then, you may wish to go easy until you get used to it, *Pat*. This one packs quite a punch.'

26

Gardner left Barnett in her office to pan relentlessly for gold.

Not only was he lightning fast with all manner of databases, but his people skills were also sharp. He always made a lasting, positive impact on others, hence an uncanny knack of calling in favours from people he'd not seen in donkey's years, people who'd have long forgotten anyone else.

She knew it wouldn't take him long.

In the meantime, she went to put Marsh in the loop, feeling confident she could grow the team.

'Dental records show that the skull in Robert's possession belonged to James Sykes. Born in Leeds in November 1967. Had he lived, he'd be fifty-seven. Ray has already dragged up the case file on his disappearance eighteen months ago. A rather short case file, I might add. I hope someone makes more of an effort to find me if I ever vanish without a trace! Although, we're still filling out gaps, the crux of it is that Sykes was a factory worker, living in a block of flats in Leeds. After failing to come in to work for a week, they made a missing person's report. There were no signs of foul play at his apartment. He had some background of depression, some brushes with the law. There was a suspicion he'd committed suicide. Like I said, early doors. We still need to digest it.'

Marsh was nodding. 'I take it from the excitement in your voice, Emma, that you think he's been murdered then?'

Excited? Hardly the right word... just trying to do my job. 'If James Sykes was murdered eighteen months ago that's ample time for his body to decompose. If he was left outside to the elements and insects, the quarry dust could be an indication of where that may have occurred. So, fingers crossed that we get a match.'

Marsh nodded.

'Still no cause of death?'

'Nothing clear. It could be starvation, or hypothermia. Maybe someone kept him imprisoned in those conditions, and he died? Intentionally or accidentally?'

'That's quite a leap, Emma...'

'Sorry. Just hypothesising. Also, James Sykes' skull was taken from that body. It was detached carefully, and the match is perfect. So, James Sykes disappears, and eighteen months later, his body is dumped on two people by a mysterious woman who has stolen Jess Beaumont's car? The notes indicate that it's something to do with their past, and some hidden truth. I don't really know what more I need at this stage... There's clearly something way off here. Suicide won't cut it with this one any more and I can't run a case like that on fresh air.'

'Okay. Let me think... there're six of you already so—'

'Five,' Gardner interrupted.

'You're forgetting the officer I already gave you to collect samples,' Marsh said.

Fair point. 'Still, six isn't enough.'

'I get that.' Marsh sighed. 'Okay, how about...'

Here it comes... six more, surely?

'Three? Yes, I can spare three,' Marsh said.

'Three?' Emma rose, her hands in the air. 'Just three? That's still fresh air!'

Marsh raised an eyebrow and waited for the hands to come back down before speaking.

'You want to talk about fresh air, Emma, then let's talk about how much of it's blowing through our coffers...'

God, here we go... No thanks! Gardner had to force herself not to roll her eyes.

'Yes, didn't think so,' Marsh said. 'Three... and I'll have to try for that. You may have to settle with two. And that includes the officer I've already given you to collect quarry samples.'

Bloody hell.

'If necessary, I'll muck in,' Marsh said.

Jesus, Gardner thought, *there really must be a lot of fresh air in those coffers if her indoors is offering to step out of HQ.*

27

The best option was to play along with Tommy's game. Blowing their identities would condemn him and Cecile.

And, if Riddick turned on Tommy physically, the odds were massively against him. Tommy was a giant, and most certainly armed.

So same outcome.

The game was horrible... brutal... but, in a way, they still had the upper hand. Tommy had no reason to believe that Riddick wasn't Jay Turner, and his suspicions over Cecile were just that. Suspicions. She *still* had an opportunity to prove him wrong and walk away.

Riddick prepped the needle.

He tried his best to ensure the dose was as small as possible without arousing Tommy's suspicions, but having experienced it himself, and watching Henry die, he knew that Cecile was still about to receive one hell of a kicking.

And, like Henry, she'd also have zero tolerance.

The risk was high.

But the risk of not doing it remained higher.

As Riddick leaned in with his needle, he made eye contact with her, trying somehow to convey that this was the best option available. He could see the terror sitting behind her eyes, but he could also see the clarity and acceptance. He also thought he detected the briefest of nods.

In fact, it was to their advantage that Tommy had insisted on Riddick using the needle; it was highly unlikely that Cecile would know what she was doing, and it may have looked very unconvincing.

Willing himself not to throw up over what he was doing, he pushed the drug into her bloodstream.

He watched her eyes turn to clouds.

His heart thrashed in his chest. *You can take it.*

Eventually, her body dropped back.

After a few minutes, Cecile merely looked at peace, and Riddick felt grateful. The terror and anxiety must have been traumatic and exhausting.

'Okay, she took it,' Tommy said. 'Good going. No stranger to it, I imagine. Still don't trust her. Let's get her upstairs. I've some cuffs. We can restrain her and when she wakes, I'm sure she'll be far more transparent. People always tend to be more truthful in the haze, don't you find?'

Riddick couldn't help himself. 'Is all this really necessary?'

Tommy sat up straight, his eyes widening.

'Sorry... she just seemed lost. Like nearly everyone else that comes to the door. A junkie.'

'Have I overestimated you, Jay?'

Riddick shook his head. 'No.'

'First rule in this game, Jay, is they're never just junkies. Everyone has an agenda. All that money? Not using the phone? She's either stupid enough to be setting herself up with some business, or she's here on behalf of someone else. Also, stupid. And, if I'm wrong, she gets a free high out of it. No great shakes. But those eyes, Jay, did you see those eyes?'

Riddick knew he'd have noticed. He felt dreadful conceding right now that Tommy, sharp as a tack, had that spot on. But it was better that he gave him something to elevate himself again in his eyes. It was the respect he'd earned from Tommy that had brought him this far.

'Yes, they were clear. Too clear for a junkie. But I checked for bugs.'

'I know you would've done, Jay. But that's just the beginning. When there's a game to be played' – he looked down at Cecile – 'you always make sure that the last move is yours. Now help me get her upstairs.'

28

When Gardner got back to her office, Barnett was just coming off the phone and scribbling down notes. He hit the keyboard again, made a few sounds of approval, and wrote something else down too.

There was a knock at the door and Rice poked his head in. 'Ready?'

Gardner looked at Barnett, who nodded.

Gardner and Rice sat opposite Barnett, readying their own notebooks.

'Interesting beginnings for our victim, Mr James Curtis Sykes,' Barnett began. 'His parents, Derek and Agnes, were social workers. In 1980, Leeds council believed the homeless issue was getting out of hand. They handpicked Derek and his wife to run a new homeless shelter, which still exists today. It's called Bright Day. They housed them and their then thirteen-year-old boy, James, and his four-year-old sister, Elizabeth, in a separate property just behind the shelter. To begin with, Bright Day achieved some acclaim for the council, and Thatcher's government.'

Rice guffawed. 'Probably for cleaning up the streets rather than helping anyone! The north of England too, eh? Now that was unusual for them lot back then!'

Barnett continued, 'At eighteen, in 1985, James finished his schooling and opted to work at Bright Day with his parents while he acquired the necessary qualifications for social work. Because of ill health, Agnes retired in 1988, and Derek in 1989 to care for her full-time. James, who'd been attending night school for the relevant qualifications, took over the gig.' Barnett checked his notes. 'That made him twenty-two. And this is where it gets interesting.'

Gardner leaned forward. 'James Sykes *only* lasted two years before he left Bright Day. The details surrounding his exit are still unclear. However, James spent the rest of his life as a factory worker, earning little. It makes you wonder why he suddenly left that job, and why his entire family had to uproot from that house behind the shelter.'

'A family of social workers, eh? What do you expect?' Rice asked. 'All sounds suspicious to me. You can't have that many do-gooders in one place. Recipe for disaster.'

'The sister, Elizabeth, wasn't a social worker,' Barnett said and sighed. 'She was institutionalised at fifteen for severe mental health issues. She attempted suicide on three occasions. However, before her seventeenth birthday, she made it out briefly, but...' Barnett looked down, clearly affected by what he'd been reading. 'She got caught up in a house fire that killed her parents and left her burned and catatonic. She still has round-the-clock care to this day.'

'Poor girl,' Gardner said. 'Is this James Sykes' only remaining family?'

Barnett nodded.

The phone rang. Barnett took the call, greeted someone called Carrie, held up a finger to apologise to Gardner and listened intently. He made more notes.

As he did so, Gardner regarded a notable change in his expression. At first, his eyes widened before a misty glaze passed over them. His face then seemed to crumple. 'Are you sure, Carrie?'

After hearing her response, Barnett gave a gentle shake of his head.

Gardner nodded over at him, trying to catch his attention. She wanted to mouth, 'Are you all right?', but he was evading her eyes.

His expression darkened further as he listened. 'Thanks, Carrie.' He ended the call.

'Ray, is everything all right?'

Barnett didn't look up. He rubbed his temples, shook his head again and then rose to his feet. He marched for the door, catching Gardner's eyes en route. 'I'm sorry. Give me a minute.'

'Of course,' Gardner said.

After he left the room, Rice said, 'Whoa. Did you just see that?'

Gardner rose and went over to the desk. She looked down at Barnett's scribbled notes.

Shelter name (1991) Bright Day. Original name—

'The name of the shelter only changed to Bright Day in 1991,' Gardner said, looking at Rice. 'Some kind of fresh start? Maybe, after getting rid of James Sykes following the controversy, the council and government wanted to put as much distance between the old and new order as they could.'

'Must have been one hell of a controversy,' Rice said. 'So, what do you think spooked Ray?'

'Something about the original name, I think... He hasn't written it down. How does Ray have any connection to a homeless shelter before 1991?'

'Beats me,' Rice said.

Gardner's office door burst open. It was Suggs, looking as white as a sheet. 'It's Ray...'

Gardner moved towards the detective 'What Cam?'

'He's in the corridor... I don't know... he's clutching his chest... We've called the ambulance.'

Shit. Gardner ran.

Knaresborough Town shivered under a white blanket.

It was a quiet morning for Jess Beaumont and Oxfam in the market square.

The perfect opportunity to slip a thriller from the second-hand bookshelf.

Jess's brain was permanently overworked, and she loved the way a writer could take on that responsibility of guiding her thoughts – it provided respite.

Unfortunately, however, the lever that usually allowed her to hand control over to an author was completely inoperable today.

She'd suffered an awful night with her father, who'd woken hourly, shouting for Daisy, Jess's late mother. And every time Jess had attended to him, there'd been more signs that he was losing the ability to recognise her. Once, he'd even hurled abuse at her, and called her a 'temptress, here to relieve him of his money'.

She didn't miss the irony. It wouldn't be long before he was in a home, and that would most certainly relieve him of all his money.

Also, someone had just informed her that the Mercedes had been recovered.

At least what remained of it.

And now she needed a new car. It was her fault, so she didn't think the insurance would be in any hurry, which meant she'd have to *relieve* her dad of some money to get one.

Temptress that she was!

Thank God she'd the power of attorney. Imagine having to tell him about his car and ask him for a new one?

The bell tinkled as the door to the shop opened. Cold air blasted her.

Wearing a fur-lined parka, Laura Wilson stepped in, kicking the snow from her boots onto the mat. She closed the door behind her and smiled over at Jess who instantly forgot about the cold. Laura always radiated warmth, and the possibility of another positive chat with her today suddenly made Jess feel more resilient in the face of recent issues.

'Like a ghost town out there,' Laura said. 'Mind you, only a fool would go out in this weather.' Her mouth curled into a smile. Fine lines appeared around her eyes. 'I guess that makes me the fool.'

Jess smiled. She wished she could approach the world with the same sincerity, grace and contentment. She stroked the sunflower lanyard. Rather than battling through every single day.

Laura strolled over to the Christmas tree beside the front desk and prodded a red bauble with her gloved hand. She raised an eyebrow. 'Have you been moving the baubles again, Jess?'

Jess smiled, making eye contact with Laura. She always found it easier to do so with Laura than with anyone else. 'They looked wrong this morning. All wrong. I couldn't relax. How do you think they look now? Be honest. I'd prefer it—'

'I'm always honest. And I think exactly what I thought yesterday morning,' Laura said. 'It looks like a queen has decorated it.'

'No... no...' Jess said, looking down. 'The green baubles were too close together. Now, the red, green and blue alternate more regularly. Can't you see?' She carried on looking down until she got an answer.

'Alternating to perfection,' Laura said. 'And, having experienced forty-eight Christmases, I can say that with confidence.'

Jess smiled and nodded. She chanced a look up and found she could lock eyes with her again for a short time.

Laura sidled along until she was at the desk, facing Jess.

'Are you here for those books you put aside? Betty came in yesterday and suggested they go back on the shelf. I told her what's what! No one has touched them since. Do you want them now?' She looked down and slipped the three crime books from beneath the counter.

Laura laid her gloved hand on the books. 'Never in doubt. And today, I have my five pounds.' She reached into her parka and slid the note over the table.

'Thanks. But like I said, you could have taken them yesterday and paid today. We trust you. I trust you. Honestly.'

'Yes, but would you have felt comfortable doing so?'

Jess looked up, shrugged and smiled. 'No. Just because rules are rules. But that's down to me, not you.'

'It's very much down to me, young lady! I wouldn't want to make you uncomfortable. The service in here is impeccable. Credit where credit is due.'

Jess blushed. 'Thanks.'

'You look tired, dear,' Laura said, opening a bag for life and slipping in the books.

Jess was still blushing. 'My father. He had a terrible night. Didn't recognise me at one point. Didn't know what I was going to do. Called me a temptress... after his money. I'm not... well, obviously, I'm not. I'm his daughter, but... do you think I'm after his money?'

'Why would you ask me that, dear?'

'Because he paid for the house, and the Mercedes, and the two-seated sofa, and—'

'He's your father, dear. If he can't buy you those things, then no one else can. My father was a prince. He used to bring me something home from work every day. Some days, it could be as wonderful as a new doll. Other days, he might bring me back some liquorice... but always something. So, if your father doesn't, what chance do any of us have?' Laura laughed. 'Now ignore my frivolous comments, and...' Laura reached over and took Jess's hand.

Jess didn't move her hand. It felt awkward, but right somehow. If that made sense. Which it clearly didn't.

'It's time to let me help.'

Jess shook her head. Filled with anxiety, she couldn't lift her eyes again. 'I can't... He won't.'

'It's time.'

'No. He doesn't know you. If he sees an unfamiliar face, he'll say horrible things. He'll be nasty. I couldn't bear it. Please... I think it'll be okay for a while longer.'

'What're you afraid of, Jess?'

'Him throwing things. Hurting you. The way he shouts. I don't want you to hear the way he shouts.'

'And yet you know what I used to do?'

'Yes...'

Laura was a retired nurse.

'And I'm not even fifty!' Laura said. 'Meaning there's life in these bones yet. I retired early because I had to take care of my father. Now he's gone, I'm at a loose end. You think your father will offer anything I haven't seen before?'

'He won't accept it. He won't. He just won't.' Jess could feel her twitches kicking in. She shook her head. 'Please... I'm sorry... but please.'

Jess could feel Laura squeezing her hand. 'Okay. Can I make one suggestion... just one, and then you can throw me out?'

Jess didn't respond. She closed her eyes, trying to force back the twitches.

'Let me meet him. Just once. Let me see for myself. I can, at least, give you my honest advice. If I can't help, I'll be honest. If he needs to go to a home, I'll be honest. And then, you can do with that what you wish. Please, Jess... it's time to let someone else in.'

Jess could feel the tears spilling out and felt a gloved hand wiping them from her cheek. For a moment, she thought of her mother. The only other person she'd ever let close. The way she'd used to hold her, comfort her and wipe those tears away. How she missed it.

And for the briefest of seconds, she was there with her again.

It felt wonderful.

Special.

And for that reason, she opened her eyes and gave Laura something she'd not given anyone since her mother had died.

She gave Laura her trust.

30

Once the hospital had run their tests and concluded that Barnett had a heart like an ox, which made sense considering the size of the body he had to power, they gave him the thumbs-up to go home.

Barnett's vehicle was still up at HQ, so Gardner offered to drive him.

'No,' Barnett said. 'I'm fine. Take me back with—'

'Not on your life,' Gardner said, pinning her debit card to the reader on the parking machine before plucking her ticket back out.

Barnett shook his head. 'Don't do this... boss... come on. If this was Phil, he'd be demanding I go back to work, *not* sending me home!'

'But I'm not Phil.' *Thankfully.* 'And I'm glad you're fine, Ray, but I'm not. Neither are *most* of your colleagues. You're a rarity in that place in that you're quite popular. You scared the living shit out of me and everyone else.'

'It was a *bloody* panic attack. Haven't you ever had one?'

'Not one that put me in hospital.'

Barnett sighed loudly. 'Cam overreacted!'

'Like I said, testament to how much he likes you! Anyway, the doctor said you need to rest. This argument is not rest.'

'They *always* say to rest.'

'For good reason.'

Communication ended abruptly when they stepped outside. The wind was bracing, and both ducked their heads beneath hoods as they shuffled through slush and snow to her vehicle. They shivered in the stony silence as Gardner whacked the heat high and negotiated the barrier out of the car park.

Gardner was desperate to know what had triggered Barnett's panic attack, but she didn't want to prod him too much. It was clearly something significant. It'd brought him to his knees – literally! Last thing she wanted to do was trigger another episode. HR would not be best pleased with her choice of actions. Neither would Barnett, who she considered a friend and a colleague.

Annoyingly, he was probably making her wait on purpose, because of how pissed off he was with her.

'Okay, can I come back in the morning?' Barnett said.

'The doctor said twenty-four hours—'

'Oh, for pity's sake, boss! Bloody doctors. I don't trust them, anyway!' Barnett said.

'Many people don't trust us,' Gardner said.

'Thinking about some people I've worked with, they're probably right not to.'

'Is someone at home with you?'

'Yes, my father.' Barnett sighed.

'Well, don't be keeping this from him,' Gardner said. 'Talk to him.'

The smirk and shake of his head suggested that he probably wouldn't.

Gardner pulled up outside Barnett's home.

He looked at her. *Come on. Speak!* He knew full well what he was doing.

'Anything you need to ask?'

'What do you think?'

'I can't believe you just managed the entire journey without asking me... Phil would've asked me while they were still running the tests!'

'Your health is more important to me.'

'Good answer.' He took a deep breath. 'Helping Hands was the name of the homeless shelter before 1991, when the council ran it. After the council relinquished control in 1991 and KYLO Ltd took it over, they released James Sykes from employment and changed the name to Bright Day. My mother...' Barnett broke off and looked away.

It really is personal. No wonder the panic attack. 'In your own time, Ray.'

Eventually, he looked back. Tears pricked the corners of his eyes. 'It's nothing I'm ashamed of... don't get me wrong... but I'd be lying if I said this wasn't bloody hard. I...' He rubbed at the corners of his eyes with the back of his hand.

She reached over and put her hand on his shoulder.

He took a deep breath. 'Before I was born... my mother was there, boss. She was homeless, and she was there. At Helping Hands.'

31

Barnett was relieved that no one was waiting for him on the other side of the front door.

He'd half-expected his father's screwed-up face. An endless quizzing over why he was back so early in the day.

Richard Barnett worried about everything, and he certainly wouldn't be finding out about Ray's trip to the hospital in an ambulance.

Richard had nursed Amina, Barnett's mother, through three years of illness prior to her death. The experience had scarred him mentally, and he had become extremely paranoid about going through it again. His son was all he had left and the focus of all his concerns.

Barnett's excellent diet and intense fitness regime didn't go far enough in allaying Richard's paranoia. If Barnett wasn't being moaned at for going to bed too late, working too hard, or drinking too much coffee, then something felt seriously amiss in this house.

Hanging his jacket up, and noticing the absence of his father's, Barnett recalled Richard was having his weekly lunch and a pint with Roger in the Crown Inn. A pint that regularly turned into many more. The old man would stumble home, dodging traffic late afternoon.

Hypocrite. It's open season on my lifestyle, but so much as a mention of your drinking and it'll be pistols at dawn.

Having unloaded on Gardner, Barnett felt less heavy than he'd done earlier, but he was far from all right. In fairness, Gardner had been right to send him home. Quiet time to get his thoughts in order was probably what the doctor did in fact order.

After making himself a green tea, he went upstairs. Perched on the side of his bed, he went for the third drawer down on his bedside table for a photograph of his mother. In the photograph, Amina Ndiaye was fourteen. She was sitting beside a tree, in a floral dress, writing in a notebook. Back in Liberia, her father had taken the photograph. Barnett had many photographs of his mother, some framed, but he'd a particular fondness for this one. He didn't leave it out, because he wished to keep this one, his favourite one, for himself. He especially liked it because of its complete lack of pretentiousness. Nowadays, people worked so hard on their poses for social media. In this photo, she was unaware of the camera. Lost in her own thoughts. A reflective expression on her face.

Shortly before her death, Amina had given him the narrative behind the image. 'I was writing poetry. I always loved writing poetry.'

Barnett had asked her why she'd stopped, to which she'd replied, 'How do you know I stopped?'

It was only after her death that her passion for poetry became truly apparent. In her belongings, there were piles and piles of handwritten verses. His father must have known, but had been happy to keep her secret while she lived. Now, after she'd gone, he'd been happy to share it with their son. Of course, that had been all he was happy to share. If Barnett broached the subject of Helping Hands, which he'd tried to, once before, in the months after her death, he'd hit a brick wall.

Or the brick wall would hit him.

No one knew how to shut down a conversation with an icy stare quite like Richard Barnett!

Barnett put the picture of his mother down and sighed. He then went into his second drawer and pulled out five notebooks. After sifting through them, he found the one decorated with pencil-drawn sparrows. He'd read all his mother's poems countless times now. When he'd suggested approaching a publisher to his father, that brick wall made an appearance again. He'd a point, Barnett accepted. After all, she'd kept it quiet in life. Would she really want it shouting about now?

Most poems were about nature, and some were about Africa. Liberia experienced devastating civil war in 1989, but she steered from the topic that led to her emigration in 1990. She'd mark her later poems with a wistful tone and a longing for the life prior to the emigration and civil war.

There were several poems that had always confused him, though.

Sad poems about losing someone.

There weren't many. Five at the most. And he still never knew the reason behind them. Inevitable then, that today's events should throw the memory of them into the spotlight again.

The person lost in these poems was innocent, but Barnett didn't know of his mother losing anyone other than her parents. He'd broached it with his father and been told that he was a fool for trying to find meaning in her flowery words. 'Give it up,' he'd said. 'The reality with poetry is that only the poet really knows what they're on about! And to be honest, I'm uncertain she understood what she was lamenting there.'

Before today, Barnett had decided she was personifying Liberia. Missing it as if it were a person she loved. But now, with the mystery behind her homeless years on his mind again, he wondered if there might be something more to it.

He reread the five poems.

The fifth, entitled 'Gone but not forgotten', speared him the deepest:

> *In the quiet, I still hear that heart, a tender song,*
> *A fragile soul, too pure, in this world not long.*
> *In the night's embrace, I feel your touch,*
> *Gone too soon, a presence missed so much.*
> *In my heart, your innocent spirit is forever strong.*

It was only after he'd finished the fifth poem, did he realise his cheeks were damp with tears.

Who's gone, but not forgotten, Mum?

32

By late afternoon, Gardner felt bloated. Not on food, as she was yet to eat since O'Brien's cereal bar, but with questions and uncertainty.

An understaffed investigation team was offering her hardly any respite. Throw into the mix countless unanswered phone calls made to Cecile, and that sad story delivered by Barnett, and it was a wonder she wasn't on her knees in a cubicle throwing up!

She looked at her watch. She guessed there was still time for that to happen.

To make matters worse, the other officers Marsh had promised were yet to materialise. At least Marsh hadn't come good on her threat to 'muck in'. Gardner was in no mood for that. Everyone would be walking on bloody eggshells.

Several hours on from Barnett's hospitalisation and return home, the only other person who had a clue as to the cause of the panic attack was Rice. Suggs and Ross were none the wiser even though Barnett had given her permission to share it with the team.

In the incident room, she explained, first, that Amina Ndiaye was an immigrant who'd arrived in the country at fifteen, following the death of her parents back home during conflict. They'd placed Amina Ndiaye in foster care and one of the foster parents had horrendously abused her. A man that'd since died in jail. Nobody had ever kept any of this from Ray.

'Fortunately for that foster parent, he died before Ray knew,' Rice interjected.

'Poor fella,' Ross said, shaking his head.

Gardner nodded. 'Don't you dare go handling him with kid gloves tomorrow, Brad, when he's back. It'll piss him off. Remember, he's made peace with these events long ago. Today's surprise would have that impact on anyone.'

Suggs and Ross stared at her, wide-eyed, hungry for information in the same way she'd been earlier.

'It turns out that Amina ran away from the foster care I mentioned earlier and started sleeping rough in Leeds. This was in 1990. She'd only just turned sixteen. She ended up at Helping Hands for almost eight months.'

Suggs and Ross nodded. It was now clear why Barnett had jumped from his skin after learning that Helping Hands was Bright Day's former name.

'Now, this is the part of the story where Ray, like us, is none the wiser. Whatever happened at Helping Hands to his mother is absolutely taboo in his household. By household, I mean his father, Richard Barnett. Amina, unfortunately, passed away three years back, and Richard lives with Ray, and is still unwilling to discuss that time.'

'Might be necessary for him to reconsider that now?' Ross said.

'My point,' Rice said, nodding. 'Sooner we talk to him, the better.'

'I agree,' Gardner said, looking between their faces. 'But with sensitivity.'

'Always!' Rice said. 'Sensitivity. With a capital S.'

'Which is why I'll do it.'

Rice smirked.

'And why we wait until Ray contacts us today: he said he'd talk to his dad this afternoon. If we don't hear from him, then I'll do it myself tomorrow.'

Rice shook his head.

'Stop it, Phil. Ray is one of us. We adjust when necessary. Who else is ever going to look out for us?'

She clocked Suggs nodding; she was glad someone seemed to agree.

Gardner concluded Amina's story, vague though it was. 'After her time at Helping Hands, Amina got lucky. She ended up in shared housing, accessing education, and met Richard. I'm glad there was some light at the end of the tunnel. Anyway, until we know otherwise, Ray isn't directly involved in whatever is going on here, having not been alive during those years at Helping Hands, so I'm not pulling him from the case. Any objections?'

Rice lowered his eyes.

'So...' She turned to the side so she could gesture at the board. 'Let's not beat around the bush, this is a murder investigation, and we're thin on the ground. I've pulled an operation name to underline this to top brass. Operation Gearchange.' It was written on the board.

Suggs and Ross whispered among themselves. Common practice. Trying to find clues and links from a randomly generated operation name. Superstition. She let it play out and then coughed a minute later.

She helped them along. 'And we certainly need a gearchange from Marsh and those further up the food chain. I'm confident that, hopefully, by the end of the day, we'll have more support.' *Three officers if we're lucky.* 'But until it's there, it's not.'

She pointed between two very different pictures of James Sykes. 'You can see the differences here in our victim, and I'm not just referring to age. Age isn't always kind to you...' She winked over at Rice, worried it'd become rather icy between them again.

He smirked and mouthed, 'Piss off.'

'But not usually this bad.' She pointed to a suited, cleanly shaven young man with styled hair wearing a suit. 'Here is James Sykes as a young man running Helping Hands.' Then, she pointed to another image of an overweight man in factory overalls with messy hair and an unkempt beard. 'And around eighteen months ago, which was the last time he was seen alive. Aged fifty-five. Barely recognisable.'

She went through his background. His parents and their social work; his upbringing in the accommodation behind the shelter supplied by the council; his movement into running the shelter at an early age; his parents' retirement. 'He ran Helping Hands until 1991. He held the position for just under two years before they removed him at twenty-four years old. He spent the rest of his working life as a low-paid worker bouncing around factories.' She continued to explain his mysterious disappearance from his home. The unlocked door. No signs of a struggle. The suspected suicide. 'Which takes us to now... James turning up in two pieces. Two *carefully* separated pieces, I might add.' She pointed at the images of the remains, and then the photographs of the notes. 'Two cryptic notes. And' – she moved her finger between images of Robert Thwaites and John Atkinson – 'two targeted individuals, who seem really inconvenienced by the whole thing and don't wish to discuss it. Anyway, this is all inputted onto HOLMES 2 for you to digest.' She pointed at the photocopied case files lying in front of Suggs and Ross. 'I copied the case files from the investigation into Sykes' disappearance. Ridiculously brief, eh? Those in charge were *desperate* to write it off as suicide.'

'Looking at that photograph,' Suggs suggested. 'They may have had a point.'

Gardner raised an eyebrow at him. 'Pack it in.'

'Sorry boss.'

'It's complete bollocks, anyway,' Rice said. 'The suicide. The investigators jumped too quick. *Suspiciously quick.* They were leaned on.'

The two younger detectives probably expected Gardner to shut Rice's conspiracy theories down, as she normally did.

She didn't. In fact, she stunned her audience by agreeing for once. 'Wouldn't be surprised, Phil. You see... let's look closer at Sykes' time running Helping Hands.' She went over to the board with a marker and wrote 1989, 1990 and 1991 on the board. 'It was council funded with extra support from the government. A lot of powerful people stood to have their fingers burned around any controversies. If something dodgy went on then, no one would have an appetite to reopen old wounds. Suicide was quick and easy closure.'

'Especially with no family left to care,' Rice said.

'So, what do you think happened in 1991?' Suggs asked. 'Why did he lose his job?'

'I don't know yet,' Gardner said. 'But if the shelter came out of council hands in 1991, then I suspect the government wanted to wash all hands of it.'

'And we know how careful they like to be, especially around elections. There was one in 1992, I believe?' Rice said and sneered. 'Best to drop all the hot potatoes, eh?'

'So, whatever *happened*,' Gardner continued. 'It was controversial. What better than a clean break? Giving it to the KYLO group to run must have made sense. KYLO wasted no time in converting the place and its name. They got rid of Sykes and Bright Day was born.'

'They washed its face,' Rice said.

'Precisely,' Gardner said. 'Or rather, completely hosed it down. James Sykes had been bad for business. For the altruistic government and its council—'

'Hey hey, self-proclaimed altruistic government and its council!' Rice interjected.

Gardner nodded. 'Either way, it was KYLO who hit the reset button to hide something from the council's time in charge.'

'But why would they do that?' Ross asked.

Gardner explained KYLO were a wealthy chemical company that had been mired in its own controversy. Pollution had been their critics' main line of attack. Recent years had seen them come under fire for single-use plastics.

'So, it's reasonable to suggest they saw an opportunity,' Gardner said, trying not to sneer like her colleague was happy to relentlessly do. 'Why not, to quote Phillip Rice, wash the face of Helping Hands, and by effect, then wash its own face?' She didn't sneer, but her tone of voice revealed contempt. 'Taking over a homeless shelter, funding it extensively, reveals their compassionate side. Their declaration that they were giving back to the community.'

'And out goes Sykes and the controversy with the bathwater,' Suggs said, nodding.

'KYLO is worth sixty billion,' Gardner said. 'They've a lot of power.'

'Bloody hell,' Suggs said. 'Why have I never heard of them?'

'Name me five chemical companies,' Gardner asked.

Suggs' mouth fell open.

Gardner smiled. 'I understand that you're not well read, Cam, but I'll let you off this one. It's not like Apple or Amazon. These guys fly below the radar by feeding the other more visible industries.'

'Poisoning the world,' Rice said.

Gardner nodded. 'Still, they'd drawn some attention to themselves over chemical dumping, so they wanted to wash themselves. Leeds' most visible homeless shelter. Clean up the streets. Feed the homeless only the best foods. Nourish them. Offer them guidance to get back into normal society. The things our government should have been doing... but clearly failed at.' She pointed back at James Sykes. 'This man remained silent until his death.'

'Paid off... I imagine,' Rice said.

Gardner stared at him. 'Maybe he finally came clean and certain people just couldn't allow it?'

'Wouldn't be the first time, would it?' Rice said. 'Although wouldn't a bullet to the head have been enough? Why the elaborate jigsaw puzzle? Skull here... rest of him here... And why the involvement of Robert Thwaites and John Atkinson?'

'Not sure,' Gardner said. 'But they're connected to all of this, and I can't wait to ask them.'

'Do we know any of what was going off at Helping Hands?' Ross asked. 'Under James Sykes?'

Gardner said, 'Not in detail. We've not had a second for a proper dig yet, but I can give you some headlines. Drug overdoses, miscarriages, reports of abuse... not totally uncommon then I imagine... transparency wasn't what it is now... but there were quite a few reports. It was like a rusty tap was turned on, and the filthy water just kept gushing out. We need to dig, dig, dig,' Gardner said. 'I'll be doing it all night, no doubt, but make sure you get some sleep. Tomorrow will be busy. I've got an appointment with the director at Bright Day tomorrow morning. I've attempted to request an appointment with KYLO, but they've tried to fob me off with someone in charge of the Corporate Philanthropy Department. I know. The Corporate Philanthropy Department. Someone explain that to me?'

'An oxymoron?' Suggs asked.

'I take it all back,' Gardner said. 'You're well read. Anyway, I'm awaiting confirmation on my request for an appointment with Harrison Hall, the CEO, and the late founder's son. Be interesting to see how long that takes! Meanwhile, let's take our investigation down to ground level for a moment. We can throw James Sykes' name at the Thwaites and the Atkinsons and gauge a reaction.'

'Wasn't Robert Thwaites a commercial solicitor in another life?' Suggs asked.

'Jesus, Cam, I really had you wrong... I'd already considered that. I've requested a list of every company he's ever worked with.'

'And any money KYLO is on there,' Rice said.

'Yes. But John Atkinson... that's a link I'm struggling with. Any epiphanies there, Cam?'

He shook his head. 'Sorry, boss...'

'Still, I've requested an entire background check on his finances, and his business dealings. In other news, forensics is still to cough up anything on the burned-out Mercedes, but the red quarry dust was a godsend.' She explained how the officer was collecting local samples. 'Be plenty of hidey holes around some of those old quarries to hide in.'

'And murder someone,' Rice said.

Gardner nodded. 'Let's hope that the gathering of samples coughs something out.'

'We need to speak to those in power,' Ross said.

'That's where you come in, Brad,' Gardner said, pointing at him. 'The Ministry of Housing, Communities and Local Government handle the homeless issue in the UK. You also must consider Leeds City Council, and their role. I need you on that flat out. I want every complaint made against that homeless shelter. And I guarantee that someone has them locked away. Batter it until you find a whistle-blower. There's always a whistleblower.'

'Will do, boss,' Ross said, suddenly looking ten feet tall. He saw the importance of that responsibility.

She saw an expectant look on Suggs' face. 'Don't worry, Cam... you've been firing on all cylinders' – *and there isn't anybody else in this room, right now* – 'I want you to investigate James Sykes' family in more detail. His parents died in a house fire. No suspicious circumstances. To me, a fire is always suspicious, especially if it kills people connected to all of this... Also, James' younger sister, Elizabeth. Now, there's a tragic story. Burned in the fire and institutionalised because of mental health. Incommunicative. So, if you could pay her a visit too, and see if there's anything there for us?'

Suggs nodded. He didn't look ten feet tall, but he looked pleased enough.

She surveyed her tiny team and inwardly sighed. 'Look, I know this operation is growing rapidly, and we're super thin on the ground' – she glanced at the board – 'but I feel something big coming together.' *Whatever in God's name that might be.* 'So, I know I'm putting a lot of pressure on you with these tasks, but you're good for it. You've proven it before in the past and you'll prove it again. There're no officers I'd rather have on this.' A lie… but a necessary one. 'Even Cam.'

They all laughed.

'Phone me whenever. Whatever time. Middle of night. Although, I wouldn't want you missing sleep because most of this is daytime work. Tomorrow is going to be a big one.'

Once they filed out, she collapsed into her chair.

She hadn't been exaggerating.

She suspected tomorrow would be a monstrous day.

And I still have the Paul and Cecile situation firmly on my mind.

She sighed.

Ah well, I can sleep when I'm dead, perhaps.

She tried to ignore the niggling thought that maybe this job would make that happen.

33

Is this what I am now?

Riddick circled to the other side of the bed.

One of them.

He looked at the handcuffs that fixed the unconscious woman to the headboard.

A monster?

His eyes moved to her pale face.

Cecile.

Pumped full of poison. By him.

Her eyes rolled beneath her lids, and she murmured. He leaned in to listen, but her words made no sense. As he drew back, he saw saliva bubbling at the corner of her mouth. He used his sleeve to dab it away. 'I'm sorry.' He moved his sleeve to his own eyes. 'For what I've done to you.' He closed his eyes and thought of his wife and children. 'For what I've become.'

When he opened them, she was staring up. 'Help me.' Her voice was hoarse and croaky.

Her eyes moved to his face. He couldn't see any recognition in them. The handcuffs rattled when she tried to pull her hands towards herself.

'I can't. Not yet. I just can't. There are too many others relying on me. On us.' He closed his eyes. In the simple act of refusal, he felt overwhelming nausea, and he couldn't bring himself to say the words. The shame was far too intense.

He didn't just think of his wife and children this time, but of the others who'd died because of him. He felt his friend Arthur's hand in his just before it slipped away, and the boy fell from the hospital roof.

Cecile next? The next good person to die from his choices?

'Help me.'

Riddick opened his eyes and saw she was panicking now, turning her head from side to side and tugging at the headboard.

'Please,' Riddick said. 'I will. But first—'

Heavy footfalls on the stairs.

His eyes snapped towards the open door. It was empty. But Tommy Rose was most certainly seconds away from standing there. He looked back down at Cecile with his finger to his mouth.

You're going to have to trust me.

He saw the tears in her eyes.

He dropped his finger from his mouth.

A big ask I know. Especially when I don't even trust myself.

'How do?' Tommy said from the door.

34

Unless it'd come from her late mother, Jess Beaumont had always struggled to tolerate touch. She'd always needed space. Autistic individuals varied massively on their needs regarding sensory input. Some of her autistic friends preferred the hugging, squeezing and the firm touching. She didn't envy them this trait, simply because she didn't want touch, but that didn't stop her considering what it may have been like, and beaten herself up over the absence of it, because beating herself up over things was one of *her* many specific traits.

It was surprising then when she threw her arms around Laura Wilson at the front door.

And a *pleasant* surprise.

It must have been the first instance in which she'd sought warmth and comfort from another since her mother had passed away almost four years ago now.

The tight squeeze must have lasted almost half a minute, before discomfort set in, and she had to break the embrace and back away into the hallway, lowering her eyes to the floor as was her default.

'Sorry for invading your space.' She touched her forehead but restrained herself from tapping it. 'Inconsiderate. Please—'

'Don't be sorry,' Laura said, stepping in and closing the door behind her. She stooped slightly and craned her neck so she could catch Jess's eyes.

It encouraged Jess to raise her eyes and make eye contact.

Laura showed the palms of her hands and moved them closer to Jess. 'May I?'

Jess nodded. Strangely, she felt no anxiety over being touched by Laura.

Laura's hands settled on Jess's shoulders. 'Please look at me.'

Jess tried and managed more than usual before succumbing to discomfort again. 'Sorry—'

'Enough with the apologies,' Laura said. 'Now, tell me, what's happened?'

After Jess had explained how awful the evening had been with her father, she felt the weight lifting. She also realised that it wasn't the mere act of sharing her troubles that unburdened her, but who she was sharing them with.

As they drank tea, Jess desperately wanted to give Laura more than just a *thank you*. A comment or two on how gracious and giving she was with her time would suffice; or maybe a reference to how at ease she made her feel, not unlike her own mother had for so many years.

But she remained at '*thank you*' and realised that would have to do.

'You shouldn't have to listen to those things your father says,' Laura said.

'I know he doesn't think those things... *not really*... I know he loves me. Or loved me before. More than anything. But... if he can say such things... call me such horrendous names... then...' She broke off to wipe a tear away. 'Are they signs of the person he really was before the illness? The person who I never saw. Was my father really like that?'

Laura reached over and put her hand on her leg. 'You can't think like that, Jess. Let him be what he was to you. Alzheimer's is cruel. The changes in his brain will be confusing him. My father was wonderful, and I know that from countless, countless people; yet the things he said were often horrendous, too. But deep down he was still the kind man whom I loved, and your father will be too.'

Jess nodded. 'I know this... thank you... and you're right... or at least you were right earlier. It's time. He must go somewhere. I won't be able to manage much longer. I replaced all his cups and plates as you suggested with paper ones, but he still throws them. And sometimes when I try to get him into his chair, so I can change his sheets, he resists. I'm worried he'll start lashing out.'

'Yes,' Laura said. 'It may come. *Probably* will come.'

Jess wiped at her eyes again. 'Will you help me? Find him a home? I'm clueless. I'm clueless about everything.' She tapped her head. 'You might as well lay me down in a bed beside him for how much help I am to anyone.' She tapped harder. 'I'm sure it's my fault he's deteriorated.'

Laura took Jess's wrist to stop the tapping. Normally, her instinct would be to yank her arm away when someone interrupted her stimming, but not this time. This time, she felt safe, somehow. 'Sorry. It's a stim.'

'I need a promise now,' Laura said.

'Yes. I'll try. No guarantees when you're dealing with someone like me, but I'll try to, and just apologise when I mess it up...'

Laura smiled. 'And that's exactly what I want you to promise! I want you to promise to stop apologising to me!'

Jess looked up at her briefly, smiling, then lowered her eyes. 'Can I promise to try?'

'Perfect.'

'Will you help me with a new car, too?'

'Of course. So, back to the other thing. Are you ready?'

'I don't know... He's... look, I...'

'This won't end in an apology again, will it?'

Jess laughed and then mimed zipping her mouth closed.

Laura released Jess's wrist and stood. She looked down and held out her hand. 'Come on, then.'

'Laura...'

'Take me upstairs, Jess, to meet your father, Nigel, and once I've met him, we can get everything in order.'

* * *

Jess was the first to step into a room that was never dark.

A small night lamp forever glowed by her father's bedside. He was already disorientated, and the thought of him waking up and not being able to see was inconceivable.

The angry, frustrated man from earlier was gone; instead, the peaceful looking sixty-two-year-old father she adored lay in his place. His features softened by slumber.

Jess looked back at Laura and beckoned her into the room before turning and moving closer to her sick father.

The bed cover had fallen from him slightly, revealing his faded blue pyjamas, his favourite set. The worn fabric marked the passing of almost fifteen years. He needed new ones, but she'd wanted to leave him with items he may recognise.

She sat beside him and took his hand. Opposite her, Laura took the single sofa chair in the corner. She smiled and nodded at Jess, suggesting that she continued her moment of affection with Nigel.

The lines on his face, which had deepened since the onset of Alzheimer's, offered a glimpse of his former self. A man who'd worked twelve hours a day for most of his life, but had always been there to tuck Jess in at nighttime. He'd never believed in autism. Jess had heard him arguing with her mother about it, claiming it to be an excuse for quirkiness and awkwardness. She recalled his words to her mother: 'She's got a unique personality. That's the only definition she needs.' Despite his denial, he never voiced his concerns to Jess. He only ever treated her with love and adoration.

She moved her fingers to the thin, grey hair resting on the pillow, and a tear came to her eye when she recalled the fullness and vitality of it when she'd been a child.

She looked up at Laura. 'I shouldn't wake him.'

Laura leaned forward in the chair. 'Then don't. I'll come again tomorrow and meet him then. We don't need to rush this. Meanwhile, I'll start speaking to the local homes.'

'Sorry...' Jess said. 'I meant thank you... just thank you. I'm sorry... I promised.'

'You promised to *try*. You're trying.'

Jess leaned over and kissed her father's forehead and stood. She released his hand.

'The photos are beautiful,' Laura said, gesturing around the room at the many framed images that decorated the dressing table, the side tables, the wall and the windowsills. 'They'll help. What you've done for him, Jess, is wonderful. He may struggle with his memories, but he's got them all around him. There'll be moments... moments when you're not in the room... in which he'll fall back into them because of these pictures.'

'I hope so,' Jess said, stroking the frame of one of the pictures on his bedside table. A picture of her sitting on his shoulders.

'Sleep well, Dad,' Jess said.

Laura rose from the chair and wandered over. She looked down at Nigel. 'You've done well with this one here. You must be so proud of her.' She stroked his hand. 'God bless Nigel, sleep well, and I hope we can meet tomorrow.'

35

Barnett's eyes bolted open, and he sat up in bed.

The sound of the front door had woken him. It meant his father was back from the Crown Inn.

He looked at his watch and cursed. He'd been asleep for hours! No way was he going to rest properly tonight. He sat upright and swung his legs from the bed, yawning.

He listened to a voicemail from Gardner asking how he was feeling. She also provided further details regarding the shelter, probably to reassure him that he wasn't being cast aside. The details made for very interesting listening.

He stepped out of bed, deciding it was now time to confront his father. At this moment, half asleep, he felt in no state to do it. But then, would he ever feel in a state to do it?

He recalled the first time he'd attempted this conversation three years back.

Following Amina's death, Barnett hadn't just recovered poems, he'd recovered a mysterious photograph too.

A picture of his mother dated 1990. She was about sixteen and standing beside two other young girls outside Helping Hands. The shelter's cheap, decrepit sign clearly visible above her. This had been

Barnett's first brush with the truth. After googling Helping Hands, he'd confronted his grieving father.

'So, she was homeless, so what?' Richard had shouted. 'She wasn't when we married, and she certainly wasn't when she had you, and she most definitely wasn't when we gave you the best possible life.'

That was all his father had considered him entitled to.

He'd tried several times over the years, and grabbed a few snippets of information, usually when Richard was drunk. The sexual abuse by a foster parent which led to her homelessness had been the most harrowing moment, and Barnett had spent days reading around the investigation. The disgraced bastard had died in jail. But her actual time in Helping Hands was shrouded in mystery, and Richard never seemed to have any inclination to shine any serious light on it.

Barnett sighed. Right now, his father would have a lot of alcohol in his bloodstream. In his experience, this usually helped. It'd loosen his tongue, at least for a short time, until the blue devils came out to play.

Barnett knew Richard's routine well. He allowed him fifteen minutes to settle into the lounge to enjoy his chaser. A glass of fine malt. Then, he joined him in the lounge.

Barnett entered a room that had changed little since the early nineties when he'd been growing up here. Undoubtedly, the happiest period of his parents' lives, hence the sentimental attachment and reluctance to update.

His father sat in jeans and a T-shirt in a single sofa chair alongside the fire. The fire was still in its infancy and was only still licking at the bigger logs. Richard's eyes were closed, and his hand held the empty glass upright on the sofa's arm.

'Dad,' Barnett said.

Richard opened his eyes and looked at his son. A smile broke on his face. 'Son. It's cold out...' He leaned forward. 'I saw your car outside and knew you were sleeping. Is everything okay?'

'Everything is fine,' Barnett lied. 'We just worried about worsening weather and opted to finish up some work at home.'

'Ha,' his father said, looking down into his empty glass with a look of disappointment. 'You know where you get that acting ability from? That ability to spin a yarn?' He put the glass down at his feet. 'Your mother.' He laughed. 'There never was a problem. *Everything is fine.* That's all she ever gave me. No matter what. One time, she got gout. Could barely walk. Took her God knows how long to get down the bloody stairs. Didn't mention it and told me she was bloody fine. Ha! I mean, where's her breaking point?' He stared down at the fire. The bigger logs crackled and spat. 'She kept saying she was fine even when she wasn't.' His face fell. 'I wonder now if she'd ever have gone to the hospital, if I hadn't had carried her, moaning in pain, to the car that morning...'

Blue devils were out already then.

'No yarn. I'm fine. Honest. Just responding to weather warnings.' Barnett realised he was playing a pointless game. When he got to the point of the conversation, his father would know full well that he wasn't fine. Then his accusation that he hadn't told the truth would carry weight.

'How was Eric, anyway?' Barnett asked, sitting on the long sofa.

'Reserved for a pint or two; loud-mouthed, obnoxious and full of opinions on pint three and four. After that, it's kind of blurred. Ranting and swearing. You know how well he does that.'

'He's well, then?' Barnett asked, laughing.

'Never better! He always makes me feel I'm doing a grand job of keeping my own emotions in check.'

'What're best friends for?'

'Exactly. That's why we pick them.'

They both stared at the fire as it grew in intensity. The top logs weren't being completely consumed, and they spat and crackled aggressively. 'Go on, son, get to the point. Home early... not working... sitting with me in the lounge... three things vastly out of the ordinary there.'

God, you can be a miserable old bugger! 'Dad. I need to know more about Mum.'

Barnett looked at him, but his dad kept his eyes on the fire.

Barnett held back a follow-up. *Just give him time to process the request...*

It was, after all, Richard's favourite topic of conversation. But it was always on his terms. And always based on his state of mind, which flickered as erratically as the flames currently did.

It'd been long enough. 'Dad, I—'

'Need? *Why?*'

'Well, want.' But it was needed, really. It'd crept into the shadows of an investigation.

'Still... why?'

What a ridiculous question! Why couldn't he ask about his own mother? Why was his old man such a pain in the arse? 'Just been thinking a lot. Been reading her poetry—'

He guffawed.

Barnett ignored this and continued, 'And I just feel there are too many gaps in... sod this! Why can't I ask? Haven't I any right to know my mum better?'

His father raised an eyebrow. 'Ridiculous, son. Tell me what you already know about your mum.'

Opposite to you! 'Kind... loving... *always* there for me.'

He smirked over the emphasis – probably detecting it was a jab.

'She was funny,' Barnett continued. 'And she'd have put a bloody Christmas tree up by now, too!'

'It's your house!'

'I'm always working.'

'Yes, about that—'

'I'll also tell you what Mum was good at. Keeping you off the six pints and a whisky afternoon binge...'

Richard's smirk broadened. 'Aye. She was.' He looked away, contemplating something, *happily*, before turning back.

'Point proven... to myself at least. You knew your mother as well as anyone could do. She was perfection. You just said so before. What gaps could we possibly fill in here?'

'Not about before she met you, though. Hardly anything about *before*.'

His father waved his hand. 'Before! Before ain't worth a great deal.' He pointed at Barnett. 'Time with you, son. Time with me. Now, that's what means a great deal.'

Barnett inwardly sighed. He suddenly felt warmer. He wondered if the fire had suddenly intensified, or whether another panic attack was on the cards.

He lowered his eyes for a moment. He'd have to go in strong. Not the best option. Since his mother's death, Richard had issues with anger and frustration. Although he'd never lashed out, he'd smashed a glass or two, shouted obscenities and sent Barnett to Coventry frequently.

Still, if Barnett didn't ask these questions, then his colleagues most certainly would tomorrow, and he wouldn't like that one bit.

Barnett looked up. As he was still wearing his suit, he could reach into his inside pocket and extract the photograph from 1990. He leaned forward and put it on the coffee table.

Richard didn't dignify it with a look, preferring, instead, to watch the fire. 'What's that?'

'Helping Hands, Dad.' As soon as he finished the words, Barnett flinched, half-expecting a glass in the face.

Fortunately, that didn't happen and, fortunately, Richard's expression didn't worsen. He just sighed. 'I thought we did this already?'

Or didn't do? Matter of perspective.

'Helping Hands is being investigated.'

Richard looked around at Barnett. 'Long time coming.'

'Wouldn't know. I know nothing about the place.'

'Ha,' Richard said. 'What I know isn't bloody good. Helping Hands... Helping sodding Hands.' He sighed and shook his head. 'Is this really a gap you need filling?'

Barnett shrugged. 'I guess we've gone beyond the point of it being a choice.'

'Suit yourself. Ask away – what do you want to know about her life before us? Before Helping pissing Hands.'

'Well, I know about her life before in Liberia. Even the horrible war stuff near the end. It's just her two years homeless. Her eight months here, in *this* place.'

'For good reason. She didn't want you to know.'

'Why not?'

'Painful. Very painful.' His father stared into the flames, which were now raging.

'She's gone. It won't hurt her now for me to know the truth.'

His father snorted and looked at him. 'You misunderstand, son. She wasn't worried about you knowing for *herself*. She was worried about the pain you'd feel.' His father raised an eyebrow and an icy chill went down Barnett's spine. 'Some things are best never given the light of day again. Her time in Helping Hands is one such time.'

'We're beyond that. I need to hear it.'

Richard rose to his feet. 'Bloody detectives. Relentless, aren't they?' He walked over to the mantelpiece for his bottle of whisky. 'I've met Eric once a week for three years at the Crown. Never ever have I drank over six pints, and one chaser.' He unscrewed the lid and topped up his glass. 'Your choice of conversation is hardly something for a sober mind.' He drank the glass of whisky in one and slammed the bottle down. Then he refilled it and walked back to the single sofa chair. He deposited the glass on the floor beside his feet.

'Seems I hold the cards here so you can lead. Why now? What's happened?'

'It's best I don't tell you—'

'*What's* happened?'

Barnett sighed and looked down. How much was he allowed to say? Very little, probably. But better he got something now than his colleagues taking a run at him. 'Do you recall a James Sykes?'

Richard's eyes narrowed. 'I recall him.'

Barnett felt a surge of adrenaline. *Bloody hell.*

'Is he dead?' Richard asked.

'Yes.'

'Good, he was a prick,' his father said, reaching down for his glass. 'How?'

'Please, Dad,' Barnett said. 'I *really* can't tell you.'

'Never mind,' Richard said, taking a sip of whisky and placing the glass back at his feet. 'Least he's dead. Guess it doesn't matter how.'

'We need to work out if his death has any connection to his time running Helping Hands.'

'I can tell you with no doubt whatsoever that it is. The man was a cockroach. And you know what happens to cockroaches... eventually—'

'Dad, pipe down! You're going to make yourself a bloody suspect!'

'Think I'd probably enjoy that where this man is concerned. Happily take the credit. That man hurt many people. I'm afraid your mother's story isn't a unique one. All those accusations that were made against the place! Surely, you're aware of them all?'

'Nobody ever proved anything.'

'Pah! Money talks. And it was a different time, I can tell you. Much easier to brush things under the carpet back then. Especially regarding the homeless. I mean, do you take the word of a homeless person these days, son? I bet you don't.'

'I listen to everyone.'

'Your colleagues?'

Barnett shrugged. 'Most of them.'

He raised an eyebrow and sighed. 'Better than hardly any of them, I guess. Because they certainly didn't listen back then!'

'There was an investigation that found nothing, with the support of the police, and—'

'You serious?' Richard said. 'Did it even take place? And if it did, how do you know someone didn't butcher it with bribery?' Richard said, his face reddening.

'I'll be looking into it.'

'Look into what? It's all gone. Wiped clean. KYLO changed the place, radically, from head to toe; it was almost as if it'd never existed. The public purse has no appetite for things that never existed. Waste of money.'

'Maybe. But we now have a murder. So, silence isn't an option.'

'Go on then, tell me what you already know.'

'Accusations of sexual abuse and drug abuse,' Barnett said. 'The problem is – it's all so common with institutions such as this. Comes with the territory. Especially online. They must bat a lot away, and the accusations become less and less powerful, I guess. It was the stuff that wasn't so prevalent in the public domain which caught our eye,' Barnett said. 'It took more digging. A cluster of events between 1989 and 1991. But as I said before, an independent investigation found it not guilty of systemic failure.'

'Paid off!'

'Maybe. And like I said, there wasn't an appetite online to keep things going like there is now. Just kind of died. These events involved two suicides, four drug overdoses and several miscarriages. Excessive numbers considering the short period...' He broke off, noticing that his father was now sadly regarding the picture of Amina on the wall.

'And she was there... your mother... for some of it, at least. Two of those deaths were good friends of hers. Those three went through thick and thin together.'

'Christ,' Barnett said, lowering his eyes. He felt a sudden, rather overwhelming hollowness inside. His gaze fell to the picture on the table.

His father must have noticed the direction of his attention. 'Yes... those two... with your mother in that picture. Isla and Britney. That was the day they arrived at Helping Hands. I thank the lord, every single day, that at least your mother made it out. I never met Britney and Isla, but she never stopped talking about those girls.' He sighed. 'In a way, I feel like I know them.'

Barnett reached out and touched his mother on the image. *I'm sorry, Mum... sorry for what you went through.* He looked at the two smiling girls alongside her. They looked so young, *so innocent.* The smiles were a lie. Young adults putting on a brave face. Desperate for help.

'Out on the streets,' Richard continued, 'Isla and Britney helped her. Remember that your mother was an immigrant. She may have dodged bullets, but sleeping on cold streets in our world requires an altogether unique skill set. They were close, son. Close as could be. Turned out that Isla was pregnant when they all went into Helping Hands. When her child was stillborn, a result of the incompetence of the medical support in the shelter, she spiralled into depression. One night, she invited Amina and Britney up to the roof of the shelter. They tried to stop her, but in the end, she just jumped.'

Barnett looked up at his father, who was now leaning forward, staring sadly into the fire. 'Then Britney ended up dying of a drug overdose a few weeks later.'

'Jesus.'

'Amina was adamant that losing Isla destroyed Britney, so that's on them bastards too.'

Barnett, who couldn't believe what he was hearing, was shaking his head as he looked down at his mother. *How did you hide so much pain from me? You didn't need to protect me from all that. I could have listened. I wish you would've told me.*

He touched her picture again and then brushed a tear away.

'But your mother was strong,' Richard said. 'Remember? Never anything wrong with her. She was like that to the end. Even when she could barely move.' He broke off, lowered his head, pinched his eyes and cried.

Barnett had only ever seen his father cry once before, and that had been on the day his mother had died. He went over, lowered himself down into a squat, and put his arm around his father's shoulders. He pulled him close and let him cry. He couldn't hold back his own tears, but he tried his best to do it in silence.

Eventually, Richard settled. Barnett released him from his tight embrace and rubbed his back instead. 'I understand, now,' Barnett said. 'I understand why you kept the truth from me. The pain she must have gone through, I—'

A stare from the damp, red eyes of his father interrupted him. 'Oh no, son... sorry... it gets worse. That's not everything.'

Barnett felt his stomach turning. 'I just assumed she got out of there—'

His father shook his head, completely pale. 'No. She was a kid, son. She was homeless with nowhere to go. No, she stayed. After all, she'd someone else to think about and—' He broke off, reached down for his whisky.

'Someone else. Who?'

Richard drank the whisky back. 'The life inside her, son.'

Barnett stood. 'What? What do you mean?'

'She was pregnant. Your mother was pregnant.'

36

After putting her children to bed, and a quick chat with Monika, Gardner eyed up her wine rack.

She then set herself up at her computer with a cup of herbal tea.

Boring, but sensible.

She intended to drag the internet for everything there was on KYLO, Helping Hands, Bright Day, James Sykes... the whole bloody lot of them! Her team was so light, and she'd already demanded that they went home and rested.

So, these hours before exhaustion finally took her were valuable.

It was also bloody exhausting trying to keep her mind from the other issue. It was constantly leeching away at the back of her mind.

Riddick.

And still no bloody word from Cecile.

So, within ten minutes of failed internet searches, while simultaneously living through several worse-case scenarios with her friends – which involved funerals – she stupidly looked for sanity in a bottle of Merlot.

She'd had an idea earlier, but had, for fear of setting a hare running, forced it to the back of the mind.

Now, she was suddenly changing her mind and feeling some-what courageous.

Half a bottle of wine would do that to you.

She placed a call to the Digital Forensics Unit down in Wiltshire. Sandra Mills was a friend of hers from home. Their relationship was close and trusting. Still, Gardner was taking quite a liberty here. There was no guarantee Sandra would help; in fact, she probably wouldn't. Still, she wouldn't shop her for the unorthodox request, so there might be no harm in asking.

Gardner must have had more credit in the bank than she'd realised, because Sandra agreed to triangulate the calls made to and from Cecile Metcalf's mobile phone to locate the area she might be. Sandra asked for at least a day. She, too, would have to call in favours to keep it below the radar. Gardner hoped to God it didn't backfire on poor Sandra. She was one of the best, and Gardner cursed the half bottle of wine for giving her the courage to put a good friend in the firing line before drinking the other half.

Drunk and struggling to stay awake now, never mind *drag* the internet for every remaining morsel, she closed her eyes—

Her phone snapped her out of it.

Immediately thinking of Cecile, she launched for it.

Barnett.

She took a deep breath and tried her best to sound sober. 'Ray?'

'Boss, I...' Barnett's tone was off. 'I spoke to my father.'

He was clearly distraught and, when Gardner heard the details of why, she wasn't surprised.

'Oh, Ray. I'm sorry. It must have been a shock.'

'I'd an older brother or sister... at least, I would've had... surely, it still counts even if they didn't make it into this world...'

'It counts. It *really* counts.'

'The pain Mum went through. I wish she'd told me everything.'

Do you? Really? Gardner thought. *I mean, it's important you know*

now, but did you need the burden of all that in your life while you were growing up?

'She protected you.'

'I can't believe she shut it all away.'

Maybe she didn't? Gardner ran her finger around the rim of the empty glass. *But she had a new life... with Richard... a new child. You, Ray. Sometimes, you have to do what you have to do.*

'She must have been sad... so bloody sad inside,' Barnett continued.

Gardner put the glass out of her line of sight. She was craving another drink and with what she was most certainly up against over the next couple of days, opening another bottle would be a dreadful idea. 'She'd have been grateful for what she found, Ray. A loving husband, and a loving son. I don't believe she was unhappy. And she probably didn't want to say anything for fear of tarnishing all the goodness she now had. Still, I can only imagine your shock... Maybe it's best if—'

'No,' Barnett interjected. 'I need to work. I can't stay in the house. Not now. And just because my mother was in that shelter, doesn't mean she's connected with Sykes' death. It was a long time ago. I don't think I'm compromised.'

Maybe not yet... but what if we establish that link?

'Please, boss, I'm begging you.'

She gritted her teeth. Her gut was to refuse him. And, normally, it'd be a flat-out refusal, no question. But how light on the ground was she? Would Marsh give her someone else? Unlikely. And even if she did, would she get anyone nearly as capable as Barnett? Also, unlikely.

'Office work, okay?'

'Thank you, boss...'

'But if the case becomes any more personal... if it becomes evident that Sykes died because of that period when your mother was there, you step down, no questions. Okay?'

'Okay.'

'And, truth be told, Ray, I need you. No one is better in the office with information.'

'I've already started.'

'Now why doesn't that surprise me?' *I imagine you did much better than me over the last couple of hours.* 'Go on, then.'

Barnett explained. Some of which she knew already.

'One of the other suicides was a Melissa Sale. She also miscarried.'

'So, we now know of two women that miscarried, Isla Holt and Melissa Sale, committing suicide?' *Patterns emerging.*

'Aye.'

'Shit... we need to get eyes on that internal investigation! I've got the request in. Any more on overdoses?'

'There were four fatal overdoses during Sykes' tenure. Overdoses are possible, but four is a lot considering that the homeless people were searched for drugs before being provided with a room at the shelter. It makes you wonder if a member of staff was bringing it in. But, here's what really caught my attention...'

This is why he's the best, Gardner thought. *If there's something to be found, Ray finds it...*

'Two of the five women who lost their children died from a fatal overdose. Tia Loom and Seren Rhodes.'

Gardner sat up straight in her chair, adrenaline flooding her body. 'So, four of the five women who experienced miscarriages never made it out?'

'That's correct. Tia and Seren, overdose. Isla and Melissa, suicide. The only person who made it out was my mother, Amina.'

Who'd now also passed, Gardner thought. There was no need to state the obvious.

'Good Lord.' Gardner took a deep breath. It was the type of revelation that demanded you were straight on your feet and into work.

Except, she was currently quite pissed, and she wondered who she could contact at this time of night.

Gardner only realised after being lost in her thoughts for a while that Barnett had gone quiet.

'I'm sorry, Ray.'

'All these poor women. Yet, my mother survived. I bet she felt so guilty. These broken people around her. Suicides. Overdoses. I wish she was still here, boss, so I could hold her... help her... tell her we will find the truth.'

Her sympathy for Barnett was immense, but if there had, indeed, been a conspiracy to silence four out of five women, why did Amina Ndiaye walk away?

And there was absolutely no doubt that a bright spark like Ray hadn't considered it.

She imagined it'd be the first thing out of Rice's mouth in briefing.

With that on her mind, she'd no choice. 'Ray, I want you to stay home first thing. You at least take the morning off. *Work from home.* I'll phone you early afternoon—'

'Boss—'

'I'm sorry, Ray. I'm sorry for everything that you've just found out. But that's my decision. Tomorrow afternoon. Sit tight and keep researching.'

And maybe, when I rule your mother out, you can come back in.

* * *

After Gardner had contacted Rice to fill him in, she cancelled the briefing anyway. It felt more logical to head straight to the Bright Day shelter first thing.

'The sooner we find out what the bastard government and the blood-sucking pricks KYLO are burying, the better,' Rice had said.

'Never been a huge fan of Ray. Stand-offish, you know? But shit, that's some weight to carry!'

'Yes,' Gardner said, appreciating Rice's sympathies even if they came dressed up in their usual bullish costume.

'One thing is bothering me...'

Here we go.

'Why did his mother get a pass, eh?'

'We'll sleep on it. See you first thing.' She hung up before he'd any more opportunities to voice his concern.

Hoping to flush some of the alcohol from her system, she drank a pint and a half of water and went to bed. She'd no hope of being fresh now, but she could try to mitigate the damage.

In bed, her mind gravitated towards Lucy O'Brien.

She'd been there for Gardner, pretty much constantly, but had been forced to take a back seat to her concerns over Riddick and Cecile, and Operation Gearchange.

After double checking her phone to confirm that she'd not missed a message, she considered whether to send one.

Their relationship was going nowhere, of course. At least, not in how O'Brien, and potentially Gardner, would really like. It was dead in the water. It had to be. It wasn't even open for debate.

Despite this, Gardner held the friendship in high regard and wanted to ensure its survival.

Would a text message this late send off more false signals though?

Oh, whatever!

Maybe it was the bottle of wine, but she rattled one off.

> That cereal bar saved my life as per. It was all I ate today! Sorry, haven't spoken all day... been flat out. Catch up tomorrow. X

She deleted the X before sending it.

She waited for a reply, but none came.

Before she fell asleep, however, Marsh came good on her promise, texting the names of three officers joining the operation tomorrow.

They were all capable.

She fell asleep with a smile on her face, especially as one name had been Lucy O'Brien.

37

1990

Elizabeth Sykes was not oblivious to the pain and suffering that plagued the lives of many. She was, after all, the daughter of two social workers who lived behind a homeless shelter and helped on the weekends.

Elizabeth would often lie awake at night, wondering if the resolve to support people in need, that featured so prevalently within her mother, father and older brother, and now, her, was genetic. Because, when she looked outwards into the vast world, she saw little altruism, little compassion, and very little desire to help from others.

Whatever the reason, she knew now that the tight grip she had on Mary's hand was in earnest. It was real and wasn't simply an attempt to pacify someone broken and lost. She felt compassion.

Mary had been induced following a miscarriage and wasn't in complete control of her senses. Still, although she was bedridden, she possessed enough sense to know of her loss, and had now cried for her child for close to an hour.

When Mary finally calmed, she asked, 'What's your name?'

'Elizabeth.'

Mary stared up at the ceiling as if trying to process something.

Eventually, her eyes moved to Elizabeth. 'A beautiful name. I'd like to call my daughter, Elizabeth. If that's okay with you?'

Elizabeth didn't know the most appropriate way to answer this question, so she went with her gut. Her gut always told her to be agreeable and kind. 'Yes, of course,' Elizabeth said. 'I'd like that.'

Mary turned her focus back to the ceiling. 'They said it was my fault. That I abused my body.'

Elizabeth squeezed her hand.

'But I didn't, Elizabeth. I swear I didn't. Since the day I found out about you, I didn't take a thing.'

The peculiar use of the pronoun made Elizabeth wonder if Mary had suddenly addressed the child that she'd lost.

Elizabeth heard someone at the door to the room. She turned and saw her brother, James, there. He had an irritated look on his face, and he closed the door behind himself when he came into the room.

James was often irritated. Fortunately, he rarely took this out on her. With his fourteen-year-old sister, he was usually sweet, and had always fed her and brushed her hair when she was much younger, and their parents were busy. Still, she'd heard him vent before now. He'd shout and swear in another room, usually, and she'd hear things being smashed. It was terrifying, truth be told.

So, she was always cautious in his presence.

'What're you doing here?' he asked her. In this moment, his voice seemed to be wound tighter than it ever had been with her before.

'I heard crying and—'

'So?'

She felt pain in her stomach. 'I – I'm sorry.'

'You shouldn't be here. Hasn't it been made clear to you?'

Elizabeth nodded but looked up at her brother with sad eyes, trying to appeal. 'But... she was crying. So much. I thought she could do with company.'

'No... she just needs her rest... she's been through a lot.' He looked over at Mary. His irritated expression morphed into one of disgust instead. He leaned back out the door. 'Nurse... we need. The medication is wearing thin.'

Elizabeth rose to her feet at the same moment his intense glare swung back onto her. 'Go.'

'I'm sorry—'

'I said, go.' James turned away and sighed.

As she made her way to the exit, Mary called out, 'Elizabeth... please, Elizabeth... don't go. Don't leave me.'

Elizabeth turned. 'Sorry, Mary, I—'

'Damn it! Go!' James hissed.

Elizabeth swung, her stomach jarring again.

'My daughter... please, Elizabeth. You're my daughter!'

James stepped forward and prodded his sister out of the room as the nurse swooped in.

Once the door was shut, Elizabeth pinned her ear to the wall.

'Listen... she's not your daughter,' James said. 'Your daughter is dead. And, as we've discussed, it was your fault. Your own selfish fault.'

Elizabeth backed away, hand to her mouth. It was at this moment that she realised that James, her brother, wasn't like her and her parents after all.

And if altruism was genetic, then James couldn't be her brother. Not really.

Because James Sykes was a wicked man.

A very wicked man.

38

Despite being assured by the doctor beside him that Elizabeth Sykes was completely unresponsive, Suggs worked his hardest to ensure his shock and dismay remained firmly buried.

With Elizabeth's one remaining eye still open, he'd take no chances.

It'd been three decades since Elizabeth, in her prime, had been caught in the house fire which claimed her parents, but the physical scars from that tragedy were as clear as ever. Her hairless scalp and face bore the intricate, rugged patterns of scarring.

Suggs was looking down on survival way beyond the odds.

Closer to the bedridden woman now, Suggs resisted an urge to pass his hand over the remaining eye, struggling to believe that it wouldn't move.

Her arms lay above the thin beige blanket that covered her. There were tubes in the back of her scarred hands.

She appeared more like a sculpture than a human being: rigid and completely frozen out from the world around her. The doctor had already informed him that the room, although quiet, could suddenly explode with activity, and she'd *still* appear in this perpetual moment of disconnection.

It was a contrast Suggs had no appetite to see.

In fact, he'd seen quite enough.

'Very few people,' Doctor Robinson had said earlier, 'if any, could survive such catastrophic burns.'

And looking at her now, Suggs concluded there was a very good reason for that. There was nothing fortunate in such survival.

'Permanent catatonia triggered by trauma is rare, but that's what we've here: mutism, stupor, rigidity,' Robinson had continued. 'Elizabeth has experienced every symptom of the condition... again, rare. Treatments are usually effective, but that hasn't been the case with Elizabeth. Even electroconvulsive therapy did little to shift the dial, I'm afraid. The condition remains chronic.'

'How does she eat?' Suggs had asked.

'A PEG tube. It's been surgically inserted directly into the stomach through the abdominal wall. It's comfortable. All nutritional needs are met.'

'Do you think she'll ever recover?'

Robinson had shrugged. 'Years ago, I thought so. But, seeing her failing to respond to any treatments for such a sustained period... well... the reality is *I don't know*.'

Now, looking down at her, and having adjusted to her extreme disfigurements, Suggs had the urge to reach out and touch her face. Reassure her. Tell her that people were here for her. And, one day, she could wake, and the support would be in place.

But, again, he maintained his professionalism.

Just before he left the room with the doctor, he took one last look back at her, and instead of pity, he felt, for the first time, a surge of respect.

Her condition was stark and sobering. Yet, something impressive emanated from her presence. The human spirit could persist and endure *even* during such profound withdrawal and with such horrendous past traumas.

So, as he left, he felt different, somehow, and spoke to Elizabeth in his thoughts.

You're strong, Elizabeth. So very strong.

39

***

'Wow,' Gardner said, driving into the Bright Day car park.

'I wasn’t wrong, was I?' Rice said from the passenger seat. 'It’s all about KYLO washing its face.'

'I didn’t dispute it. I just didn’t expect the face to be so chiselled, clean-shaven and drenched in expensive aftershave.'

After Gardner parked, she admired the architectural flamboyance. Its exterior was a striking blend of glass and steel, which was angled to reflect the sky rather than the dilapidated urban surroundings.

'It’s been here almost twenty years,' Rice said, fastening up his jacket. 'I remember the press conference... *a beacon of hope and modernity in a broken area.* Look around you, boss. Still looks broken to me. Shit, as ever, to be fair.'

Gardner glanced at some dishevelled shops: most a mess of peeling paint, some boarded up and covered in graffiti.

The snow wasn’t falling yet, but the cold still bit. Gardner wrapped up tight and slipped on gloves before opening the door and bursting their warm bubble.

Gardner and Rice approached the large, transparent glass façade that framed the entrance. The passersby could catch glimpses of the warm and welcoming interior. 'Imagine turning up and it being full,' Rice said. 'Here's what you could have won...'

Gardner didn't respond.

'You ever watch *Bullseye*, boss?'

'No.'

'Guess you're younger than me.'

'I know what it is, just didn't watch it.'

She considered what she already knew about Bright Day. It'd kept the philosophy of Helping Hands in that it was a shelter aiming to get you off the streets rather than just rush to your aid; therefore, residents stayed for a considerable length of time while the institute came good in its promise. Those committed to coming to Bright Day, and changing their lives, would first be on a waiting list, and then would be interviewed to gauge their willingness to be reintegrated into society. It wasn't a shelter, as Gardner had understood shelters. It was more of a rehabilitation centre.

Not that they didn't provide emergency shelter. Pregnant women, and people over, or under, a certain age, weren't turned away. Health conditions would also be a factor. And, if Bright Day were at full capacity, someone would arrange transport to shelters in other areas. She explained all of this to Rice.

'So, they lay on taxis!' Rice said. 'Well, it's not like they can't afford it. You know it's all a PR stunt, don't you? Refuge and renewal... renewal... You saw the area?'

Gardner nodded and looked up at the bold sign. *Bright Day.* And beneath it, but not in small letters. *With KYLO Ltd.* She spotted the proud use of solar panels which adorned the roof and then thought of the company's controversial background in single-use plastics.

The world was awash with irony.

Inside, a large, real Christmas tree, dripping with expensive decorations and lights, towered over the reception area. A receptionist dressed as an elf asked Gardner and Rice to sign in on the screen and indicate that they were here to see the manager, Miranda Reikh. The screen took snaps of them, and they were handed stickers with their images on. They also received lanyards from the elf receptionist.

Rice smiled at the receptionist and held up his lanyard. 'What? I don't get one covered with tinsel like you?'

The receptionist chuckled.

'Like you celebrate Christmas,' Gardner grunted as they went to sit and wait for Miranda.

'Because I've no one to celebrate it with,' Rice said. 'Now, if the elf on the shelf over there is at a loose end...'

Gardner rolled her eyes. 'Not only is she half your age, Phil, but she also has a happy, carefree demeanour. Don't ruin her life.'

Rice laughed, while a thought ambushed Gardner. *Half your age. Like O'Brien.*

The world, indeed, was awash with ironies!

The door into the main building buzzed, and a security guard came into reception, wielding a handheld metal detector.

'Does he know we're police?' Rice said with his eyebrow raised.

'Whatever,' Gardner said. 'Don't make a scene. It's just a scan.'

Rice shrugged.

After scanning them, the guard said, 'We need to check your bags.'

'Do you know we're police?' Gardner said.

'Yes, but, it's policy and—'

'You're not looking through my bag,' Gardner said. 'Do you have a locker?'

The security guard pointed back at the reception. 'Behind reception, they've lockers. They'll give you the key.'

While Gardner was handing over her bag, Rice hissed, 'You always make a scene, boss.'

'Piss off before I make another with you.'

The guard led them into the interior.

Gardner assumed this to be the heart of the complex. The open-plan entrance hall rose three floors to a ceiling illustrated with biblical artwork from the Renaissance. It wasn't unlike some of the artwork in the Sistine Chapel.

'I've seen it all now,' Rice said.

'I've seen a need for an interior designer,' Gardner said, looking at the contemporary art adorning the walls, and striking a ridiculous contrast to the ceiling.

If you needed any more evidence that the place was no longer council run and feasted on one of the heartiest private budgets known to man, then you only needed to count the staff. There were a healthy number of suited security officers prowling, as well as many staff in white scrubs.

The place was busy, presumably with the homeless residents. Some engaged in conversation, others read, several played board games.

Although the clothing varied dramatically between the residents from T-shirts and leggings to white blouses and jeans, there was one striking similarity. They were all clean and appeared remarkably happy, considering the shit card life had dealt them.

Gardner surveyed the shelter with awe.

The place was a calm, inviting bubble, completely closed off from the harsh winter outside. For the homeless, this place must feel like paradise.

After passing by a state-of-the-art canteen, which was an open design, and fully staffed and awash with activity, Gardner couldn't resist a comment. 'Impressive.'

'Some... well, many... residents have trust issues,' the security guard said. 'If the residents can see their food being prepared, it reinforces transparency and trust.'

Gardner nodded.

Rice whispered in her ear, 'And here's me thinking they'd just be bloody hungry and grateful for a bite to eat.'

Gardner caught the smell of bacon. *I'd be grateful for a bite of that*, she thought, her stomach rumbling.

The guard led them down a corridor and knocked on an office door. When there was no answer, he opened it. 'Mrs Reikh said it was okay to wait in there if she wasn't back.'

Rice plonked himself down on a chair, peeled off his hat and gloves, and said, 'I hope they're laying on coffee... bet it's good here. Probably got its own Starbucks.'

Gardner, meanwhile, circled the room, regarding the certificates and awards.

Most impressive was a row of Community Impact Awards. They accounted for nearly every year in the last decade. Each certificate reflected the same achievement. Significant contributions to reducing homelessness in Leeds.

There was a cabinet filled with silver plaques. Gardner read a handful. Her attention was mainly drawn to the 'Social Innovation Award' for a unique approach to homeless support, via integrating technology and human care.

'Impressed?' Rice said, looking over at her. He followed his question with a yawn.

'In a way,' Gardner said. 'It may be a PR stunt, but at least it's here.' She looked at a line of pictures of the same woman, presumably Miranda Reikh, alongside different people, either dressed in business attire or work clothing. 'Looks like they've got a fair number of homeless people back up and running again.'

'Apart from the two suicides, four overdoses, and how many miscarriages?'

'Five we know of, but it was a completely different era. Different company.'

'Come on, boss... KYLO knew about it. The bastards were complicit.'

Gardner watched the door swing open before Rice had finished talking. Unfortunately, he'd been gibbering away, so he didn't cut himself off in time.

Miranda Reikh, the woman in the photographs, dressed in a tailored business suit, strolled in. 'Complicit bastards?' she echoed. 'Who might they be, then?'

Rice swung around in his chair, red-faced.

Gardner inwardly sighed. *Pillock!*

Miranda passed a severe look between the two detectives. 'Ma'am,' Gardner said. 'I'm sorry for—'

Miranda waved her away and laughed. 'Don't... I'm winding you up. Not about to get stuck into the police. I've a lot to be grateful for over the years. You've helped with some of our more difficult residents. You'll have to excuse me if I seem wired. We've just had early morning bingo with some residents, and Si, our chief resident doctor, the old bugger, practically delivers a stand-up routine when he's drawing the numbers.'

Gardner nodded. 'Still, I'm sorry... it was unprofessional.' She waited until Miranda wasn't looking at them and was heading around to her side of the table, before glaring at Rice and nodding her head, clarifying that he should apologise. *You bloody dimwit.*

'Sorry, ma'am,' Rice complied. 'Been a trying couple of days.'

Miranda waved it off, sitting down. 'No... seriously. You're detectives. Who wouldn't need to vent under that pressure? You've a murder to solve... as you pointed out on the phone to me last night, DCI Gardner.' She joined her hands in front of herself. 'So, please, take a seat and tell me what I can do.'

Gardner looked up at Miranda, who seemed remarkably nonchalant, and far too jovial, for someone who managed a company that had a connection to a murdered man, and a history of controversies.

Gardner had already asked Miranda questions the night before regarding her personal relationship with James Sykes. She'd claimed, 'He was gone long before I got here.' The dates of employment had certainly backed that up. She'd also claimed to 'know very little about the controversies', but 'she'd do some digging'.

'Well, Mrs Reikh—'

'Enough of that now, please. Miranda!'

'Of course, Miranda. Well, you said you'd do some digging last night.'

'Yes. And I did. For several hours. But you know...' She broke off and sighed. 'Look. I know this is going to come across as vastly unhelpful, but I'm not doing it purposefully... the reality is this, DCI Gardner: Bright Day isn't Helping Hands. Not at all. They levelled the entire building before constructing this, and, well, it took the soul of the place, too, if you understand what I mean. In my mind, this is a completely different company.'

'Be that as it may, Miranda, you may be the only party privy to what actually went on back then.'

'Not really, no. I started working here in 1995. That was four years *after* Helping Hands had died its *necessary* death.' She clapped her hands. 'Gone... completely.'

'Documentation?' Rice asked.

'Certainly not in my possession. And back then, they'd have handwritten a lot... I know there were computers, but the place was quite old school... or so I've heard. Look, I don't want to be the bearer of bad news, but I think you're up against it.'

No shit, Gardner thought.

'And your place rose from the ashes like the phoenix?' Cue Rice's sarcasm.

Gardner inwardly sighed.

Miranda laughed. 'No... because that would imply we're the same organisation. We're completely different.'

She'd have an answer for everything. Having seen the photos on the wall, Gardner already knew what she was dealing with here.

A politician.

Gardner said, 'Technically, you're different. But, when you took Helping Hands from the council, and demolished it, you sacked James Sykes, our victim. I repeat, Bright Day sacked James Sykes. That connects Bright Day to the murder, and I'd like to know what happened to cause that event.'

Miranda sighed. 'In that case, the truth lies with my predecessor, Mark Cosgrove.'

'Yes, but he's been dead for fifteen years,' Gardner continued. 'Which means, as his replacement, we really need your help in looking at that era in the company's history? At least until we speak to your board. KYLO...'

She guffawed. 'Let me know if you manage it. Sometimes, they take over a week to get back to me about anything! They can be a bloody nightmare. Mind you, I guess, I'm not waving a murder in front of them. Saying that, I've waved no real controversies in front of them in close to thirty years. No drug overdoses, accidental deaths, significant crime.'

'No deaths?' Rice asked, his tone incredulous.

'Natural ones, of course.'

'No one will dispute the impeccable job you may have done, Miranda,' Gardner said. 'This predates you. But we need your help. Rather desperately. And it's in everyone's best interests.'

She nodded. 'I know we've our critics. KYLO Ltd isn't the most glamorous of sugar daddies.'

Gardner felt her frustration grow. Miranda was just being defensive now. And the interview was stumbling.

'And KYLO has had their fair share of controversies themselves,' Miranda continued, making more defensive manoeuvres. 'But I'll say this straight. What we do here is nothing short of miraculous.

Comprehensive support services, counselling, job training, health care. We change the lives of these people... we really do.'

Gardner nodded, desperate to keep her irritation in check. *Jesus wept, woman, we're not putting you to the sword.*

But still she continued, 'We've local and national recognition not only for our temporary refuge, but our success in long-term solutions.'

Beside her, she could sense Rice fidgeting. Any second now there'd be a quip over Miranda's quest for a knighthood.

'We treat every person with dignity,' Miranda said.

Rice sighed. Gardner's neck prickled with anxiety.

'Sorry?' Miranda asked, glaring at him.

'Listen,' Rice said. 'As my colleague said, we're not disputing any of that. We're *concerned* about the period in which people weren't being treated with dignity and offered no long-term solutions. Apart from death.'

Gardner dropped her head. It was all she could do from keeping her anger in check.

'That's a bit strong...' Miranda said.

Gardner glared at him and then softened her stare for Miranda. 'We need your help, Miranda. We've a series of reported incidents between 1989 and 1991, which made it into public record, flashed up on the media's radar for a brief period, and then disappeared without a trace. In particular' – she opened her notebook – 'the suicides of Melissa Sale and Isla Holt. The fatal drug overdoses of Tia Loom, Seren Rhodes and Britney Lowe. There were also a number of miscarriages. That's a lot of tragedy.'

'I agree. Heinous.'

'All in an eighteen-month period.'

'I couldn't imagine,' Miranda said. 'The level of incompetence. That's why James Sykes was sacked, no doubt.'

'Got off rather lightly,' Rice said.

Well, until recently, Gardner thought.

Miranda raised an eyebrow. 'Didn't the report disqualify systemic failure?'

'The report is something we're looking into. Yet, you just referred to incompetence. Isn't that systemic failure?'

'In my opinion, yes, but as I keep stressing, it predates me. I *genuinely* know nothing about it. No one in the company has ever made that information available or spoken about it.'

'I'm not surprised,' Rice said. 'Not your finest hour.'

'Not our hour at all!' She was red in the cheeks now.

Before coming here today, Gardner suspected this brick wall. But now she'd run into it, she felt bitterly disappointed. It wasn't that she didn't believe Miranda – she was most certainly telling the truth. She was a yes-man, deliberately kept in the dark. The place needed a clean break. Nothing was cleaner than someone who knew nothing about what came before.

But then a thought occurred to Gardner.

A possibility.

A long shot, yes, a massive long shot, but who knows?

Maybe there was some crossover between the eras in staff? In the lower echelons, perhaps? In an area KYLO had been careless about wiping clean. Unlikely, but what the hell? 'Is there anyone still here who worked for Helping Hands in the past?'

Miranda chewed her bottom lip as she considered. Eventually, she said, 'Yes... just the one. Our cleaning manager, Col Brooker.'

'Is he working now? It would be good if we could talk to him.'

Miranda looked uncomfortable. 'Are you sure that's necessary? I'd be surprised if he knows any more than I do.'

'Still,' Gardner said. 'Best to be sure. So is he here?'

Miranda paled. 'Yes, but...'

Gardner sat up straight. 'Miranda?'

'I must speak to the board. My employers, first. They may not like it...'

'Miranda, we're the police. We don't need to wait for permission.

Besides, you told me it was almost impossible to get in touch with them?'

Miranda sighed. 'This is going to get me in trouble.'

'If there's nothing hidden, there's nothing to worry about.'

'And,' Rice said, 'if there is something hidden, would you really want to work for a company that disciplines you for pointing us in the right direction? To the truth?'

It was the best point Rice had ever made.

Miranda rose from her seat to go and collect Col.

40

Barnett tried his best to sit still.

Before Gardner's secondment up north, the team frequently experienced disorganisation and division. Rice and Riddick wound up the community, while some of the older detectives had forgotten how to put in a shift.

Gardner had built a formidable team up here.

His respect for her went beyond words, and he didn't want to betray her trust. However, she'd left him with all his clearance intact. Combine that with the multitude of favours he could call in, and it wasn't long before he made two significant discoveries.

The first discovery involved Robert Thwaites. During his time as a partner in Long, Oakes and Thwaites Ltd, Robert had acted on behalf of a small, up-and-coming company called Penstone Ltd. In 1991, Penstone had used Robert, on an expensive fee, to assist Leeds council, and the government, in fighting off the accusation surrounding systemic failure at Helping Hands, following the two suicides of Melissa Sale and Barnett's mother's close friend, Isla Holt.

Penstone was a small company dealing exclusively with promising new technologies... or so they claimed. One look at the major shareholders gave you the truth. Some shareholders were relatives and associates of shareholders in KYLO.

So, Thwaites and Penstone (or KYLO in disguise) brought an end to the accusations with out-of-court settlements for the relatives of Melissa and Isla.

Then, after saving Helping Hands, the press expected Penstone to make a move for the shelter.

Not so. The company dissolved because of poor profits. The press quickly lost interest in this immoral company. Government blushes were, for now, spared. Several months later, KYLO got their reward. Theirs was the winning bid for Helping Hands. The connection between KYLO and Penstone had swerved the press, as had been their intention all along.

Barnett felt sick to the stomach.

Not only had KYLO discreetly helped cover up for Helping Hands before taking over and sacking James Sykes, it had also then ordered, *out of the goodness of its heart*, an inquiry into the media's persistent accusation of systemic failure!

KYLO had paid for it. What heroes! No need for them to be biased, eh? It'd been *before* them, after all.

They'd taken the absolute piss.

When Helping Hands came back in the clear, the media quickly lost interest.

The slate was clean.

Barnett phoned Gardner. After hitting her voicemail, he sighed, and then delivered the news. Someone needed to get to secretive Robert Thwaites pronto and tell him his connection was rumbled. Unless Gardner got back to him shortly, that someone would be him.

The second discovery came following a phone call from Janice Knowles of the local council. She informed him she'd sent over all she had on the history of John Atkinson's property. After informing her he owed her a large bottle of red, he hit the computer and looked over the documents.

What he found nearly knocked him over.
The straw that broke the camel's back.
I love you boss, but no way I'm sitting on my hands!
He grabbed his coat and left the house.
Outside, he found Lucy O'Brien on his doorstep.

41

The cleaning manager, Col Brooker, wore glasses, and ironed blue overalls with no noticeable stains. He sat where Miranda had sat only moments before with his head lowered slightly and his eyes wary.

Miranda had quickly descended from a jovial, proud manager to a bag of nerves and had opted to leave the room. No doubt with the false hope that if she didn't witness this interview, she may be able to distance herself from it ever happening.

Unlikely.

KYLO didn't seem like the type of company that had wandered blindly through this world thus far.

Col, who'd already been briefed, was aware of what this was about. 'Can we ask you some questions, Mr Brooker?'

Col looked between the detectives' faces several times. She half-expected him to growl.

'It was a long time ago. I was a young man. Not sure what use I can be,' he said, straightening up, seemingly bracing himself for an unpleasant conversation.

Gardner nodded. 'I appreciate that. But someone has died,

possibly been murdered, and we don't know if anyone else is in danger.'

Col's suspicious expression morphed into a curious one.

'DI Rice, the photograph, please,' Gardner said.

Rice slid two pictures of James Sykes over the table. One from 1990, and the other from two years ago. 'Do you know this man, sir?'

He touched the younger Sykes. 'I knew him, of course.' He looked at the other. 'Is that James Sykes, too? Wow, he certainly put on the timber, eh? Wait...' He looked up. 'Is he the dead man?'

Gardner nodded.

'Shit,' Col said. He rubbed his forehead. 'Fancy that.'

'Surprised?' Rice asked.

'How could I not be? And to be honest, I don't know of anyone who's been murdered before.'

'We'd appreciate it if you tell us everything you can remember about that time when you worked for the Sykes family. Between 1986 and 1991.'

'Bloody hell. Such a long time ago.' Col nodded. 'I'll give it my best shot. But wait, you don't think I—'

'You're not under any suspicion, Mr Brooker. We just desperately need some answers.'

He rubbed his head again. 'Okay, well, let me see. I remember cleaning a lot of floors. And a lot of toilets. Place wasn't what it is now. I was one of three cleaners back then. Now, I'm a manager of about twelve. Yes, the place is bigger, but that place was old... had a way of getting dirty, quick. You know what I mean?'

Gardner nodded.

'Manager,' Rice said. 'You've gone up in the world?'

Rice's words were weighted. A suggestion that Col had been well looked after by manipulative employers was clear as day. Col would have to be a fool not to pick up on it. And so far, he seemed anything but a fool.

'Ha. If you can call it that. I've put in my yards for that extra hundred a month. Hardly a king's ransom, eh? You don't have to worry about my integrity, sir. Look... I'm a different person now, anyway. Back then, well, I was barely a kid, working for rent and beer money. You know how it is. The Sykes family thought I was loyal when most people walked. Really, I was just too busy thinking about the beer and the Saturday nights to go job hunting. Bit different now, like! Not only am I glad of my job, but I'm also still a way off retirement and need to keep it!' He stared at Rice as he said this. Two people could play at sparring with weighted words. 'There'd be a queue around the block if this vacancy came up, I can tell you. It's a good gig.'

Gardner pointed at the picture of the victim. 'Do you think it's possible that Sykes may have been killed because of his connection to what went off here between 1989 and 1991? You recall the accusations levelled against them?'

'Of course.' Col looked thoughtful for a moment. 'Wouldn't surprise me if the past caught up with him. Does with us all. The man wasn't the kindest soul. Spoke to most people like shit. Including myself. I'd no love for the man. Mrs Reikh is the best employer I've ever had. Treats everyone with respect, know what I mean? Staff and residents alike. Is any of this likely to get her in trouble? I'd hate to see that happen...'

Gardner inwardly sighed. She couldn't lie. Who knew how KYLO would react to Miranda pointing out a potential whistleblower?

Best to shift on from his question. 'The next photo please, DI Rice.' Isla Holt.

Col flinched.

'The next, please.' Melissa Sale.

Col looked away. 'Tragic, I know.'

'What was your experience of these events?' Gardner asked.

'My experience!' He guffawed. 'I saw what was left of them! Not sure I'll ever forget that.'

'You know why they did what they did?' Gardner asked.

Col lowered his head. 'Traumatised by what they lost, I guess.'

'So, you know about the miscarriages?'

He creased his brow. 'Miscarriages? I thought miscarriages came early.'

'Twenty weeks,' Gardner said. 'Why?'

'Then, these weren't miscarriages. These lasses were massive. Bigger than my wife, and she got to forty weeks.'

'Women can present differently—'

Col shook his head. 'No. These girls were much further gone than twenty weeks. To think otherwise would make you an imbecile.'

Gardner and Rice exchanged a glance. Gardner continued, 'The press reported five miscarriages.'

'Yes, I know,' Col said, looking around the room, an anxious expression spreading over his face. 'I remember. I also remember that it wasn't just five either...' He broke off.

'Mr Brooker?' Gardner prompted.

'I knew of six.'

Gardner inwardly sighed.

'Did you not think to say anything?' Rice asked.

'To the press?' Col asked, arms raised. 'Not only would I have lost this job, but I also probably wouldn't have got another!'

'What about that integrity?'

'I told you already, fella, I was a young man. Different outlook.'

Gardner looked down at her notebook and read out the names of those who experienced 'miscarriages'. 'Isla Holt, Melissa Sale, Seren Rhodes, Tia Loom and' – she paused, a knot in her throat – 'Amina Ndiaye. So, you're saying that those five women actually gave birth here?'

'Well, I can't remember all their names, but all gave birth, and a sixth, too. The babies must have been stillborn.'

Jesus wept, Gardner thought, shaking her head. *What happened to the bodies then?* Miscarriages occurring before twenty-four weeks don't have to be officially registered, whereas stillbirths would require a body and then a death certificate within forty-two days.

To Gardner's knowledge, there'd been no registration of these five, *now six*, losses at the registry office.

What had Helping Hands been playing at?

'Can you remember the name of the sixth resident who lost a child?'

'Mary Evans. I know that because she was nice. She used to talk to me. Until the experience... then, she just, I don't know, suddenly left. Never heard from her again. I hope she made it.'

'Me too,' Rice said. 'Whereas only four of the other five residents made it.'

'I know. A real crime. Depression is a killer. Clearly, James Sykes and those others should have done more to support them. And that's why he paid the price with his job, and this place had to rebuild.'

'Did you ever speak to Amina Ndiaye?' Gardner asked.

'Not really. I remember her, though. She was timid and quiet. And was up on the roof when that Isla jumped. She, like Mary, suddenly left too.'

Were they paid off? Gardner thought. *For their silence?*

'Didn't you think it was strange that six women experienced the same thing?' Rice asked.

Col's expression grew sombre. 'A lot of them had drug dependencies. Sad... but I assumed, rightly or wrongly, that the treatment of their bodies throughout pregnancy led to this outcome and—'

'They were in a shelter where they didn't have access to drugs,' Rice said, his tone slightly accusatory.

'At least they shouldn't have had access,' Gardner said.

Col shifted uncomfortably in his seat. 'Look... I was the cleaner. But, you know, times were different. It wasn't like it is now. They could have got hold of drugs, I guess. It looks like Fort Knox now, but it wasn't then.' He paused and gazed down at the floor with a haunted expression.

Gardner noticed a subtle change in Col's demeanour, a slight tremor in his voice as he continued, 'I found her, you know. Melissa Sale.' He looked up, his eyes glistening with unshed tears as he fixed Gardner with a haunted stare. 'She'd used her bedsheets to hang herself.' Col's voice cracked, and he lowered his head, his shoulders shaking as he fought to control his emotions. The weight of the past seemed to bear down on him, the memories of that tragic discovery still raw and painful.

Gardner exchanged a quick glance with Rice, silently communicating the need to tread carefully. Rice nodded almost imperceptibly, acknowledging the unspoken message.

As Col struggled to regain his composure, Gardner took the opportunity to collect her own thoughts. The council must have done a bloody good job of selling the story that these six women experienced miscarriages, because this place never would've got its revamp if news came out about unregistered stillbirths.

Miscarriages were a private medical matter between the patient and their healthcare provider. 'Who was the healthcare provider at Helping Hands?' Gardner asked.

Dabbing his eyes again, Col looked up. 'I recall the nurse here. A young lass. Stern looking.' Col seemed deep in thought. 'Not too pleasant... I'm sorry, the name escapes me.'

Gardner made notes and nodded. 'What happened to her?'

'She left at the same time as James Sykes. There were rumours they were at it. Some of the other staff spotted them a few times... getting rather too close for comfort... if you get my meaning.'

Gardner circled 'nurse'. Finding her was an absolute priority.

'They clearly wanted to keep a lid on these stillbirths,' Rice said. 'So, how did you know about them?'

Col's face creased up, angrily. 'There weren't many of us working here then. Like I said, most other cleaners were in and out. There was me, Lance and a few others. If you were a mainstay, you got talking to residents. They'd tell you things. As did the other long-term staff.'

'So, the information was in a tight loop. A tight loop you were part of. Why did it never find its way out of the tight loop to be dealt with properly?' Rice pressed.

'It did, didn't it? The media reported on it. They were under investigation.'

'Not for stillbirths,' Gardner said. 'And did you know KYLO activated the independent inquiry itself? Trustworthy?'

Col shrugged. 'I'm a grunt now, and I was a grunt then. I was a bloody cleaner on minimum wage with sod all qualifications. Couldn't even read properly till I was in my twenties! Truth be told, I thought little of the miscarriage/stillbirth difference at the time. I just thought it the same thing. Like I keep telling you, I was practically a child. What did you want me to do, kick off about it ten years later when I was more educated? Things move on, don't they?'

Often it doesn't for people who've had their lives broken, Gardner thought, but there was no point in playing the blame game with a man who'd been naïve and young. At least he was cooperating now.

'I know you said you never saw Mary Evans again, but I don't suppose you know where she could have gone?' Gardner asked, knowing it was a long shot.

Col shook his head. 'No... I really don't.'

Gardner nodded. There was still something relevant here, she could feel it. The man sitting opposite them was different to the man who'd worked here in 1989. In that, he'd grown up, had his own family, and developed compassion and a conscience. The talk of suicide, stillbirth and lies had stirred him up. He'd shed tears. A few times, he'd flinched.

There would never be a better time to get that relevant nugget. And she wasn't leaving without it.

Thousands of homeless people must have passed through the doors of Helping Hands between 1989 and 1991. A goldmine of witnesses. A goldmine that would've gone untapped by KYLO's supposed independent inquiry. The man opposite her, Col, was clearly desperate for her to tap that goldmine. Get at the truth another way. Protect his job.

But how many hours of manpower was that? How thin on the ground was she already?

No.

She needed it now.

And to get it, *good cop* would have to stay in the room, and *bad cop* needed a time out. 'Phil, could you check in with Lucy? Update her.'

Rice, of course, looked pissed off, but he'd know that the sensitive, compassionate card was on the way, and that his time in the game was up.

He left the room. Gardner heard him growl. She knew it wasn't part of the act.

'This story is evolving into a very sad story, Col. It's the potential to be one of the saddest I've ever heard. I'm praying every second, it'll not get worse, but I know it probably will do.'

He looked down at the table, shaking his head.

'But if any of this' – she waved her hand over the pictures of Isla Holt and Melissa Sale – 'makes you feel like I currently do—'

'Of course it does. I saw them both, *after* they, you know—'

'So then, get it off your chest. For Isla, for Tia, for Melissa, for Seren, for Amina, and, *for Mary*. Get it off your chest.' She really emphasised Mary, knowing his fondness for her. 'Right now, at this moment, they only have us. Me and you. No one else.'

He closed his eyes. He was cracking.

'Roles reversed, Col. Would you want them to drop their heads?'

'Okay.' He looked up. 'Because there's someone else other than us *here*. My *bloody* wife. I've always been good at dropping my head; Lydia, less so. She died two years ago and made me the happiest man alive for a very long time.' He made no attempt to dry his tears this time. 'So, I know she's watching, and I know I owe it to her.' He looked off to his right at her imagined presence. 'It's going to cost me, love.' He looked back at Gardner. 'As it's going to cost Miranda. These people who run this place... they're not like us. They're not like anyone you've ever met. We're disposable, and I've always accepted that... and plodded on. But, I guess their biggest mistake was considering these' – he waved his hands over the pictures – 'these children... disposable, too. Because we can't have that, DCI Gardner, can we?' He smiled and wiped a tear away. He looked to his right again. 'And neither can Lydia.'

'Thank you,' Gardner said.

'You won't thank me after hearing what I've to say.'

Gardner nodded. A chill ran down her spine.

He looked down as he spoke. Ashamed of the secret he was divulging. It'd clearly burned inside him for so long. 'In the old building, there was a room at the back of the second floor which had a fire escape. It was possible to leave the building via that room. James Sykes never gave me permission to clean that room... oh God... what I'm about to say... I can't believe this is the first time. It makes me a mons—'

Gardner reached over the table, touched his hand and interrupted him. 'It makes you one of the thousands manipulated and silenced by the bigger monsters.'

He nodded, lifted his glasses and wiped away tears.

'I convinced myself it was nothing. The problem was, I went on convincing myself, every single day, until, well, you know... your life moves on...' He held his hands out. 'The world around you changes for the better... seems to, anyway... and you start thinking you're part of something good... deluding yourself... until' – he nodded at Gardner – 'someone walks through the door, pulls the blanket away and makes you realise you're just part of the *fucking* lie.'

Gardner took a deep breath.

'No,' he continued. 'I didn't have James Sykes' permission to clean that room, but I cleaned the adjacent ones. And, frequently, I heard something coming from the room that was off-limits. And now, as we talk about those stillbirths, it's all so blindingly obvious.'

Gardner knew what was coming. She wanted to close her eyes but forced them open for fear of stopping him.

'That those babies I heard crying may have been those stillborn babies.'

Gardner couldn't help but close her eyes now.

She just needed a moment's separation from the room around her.

She heard Col's voice through the darkness. 'Except they were never stillborn, were they?'

42

'Checking up on me?' Barnett asked with a smile.

'About the size of it,' O'Brien said, returning his grin. 'Look, the boss was worried about you. She just wanted me to poke my head around the door and see if you were feeling any better. Except I find you on the wrong side of the door.'

'Am I not allowed to go for a walk?'

'Are you sure that's all it is?'

'Really? You think I'm going to go off on one like the boss's ex?'

'Paul and the boss never dated,' O'Brien said, looking annoyed over his comment.

Barnett frowned. *What's that all about?*

'I know. I was being sarcastic.' *And you usually love a bit of sarcasm with the rest of them, Lucy...* 'Lighten up. You want to tag along while I go rogue? I'm onto something big.'

She hoisted her phone out of her pocket.

'Good luck getting through to her,' Barnett said. 'I already tried.'

Barnett shut his front door behind him and sidled around O'Brien and made for his car.

He opened the door. 'Now, you've two options. You can follow me, panicking over what I'm up to, while frantically trying to contact the boss... or' – he pointed inside the car – 'you can hop in here with me, so I can tell you what I've found out today on the way to John Atkinson's farm.'

'Atkinson's farm? Why?'

Barnett climbed into the vehicle and closed the door.

By the time he'd clicked his seat belt, started the engine and slipped into reverse, he was unsurprised to see O'Brien in the seat beside him, looking at him eagerly.

* * *

Barnett indicated right to take the icy entrance road up to Atkinson's farmhouse.

'So, Penstone Ltd was an arm of KYLO?' O'Brien asked.

'Yes.'

'And Penstone enlisted Robert Thwaites to defend Helping Hands. Wow. So, he'd have been involved in paying off those raising grievances?'

Barnett nodded as he negotiated the icy road.

'Bloody hell.'

'Yes. So KYLO spends money to spare the council's and the government's blushes, and so is given the advantage in the later bid for Helping Hands.'

'And no one bothered to link Penstone and KYLO until now? Until you?'

'Seems not,' Barnett said.

'Jesus. Someone in the government must have known someone in KYLO to put this whole idea in their heads.'

'Makes sense,' Barnett said, nodding. 'KYLO would then have their community crowd pleaser without a lengthy bidding war, while paying over the odds. The government distanced themselves from their hot potato. And then KYLO ordered an independent inquiry into systemic failures to silence the media.'

'But everyone knows independent inquiries can be bullshit?'

'Yes, but why did KYLO need to lie? Remember, they were unconnected to the old guard. Penstone had evaporated at this point. No one was suspicious of them.'

'I can't believe no one has rumbled this until now.'

Barnett grinned.

'You're not as good as you think you are.'

'Bloody hell. Would it hurt for a little pat on the back?'

'Later. Big pay day for Robert then.'

'Yes. Imagine it'll keep his lifestyle funded until his last breath. He must genuinely love storytelling. No chance he needs to keep working for coppers in a hat!'

'But... who made the accusations and were paid off? Four of the five women who miscarried had died...'

Barnett glared at her. 'I know what you're thinking, but my mother wasn't involved. The accusations came from the families of Isla Holt and Melissa Sale. All pulled out *after* being bribed, I imagine. There's no mention of Amina Ndiaye – my mother. She'd nothing to do with this corruption. My mother would never have accepted a bribe. I know – I tried to negotiate often with her as a kid!'

'Okay,' O'Brien said, nodding.

But Barnett could tell from her tone that she wasn't convinced. How could he blame her? Still, right now, he knew... deep down... that she just couldn't be.

Both she and his father were the most upstanding people he'd ever known.

'So, why are we here and not at Robert's home?' O'Brien asked.

'Because John Atkinson has been lying too.'

He quickly explained to her what he'd discovered as he parked up.

'Unbelievable...'

He smiled. 'Just say it. "Ray, you're a genius."'

She pointed at the farmyard. 'This is massive. We can't go in there until we've spoken to the boss.'

'Okay.' Barnett tried and again hit voicemail. He left her a message explaining what he'd now discovered about John Atkinson's farm.

He looked at O'Brien. 'She's fully in the loop.'

'I don't know...'

'She'd want us to do this.'

O'Brien sighed and got out of the car as she followed Ray to the farm.

* * *

John Atkinson answered the door to them. Barnett already had his identification out. Despite this, John threw him a confused look. 'Don't recognise you... Where's the older lass with the attitude?'

Barnett looked at O'Brien with an eyebrow raised and then back at John. 'DCI Gardner is busy, I'm afraid... we're part of her team though. The one investigating the *suspicious* presence of a body on your property.' He enjoyed the use of emphasis after John had greeted him so disrespectfully. 'Is it okay if myself and DC O'Brien come in? We've some questions.'

'Questions... questions...' he murmured, backing away. He turned and waved them in. 'Doesn't matter how many times you ask them, and it doesn't matter how often you reword them, the answers will stay exactly the same.'

I've some new questions, Barnett thought, exchanging a look with O'Brien. *Brand new ones.*

He noticed O'Brien's dubious look in his direction. It seemed she remained concerned about him going off-piste despite Gardner's instructions. Hopefully, when they reached the end of the case, concern would turn to appreciation over the fact that he was doing his job.

The lounge wasn't warm enough for Barnett's liking, so he didn't take off his jacket, and neither did O'Brien. He watched John walk over to stand by the mantelpiece and regard a picture of a young lady on a tropical-looking beach. Barnett assumed this to be Clara Atkinson. Their daughter who lived in Thailand.

John looked down and nudged the grate in front of the weak fire with his foot.

He held back on the suggestion that he should throw on some more wood.

Farmhouses, Barnett thought, eyeing the many farming tools that decorated the walls, *always so chuffin' cold*.

Barnett met John's suspicious eyes. He grunted. 'What're these questions, then? You can sit if you want,' John said.

'You sitting too?' Barnett asked.

'I'm okay here. My back is shot. I stand pretty much all the time these days.'

'Sorry to hear that,' Barnett said, and nodded. O'Brien sat alongside him. 'Where's Mrs Atkinson?'

'Jen's asleep. It's all been rather hard on her. She suffers, you know. Mental health problems.'

'I'm sorry to hear that,' Barnett said.

'Are you?'

'Yes... *we* are, sir,' O'Brien said.

He rolled his eyes. 'Well, fortunately, we're expecting Clara home tomorrow. Make things easier.'

'That's good to hear,' O'Brien said.

'Anyway, can we get to it? I've got tonnes to do.' He raised an eyebrow. 'Questions?'

Barnett nodded and pulled out his notebook. He readied a pen and looked down at the blank page. 'Thank you. What can you tell me about Froisters Chemicals Ltd?' He only looked up after finishing the question.

John paled.

'Mr Atkinson?' Barnett prompted.

He shook his head. 'Who?'

Barnett flicked open his notebook and made a show of tapping the name. 'Froisters Chemicals Ltd.' He looked back up at John. 'What can you tell me about them?'

John turned and prodded the metal fire grate again with his foot, even though it was already in place. 'Never heard of them.'

'Sorry, sir,' Barnett said. 'But you were on their payroll for several years?'

John carried on prodding the grate. 'Ah... Froisters Chemicals?'

'Yes... that's what I said, wasn't it?'

'Sorry, I must have misheard you.' He turned back. He tried to appear confident now, standing up as straight as his bad back would allow, and tensing his jaw.

'So, what can you tell me about them?'

'It's been a fair number of years. I mean. How many years? Maybe you can tell me?'

'1990.'

'Bloody hell. Over thirty years!'

'Whatever you can remember will help. Start with why they paid you.'

'Ha! Hardly on their bloody payroll! If I remember correctly, they paid me a pittance.'

'For what?'

'Rent.'

Barnett nodded and made a note. 'And that was between April 1990 and March 1991?'

'If you say so. Was a long time ago.' He raised an eyebrow. 'You have the right to poke around all my financial details?'

Barnett nodded. 'We're investigating a murder, sir.'

'How many times? There wasn't a murder *here*. Those old remains were dumped on us. Do I need a solicitor?'

'Up to you.' Barnett closed his notebook and waited.

'Get to the point,' John hissed, waving his hand in the air.

'You sure?'

'Yes.'

Barnett opened the notebook again. 'I have the amounts paid.'
He read the sums out. 'Doesn't sound like a pittance, especially back
in 1990. Can you tell me though why Froisters Chemicals were
renting off you?'

John clucked his tongue, making a show of recalling the information. Complete bullshit, of course. 'They saw I'd a stretch of unoccupied
land south of my property. They approached me and offered me money.'

'Why?'

John shrugged. 'Why? They wanted to build a temporary
facility.'

'And did they?'

'Yes. A right ugly, bloody thing. Took them a few months to get
up, corrugated iron.'

'What for?'

He shrugged. 'How do I know? Not my concern.'

'But it's your property,' Barnett said. 'Surely that makes it your
concern.'

John sighed. 'Experiments, I guess. Testing safe chemicals, they
claimed. Okay?'

'And you were okay with that? You trusted them?'

'Yes. I recall they showed me documentation – it all seemed
legitimate.'

'Okay...' Barnett said, making a note. 'And then what happened?'

'What happened?' John widened his eyes. 'Nothing! They stayed
for however long it says in your little notebook and then pissed off.'

'And you saw nothing they did?'

'No.'

'Where's this facility?'

'They asked if I wanted to keep the corrugated iron facility for storage, and I told them to piss off. So, they took it all down quickly, and did just that... pissed off.'

'Do you know a KYLO Ltd?'

John rubbed his stubble. 'The name sounds familiar, but... no... I can't place it.'

'Well, Froisters Chemicals Ltd is a company owned by KYLO. The company is still going strong, actually.' *Unlike Penstone Ltd.* 'So, you may recall KYLO from the documentation?'

'Maybe.' He kicked the grate gently with the back of his foot this time. 'Vaguely.'

Barnett nodded. 'How about your old documents and files from 1990 – would you be able to dig them out for us?'

'Thirty-odd years ago! You'll be bloody lucky.' He sighed.

Barnett fixed John with a stare.

'Okay,' John said. 'Whatever. Is that all, then?'

'No.'

'Jesus.' John rolled his eyes.

'In your statement,' Barnett continued. 'You confirmed you knew Robert Thwaites.'

'As an acquaintance, yes... not as a friend.'

'But you went to school together?'

'Yes, but that doesn't make us friends.'

Barnett nodded. 'Okay, acquaintances. That's okay.'

John nodded. He was paling again and was rubbing the small of his back.

'Are you okay?' O'Brien asked.

'Yes... just my back. Look, I'm not feeling the best.'

'Did you have any business dealings with Robert Thwaites, Mr Atkinson?' Barnett asked.

'How many times! He's an acquaintance! I say *hello* in the street. What call have I for an oral storyteller?'

'He wasn't an oral storyteller in 1990,' Barnett said, reaching into his pocket and pulling out a folded piece of paper. He put it on the table alongside a vase of wildflowers.

'What's that?'

'The contract agreeing that twelve-month rental.'

John shrugged.

'The company that drew up the paperwork was Long, Oakes and Thwaites Ltd. In fact' – Barnett pointed at a signature – 'it's the partner, Robert Thwaites, who has signed the contract. So, if he brokered it, I guess you and him were in fact doing business together.' Barnett sat up straight and regarded John. 'Is this jogging your memory at all, Mr Atkinson?'

John leaned back against the mantelpiece, paler than ever. His legs were dangerously close to the fire. It was fortunate the grate was in place.

'A long time ago,' John said. The strong conviction in his voice that had been so stark was ebbing away. 'Look... I don't think we met on that. He drew up the contract, and I agreed it. No... I don't think we met. What does all this matter?'

'Just that you told us you barely knew him, and yet, he must have known all about you and your property. He brokered a rental contract for you... for... well, I'll be frank now, Mr Atkinson, a mysterious project.'

'Chemicals, lad,' John said, looking angry. 'I told you.'

'But why would an animal farmer allow chemical experimentation on his farmyard?'

'It wasn't like that. The structure they built was well out of the way of the animals... and no harm ever came from it.'

'Apart from it being an eyesore?' O'Brien added.

'Yes...' He glared at O'Brien. 'Apart from that.'

'So,' Barnett said, reaching over and touching the contract again. 'We've a clear link between you and Robert. It's not even the link to Robert that has us reeling. It's the link to KYLO which concerns us most of all...'

'Like I said, I barely know who KYLO is. Familiar, yes... but it's not like I've anything to do with them now, or really did then, to be honest.'

'Still, the victim James Sykes had something to do with them, didn't he? They sacked him when they took control of Helping Hands homeless shelter and converted it to Bright Day.'

John held his hands up. 'Things I know nothing about.'

'But all these connections, John? These can't all be coincidences! Now, it's clear we're close, and it's becoming obvious that you've been deceiving us. Rather than obstruct justice, take the opportunity, Mr Atkinson, to complete this picture. Buy some good grace. Help us.'

John's eyes moved to O'Brien. She pitched in. 'You were scared, worried about your wife's fragile state, and you've omitted important details. If you're completely transparent, there are many people who'll have your back. *We'll* have your back.'

John was shaking his head. He turned and picked up the photograph of his daughter now.

'Mr Atkinson,' Barnett said, standing up. 'Think of Clara. Think how this will reflect on her when everything is out. Transparency. Owning the truth... it's the key to a better—'

'I am thinking of her,' he hissed. 'I'm always bloody thinking of her! That's the issue!'

O'Brien stood now. 'Mr Atkinson—'

'I can't talk to you any more. Don't you understand? It'll do more harm than bloody good. Please leave.'

Barnett sighed. 'If we leave now, this is what'll happen. With all this deceit, suspicion, coupled with the fact that the body was found on this property, we'll inundate your entire estate with search teams before the day is out. Is that what you want? Think of the excessive trauma that will bring into your family. The media scrutiny! The truth is coming with or without your support. Make it with...'

John lowered his head, rubbed his temples and then looked at his daughter's photograph. 'I'm sorry,' he said. 'Listen, before I say anything, this is all on me.' He began to turn. 'It had nothing at all to do with Jen—'

A sharp, loud explosion rattled the air.

John was pitched to the side.

As the intense boom continued to reverberate around the lounge, Barnett watched, wide-eyed, as John thumped down to his knees and then went to the floor face first.

Barnett looked right.

Jen Atkinson, wearing a nightgown, was coming through an open door, holding a shotgun. Her face was expressionless, and she moved, ghostlike, across the room, barely making a sound.

He searched for rational thought, but found only overwhelming panic...

Lucy!

He flicked his head left, sighted her ashen face. She had her hand to her mouth.

'Get down!' he shouted.

She didn't move.

'*Now!*'

He looked right again in time to see Jen discharge the shotgun a second time.

43

Gardner's head rattled as she exited KYLO's glass fortress.

Revelations such as these would do that to a person.

Her winter wear did little to fend off the ice-cold wind that they'd to battle with to get into their car. The weather was turning for the worse again. She could feel the icy sting of snowflakes on her face. It wouldn't be long before the world around her was forced into another standstill.

Not the best time, to be honest. This was the first time she'd felt anywhere near the truth since the skull had emerged from Robert Thwaites' treasure chest, and she wanted nothing coming in the way of this final sprint to the end.

In the car, shivering, she filled in Rice on the rest of Col Brooker's story, while cranking up the heat.

He shook his head with a stunned expression. 'Is he telling the truth?'

'Yes. I think he is.'

'So... potentially we've six... *six*... lost babies.'

'*Stolen*.'

'I wish he *was* lying,' Rice said.

'I do, too, but he's just admitted to turning a blind eye to one of the most atrocious things I've ever heard. He's not about to tell a lie that paints himself in that way.'

'I guess so.'

Gardner heard her phone buzzing from the door compartment. Realising that she must have left it in her vehicle while she was in Bright Day, she reached for it.

'Stolen babies. Not that they're babies any more. They'd be in their thirties,' Rice continued. 'Where the hell are they?'

Two missed calls from Barnett.

And no calls from Cecile.

Shit.

She had to be in serious trouble. There was no question any more. Contacting Sandra Mills in Wiltshire last night had been a good move.

'We'll find them,' Gardner said to Rice as she dialled up her voicemail.

'And can we burn KYLO to the ground?'

'We'll try,' Gardner said, knowing full well how difficult that would be.

With widening eyes, Gardner listened to Barnett's messages. Barnett's *breathtaking* messages.

Rice lost patience quickly, especially when he heard Gardner mutter and curse under her breath and rub at her temples. Every time he hissed, 'What is it?' she silenced him with a raised finger.

Afterwards, she dropped the phone to her lap, shaking her head, and explained Barnett's discoveries regarding Robert and John. And as Rice took his turn to mutter and curse under his breath, something occurred to Gardner.

Something from her visit to the homes of John and Robert.

Ruby May Thwaites.

Clara Atkinson.

The daughters of the two key players with a story to tell were both thirty-three.

It wasn't a difficult calculation.

They'd have both been born in 1991.

Immediately, she became convinced that Ruby and Clara were two of the missing babies.

She voiced this to Rice. His eyes widened.

Then, she attempted to contact Barnett back. Voicemail.

'*Shit!*' she thought out loud. 'Okay... so he's quizzing Atkinson. We'll pick up with Thwaites first.' She reversed her car. 'Meanwhile, Phil, contact the local registry office. I want the birth certificates for Clara and Ruby May.'

44

Barnett looked to his left on the sofa they sat on.

Blood speckled O'Brien's face.

But she set her jaw and widened her eyes. *Admirable*, Barnett thought. She wasn't folding. *Yet, at any rate.*

He gave her a nod, attempting to reassure her. She returned it.

Not that reassurance meant much when someone clearly suffering from mental illness was pointing a shotgun in your direction, after proving that they were prepared to kill.

Barnett moved his eyes over John Atkinson. Shot twice in the back. Once while he was turning from the mantelpiece, and the second while he'd been face down on the floor. Had he been dead before the second shot?

One thing was for certain: he was dead now.

John's eyes were wide and unseeing, and the surrounding blood was growing over the parquet floor at an alarming rate. In one hand, he still clutched the framed photograph of his daughter Clara.

Barnett then looked at Jen Atkinson, who stood off to his right, pointing her shotgun at them.

Her complexion showed a noticeable pallor. The portrayals of insanity in those old books he'd been forced to read at school came to his mind. Lady Macbeth, or Bertha Rochester in *Jane Eyre*. Jen's eyes looked as they'd done when she'd shot and killed her husband. Vacant.

They'd only flickered into life, briefly, when she'd chambered another two shotgun bullets.

Barnett had already tried to speak to her, and each time, she'd simply hushed him, raising the shotgun slightly, to signal that she was ready to discharge it.

She was yet to look Barnett directly in the eyes. Mostly she stared off into space and had maybe glanced at her dead husband twice. Still, she didn't need to look at them to keep the shotgun in their direction and, if she fired, the buckshot would make a mess of them both.

'Mrs Atkinson—'

She gave another shush and waved the shotgun.

What could they do? They had to communicate... surely... they couldn't just wait here until she plucked up enough resolve to vanquish the room of any witnesses?

She'd obviously killed her husband over what he was about to reveal. Why would she let them walk away now so they could make that discovery elsewhere?

'Mrs Atkinson, let us help you,' O'Brien said.

Jen shushed again, her eyes still unmoving.

Barnett's stomach was in knots, and he could feel his heart thrashing in his chest.

This was all his fault! He wasn't even allowed to be here, and he'd only bloody well gone and dragged O'Brien into danger.

What a dickhead...

'We can stop this situation getting out of hand,' Barnett said.

'I *said* be quiet.' Jen's first words. Delivered with venom. Barnett, expecting blackness to descend at any second, felt his insides collapsing.

'Whatever your husband has done,' O'Brien pressed on. 'We can put it right. He said you weren't involved, and we believe him—'

'Shut up!' Jen came closer, waving the shotgun. 'I said shut up!'

Barnett held up his palms. 'Okay... okay... Mrs Atkinson. You've made your point.'

Stunned he was still alive, Barnett glanced at O'Brien again, and told her with a brief shake of his head that enough was enough. The woman was desperate. One more outburst would be all that was needed.

Barnett lowered his head to show that he was submissive, while glancing at Jen out of the corner of his eye.

She still had her eyes on them and looked more thoughtful than moments before.

They were going to have to wait for calm and make some kind of move.

'It's over...' Jen said. 'Clara can't know. She *must* never know.'

Instinctively, Barnett wanted to question what this was, but kept his head down. Fortunately, so did O'Brien.

'Oh God, she's coming tomorrow. She's *here* tomorrow.' Jen shook her head and looked distraught. Despite the shotgun still being pointed in their direction, she suddenly seemed less focused on it. Whether that was a good thing or a bad thing, Barnett didn't know. An accidental discharge or an intentional one – the outcome would most certainly be the same.

'John would've told her, eventually, anyway.' She looked back down at her dead husband. 'He was always threatening to. The guilt, you see. It consumed him. Even so, I never thought he would. That he *could*. But he buckled just now. Because you threatened to search the farmyard.' She shook her head.

What's in the farmyard?

Jen continued, 'I'd vowed to die before Clara knew the truth, and the vow applied to him, too. He *knew* that.'

There it was. They'd received confirmation of their doom. Everyone dies before the truth comes out.

Think, Ray, bloody well think!

'Jen,' O'Brien said. 'We can help you, and we promise to keep Clara safe—'

'Hush... damn it.' She suddenly looked more animated. Barnett wasn't sure that was a good thing.

'I need to think!' she hissed, pacing back and forth.

The weapon was momentarily off them.

Was this their chance? Barnett took a long, deep breath through his nose. He put some tension in his legs, preparing to spring. Right now, the distance was too great, but if she came closer, he could get to her before she spun and got a shot off...

Here she comes...

Barnett prepared to launch—

But then she lifted the gun and turned it on them again.

Shit!

'No... no... it must end. *Tonight.* Now. Clara can't ever know.'

Frustrated, Barnett hissed, 'At least tell us why you're doing this!'

Jen creased her brow. Her internal conflict was clear. She was clearly taking aim, but something was keeping her from pulling the trigger.

'Do you want me to tell you that your actions are right... that you're justified?' Barnett said. 'Are you waiting for some kind of approval?'

'I don't know... shut up... just shut up.'

'Tell us what is in the farmyard. You owe us that much at least. If you must do this, give us your justification.'

Her top lip trembled as she creased her face further.

Shit, Barnett thought. *She's building up the courage. To do to us what she did to her husband—*

She straightened up and uncreased her face. 'You're right. It's fair for you to know... to understand. Come with me and I'll show you.'

45

On the journey to Robert Thwaites' home, Rice confirmed the registered births of both Clara Atkinson and Ruby May Thwaites. Both had been home births in 1991, several months apart. Interesting, both had been born at the back end of the council's ownership of Helping Hands, after Robert's successful stint on behalf of Penstone, but just before Penstone was dissolved, and KYLO submitted their bid. Stood to reason that they could be the last of the stolen babies *if* Gardner's suspicions over James Sykes were right.

Gardner parked, and Rice pointed at Robert's house. 'Time for the great storyteller to tell his true story.'

'James Sykes' killer's intention all along,' Gardner said. *'Out the truth.* It was crystal clear in the notes.'

Rice was shaking his head. 'How the hell did Robert Thwaites end up with one of the stolen babies?'

'Think about it,' Gardner said. 'James Sykes had stolen and, by the time Robert was on the scene, had sold four babies. Although nothing has been flagged financially on Sykes yet, there are plenty of other ways to hide money and income – we'll find the truth about that. In fact, I wouldn't be surprised if the money was taken back from him by KYLO once they'd found out. Anyway, following the accusations of systemic failure levelled against Helping Hands by the families of those poor girls who took their lives, and the media fervour, enter Penstone and Robert Thwaites, on behalf of KYLO and the council, to investigate. He's one remit. This big, *sickening* mess needs to go away. Save the government from embarrassment and pave the way for KYLO's takeover. So, Robert acts quickly with the four sold children. He uses the money of powerful people to pay for the documentation to be put in place, in case anyone came looking in the future.'

Rice nodded. 'I see. The stillbirths had never been registered. So, fake birth certificates could be registered.'

'Precisely. Okay...' Gardner said, 'now this may be a leap, but I'm betting he'll confirm this for us before the day ends... while Robert was cleaning up Sykes' mess, stopping that controversy becoming a full-blown scandal of stolen babies and the like, he saw an opportunity. A golden one. Maybe, all the babies had yet to be sold...'

'Bastard.'

'Yes.' She gritted her teeth and took a deep breath through her nose – she simply couldn't wait to hear this from Robert's mouth if it was true. *Lying bastard.*

'A baby of their very own,' Rice said. 'What a fairy tale. Maybe they couldn't have them?'

'Good point. Easy to confirm when we've their medical records.'

Rice looked at the house with narrowed eyes. 'Two birds with one stone for Robert. The fifth baby off the radar, and...'

'He builds his own family,' Gardner said.

'It's a win-win for a scumbag. John Atkinson takes the final baby?'

'Possibly. John Atkinson is a school friend of Robert Thwaites. He's a little down on his luck, financially. Robert throws some work his way in terms of KYLO needing somewhere for their smaller firm,

Froisters Chemicals, to carry out some experiments. Illegal, most likely. We can pick them off on that later. Let's stick with the babies. What if... another *similar* opportunity presents itself? Maybe, John, too, is struggling for a family? Maybe, this is part of the payment for housing illegal chemical work? Maybe, he just went all out and blackmailed them for one. Or, maybe, Robert just entrusted his friend with one, too? Let's hope Ray and Lucy have got to the bottom of it with Atkinson.' She didn't voice her annoyance that Barnett was going against her orders to visit Atkinson. The last thing she needed to do was provide Rice with ammunition to use on Barnett during future altercations – they weren't the best of friends as it was. She'd deal with that later, discreetly. Another thought occurred to her. 'Who's on the birth certificate for delivering the baby?'

'An L. Wilton.'

'Made up, no doubt.'

'Almost certainly.'

'So, as soon as we finish up with Robert, we will rule that one out.'

Just before stepping out of the car, her phone rang. She answered. It was Ross.

'Brad?'

'I've sent you an email, ma'am. It's a list of all the shareholders in KYLO over the last forty years as you requested. It hasn't fluctuated, but there was an interesting change around the time that KYLO took control of Helping Hands from the government. One of the major shareholders pulled out in the preceding week. Sold all his shares. Might mean nothing, but...'

'Go on, then,' Gardner said, readying her notebook. 'Who was it?'

'His name was Neville Fairweather.'

Gardner didn't write it down.

Didn't need to.

The name was already ingrained in her conscious mind from events earlier this year.

Not that she'd be able to write now if she wanted to.

Her hand, and body, were frozen.

46

1990

Elizabeth Sykes had been torn from her world by the roots.

James was not who she'd believed him to be. Everything she'd ever believed about her family was in doubt.

She desperately needed order.

She sought it out.

Her boyfriend, Felix, was attentive. He listened. He cared.

So, despite being only fourteen, she gave herself to him in the ways he wanted. He was eighteen and had needs, she guessed. She was happy to do this. It was something, at least. Something she felt she could understand and hold on to.

Then there were her trips to see Mary Evans.

Daily, she sneaked visits to the bereaved young mother. Held her hand. Kissed her on the forehead. Told her that she was starting to look better... healthier... told those white lies.

But were those trips for Mary, really? Or were they for herself?

Mary was compassionate and doted on others. For most of her life, others had exploited these traits in her, which partially explained why she was now where she was.

So, was this just another selfish act by Elizabeth? Using another?

But it became addictive. That attention shown by Mary.

Yes, she had her boyfriend, but lately, he'd been so preoccupied with sex that he'd become less and less interested in her, and what made her tick. Her ambitions... her interests...

Mary always listened. Mary was always fascinated.

Their friendship grew.

But Mary was deteriorating. Her skin was paling, and she was losing weight. Her speech became slurred.

Once Elizabeth had tried to broach it, but Mary had brushed it aside. 'I'm well taken care of. Your brother, the nurse, they take good care of me.'

And it was at that point that the true extent of her brother's evil had dawned on her.

He was giving her drugs again.

For days, she'd considered telling her parents, going to the police, but her brother, although irritable with others, remained jovial with her, and doubt crept into her mind.

Then, as if by some miracle, Mary Evans' health improved!

They continued talking and Elizabeth watched the colour returning to her.

One day, she gave her the news. 'Things have changed. Massive things. I've come into some money. A rich relative... anyway... forget all that. I've a chance. A second chance.'

Despite being a little strange, Elizabeth was over the moon for her.

So Elizabeth, although sad to be losing someone special from her life, said farewell to her.

She planned to get in touch when Mary settled.

But, of course, she never got round to that.

Falling pregnant completely preoccupied her.

47

Doctor Ruben Robinson watched as the nurses disconnected all of Elizabeth Sykes' machines.

After someone's passing, the nurses were usually so quick and efficient at cleaning up. They reserved all emotion and compassion for those who still lived, only to fully consider the loss later, in the dark hours, when they lay awake contemplating the day.

Robinson was no different. Life and death were part of the job. Too much of an emotional response was a one-way ticket to early retirement.

Today, however, the nurses moved more slowly, and elegantly. It felt different somehow. And, as he observed Nurse Rhodes removing the PEG tube, he succumbed to a rare moment of reflection.

Elizabeth Sykes had been an enigma. A tragic tale scarred with intrigue, in much the same way that her body had been so badly scarred by the flames.

To survive the fire had defied the odds. To live for three decades since, truly impressive. To never once emerge from a state of catatonia, a startling anomaly. And now, to die without warning? No infection, no presentable heart or breathing problem... well, in a way, it could be said that the story of Elizabeth received a fitting conclusion.

He sighed.

He knew now that the unthinkable may just happen and he'd miss her.

For so long, for so many days, she'd offered him mystery on his rounds, when his day was so often black and white.

He moved over and looked down at the scarred woman and sighed a second time. Nurse Rhodes looked up at him. 'Our longest resident.'

Doctor Robinson nodded. 'And we never got to talk to her.'

'No... but she spoke... just before she passed.'

'I thought she was alone?'

'No,' she said, pointing up at the camera in the room's corner. 'They record for twenty-four hours before restarting. I'd a quick look before you arrived.'

'And?' Robinson said, raising his eyebrow. Even in death, the mystery of Elizabeth Sykes continued.

'Sorry.'

'Why are you sor—'

'No, doctor, *sorry*, that's what she said. Over and over.'

He looked down at Elizabeth again. At her pale, scarred face, and the thick skin where her eye should have been. 'I don't think you'd anything to be sorry for, my dear.'

'That's not all. She said a name...'

'Interesting... who was it?'

After the nurse had told him, he creased his brow, perplexed. 'Odd.' He then raised an eyebrow and looked down at her. *I'm going to miss you, Elizabeth... you really did interest me.*

He placed a hand on the nurse's shoulder. 'Thanks, dear. I'll contact the detective.'

48

Under a sky smeared with shades of grey, Barnett and O'Brien marched into the white expanse at gunpoint. The snowfall muffled the world into a hushed silence.

They'd exited through the rear door of the farmhouse on the opposite side of the property to where the burned-out vehicle and James' remains were discovered.

Secret barns peppered their path. Dark wood twisted into different shapes, a stark contrast to the relentless purity of the snow.

Barnett kept looking to his right at O'Brien. Each time, she met his eyes, then returned her gaze forward, stoically. They didn't dare whisper to each other. The quiet would betray them. Jen had readied herself to do what she must.

The terror was so overwhelming and his heartbeat so fast that only after the fifth barn did Barnett realise he was freezing. He lifted his hood up, but it did little to help. Winter fingers clawed at his cheeks.

Twice, he chanced a look back at Jen. Trudging through the snow, Jen looked more focused and committed than she'd done before in the lounge, and she marched relentlessly.

By the time they passed the sixth wooden structure, Barnett

became convinced that they'd left it too late to fight back and that they both were going to die. Didn't that make the rest of this march futile?

He stopped, turned and stared. His fast breaths conducted a ghostly dance in the air. When he realised he was still alive, he exclaimed, 'You need to tell me where we're going.'

Her eyes widened, and she raised the shotgun higher so she could take aim.

His mind raced uncontrollably. His thoughts were fragmented... chaotic... yet all around him, the surroundings glowed white and peaceful. He was about to die. Become part of this quiet silence.

He thought of his mother's suffering and his father's pain.

And he realised that he'd maybe been selfish. The trauma Amina had lived through and passed on to his father, and all Richard Barnett had ever wanted to do was protect Ray from those same experiences. That same pain. Guilt joined his fear, and he wished he could just have five more minutes with his father, but this had to end now.

'I won't take another step unless you tell us where we're going,' Barnett said.

She adjusted the gun to the left, so O'Brien was in its crosshairs instead. His heart sank. This was his fault. He'd broken the rules and dragged her here. She didn't deserve this. This was on him, and he needed to keep her alive.

'The next barn,' she demanded.

'So you can kill us?' O'Brien asked.

'It's okay, Lucy,' Barnett said.

She looked at him. Her eyes were wide.

He tried again to reassure her. 'We'll be okay.'

A complete lie, and she knew it.

'The next barn,' Jen said again. 'Now.'

Barnett and O'Brien turned, and they continued onwards towards the hulking structure ahead. Barnett took several deep breaths, trying to replace his fear with bursts of adrenaline. They made his senses more acute. He heard his boots crunching into the snow. He glanced down at their feet, looking at the footprints.

Maybe the shotgun blasts at the farmhouse had been heard elsewhere?

If someone does come, they could follow our trail?

He focused so desperately on these long shots that they felt more and more realistic. But, deep down, he knew there was only one option.

He had to save O'Brien, even if it cost him his life.

He owed her that much.

Just before he reached the barn door, he turned, leaning close to O'Brien as he did so, whispering, 'Run when I tell you.'

'What did you say?' Jen asked.

Barnett shook his head. 'I told her she'll be fine.'

Jen marched forward, using the shotgun to gesture for Barnett to put his hands in the air. Once he'd complied, she rustled in her pocket, knelt to the ground, still moving the shotgun between them both, and laid a key on the surface of the snow.

Then she stood and backed away.

'Open the door, and head to the back of the barn.'

Barnett and O'Brien looked at one another.

'Now.'

'*Why?*' Barnett asked.

She lifted the gun and pointed it at O'Brien again. 'Now, or I swear to God...'

'Okay... okay...' Barnett said. He swooped for the key, looked at O'Brien again, gave her a knowing nod, and then turned.

At first, he found it incredibly hard to open the door. The key might have been a small piece of metal, but right now, it felt like the anchor to a ship. Weighting him down with both the unknown, and the near certainty of his impending death.

49

On Robert Thwaites' doorstep, Gardner thought of DCI Michael Yorke. Her colleague, her mentor, her *friend*, from Wiltshire. Yorke was a true leader, and she recalled his advice to her when she was first promoted. 'When it comes to your team, you can forget about *your* emotions. Any fluctuation, and you'll lose control. You're a straight line from now on, Emma. A straight line.'

A straight line!

Right now, her bloody line was as crooked as hell and she'd spear anyone who rubbed her up the wrong way.

She shook her head. Neville Fairweather was a former shareholder in KYLO. What a thing to just find out.

Fairweather was the biological father of her close friend, the late Collette Willows, who'd died in the line of duty. Well, it went on record as in the line of duty but Gardner believed it'd been preventable.

Believed? It bloody had been. Leaving her in a vulnerable situation.

Fairweather was a rich, powerful man who'd stalked Gardner from the shadows. *Stalked. Yes... what other word was there for it?* However, he'd since confronted her, although what he wanted was still entirely unclear. He claimed not to hold Gardner responsible for his daughter's death and the reasons for his interest had something to do with Emma's own brother Jack who was currently in prison. Eventually, Fairweather claimed, he'd need Gardner's help.

Fairweather was adamant that he was operating in the best interests of everyone. *Who was everyone?* Gardner certainly didn't feel like she was part of that exclusive group.

And now here he was. The wily old bastard. Mixed up again with Operation Gearchange.

Fairweather a former shareholder in KYLO.

Bloody hell!

Gardner had Fairweather's number. She'd been told only to use it if, and when, Jack got in touch with her. Jack was in jail and had made no contact with her yet. Long may that continue. Her brother was sociopathic and dangerous.

Believe me, Neville, as soon as I've finished with Robert Thwaites, I'll contact you. You can bloody well count on that!

Having given up on the doorbell, she knocked hard on Robert's door for a third time.

'Steady on, boss,' Rice said. 'You'll take it off the hinges!'

You're a straight line, Emma. A straight line...

Robert answered the door with a bewildered expression on his face. 'Sorry, didn't hear. The bell is on the blink.'

Gardner felt her irritation surge. Enough was enough. No more beating around the bush. It was time for *his* truth. 'We need to speak again, Robert. *Now.*'

'Cassandra is at Pilates... maybe you'd like to do it later—'

'You, Robert. *Just you.*'

He looked startled by her tone and raised his hands in submission before turning away and leading them in. As Gardner followed him, Rice at her side, she inwardly ordered herself back into Yorke's suggested straight line. If *her* impatience flared, then she could be certain that Rice's would too.

'Would you like a drink?' Robert said at the lounge door.

'No, thanks. We'd like to get straight to it.' They assembled on the sofas. Gardner glared at him and then looked up at the picture of Ruby May on the mantelpiece, standing in front of the Sydney Harbour Bridge.

She stood up again and marched over to it. She regarded it for a moment. 'Such a lovely looking young woman, Robert.' She didn't look back at him, her gaze remaining on the photograph.

'Yes, I—'

'You must be proud.'

'I am,' Robert replied, a hint of confusion in his voice. 'What's this concerning?'

'Just trying to work out who she looks most like,' Gardner said, her words hanging in the air like a challenge.

Robert didn't respond, the silence stretching between them.

Gardner reached out and picked the photograph up, her fingers curling around the frame. She turned, the photograph held tightly in her grasp.

'What're you doing?' Robert asked, alarm creeping into his voice as he rose to his feet.

'Please sit back down,' Gardner said, her voice calm but firm.

Robert hesitated for a moment before slowly lowering himself back onto the sofa, his eyes never leaving Gardner.

Gardner could see the look of admiration in Rice's eyes, a small smile tugging at the corners of his mouth. He enjoyed it when she raised the temperature, when she took control of the situation.

She handed the photograph to Rice, her eyes still locked on Robert. 'What do you think, Detective Inspector?'

'I'm not too sure... she's her own look about her, definitely—'

'I must object,' Robert said, rising to his feet, his voice strained with barely contained anger.

Gardner's head snapped towards him, her glare fierce and unwavering. 'It was a home birth, wasn't it?'

The intensity of her glare was enough to make Robert falter, and he slowly sank back into the sofa, his face pale and drawn. 'Yes... what's this—'

'Come on,' Gardner said, rolling her eyes in exasperation. 'You must have known we'd get here eventually?'

'Sorry, I—' Robert stammered, his voice growing weaker with each word. 'We checked Ruby May's birth certificate.'

'Why?' His voice was barely above a whisper.

'A couple of things. We noticed your daughter was the same age as John Atkinson's, give or take a few months.'

'Coincidence,' Robert said with a shrug, trying to appear nonchalant, but the tremor in his voice betrayed his unease.

'Coincidence?' Rice said. 'Both of you getting a piece of James Sykes and a note. That a coincidence, too?'

Robert's face twisted into a scowl. 'The tone from both of you is all off here,' he said, his voice growing defensive.

'You also both had the same midwife,' Gardner said, her voice low and steady. 'Three out of three on coincidences.'

Robert opened his mouth, ready to defend himself, but the words seemed to die on his tongue. Instead, he took a deep, shuddering breath, his shoulders slumping in defeat.

'*Why don't you tell a true story, Robert?*' Gardner asked, quoting the cryptic note word for word.

'I need a solicitor.'

'You're a solicitor,' Rice said.

'Which is why I know how important it is to get one who specialises in this area, you smug—' He broke off in time.

'You need to stay in control,' Rice said. 'If you want the arrest to go smoothly.'

Robert's eyes widened.

Gardner said, 'My colleague is right. You're about to be arrested. You can take this opportunity to plead your case first, but I'm not waiting around for a solicitor. I'm happy to just take you to the station.'

'Are the neighbours in?' Rice raised an eyebrow. 'This could all be done without drawing too much attention. Cassandra probably wouldn't like that.'

Robert lowered his eyes. It'd be sinking in now that his time was up.

'Help us with this,' Gardner said. 'In late 1990, your company acted on behalf of Penstone Ltd to fight accusations on behalf of Helping Hands. Successfully I might add. I'm assuming the pay-offs were substantial. After all, you had the backing of a cash cow in KYLO.'

Robert shook his head.

'You also acted on behalf of Froisters Chemicals Ltd to lease property from John Atkinson. Froisters was an arm of KYLO.'

'Lots of connections to KYLO there,' Rice said. He made a show of looking around the impressive lounge. 'Lots of money in KYLO. Makes sense. Also, James Sykes worked for KYLO. Now he's dead. Another coincidence?'

'*I* certainly didn't kill him,' Robert hissed, glaring at Rice.

'Are you confirming that KYLO employed you on those two occasions?' Gardner asked.

'No comment.'

'How much did they pay you?' Rice asked.

'No comment.'

'But you acted on behalf of the homeless shelter when the families of Isla Holt and Melissa Sale demanded the truth?'

'I acted on behalf of a lot of companies.'

'You're saying you can't remember?' Gardner said. 'Strange. A case like that would surely stick in someone's mind. It had media coverage.'

'No comment. I want to phone my solicitor.'

'I'm assuming you knew about the six miscarriages, too. The media flagged them up.'

He looked like he was going to throw up.

'Turns out they weren't miscarriages. That the children were stillborn.'

'Who said?' Robert creased his brow.

'Piqued your interest, eh?' Rice asked. 'We've someone who remembers. No doubt we can find more people who remember.'

'So, if they were stillborn, why were they not registered at the registry office?' Gardner asked.

Robert reached over for his mobile.

'We also have reason to believe that the babies may have survived. A witness that heard them crying.'

Robert dragged his mobile towards him. 'I'm phoning my solicitor.'

'You can do it from the station,' Gardner said. 'I'm arresting you on—'

'No!' Robert shouted.

Rice rose from his seat.

Gardner regarded Robert.

'No!' Robert's eyes swung back and forth. He looked like a rabbit trapped in someone's headlights. Gardner held up her hand to tell Rice to hang back.

The truth was close. And even though she knew the truth now, she wanted to hear him say it.

Robert dropped his phone and put his face into his hands. He stayed there for about half a minute before looking back up. 'Just know that this is on me... and not Cassandra. She'd nothing to do with it. If you do that, I'll tell you everything.'

'Whose child is Ruby May?' Gardner asked.

Robert put his face in his hands and cried.

Gardner and Rice exchanged a glance.

'I manipulated her into doing it... she was so desperate for children. I lied to her. Cassandra is innocent! Although she knew that I'd pulled strings, she was clueless about Ruby's origin.'

'Cassandra is on the birth certificate, Robert. She's lied about giving birth to that child.'

'Please...' He looked between them with tears running down his face. 'Please... I'll give you everything. *Anything.* Just protect Cassandra. Protect the mother of our child!'

'But she's not her mother, is she?' Rice said. 'Who was Ruby May's real mother?'

Robert slipped from the sofa to his knees, sobbing.

Gardner exchanged another glance with Rice.

Robert leaned forward and swooped up the picture of Ruby May that Rice had set on the table. He clutched it to his chest as he cried, 'She *can't* ever know... Ruby can't ever know... it'd destroy Cassandra.'

You should have thought about that before you stole her.

'It'll destroy our family. Please, I beg you... just take me and leave them *both* alone.'

'It's not how it works,' Gardner said, but then he was far from rational now, so she was wasting her breath. 'Who's Ruby's actual mother?' Gardner asked.

'Dead!' Robert pleaded. 'What life would she have had in the system? Can you not see that I thought I was doing the right thing?'

'No, I can't. Who was the mother?'

'They found her hanging. Suicide. Is that really what Ruby needs to know? Is that what you're going to make her live with?'

'Melissa Sale,' Gardner said, recalling the second suicide. 'That was her name. One of many sad and lonely women, that came to that shelter for help. One of many sad and lonely women that this system failed. One of many sad and lonely women that you exploited...'

...you evil, snivelling bastard.

50

The lock gave way with a metallic groan.

Trembling, Barnett pushed the old barn door open; the hinges protested with a grating sound. It'd been a while – a long while – since someone had been through this door.

He checked over his shoulder for O'Brien. She was mere inches behind him. Was now the time to order her to run?

He caught sight of Jen's wild eyes, and the glint of her shotgun.

No. Too close.

Barnett turned back and went inside the barn.

The air was rank, and Barnett gagged. Although, it could very well be the fear that caused the reflex, rather than the stale air.

The rows of empty pens lining the sides of the barn spoke of an era when it had harboured animals. As he passed them, he glanced down at the wooden barriers worn by time, and then the ground, which was a patchwork of trodden earth and scattered straw.

He paused midway into the barn and leaned against a barrier.

'To the end,' Jen hissed.

Walking into this icy tomb was suicide. He didn't know what awaited them further inside, but it couldn't be anything good. And to think they were walking away after seeing whatever it was would be pure delusion. She'd gunned down her own husband to protect whatever this secret was. She wouldn't be letting two police officers walk free after they knew.

It had to be now or never.

'Now,' Jen said.

'Not until you tell me *why*.'

'I told you: I'll show you. Just a bit further—'

'No.'

'Turn around, then.'

Barnett steeled himself. Now was the moment. Charging her down while she wielded a shotgun was perilous, but if anyone was getting out of here alive, a chance had to be taken. The likelihood of him taking her to the ground, and taking the gun from her, was minimal, but even if she got a shot off, he may get fortunate and only be winged. All of this provided an opportunity for O'Brien to run.

It was his fault she was here.

This was *his* sacrifice to make.

He turned and saw that she was pointing her shotgun at O'Brien's head.

Shit. That trick again.

Well, it'd worked outside the first time. Why wouldn't she do it again?

He raised his hands. '*No*... okay... you win. I'll go... lower it...'

Jen didn't look at Barnett. She kept her eyes firmly fixed on O'Brien, who was trembling.

Barnett edged forward. Jen must have caught his movement out of the corner of her eye and jabbed the shotgun against O'Brien's forehead. 'Stop yourself!'

'Okay... okay... please.' He put his hands together, begging her. 'Please.'

'Go.'

'And do what?' Barnett's heart raced; he flicked his eyes back and forth between the quivering face of his colleague, and the cold, grim face of the woman on the edge. 'See *before* it's gone. All gone. Before I burn everything to the ground.'

'Just do nothing yet, okay?' Barnett said.

O'Brien spoke, her voice quivering. 'Mrs Atkinson, we can still help—'

'*Don't,*' Jen hissed, pushing the shotgun against her head again. 'Just don't.'

'Okay.' Barnett turned. There were three more pens.

'Back one, on the left.'

Barnett walked. This was a complete disaster. He felt like throwing up. With every footstep, he expected to hear the shotgun discharging. He just hoped it came in his direction rather than O'Brien's.

He glanced up, regarding the shafts of light piercing through the cracks and holes in the barn's structure. It made shadows dance around him. Long, haunting ones. But they didn't scare him. The only thing that terrified him now was the woman, radically out of control, about to end their lives.

He passed another pen. He was at the penultimate one. The stench of rot was more pronounced here. Expecting the worst, he tried to squint and see into the adjacent one but made out only a mound of hay.

'It wasn't my fault,' Jen called out behind him. 'She came here. You understand that. She came here and, God rest her soul, I just couldn't... I just couldn't let that happen. Let her destroy everything.'

Who came here?

'This wasn't on us, do you hear? This wasn't on us. She never knew. Someone told her.'

Told her what?

He wanted to shout back, but his concern for O'Brien was overwhelming now, and his eyes were fixed on the mound of hay as he neared.

'Mary Evans said she was here for her daughter. A lie, don't you see? Clara's my daughter. Hasn't been any other way since as long as I can remember and can never change.'

Barnett took a deep breath. Hidden in the hay, half-buried and partially obscured, were human remains.

'This isn't my fault. Whoever told her is to blame for this. John couldn't understand this... he couldn't live with it... I desperately wanted to believe that today would never come. But deep down, I knew. I just knew. The past never stays buried, does it?'

Barnett was still regarding the remains. His hand to his mouth. The presentation of these bones was different from the ones in the other barn. The others had been intact, presented with some dignity. These were smashed and scattered.

'And I'm sorry now, for what's got to happen, I really am. But Clara can never know.'

'*No.*' Barnett turned back.

O'Brien was looking in his direction, quivering, with the shotgun still against her head.

'Jen, put the gun down,' Barnett said. 'This has gone far enough. You'll make it worse. This can't be stopped now.'

'It can,' Jen said. 'I'll burn everything. This. The farmhouse. Us. No one will ever realise. Clara will never find out.'

'Think, Jen,' O'Brien protested. 'Think about it. What we knew coming in today, others know too. Like you said, the past can't stay buried. This isn't the way to protect Clara. Nothing can protect her from the truth now. I'm sorry, but that's the reality. If you do this, you'll only make it worse for her.'

'No... you're wrong!'

Barnett heard something from over near the remains. He flicked his head back, seeing a rat emerge from behind the hay. It was massive. The rat eyed him up, and then bolted when it heard the booming sound of the shotgun.

51

After his emotional collapse, Robert Thwaites verified that he'd demanded Sykes give him Melissa's child as further payment for saving him from prison.

'Looking back, I think I was atoning for the harm I'd caused covering up this whole situation. It tore me to pieces getting that bastard Sykes off with everything he'd done, but I thought that if I gave this girl a home, instead of letting her go into the system, then I'd be doing some good.'

Nonsense, Gardner thought. *You were looking after number one. There was no buyer for the fifth child, yet you saw an opportunity. The game was up for Sykes anyway – you couldn't possibly let him off and find a buyer. And you certainly couldn't allow the baby to go into the system, because that would be the same as admitting the truth, something you'd been paid handsomely to bury. If anything, you helped James again – by taking all responsibility from him.*

'And the sixth baby went to John Atkinson. A friend of yours. Someone else struggling to have children. Who was the mother of the sixth child? We've the list if it'd be easier to hear them read out?'

'No... it was Mary Evans,' Robert said, rubbing his forehead. He fixed Gardner with a stare. 'A homeless drug addict. What life could she offer?'

'So, you brought your friend John into the loop,' Gardner said.

'Did he pay for his daughter, or did he score a freebie like you?' Rice asked.

Robert glared at Rice. 'John allowed KYLO use of his land for many, many years following the expiration of the first contract. But again, I knew he'd give Clara a good life. It was my choice.'

'It was *never* your decision to make,' Gardner hissed.

'Was Mary Evans never any the wiser about the fact that her child survived?' Rice asked.

'None of them were,' Robert said. 'James Sykes ensured they were that pumped full of drugs when they were induced. They didn't know the baby was being stolen. The nurse had already told them the baby had died... inside...' He hung his head in shame. 'Any that suspected they heard the baby crying or felt the baby's movements were told that they'd hallucinated because of blood loss.'

Gardner shook her head. 'How many lives destroyed for money, for KYLO, for *you*?'

'I'd no part in that process,' Robert hissed.

'By covering it up, you'd one of the biggest parts!'

'It's been hard, but I've made some peace with it. Those six children were given a chance when they had none.'

'Maybe, if people like you were protecting the systems in this country, instead of abusing them, they could have had wonderful lives,' Rice said.

Gardner shook her head. 'How do you square it with the depression that came because of this atrocity? Suicide, drug overdoses... four innocent women died because of what Sykes did. And the two that survived. Amina and Mary? They would've walked away empty. Hollowed out—'

'They were paid well for their silence.'

Gardner sucked in a deep breath.

Paid well.

She thought of Barnett, and her blood ran cold. 'You're lying.'

Robert squinted. 'Why would I lie? Yes, I know what happened with Amina Ndiaye. She built a new life because of that money. That's one of the few good things to come out of this sorry—'

'*Listen,*' Gardner said, pointing at him. 'Nothing good has come from this. It makes me sick to the stomach to hear you even suggest it.'

Robert shrugged. 'Mary Evans, unfortunately, spent her money on drugs and hit the streets again. I doubt she'd have made an excellent mother.'

'How do you even know that? Children change people,' Gardner said.

'It clearly hasn't changed you,' Rice hissed.

Gardner nodded in agreement. 'So, did Mary and Amina know their children had survived?'

Robert shook his head. 'No... but we still paid them significantly to sign non-disclosures. We never wanted them speaking out against Bright Day should they remember anything or start to suspect something. But, we were very confident that they had no idea about their children.'

Gardner sighed as she lowered her head. Amina hadn't intentionally walked away from her stolen child for money, which was something. But it wouldn't stop Barnett being absolutely devastated.

'I'm not usually lost for words,' Rice said. 'But the way you've treated the vulnerable... I can't even comprehend it. Boss... can I have the honours of this one?'

Gardner rose to her feet. 'Be my guest, Detective Inspector, but sit with him until the other officers arrive to transport him. Do it when they arrive. I *really* need to contact someone first. Ah, one last question,' Gardner said. 'With everything we have, there isn't any more point in lying. So, tell me, did you have anything to do with James' death?'

He shook his head rigorously. 'Nothing.'

'Any idea who did?'

'Honestly... *no*...' He rubbed his face with his hands, his fingers digging into his skin, as if trying to physically wipe away his despair.

Gardner nodded and turned.

Robert called out after her, 'She's had a good life, DCI Gardner. Ruby May. And so has, Clara, and all the other children. I've checked up on them. None of them have ever wanted for anything.'

Gardner stopped, rubbed her eyes and turned back. She looked long and hard at Robert. She felt a curious mix of rage and sadness.

She pointed at him. 'I'm glad they were happy. I really am. But six lives were ruined. For Isla, Melissa, Seren, Tia, Amina and Mary. Mr Thwaites, you never deserve to see the light of day again.'

'I won't go to jail. The things I can give you on KYLO,' Robert said. 'It'll be in the interests of your seniors to listen.'

Again, Gardner felt her blood run cold. His threat wasn't empty.

'Maybe,' Gardner said. 'Maybe you'll walk free. Except... how free, and how light will those days be – when your daughter learns the truth about you?'

His face fell.

52

It took Gardner a few minutes to compose herself in the car before she contacted Neville Fairweather on the number he'd given her.

Unsurprisingly, there was no answer.

She unleashed a voicemail. 'Six stolen children. *Six*. And KYLO, the company you were a shareholder in, covered it all up. *Abduction!* You knew, didn't you? How could you? All your nonsense about the greater good. This stinks. Four women died. You *must* have known. And what of the two mothers who survived? Mary Evans and Amina Ndiaye. Were you complicit in paying for them to sign NDAs? You as good as bought their children from them. You talked to me about a world we can't see. A world that needs order. Is this what you're referring to? KYLO? And is this the order? You give me this number to help you protect my brother. A brother I don't really have any desire to protect, anyway. It's bullshit. Who're you? What do you want? Listen, Neville. You've one hour to phone me back, or I'm taking you down. So, help me God, I'm taking you down.'

Out of breath, she hung up and closed her eyes.

She thought of her own daughter. Thought of that moment when she first held her and gazed down into her eyes.

Anabelle.

She rubbed the tears from her eyes. And then she knew one thing for certain. The person who'd brought this to light, who'd set this whole thing in motion.

That person was a mother, too.

Ahead of her vehicle, Robert was being led out in handcuffs by two officers. Rice had made his arrest.

Glancing in the rear-view mirror, she saw an elderly couple on their front doorstep watching the show and smiled wryly.

What'll the neighbours think, eh?

Gardner's phone rang as a Land Rover drove up the drive alongside Gardner. She caught the profile of Cassandra.

She answered the phone to Fiona Lane. She doubted it was to catch up following recent disagreements, which meant only one thing, really. 'We've got a match, Emma! We've got a bloody match on that quarry dust!'

Fiona said she'd put everything in motion. That meant PolSA, the Police Search Adviser, would orchestrate a thorough search of the abandoned quarry for any peculiar activity.

After the call, Gardner watched Cassandra Thwaites, fresh from Pilates, jogging up the drive to her husband in full lycra.

The officers escorting Robert stopped, allowing him to speak.

After, she collapsed to her knees, and Rice knelt to read her her rights.

How could you ever think that something like this could stay buried?

Gardner hated to see lives destroyed.

Robert and Cassandra deserved their train to hell, but Ruby May and Clara, what sadness awaited them?

Yet, now it was unavoidable. Made necessary by their parents' lies. Because the suffering of those mothers was unthinkable.

Indescribable.

Her phone rang again. She expected it to be Fairweather. It wasn't.

She answered. 'Ma'am, we—'

'Emma,' Marsh interrupted her. 'There's been an incident at the Atkinsons' farmhouse.'

Barnett... O'Brien... She felt as if all the air had been sucked from her body. '*What?*'

53

The Atkinsons' farmyard pulsed with blues and twos.

Shots fired.

That was all Marsh had known.

Gardner threw herself from the vehicle and ran towards the flurry of activity, her feet joining the rhythmic dance of blue hues.

She passed a paramedic, who was shining a light into Jen Atkinson's eyes, while a tall, suited female officer she didn't recognise stood alongside her. Jen was cuffed.

'What's going on?' she asked the small huddle.

'I'm not too sure, ma'am,' the officer said.

The paramedic remained focused on Jen, giving a slight shrug to show that he was with the officer in not having much of a clue.

Gardner sensed Rice coming up alongside her and felt the scar over her chest tingle; a wound in the line of duty from long ago, and an indication that things weren't as they should be.

She tried to slow her breathing, knowing that a panic attack loomed, but this just made her aware of her thrashing heart, and the impending spiral into chaos.

'Jen... what's happened?' Gardner asked.

Jen, pale faced and nonchalant, didn't move her eyes, even when the paramedic switched her light off.

'We know *everything*,' Rice said, trying to rouse her. 'We know about Clara.'

It didn't work. Jen wasn't with them. She seemed dead behind her eyes.

Gardner was still focusing on her breathing, trying not to confront any hideous possibilities as to what may have happened.

Still, simply by trying, she was acknowledging.

Shots fired.

She thought of Robert's tearful reaction when he'd realised the game was up.

How had John and Jen Atkinson reacted to O'Brien and Barnett?

Shots fired.

She clutched the scar on her chest, and squeezed her eyes shut, forcing back a sudden need to vomit.

Then, she heard a familiar voice calling for her, and opened her eyes.

'Boss!' Barnett called as he exited the farmhouse, hand in the air.

'Thank God... thank God...' She turned and started to run in the direction of Barnett, who trudged out in the snow, head lowered, appearing in sharp contrast to the dynamic, kaleidoscopic effect of the lights being reflected on the frosted windows.

Almost slipping over, but refusing to slow her pace, Gardner drew close to Barnett. He raised his head. She immediately saw the sadness in his eyes, and she froze.

Lucy?

Oh no... no, no...

Lucy...

Images of O'Brien sliding cereal bars over a desk towards her, large smile on her face, a twinkling in her youthful eyes, made her lower her head.

Rice caught her up a second time. 'Bloody hell, boss. Some of us don't run every morning—' He broke off, clearly seeing the terror on her face.

O'Brien: the first person who'd been there for her when Fairweather had paid her and Monika a sinister visit, leaving Gardner terrified for her children. The only person who really *heard* Gardner, who *listened*, in a world where no one paid the slightest attention.

'Awful,' Barnett said as he drew close. 'Jen killed John...'

'Lucy?' Gardner asked.

But he didn't hear her. Too preoccupied with his own train of thought. 'Jen killed Mary Evans, Clara's real mother... and—'

'Lucy?' Gardner exclaimed, raising her head.

She sighted O'Brien at the door of the farmhouse.

Her heart leapt as she scrambled forwards, swerving Barnett.

In case this was a cruel trick of her imagination, Gardner kept her eyes fixed on O'Brien, unwilling to risk even blinking. When she was close enough to conclude that her mind wasn't deceiving her, she launched again and threw trembling arms around O'Brien. 'Thank God,' she said. Embracing Lucy at the door, she felt both happiness, and sadness over the fact that she'd never had chance to do this with her late colleague, Collette Willows.

_____

54

Shivering, Gardner and Rice listened intently to O'Brien and Barnett as the snow swirled down around them.

After finding out that Mary Evans, Clara's mother, had been murdered to protect the lie, Gardner shook her head and sighed. So much tragedy because of James Sykes.

It was saddening to think that he'd never see a courtroom.

She glanced over at Jen Atkinson and thought of Robert and Cassandra Thwaites. She also thought of all those other as-yet-unidentified people who'd purchased stolen children.

Not everyone would escape the judge's hammer.

'It was clear Jen wasn't backing down,' O'Brien said. 'You could tell from her eyes. She was locked into her plan. It was clear she'd die rather than let Clara know the truth. And just like her husband, we were expendable.'

Gardner felt a shiver run down her spine. _How close I came to losing you..._

She glanced at Barnett.

Both of you.

'She planned to burn everything,' O'Brien said. 'I told her it wouldn't solve anything. But she was locked in, you know. Like I said.'

'So, you went for the shotgun?' Gardner said, shaking her head.

'There was no other option,' O'Brien said. 'It went off, but no one was hurt. Then, Ray restrained her.'

She stared at Barnett. He looked embarrassed about ignoring her instructions, lowered his head, and said, 'I'm sorry, boss.'

'Not now,' Gardner said, trying to keep the frustration out of her voice. 'At least you survived. Against shit odds, too. Right now, you've been through enough.' *And you're about to find out that Robert Thwaites paid your mother off, and you've a half-brother or sister out there, somewhere.* Heavy. 'But later, Ray. We need a serious talk.'

He nodded.

'Okay, briefly,' Gardner said. 'This is what we now know after speaking to Robert Thwaites.'

She explained what they knew and looked at Ray as she told him that his mother, Amina Ndiaye, was given a settlement. 'But Robert assures me she didn't know about her child being alive.'

Barnett nodded as Gardner spoke, trying to keep himself stoic, but he looked as if he'd crumble at any second. 'It's true. She'd never have walked away from a child.'

'I believe that too,' Gardner said. 'But you can't blame her for taking the money. Think about how desperate she was. How much she must have longed for a way out of that life.'

Barnett continued to nod before looking up at Gardner. 'But do you think my father knew about the NDA?'

'I don't know.' Gardner put her hand on Barnett's shoulder. It was hard to be angry with him now. She could only imagine the turmoil.

Barnett thanked her with a gentle smile. 'Don't worry, boss. I've an older brother or sister to hold it together for.'

She returned his smile.

'Before, I was convinced that whoever set this in motion and possibly killed Sykes had to be a mother,' Gardner said. 'But there were six mothers.' She looked at Barnett again as she said the next part and softened her tone. 'And they've all passed. Mary was the last to die, and judging by her remains, that wasn't that recent.'

Gardner looked over at Jen. *Dead behind the eyes.* 'You said, Lucy, that Jen had said someone had told Mary she had a daughter. That because of this, she came here, and well... unfortunately... Did she give any clearer sign of who that might be?'

'No. Just that *someone* told Mary.'

Gardner sighed. 'I've a feeling that we're not going to get much out of Jen Atkinson, but we'll have to try. But first, we need to check out this quarry.'

'Do you think it could be one of the fathers?' O'Brien said.

'Possibly. Who knows who Sykes' potential murderer has told? Shit... the field just keeps widening. We need to narrow it down.' She pointed over towards Jen. 'Let's hope she can do that, or there's something at the quarry.'

Or that lying bastard, Neville Fairweather, comes good.

'Now both of you two over to the paramedics,' Gardner said.

'I'm fine...' O'Brien said.

You've just had a shotgun waved at you. 'Now.' Then, after the all-clear, Lucy, can you grab Cam, and interview Jen? Doctors may pull the "she's in shock" card, so you may have to throw some weight around.'

Barnett glanced at Gardner.

'Don't even ask,' she said and then looked at Rice. 'Ready for the quarry?'

55

The Police Search and Advisory Team had already set up cones to mark out a makeshift path through the quarry, to prevent any officers from straying into disguised holes, or worse still, deadly precipices.

As Gardner and Rice neared the central point, a collection of disused workmen's huts, the presence of PolSA grew thicker. Four by fours that could tackle the deep snow, and bright, artificial floodlights that pierced through the dimming light of the day.

They moved past officers with glaring reflective vests and keen German Shepherds. Gardner showed her ID to log in. Up ahead, she recognised Fiona, clad in a long, sheepskin coat that must have set her back a few quid, and a threadbare bobble hat pulled down tight on her head.

'I just heard about the shooting,' Fiona said. 'Is everyone okay?'

Gardner nodded. 'Surprisingly.'

'I was just about to text you. We've found something *significant*,' Fiona said, turning. 'Follow me.'

They weaved a path between the cones, feet crunching in the drifts, into an area of snow-covered dilapidated workmen's huts. The exposed wood which comprised the sides of the huts was worn and weathered. They approached a small patch of white-suited forensic officers, squatted and huddled around something.

'You need to get suited up if you want to get any closer, but you can see it from here.'

'I can see a lot of backs,' Rice said.

Fiona called over, politely requesting that one of her team stand and move.

Gardner could see an overturned mining cart, crested with snow. Something was attached to the spike, winding off, snake-like, across the ground. 'Chains?'

'Yes,' Fiona said. 'Until we run samples, I can't confirm that someone was chained here.'

'Why else would they be there?' Gardner said.

'Yes,' Fiona said. 'Especially when you take into account what's in *that* hut.' She nodded at the dilapidated structure nearest to them.

'Get me a suit please,' Gardner said.

* * *

Suited up, Gardner and Rice stood beside the closed door of the hut.

A heavy chain, thick with rust and ice was fixed to the outside.

'It's already open,' Fiona said, reaching round. She pushed the door. It creaked and the chain clattered against the wood, echoing off the stone walls around the quarry.

Only on entering the gloomy hut did Gardner fully comprehend how fresh and sharp the air had been outside. Here, it was musty and stale. An artificial light had been set up in the corner.

It looked as if the hut had been cleared out, except for a simple wooden bench, being poked and prodded by two SOCOs.

Fiona gave an order and the SOCOs allowed them access.

Gardner approached the table.

She saw a tool she recognised from another case she'd worked on long ago. A tool which had a sturdy handle, designed for a surgeon's confident grip to allow precision, and a blade, a specialised curve of gleaming stainless steel, complete with the teeth required to get through bone.

A bone saw.

Gardner saw everything.

James Sykes, chained up outside to die, abandoned to the elements. Left to rot.

Then, his remains, laid here on this bench, for the skull to be separated from—

'Wait,' Gardner said. 'Why is a bone saw necessary? I was told that the skull could be gently separated from the body at the atlanto-occipital joint?'

'Yes,' Fiona said. 'Unless decomposition wasn't fully complete. A bone saw could be used to cut through any remaining connective tissues or small bone projections.'

'Bloody hell,' Rice said.

'She wanted us to find this,' Gardner said, edging closer. 'She's left it on display. She's completing the narrative, herself. Guiding us to the truth.'

'She?' Rice said.

'I'm still convinced it's a mother, Phil... we didn't know about Mary Evans until we spoke to Col, maybe there's a seventh. *Another* victim of Sykes and the wealthy idiots that protected him.'

'But why are you so convinced?' Rice asked. 'I don't feel the same way.'

She looked up into Rice's eyes. 'You don't have a mother's instinct.'

She then looked down and regarded the bone saw. 'Wait... what's that?' She pointed. There was something small and white poking out just beneath it. *Bone?* Fiona waved a colleague over. The SOCO who answered her request, took a deep breath and turned the bone saw over, carefully. There was something folded stuck to the underside, the corner, which Gardner had seen, poking out.

The SOCO carefully removed it. 'Blu Tack,' the SOCO said, and then opened out a note.

Gardner leaned in so she could read it too.

There was a list of names. She recognised the first one immediately.

Mary Evans.

Next to Mary Evans was written: *Clara Atkinson.*

It was a list of the victims. The women who'd had their children stolen. Along with the real names!

Melissa Sale: Ruby May Thwaites

Amina Ndiaye: Clarissa Trent

Isla Holt: Dalton Hargrove

Seren Rhodes: Jarvis Redfern

Tia Loom: Sienna Marlowe

Then came a last name which made the breath catch in her throat.

Another mother. A seventh mother. As Gardner had predicted.

'Elizabeth Sykes.'

'James' younger sister,' Rice said. 'What was her child called?'

Gardner shook her head and pointed. 'That space is blank.'

'He took his own sister's child. Are you as disappointed as me that this bastard is dead?'

'More than you could imagine.'

'You know that this means you're wrong, though,' Rice said. 'It can't have been the seventh mother, Elizabeth, who put this in motion.'

Gardner nodded. He was right. Elizabeth had been catatonic for decades, and this morning, she'd passed. How?

Unless...

She hoisted her phone out, saw that she had enough bars to make a call, and contacted Cameron Suggs.

'Boss?'

'This is what I need you to do... now.'

56

How quickly things could change.

There was a time, not so long ago, when seeing her mother bedridden, close to death, would've broken her heart.

When she'd have been moved to tears by the sight of her broken father, hunched and inconsolable, beside his wife.

But now such responses were laughable in the face of what she knew.

Her brother, James, had taken something from her. Something he'd no right to take. And her parents – her parents! – had known.

They'd known.

And then, on her brother's say-so, they'd had her committed.

Two years she'd spent trapped in that institution.

Two long years.

Pumped full of drugs... electricity poured into her brain...

She'd made it too easy for her family to betray her.

Cutting herself... attempting suicide... she should have been more sensible. She should have dealt with her brother when she was fifteen, instead of becoming lost to emotion.

And her parents? How could they?

Trying to convince her that her baby had died before it was born.

Yet, that nightmare, the same nightmare she'd had every night for the first year... looking out through a swirling haze... watching... as her baby girl was carried away... crying.

It'd seemed so real.

And the cost of telling the doctor?

More ECT, more drugs, and another year.

At least, now on her deathbed, her mother admitted it. 'That infernal woman shouldn't have told you, Elizabeth, dear. Look, it was for your own good. You weren't even fifteen.'

It didn't help. In a way, seeing the admission pass through her lying lips filled her with even more hate.

And her father? Always so weak. Always happy to bend. 'Listen to your mother.'

'James took my child off me... your granddaughter!'

'You were a child, too,' her mother croaked. 'And I was too sick to care for another baby.'

'He took them all, though... I know... James took all those children and sold them to wealthy bastards. Mary Evans! She was my friend, too.'

Behind her, she heard the bedroom door creaking open.

She turned to look at her brother. He'd put on a lot of weight in the time she'd been away. His face was pale, and he coughed, regularly. She'd like to think that the choices he'd made were a cancer eating away at him, but she knew that wasn't so.

The jovial big brother, who'd always had a smile, had been a liar, and a monster, and this was simply his true form exposed.

'Are you part of this family or not, Elizabeth?' James asked. 'You talk about Mary Evans as if she's more important to you than your own blood.'

'She was desperate... she lived on the streets... she was addicted to drugs... and you took her child.'

'And now she's content. And knows nothing about the—'

'How could you?' Elizabeth asked again, turning her gaze to each family member. 'For money?'

'You were fifteen,' her mother repeated.

'Go to your room,' James said.

'I'm seventeen, you can't tell me what to do—'

'You're sick. And have been released into our care. Now, go to your room,' James hissed. 'Or do I contact Doctor Caine?' He pointed a finger.

'How many children? How many did you take? How many did you sell?'

James came into the room, hand raised, ready to slap her. She flinched and closed her eyes, preparing to receive the blow.

'Stop!' her father hissed.

When she opened her eyes again, she saw her father was standing. 'Stop, both of you.'

Elizabeth couldn't help the tears now. Tears of complete disbelief. This idea that the evil was inside the whole of her family. 'Did you know, Dad? Did you know about all those children?'

She saw a flash of shame in his eyes before he replaced it with a narrow, steely glare. 'Those children have had better lives. I made sure of that.'

Elizabeth shook her head. 'So, you knew all along. How could you? For money? For bloody money?'

Her father raised a finger. 'Listen, Elizabeth. The government left us with nothing when we retired early. Nothing. Everything we did for everyone, for all that time, and what did we get? Not a penny. Now, you've this roof over your head. And that care you received for two years – do you think that was free? Someone had to cover the costs. The best facilities you can imagine. The best care to get you well again. You think the NHS would've taken care of you for two years?'

'So, you've kept me locked up... protected your secret.'

'Shut up, Elizabeth,' James said. 'Shut up, or I'll call the doctor now.'

'To lock me up again. Will that be your answer forever?'

'You're not being reasonable,' her father said. 'They'd better lives. They're still having better lives. If you slow down to appreciate that, you'll understand that everything is best left alone.'

'My daughter... where's my daughter?' She thumbed her chest.

'She went to a wonderful home,' James said.

She folded over as if she'd been struck in the stomach.

'I'm sorry that you found out,' James said. 'She'd no right coming back and telling you.'

'I knew she could never be trusted,' her mother croaked. 'You never listened.'

'Who did you sell my daughter to?'

'No good will come of that,' her father said. 'Now go to your room, Elizabeth, before I let your brother make that phone call. And only because I care, mind. Care that you're a danger to yourself.'

'Please,' she begged. 'My daughter?'

'God love us,' her father said.

'Your room... now!' James shouted.

And it was then, in that moment, surrounded by so much malevolence and evil, that she decided that not only did she want to die, but she also wanted all of them to die too.

She thought of her father's words: Now, you've this roof over your head.

And with a nod of her head and a brisk exit from the room, she determined to burn it all down.

57

Now that they had the names of six stolen children, Gardner returned to her vehicle parked alongside the quarry and contacted Marsh. At this stage, she wouldn't ask for more personnel. She was simply going to expect it.

Marsh agreed to some officers to speak to all the potential abductees on the list.

After ending the call to Marsh, Sandra Mills, from the Digital Forensics Unit in Wiltshire, contacted her.

Gardner felt as if she was currently in the eye of a tornado.

'Emma... I've sent you the image. I've narrowed the calls Cecile Metcalf made to you down to a one-mile radius. It's a reasonably packed urban area. That's as much as I can offer on my end.'

'You've gone above and beyond,' Gardner said. 'Thanks.'

'As soon as you've got clarity on the situation, can you give me a buzz – let me know how it pans out? Always had a lot of time for Cecile.'

'Of course. I'm sure she'll be fine, Sandra,' she said, wondering who she was trying to convince here. 'Thanks again.'

Rice wasn't yet in the car. He was busy talking to some PolSA officers he knew personally. She checked her email and located the information that Sandra had sent through.

Now what?

Her situation up here was vastly different from how it was in Wiltshire. She, unlike Barnett, had very few favours to pull in. Going in gung-ho on ANPR or even overhead drone surveillance to scour that radius for Cecile's car would be sure to draw in unwelcome attention. And, after Cecile had pointed out what Riddick was potentially involved in, the last thing Gardner wanted to do was to start a shitstorm in case she was mistaken. She herself, at the pinnacle of Operation Gearchange, couldn't go off-piste. It'd be too suspicious.

Now she'd more officers seeking the abductees, maybe she could ask someone closer to home?

Rice was out of the question for obvious reasons. Barnett, too. O'Brien was chasing down an interview with Jen Atkinson. She had Suggs looking into her hunch. This left Ross. She phoned him. 'Something has come up, Brad. Maybe something, maybe nothing. Concerning someone who used to work at Bright Day.' She scrunched her face up. Lying like this burned her immensely. She gave Cecile's car details. 'I've sent a radius over. Could you just drive around the area, locate the car, pop a pin in maps and send it over? I'll take it from there. Don't engage, please. And don't waste your time running it through the system again – just hit the ground. Is that okay, Brad? This is for me to pick up. No one else.'

'Err, yes, of course.'

This must sound suspicious as hell, but needs must...

'Just pop a pin and head straight back. Okay?' Gardner repeated.

'Yes. I just heard about the shooting. Is everyone okay?'

'Everyone is fine. That's why I'd prefer you just kept a low profile.'

'Sound.'

Rice hopped back in the car as she took a deep breath. 'Anything, boss?'

'Not yet.' Her phone rang. 'Could be it.'

It was.

'Cam?'

'You were right, boss. I just got off the blower with Doctor Ruben Robinson. He consulted Elizabeth's medical records. After the blaze, she had countless surgeries and tests. It's recorded that she'd never given birth...'

Yet, Elizabeth was on the list...

She told Suggs to hang tight and then turned to Rice. She explained what she'd just found out.

'So, what're you saying? That Elizabeth Sykes shouldn't be on the list?' Rice asked.

'One option. The other option is a bit more dramatic.'

Rice guffawed. 'A bit more? Are you suggesting that the person in the hospital wasn't Elizabeth Sykes? That would be a hell of a lot more!'

Gardner stared at him, allowing it to sink in that this was indeed what she believed.

'Boss! Come on... There's a motherly instinct and then there's—'

'We any closer to finding the midwife who delivered these children in the shelter?'

'You know we aren't.'

'Yet, we've a name on those birth certificates for Clara and Ruby May?'

'L. Wilton. We concluded it was fabricated, remember?'

'Not concluded, Phil. We said it was a possibility.'

'I already phoned it in with the registration number. It didn't match any name.'

Gardner thought about it. 'But there's someone else. There must be.' She closed her eyes, replaying the interview with Col, the cleaner, at Bright Day.

I recall the nurse here. A young lass. Stern looking. Not too pleasant...
I'm sorry, the name escapes me.

She reminded Rice. 'We need to find out who that nurse is that Col was referring to... Wait a minute... let me see that birth certificate for Clara Atkinson.'

Rice showed it to her on his phone. She zoomed in. 'L. Wilton.' *Except...* the *t* was smudged. She looked at the registration number. Again, slight smudging. There was a three that could have been an eight. Another number also looked ambiguous. She pointed it out. 'Did you try different combinations?'

'No. That's definitely a t, and those numbers are three and seven.'

'Where's the other certificate – for Ruby May Thwaites?'

He searched through his phone, and his face paled. 'Err... shit.'

She snatched the phone off him.

L. Wilson with a one and an eight.

'Idiot. Why didn't you check both?'

'Because it looked clear to me.'

'You need to get your bloody eyes tested... Get on the phone now and find out if an L. Wilson with that registration number used to work at Helping Hands and if it is...' She paused. *She wanted it fast.* 'Get Ray on it, immediately, and find out where the bloody hell she is.'

'Is that a good idea?'

'Probably not... but you're my only other option... and after that woeful spot of incompetence, I'll take my chances with the emotional one.'

Rice turned from her, growling, as she started the engine.

58

Following a severe weather warning, Oxfam had closed early, and Jess Beaumont had returned home just before sunset.

She found her father awake, upstairs, and in better spirits than he'd been in a while.

Nothing gave her greater pleasure these days than in those few moments when he still recognised her.

The broad smile on his pale and withered face suggested that this was one such moment.

To see him like this, after so many days, filled her heart. When he proffered his hand, she took it, gratefully. And, as the skies darkened outside, and the snows thickened, she hunkered down with the man that had brought her so much joy in her younger years. Here was one father who'd given more time to her than his work, and she was happy to tell anyone who asked.

'Merry Christmas Little Miss Jess,' he said. His nickname from a bygone era. A time when they'd hunker down and read together. 'I hope you're taking good care of yourself in this weather.'

Her father had been an architect in his earlier years and was partly responsible for the multitude of modern buildings that adorned the city centres of England. She often marvelled at the contrast between his contributions to the contemporary landscape and his current state. As an elderly man, he now belonged to an older generation, ready to pass the baton to the younger ones who would shape the future, just as he had helped shape the present with his architectural designs. 'Will you read to me?' he asked.

Seeing him reconnecting with their past together warmed her heart.

'After all, you owe me Little Miss Jess,' he said.

'Two hundred and fifty-three books between the age of seven and eleven,' she said. 'I remember every single one.'

From the age of seven, she'd consigned every book her father read to her, beginning with *The Hobbit*, to one side of her bookshelf. The last book, number 253, had completed the circle nicely. Book three had been *The Return of the King*, the conclusion of the *Lord of the Rings* trilogy.

Her father smiled again. 'Two hundred and fifty-three wonderful books.' He seemed so lucid. So clear. There was no anger or frustration. 'Two hundred and fifty-three wonderful memories.' He squeezed her hand, gently, with the little strength he had left.

And then she realised something that she'd forgotten in these past few turbulent days.

She really loved this fading old gentleman. And this was how she'd like him to go.

The *way* she'd always expected him to go.

But then, she guessed, most people would hope for the same thing.

The horrors of Alzheimer's and other traumatic illnesses were for others, until they finally caught up with you, or someone you loved.

She sat, reading from one of his favourite Charles Dickens' books, *Great Expectations*, while he nodded and sighed, smiling regularly.

Her plans to put him into a home again fell to doubts.

Maybe the spells wouldn't return? Maybe he could remain this calm, fragile being, until his final breath?

'You know, Little Miss Jess, we were blessed – me and your mother,' he said. 'Because of you.'

Jess always struggled with eye contact with most people, apart from her parents. With them, it was like a key slipping into a lock. They understood her atypical way of thinking and she felt safe in their presence. However, her eyes dropped in this moment, because of guilt over the plans that she'd been making with Laura. 'Dad, I—'

'You almost didn't happen, you know. *Almost.* We were told we couldn't have children.'

'Really? Then how did—'

'Circumstances aligned for us rather spectacularly. And you were everything we could have hoped for, Little Miss Jess. Everything. And you were so different. But all the better for it.'

He'd spoken before of *circumstances aligning* and she'd always considered it a rather funny expression. She'd always thought he was referring to conception. The moment the sperm met the egg. For obvious reasons, she'd not quizzed him over it. Of course, she regularly spoke matter-of-factly – it was her way, after all – but sex talk with your father? A bridge too far.

But now he was saying they'd been unable to conceive.

She read until his eyes closed, feeling a mixture of warmth over her father's rare moment of contentment, and the cold from the guilt bubbling away inside, when the door to her father's room opened, and she almost burst out of her skin.

Laura stood there, wearing her winter coat, with a handbag over one shoulder.

'Sorry, dear, did I make you jump? I knocked gently downstairs, for fear of waking your father. When no one answered, I wasn't sure if you were in, so I tried the door. It was unlocked.'

Jess was certain that she'd locked it, simply because she always locked it. It was like those bloody car keys all over again. These mistakes were out of character and didn't fit well with the way she operated so pedantically.

She wondered briefly about early-onset Alzheimer's, but then shook off the negative thought and smiled up at her friend, forcing herself to make eye contact. 'Would you like a hot drink?'

'That would be lovely. I've so much to share with you. I've been hard at work today, and I feel that we've quite the option available for Nigel here.'

The guilt within Jess bubbled more fiercely. She stood, staring down. 'He's been lucid. Clear. I've been reading to him. He's not ready. I think he can spend more time here, with me—'

'But we've spoken about this, Jess.'

Jess nodded, and joined her hands, circling her fingers, suddenly filled with anxiety. 'Yes, but you should have heard him talk. Remembering my childhood and everything.'

'Fragments, dear, fragments. And while those fragments give us hope. Eventually, they too will go. Look... why don't you get us both a cup of tea? I won't lie. I'm frozen solid.'

Jess nodded, stood, and Laura followed her to the top of the stairs.

'Actually, do you mind if I just use the little girl's room?' Laura asked.

'Of course not,' Jess said. 'It's at the end of the corridor. Can I take your coat and bag?'

'It's unnecessary, dear.'

'Please,' Jess said, her eyes darting from side to side. 'They need to go by the door. I'll put them there.'

'Of course,' Laura said, peeling off her jacket and bag. She handed them over. 'Whatever makes you comfortable.'

Downstairs, Jess laid the coat on the back of the sofa, and the bag on the sofa itself, while she went to put the kettle on. Afterwards, she carried the coat through and hung it up. She also checked the front door. It was indeed unlocked. How strange. She locked it and went to make tea.

As she waited for it to brew, she stared out the kitchen window at the heavy snow and recalled building a snowman as a child with her father.

Whenever she stumbled on happier memories, she enjoyed spending time with them, so she did just that. She relived the moment they rolled its torso together, laughing as it grew. She recalled the moment they decorated its face with stones, and a spatula stolen from the kitchen—

'Jess?'

Jess drew back from her memory and turned to see Laura in the kitchen doorway.

'Sorry, I was just away with the fairies...'

'I was just about to apologise for taking so long,' Laura said. 'But it was clear you hadn't noticed, dear.'

'No... I... that's okay.'

Laura looked embarrassed. 'I have to confess, Jess. Your father woke.'

'Oh God, really?' Jess said, she moved for the door. 'Is he all right?'

Laura put a hand on Jess's arm. 'He's fine. He's asleep again. I merely stopped in to introduce myself. You know, he thought he recognised me at first.'

'Strange... I guess. He gets confused. So confused.'

'Anyway, I introduced myself, told him about how wonderful you are, Jess, and how he should be so proud of you, and off he went again. All calm now. Completely dead to the world. Didn't look like he'd be waking again. Please, sit. I'll carry the tea through.'

'Thanks.'

Jess sat on the two-seater. She looked down at Laura's bag sitting beside her and was just about to reach for it. The tea appeared over the back of the sofa.

'Well,' Laura said. 'We really took our time. You with your daydream. Me with your father. The tea has gone rather lukewarm. Should I warm it?'

'It's okay for me,' Jess said, taking the tea. She took a mouthful.

'Then it's okay for me, too.'

As Laura came around the side of the sofa, Jess finished the tea in several large mouthfuls and leaned to deposit it on the floor.

When she sat back up, she saw Laura was about to sit on the bag.

Jess reached for the strap and tugged; unfortunately, the bag itself slipped from the sofa, and the contents spilled out.

'Sorry... sorry...' Jess said, pushing herself from the sofa and falling to her knees. 'Such an idiot... *such* an idiot.' She stopped herself short of hitting her head, so she could reach for the contents of the bag—

Her breath caught in her throat.

Her car keys.

Then her mind flitted back to several days earlier, when Laura had offered to help carry some boxes into the storage room. Jess had been in the process of hanging shirts onto a rack. She'd told Laura that the key to the storage room was behind the counter.

Laura must have taken her car keys from her bag when she'd put the boxes into the storage room... but... but...

'It makes no sense... no sense.'

'Leave them... come and sit down, dear.'

Jess looked up at Laura. 'Did you take my car keys?'

'I did, yes. And a house key, too. Please come and sit.' She patted the sofa. 'I don't want to lie to you any more. Sit and I'll tell you everything.'

Jess stood. 'Go away. Please go away. Now. Or I'm phoning the police. I'm an idiot... what have I done? What have I done? Who've I let into my house? Wait... my father... is he okay? What have you done to my father?'

'Nigel Beaumont isn't your father.'

'I don't understand... I don't understand... I don't understand...'
She repeated herself three times, something she did when under
extreme stress.

'But there's no need to worry about him any longer... in fact,
Jess... there's no need to worry about much for too much longer.
Things are just about finished.'

Now, she turned in a circle. Again, she couldn't help herself. It
was another reaction to stress. The need to turn. Spin as quickly as
she could. Tear the poison from her mind with dizziness.

The world around her blurred.

When she got into this state, there was only one person who
could pull her from it. Clutch her. Hold her tight and squeeze the
poison, the stress, from her mind.

Her mother. 'I *need* my mother. I *need* my mother. I *need* my
mother.'

She fell back onto the sofa, her eyes squeezed shut.

'I'm here, dear,' Laura said. 'I'm here.'

59

Gardner sat alone in her office, head in her hands, while Rice readied the incident room.

Her anger with him was thawing; he'd apologised twice on the way back. Apologising was quite a step for Rice; he was clearly contrite over his incompetence.

She stared down at her phone, willing it to ring. She was waiting for so many calls.

Would Ross find Cecile's vehicle? Would Neville Fairweather call her back? Would Barnett strike gold on L. Wilson?

Not forgetting KYLO and all those bloody bigwigs!

Why were all those shareholders and leaders so bloody hard to get in touch with? Miranda hadn't been wrong when she'd said that they were elusive. Right now, all of them were working outside of the country, and none of them were returning calls.

It was a pain in the arse going through Interpol to get law enforcement support internationally, but if she got to the end of the day and this operation was rumbling on, then that route would be a must.

There was a knock at her office door. She stood, half-expecting

Marsh to swan in, with a frustrated expression on her face, declaring, 'All of this from a bloody skull in a thespian's treasure chest!'

But it wasn't Marsh. It was Barnett, holding his notebook.

'Okay... Laura Wilson is a registered nurse with training in midwifery,' he began. 'The number on the certificates is *accurate*.' His emphasis was used to embarrass Rice.

You don't need to bother, Ray. He's embarrassed enough.

'She worked at Helping Hands for that two-year period with James Sykes between 1989 and 1991. She *left* with him.'

Gardner recalled Col's comments: *There were rumours they were at it. Some of the other staff spotted them a few times... getting rather too close for comfort... if you get my meaning.*

Is that why she helped him with his atrocities? Was he manipulating her?

'Some background on Laura. Her mother died young and she was taken into care at eight, when her father died from his drinking and drug habit. With no other living relatives, she entered the system. Which served her reasonably well. She moved around between foster parents, but never caused a great deal of bother, and even gained training to become a nurse and midwife. After spending a year in the NHS, she took the job at Helping Hands when she was twenty-two. She was relieved of her position when KYLO took control of the facility just prior to its conversion to Bright Day. The reason cited was inappropriate relationships, and there's a statement from her admitting to a long affair with James Sykes. She'd even admitted to sexual relations with him in the workplace itself!

'I contacted the person who took his statement. Philomena West, who once worked for KYLO in the Human Resources department. She remembers the interview well. She said that Laura seemed rather weary, and forlorn, which is to be expected when losing your job, I suppose... but Philomena thought it strange how she remained defensive of Sykes even though the affair was over, and he'd cost Laura her job. Philomena said that Laura couldn't drop that "doe-eyed, wistful look" that she associated with people in love, or obsessed, or... and these were the words she used... *emotionally drained*. You think Laura was helping Sykes abduct the babies?'

Gardner nodded. 'Without doubt. I don't think Sykes himself was inducing the births. Plus, someone had to tell the pregnant women that they'd lost their babies and that the birth needed inducing. Unlikely, they'd listen to Sykes on that one... however, enter the resident nurse trained in midwifery and it becomes an easier sell. Also, she'd have been knowledgeable about the pharmaceuticals required to keep the mothers out of their minds throughout the process.' Gardner shook her head, nauseated. 'I dread to think how these monsters sold their evil to these poor women when they came round...' She stood, placed her hands on the table, still shaking her head. 'Did they tell them that their children's remains had been disposed of before they could say farewell to them? That they were too malformed for them to even hold?'

'Surely not...' Barnett said.

Gardner raised her head. 'You think that evil has limits?'

He lowered his head.

Gardner stood up straight, feeling desperately guilty, having momentarily forgotten how personal all this was for Barnett. For what Amina Ndiaye had potentially gone through.

'I'm sorry, Ray, I wasn't thinking...'

'It's okay, boss...' Barnett lifted his head. 'No kid gloves. I'm focused. I won't fold... I *can't* fold. The truth is what Mum would've wanted.'

You shouldn't be anywhere near this, Ray. Jesus, Emma, you shoot Phil down for his incompetence and then display a fair amount of it yourself. Hypocritical.

But when Barnett continued with his detailed findings, Gardner soon remembered why she was throwing caution to the wind.

'We know Laura agreed to give her name and ID to the birth certificates for the fictional home births,' Barnett said.

'I expect that agreement was part of a healthy severance package after Robert came in to clean house?' Gardner suggested.

Barnett nodded. 'Sounds workable. Still, Laura was anything but healthy. She fell into a depression. A bad one. Her father's demons became her own, it seemed. She abused drugs and alcohol and when she became broke, she ended up homeless.'

Gardner stood and paced, thinking out loud. 'Maybe, once the cloud of manipulation rose, the horror of what she'd been part of must have hit her like a train?'

But was she being too kind to Laura Wilson here? Was she giving her excuses for her heinous behaviour?

Maybe she just got what she deserved?

Barnett looked at his notes. 'No one hears from Laura again until 1995. Four years after sleeping rough, she rented a house in Leeds and took some nursing refresher courses.'

'Moving from the streets to rented accommodation and study? Who funded that?'

'She did.'

'Wow, that was some skilful begging,' Gardner snorted.

'Maybe she had some of that money left from KYLO?'

'After four years on the streets? Doubt it.'

'Stolen?' Barnett asked.

'Carry on for a moment, Ray, and then I'll tell you what I think.'

'Intriguing! Laura hired herself out, freelance, to private companies that serviced the wealthy elderly in their homes,' Barnett continued. 'No marriages or children. She hasn't worked in over ten years and, at fifty-six, is still too young to qualify for a state pension.'

'And yet she still has money?'

'She owns a property. An expensive one at that. Shall we take a drive out there?'

Gardner smiled. 'Nice try, Ray. You're still due one bollocking, and you're officially off this case – so you'll be staying here.'

Barnett looked disappointed, but he gave a brief nod of acceptance. 'You were going to tell me what you think.'

'Hear me out before you shake your head, Ray. Laura Wilson had
no money, yes? Four years after being on the street, she comes back
with enough to build a new life. I don't think Laura ever built that
new life. I think someone else built it in her place.'

Barnett didn't unknot his brow. 'So where's Laura?'

'Dead... she died in a hospital bed this morning.'

'Died... when...' Realisation opened his brow. 'Elizabeth Sykes.
She died this morning. I—'

'According to the list we recovered, Elizabeth Sykes had a child
stolen, too.'

Barnett rubbed his temples as he thought and then fixed
Gardner with a stare. 'Elizabeth Sykes. The woman that died this
morning, never had a child.'

Gardner nodded. 'Someone wants us to know that. The person
who left that list. The person who put this whole thing in motion. I
think that's Elizabeth Sykes. Because Elizabeth Sykes was never
lying in a hospital bed. If you need an identity... why not take the
identity of the person who ruined your life? And why not kill her
too? Just like you'd eventually kill your brother – the other person
who ruined your life.'

Barnett was nodding now. He saw it too. 'The house fire... Do you
think Elizabeth somehow got Laura there, intending for her to die?'

'Yes, I do... except, Laura didn't die. With the state she was in,
Elizabeth felt no need to finish her. She was probably happy to let
her suffer.'

'But Elizabeth would've killed her own parents in that fire, too...
Really?'

Gardner nodded. 'It's the hardest part to get my head around, but
listen, what if they knew? What if they were aware that Sykes had
taken her child? What if they were in on it? For social workers, they
retired into a big, lovely house, and seemed well-off at the end.'

'I looked into their pensions. Wasn't a king's ransom. They retired early.' Barnett said. 'They'd have struggled to cover their lifestyle, especially with the mother's health. I assume Sykes was giving them money?'

'He most certainly was,' Gardner said. 'But would they have been oblivious to where it was all coming from? Maybe they didn't ask questions? But if they did, and they knew, and they knew about Elizabeth, too, then we've a motive for her rage. For the fire. For the murders.'

'I don't know, boss...'

'You need more,' Gardner said. 'Elizabeth was institutionalised for two years. Her treatment programme included lithium and ECT. This suggests complete mental instability. Also, who signed off on having her committed? All three of them. Mum, Dad and James. Think about that. It'd be hard not to feel betrayed. Also, how do we know the family didn't push this to get her out of the way until she calmed down? Maybe she'd discovered what was going on?'

'It's all very messy,' Barnett said.

'Yes... precisely... far too messy... which is why you need someone to put it all together. Seems Elizabeth Sykes has taken it onto herself to do just that. Why else has this all suddenly exploded again?'

'But wouldn't she set out to find her child?'

'Maybe she did. Maybe she has. Everything would've been easier with a new identity, a nurse's qualification and some money in the bank.'

'Money in the bank... wait... James Sykes. He must have earned a fortune. No doubt, KYLO probably clawed some back, but let him keep some for his eternal silence. Yet... he ends up a factory worker for the rest of his days? Why? Why did he not seek a Caribbean island? Because she stole that money from her brother before she burned the house?'

Gardner nodded.

'But why didn't she burn him, too?'

'Maybe she needed him alive because he knew where her child was... Perhaps he was just out? If she'd killed him the next day, after the house fire, imagine the questions that would be asked. The links that could be made?'

Barnett shook his head. 'It's such a long time ago now, though. If it's Elizabeth, why wait almost thirty years for revenge?'

'Patience? Fear of KYLO closing ranks if she chased them immediately? Pushing the truth even further into the darkness? No, letting everything return to the status quo, over time, would've helped.'

'But thirty years?'

'I know... I get that... Seems so long. It may have taken that long for her to untangle it all. Elizabeth vs KYLO? Wouldn't be an overnight fix. I suspect she needed to find out who her child was first.'

Barnett said, 'But how do we verify or prove any of this until someone starts answering questions?'

'Agreed... so give me her address, and I'll go and ask them.'

60

1993

Elizabeth watched her alarm clock until the LED display switched to 01.00.

Suitably wired on Pro Plus, she rose from her bed.

Her parents would be asleep now, and her brother was at his girlfriend's, so she moved through the house, removing the batteries from the fire alarms and the carbon monoxide detectors.

In the kitchen, she prepared a warm meal, and a hot drink, which she set at the dinner table. She sprinkled the contents of several sleeping pills, taken from her dying mother's supply, into some soup.

After checking the time again, she went to the front door to wait for Laura.

It'd be a disaster if anyone saw her lingering around outside.

As she waited, she thought of all those years as a child in which she'd admired Laura Wilson.

Despite being underweight, and quietly spoken, rather like herself, Laura had carried herself with great poise. Some saw it as a stern, almost aggressive demeanour, but Elizabeth believed it to be a steely determination in a man's world.

Laura had been broken by her involvement. She'd spiralled into addiction, and eventual homelessness. Not that Elizabeth felt any sympathy.

After being released from her institution last week, Elizabeth had located her, sleeping rough in Leeds City Centre. Elizabeth had paid for some accommodation and food for several evenings.

Laura, wracked with guilt, had confessed all, in detail, to Elizabeth.

Elizabeth had nodded sympathetically to coax everything from Laura, but inside, her heart was in flames. It was then, at that moment, she wanted Laura to experience, like her, how it felt to truly burn.

You should have known better, Laura. You were orphaned, bounced between foster homes... yet, even with nothing, you carved out chances...

The world gave you hope, Laura, and how did you repay it?

By destroying the lives of others. Lives that shared similarities with yours.

But don't believe that depression, addiction, homelessness, is a big enough price to pay for what you've done. Please, don't believe that.

Not for a second.

Laura arrived and Elizabeth embraced her at the front door.

Hold tight, Elizabeth. This act... this nauseating display of forgiveness and affection... it'll end soon.

'Thanks... again...' Laura said, speaking quietly, so as not to wake Elizabeth's parents. Elizabeth had told her that James wasn't in this evening and was staying at his girlfriend's. She'd never have come otherwise. 'Are you sure that James—'

'He's out.'

'I haven't eaten all day.'

You're desperate... I understand, Laura... but there it is again. That uncontrollable impulse to use others.

'Come and eat,' Elizabeth said and watched her eat the food she'd already prepared.

Afterwards, Laura started to cry. 'I don't deserve this.'

No, you don't.

'He manipulated me.'

Elizabeth nodded, offering a sympathetic look. Not an excuse.

'I wish I could give you more. I wish I could tell you where your child was.'

Elizabeth considered the pages of notes she'd scribbled down during Laura's confession in the hotel room. The locations of the children remained a mystery. Although heavily involved, the details of the transactions made with the purveyors of children had been a guarded secret by James, and she'd not even been paid well for her contributions!

But, with time, Elizabeth would unlock the truth and bring accountability to everyone who deserved it. And she'd find her own daughter.

It'd happen. She knew that now. As certain as the sun rose. One day, justice would be served, and she'd be reunited with her daughter, and save her from this vile world.

After Laura had eaten, they sat together on the sofa in the lounge for a while.

Laura let her head droop on Elizabeth's shoulder.

Repulsed, Elizabeth ran her fingers through her matted hair.

'You know you can never do anything, Elizabeth. You know that they'll kill you if you try.'

'Who?'

'The company that closed all of this down. They're powerful. So, so powerful. I'm sorry I can't give your daughter back to you, Elizabeth. But if you confront them, they'll silence you.'

Let them try.

'So, tell me, again, about my daughter,' Elizabeth said, stroking Laura's hair.

Tell me again, you lying bitch, about the girl who was too deformed for me to look upon.

Laura, through a mouthful of tears, told Elizabeth about how her daughter had a lot of dark hair, and a beautiful button nose.

I dreamed about her. I saw her. I saw you carrying my crying child away from me.

It wasn't long before Laura was asleep.

She stared down at the nurse.

She was older, of course, but they had similar slight builds. Their hair was also the same dark brown, and their eyes, green.

She stroked her face.

Soon... you'll be all gone. And I'll find them all. The children... the parents... all of them. Even if it takes decades.

She headed upstairs to her brother's room.

Having spent the last couple of nights searching it, she knew exactly where to go.

The back of his wardrobe.

So much money.

Two bags full.

More than enough to lie low, until a suitable time to emerge from the shadows. Laura had dropped from the radar two years ago, so maybe she'd leave it another two years before taking on her identity. Time for her to research new passports, and photo identities. She lifted the bags and smiled. She certainly had enough to fund such illegal processes.

Moving forward, if she needed to make the money last, she could get a job as a nurse. It may be prudent to do some refresher training, because it'd be all new to Elizabeth, and she imagined those long shifts were full of challenges. But this was something for later. Much later.

As she carried the heavy bags downstairs, she thought of the private investigators she could now afford to help root out the truth.

She knew it'd be a long, arduous road.

But if it took years, so be it.

If it took decades, so be it.

Downstairs, she took one last look at Laura, sleeping on the sofa, and then grabbed the petrol canister she'd stored around the back of the house.

Then, she doused the stairs in petrol, and set her home alight.

As she walked, leaving three poisonous entities to their demise, she thought of her brother.

The evilest of them all.

She could wait.

She'd watch over his life, ensure he was miserable, and when she finally knew everything, she'd tell him that it was she who ruined his life. Then, he'd die knowing that the truth was coming, and his whole existence was a shameful mess.

Oh, how I'd love you to suffer.

Just like she'd done.

From a distance she watched the house burn, and the monsters die, and realised that the pleasure she felt wasn't normal.

Her bloodline was not how she'd always believed it to be.

The Sykeses were evil.

And the world would benefit – it truly would – when they no longer sucked like leeches from the world around them.

The drugs worked quicker than Elizabeth had anticipated.

Jess was working hard to keep her eyes open, so Elizabeth moved frantically with the truth.

'I could sense that you knew, dear, deep down. When we embraced... when I touched you... when you looked at me. The connections burned. So, I know that this isn't as shocking to you as it could have been. I doubted you would've given me those keys to the storage room... or let me into your home... or into that imposter's room upstairs... unless you *knew*. Unless you genuinely felt it.'

'Dad...' Jess managed, drool bubbling at the corner of her mouth. 'Dad... is he okay?'

'I've told you, dear, he wasn't your father. A man, a beast, who paid my brother, your uncle, another creature, to take you from me. And that imposter has gone now, along with your uncle, and some of the others. These are people who believed they were above what nature intended. They weren't natural... not in the sense that they should be... and we, too, dear, are the same. Must be the same. We carry the same genes. The same blood. We are both Sykeses.'

'My life... a lie,' Jess managed. Her eyes closed.

Elizabeth reached out and placed a hand to her cheek, attempting to rouse her.

Jess opened her eyes.

'Not any more,' Elizabeth said. 'Be empowered by the truth as the truth empowered me, dear. It gave me strength, patience. It took me so long to untangle the web. KYLO... the government... they were sealed containers. For so long, the private investigators baulked at my requests because they feared for their own safety. But eventually, I found someone who helped. And he found threads... threads he could pull... and eventually, dear, the truth began to untangle. James lived far longer than I intended. He couldn't die until I had everything, you see. Every part of the story. His death would risk my exposure before it was finished. But he suffered. He lived a life of wanting, a life of crawling around for pennies to survive. I told him this before I chained him to an old cart and listened to him beg for food and water for days... and then I watched him rot.'

She noticed Jess's eyes were closed, so she squeezed her arm this time.

Jess opened her eyes, weakly.

'There were times when I considered failure, quitting, ending myself before it was finished, but I persevered. A few strokes of luck there, and several people who emerged in later years, now willing to help, and the truth just came faster and faster. And I found you. I found you, Jess.' She leaned forward and kissed her forehead. 'Twelve months ago... I found you. You were the hardest and final piece. The best for last. And with that, it began, and today, it ends.'

Jess's eyes were closed now, and Elizabeth was disappointed with the speed of the drugs. 'What a thing for you to find out. I'm sorry for that, but you deserved the truth. The life they gave you was, as you said, a lie.'

Jess managed to say something.

Elizabeth leaned in. 'What was that, dear?'

'Circumstances... aligned...'

'Circumstances?'

'Aligned,' Jess said, and her head slumped to the side.

Elizabeth sighed. Maybe, after all, it was for the best, that Jess didn't know what came next.

Elizabeth had believed it may have offered her peace, *closure*, in this final moment, but Jess had been different from how she'd always imagined her. Reserved and awkward. With a range of idiosyncrasies that made her anxious.

The closure may have caused her fear.

She stroked her sleeping daughter's face. 'Maybe it's for the best. You're so loveable, dear. So unlike the rest of our kin. But I know it lies within you. It lay within me without my knowledge. And it most certainly lay within my parents, and James. I wish I could have been there to prepare you for the burden you carried, but I wasn't allowed that. And now it's too late. I can't protect you, like no one protected me. I'll give you peace. You'll never face the rage I faced. The devilish instincts. It's my responsibility to stop you evolving into your uncle... your grandparents... into me...'

Elizabeth stood and moved to the front door, thinking of all the truth that was coming to those stolen children, and the judgement that was coming to the fraudsters who'd paid her brother.

She also thought of Robert Thwaites, trying to erase the truth, predicting that he'd die where he belonged. In jail.

She hoped the world would find a way to tear down KYLO, too, but knew that was rather ambitious thinking, considering their power.

Outside, she retrieved the petrol container she'd left by the front door on the way in and took it into the house.

As she drenched the rug in front of the two-seater sofa, she looked down at her sleeping daughter.

Gentle... innocent... harmless, even.

Hard to believe that the same blood is in your veins as mine.

Elizabeth thought of the night she'd killed her parents, and her belief that the world would benefit when the Sykeses no longer sucked like leeches from the world around them.

She pulled out her lighter. 'I won't leave you to the same fate... but, at least, dear, you can finish your life in the same way you started it. With me.' She knelt and lit the rug. 'Your mother.'

62

Barnett sat alongside Gardner in her vehicle as they headed back into Knaresborough.

She wanted to be close to Laura Wilson's property when response arrived there. En route, she'd drop Barnett at home. He'd left his car at the Atkinson farm when the paramedics advised him not to drive until he'd calmed from his near-death experience. O'Brien had accompanied him back to HQ in a taxi.

The journey was slow, because of the weather, and she had to be vigilant, but she still threw several concerned glances in his direction.

'You don't need to worry,' Barnett said.

'When it comes to personal issues, I've got my fair share of history, you know.' *A sociopathic brother who tried to brain me as a kid for example.* 'If you ever need to talk.'

'Clarissa Trent,' Barnett said, looking at Gardner. 'My sister.'

'I know,' Gardner said, nodding and indicating to change lane on the carriageway.

'Wow... she'll probably know by now.'

'Yes. Marsh sent officers to inform them,' Gardner said.

'Wonder what Clarissa thought? How she feels?'

'She'll be stunned at first, I imagine.'

'I hope she doesn't think Mum abandoned her.'

'Why would she? The narrative behind what really happened is compelling. Your mother's hardly to blame.'

'But is she completely blameless?' Barnett asked.

Gardner indicated off into Knaresborough. Who knew for sure? But Gardner couldn't see it herself. Amina would've taken the money, because, well, *why wouldn't you?* She wouldn't have known the truth.

'I think she *knew* she had a child out there,' Barnett said.

'It won't do you any good to think like that. And how could she possibly know?'

'She wrote poems, boss. About losing someone. She knew something had been torn away from her. That something unjust... unnatural... had happened.' He shook his head. 'Maybe I'm overthinking it?'

Again, who knew? *You'll drive yourself mad thinking about it, Ray.* 'Losing her child to death, in itself, would've felt unnatural to your mother. As if something had been torn away. She may have suspected nothing.'

'What do they say though, boss? That a *mother knows.*'

'Maybe... but I know this, Ray, so listen carefully. I know Amina Ndiaye's son. Very well. And if she was anything like him, which I'm sure she was, she wouldn't have turned her back on the truth. In fact, like her son, she'd have stopped at nothing to find it.'

He nodded, looking tearful. 'Thanks boss. I hope Clarissa wants to make contact.'

'She will. In her own time. Just let her come to you.'

The phone rang. It was response. Laura Wilson wasn't home.

Frustrated, and desperate, she used every part of her willpower to stop herself hitting the steering wheel. The individual beside her right now was rather sensitive. It was better to avoid sudden moves.

She parked beside Barnett's house.

This time when her phone rang, her blood froze.

'You all right, boss?'

'I don't know, yet.'

She answered the phone. '*Neville.*'

'Hello, Emma.'

63

Neville Fairweather had got straight to the point.

She shouldn't have contacted him yet.

He admonished her for it, but she fought her corner, explained that this was his one chance to prove himself to her... prove that he, like all the others, wasn't a monster.

He'd sighed and relented, but not without ensuring he snared another bargaining chip. 'After this... you must come good on our deal.'

Except, she still had no real idea as to what that deal was.

She agreed anyway; she was tired, and so desperate to find Elizabeth Sykes and put a stop to this madness.

'I removed myself as a shareholder from KYLO when they decided to bid on the homeless shelter.'

'Because you *knew*. You knew what was going on there.'

'I repeat, I *removed* myself.'

'Knowing makes you complicit.'

'Emma... if any of us were judged on all the things we knew... it'd be a busy courtroom. Have you seen Bright Day, itself? The building?'

'Yes... it's interesting.'

'Sleek, eh? A modern masterpiece. Have you looked into the person that designed it?'

'No, why—'

'Goodbye, Emma. Next time we speak, it'll be about what I want, *not* what you want.'

And then he was gone.

She turned to Barnett. 'Find out who designed Bright Day's building.'

Barnett nodded. He hoisted his phone out. His finger moved swiftly over the screen as he researched. Fast. Efficient. A natural.

He looked up, his eyes wide. 'Nigel Beaumont.'

Gardner started the engine. 'Father of Jess Beaumont. Which puts him in Elizabeth Sykes' crosshairs. With that sweet girl, Jess Beaumont, caught in the middle.' She checked the mirror and drove out. 'Clara Atkinson was not the last baby born there. Jess Beaumont was. And Nigel was the last bastard to benefit.' She glanced at Barnett, who was fastening his seatbelt. 'You're coming because I don't know where Elizabeth Sykes is. But if everything is in order, and she's not at the house, you stay in the vehicle. Understand?'

64

But everything wasn't in order.

'Shit! Jess's home! Can you see it?' Gardner said.

At this distance, near the end of the road, the front windows of Jess's quaint home flickered in the gloom of the dying day.

'It's on fire!'

'Phone it in _now._'

While Barnett radioed in to have emergency services sent out, Gardner screeched to a halt and pounced from the car. She darted towards the home. From within, the fire alarms squealed. The flickering flames through the glass were ominous, as was the smoke weeping out of the house.

It may not have been a raging inferno yet. But it wouldn't be long.

She tried the front door. Locked.

Shit!

She barged it. Once... twice... she stumbled back, shooting pains flying down her arm.

The door had barely moved.

'Stand back,' Barnett hissed.

She stepped to one side. Being a large man, Barnett could grip a solid, fixed canopy sheltering the front door. With support, he thrust his foot into the door. Once... twice... it splintered... three... four... it burst open. Smoke swirled and danced before escaping its confines like some dark spirit. The sound of the wailing alarms was suddenly ear-piercing.

Covering their mouths, Gardner and Barnett turned away.

Gardner looked at Barnett, her heart pounding in her chest. 'Look, you stay out here and wait for emerge—'

Barnett, jaw set, eyes wide, shook his head, had already turned. He shot in past the hanging door.

Predictable.

Covering her mouth, she followed him.

'Jess!' Barnett called.

No reply.

Gardner tried as well. '*Jess!*'

Nothing.

And the alarms were so bloody loud...

Coughing now, Gardner looked inside the burning lounge. The black smoke was swelling, so it was difficult to see clearly. There was a large blazing rectangle on the floor, which Gardner recalled as the rug. Some of the wooden floor that covered most of the lounge had caught and the flames were already licking at the walls on the left side of the room. Jess Beaumont lay, presumably unconscious, on the sofa to the right of the room. *Why had she not woken? Had she succumbed to the smoke?* The edges of the sofa were catching and would certainly be close to eruption.

'Jess!' Gardner shouted, starting forward, keeping to the far right of the room where the flames were yet to spread.

Barnett, coughing, came out of nowhere and thrust out a hand to stop her.

She watched him, hand over his mouth, take long, fast strides over the smouldering wood, hoping his trousers didn't catch, and the floor didn't give way. She covered her own mouth, coughing, her mind awash with potential outcomes. None of which were positive.

Barnett got to the sofa. He had to stop and lean over to grab Jess. 'Ray!' Gardner shouted, watching the flames scratching the sofa lick his legs, too. 'Hurry!'

She heard Barnett grunting as he scooped up Jess, uncertain whether his noises came from pain or exertion. Probably both.

At that point, a sudden force pushed Gardner backwards into the hall through the front door, and the wall knocked the wind out of her chest.

She looked up into the wild eyes of her assailant.

'*Elizabeth!*'

Gardner's eyes fell to the kitchen knife in her hand, and, for one terrifying moment, she thought she'd been stabbed. She touched her chest and saw there was no blood on her fingers, recalling the time, years ago, when a blade had punctured a lung, and she'd almost died.

'Elizabeth... *please* listen,' Gardner said, lifting the palms of her hands, showing that she was unarmed.

'You're early,' Elizabeth hissed. '*Too* early.' She lashed out.

Gardner felt a searing pain in her temple and lifted her hands to her face to protect it. She slipped to the side, along the wall, and uncovered her eyes. Elizabeth was no longer in front of her.

'Ray,' she shouted. 'Elizabeth is *in* here.'

Gardner sprang forward back into the lounge.

Over the shoulder of Elizabeth Sykes, who had the knife raised, she saw the face of Barnett, contorted in pain, as he held Jess Beaumont over one shoulder in a firefighter's lift.

He'd no time to act.

Gardner charged and crashed into Elizabeth's back. The two of them went down together onto the smouldering wood beside the flaming rug.

Elizabeth screamed in agony. Her body protected Gardner from burning, too. Gardner's instinct was to hold Elizabeth down, restrain her, but that would surely kill her. She tried to scramble up off her without touching the flames. But the heat was intense, and the smoke was overwhelming.

And then the screaming intensified.

Elizabeth's hair had caught fire from the rug.

Barnett's hand was suddenly hanging there in front of Gardner's face. Instinctively, she reached out and gripped it.

Barnett yanked her upwards with no effort of her own. She saw that he still had Jess slung over his shoulder. God, how strong was he?

'Elizabeth!' Gardner shouted, looking down.

Elizabeth had turned onto her back, hair flaming, face smoking, waving the blade in the air.

Barnett was tugging Gardner away by her hand. 'Come on,' he hissed. He, too, sounded in a great deal of pain. '*Now.*'

Gardner slipped her hand free and hissed, 'Get out, Ray.' She reached down for the writhing woman. 'Please, Elizabeth,' she coughed. 'Please take my hand.'

Elizabeth was still waving the knife as she burned. It was unclear whether she was comprehending Gardner's request.

Gardner yanked her hand back. The blade narrowly missed.

'Boss,' Barnett shouted in. 'Leave now!'

Elizabeth screamed again. She seemed to shout something, but the words were difficult to understand over the wailing alarms and her own agony. And what she could make out sounded like nonsense.

She reached down again, and this time, she felt the sting of the blade.

It was no use. She wouldn't accept help, and she was being rapidly consumed by the fire.

Despite her impending death, Elizabeth shouted again and again, but the words still seemed to make little sense, and then... it was all brought to a sudden close. Barnett's hand landed on her shoulder, and before she knew it, she was in the garden, coughing her guts up.

Barnett slumped down, moaning in agony and coughing, rolling in the snow. Smoke rose from his trousers as he moaned in pain. Beside him lay the prone form of Jess Beaumont.

Gardner looked at her hand. The cut ran down the centre of her palm. It bled freely, and would need stitching, but her injuries would be nothing compared to Barnett's. She rubbed at her forehead with the back of her hand and saw there was blood there, too.

She glanced at the house, seeing that the flames that had claimed Elizabeth Sykes had grown more ferocious. It was consuming the detached house. She could hear the fire engines. The neighbours were out in their own front garden, watching in horror as the fire tore through the building.

Her eyes moved up to the glowing bedroom window, and she realised that they'd spared no thought for Nigel Beaumont. The chaos of Elizabeth and Jess had taken all their attention.

The fire engine arrived, with several ambulances in tow. She ensured the paramedics got to Barnett and Jess first. And then, as she watched the firefighters work on the house, the words that Elizabeth had been shouting seemed to take on some clarity.

It's inside of me.

Gardner looked up at the house.

Of us.

She heard something collapsing within the structure.

Let it burn.

Gardner sighed. *Elizabeth, what have you done? It should never have ended this way for you.*

Her phone buzzed in her pocket.

She looked at it as a third paramedic came towards her. It was a message from Ross. A Google map with a pin.

'I'm sorry,' Gardner said, running for her own car.

'Wait, please,' the paramedic called. 'Smoke inhalation is—'

Gardner didn't need to hear the end. She knew smoke inhalation was deadly. She wasn't an imbecile.

Maybe it was the adrenaline, maybe it was the tragedy of Elizabeth Sykes, but right now, nothing in the world, *nothing*, seemed as important as getting to Cecile and Riddick.

Unable to bear the sounds of crying children, Riddick was doomed to spend the entire evening awake with his hands to his ears.

He'd even pushed his blood alcohol level excessively high, hoping to black out for a time. It hadn't worked.

The cries of anguish kept on, and he soon became plagued by images of his own dead children.

Add to that, Tommy had *insisted* he sleep on the hard floor beside Cecile for the night. Tommy, of course, still didn't know her actual identity, and still referred to her as *Pat*, or that *suspicious bitch*. But he'd been so busy with the trafficked children to attend to it. In a way, this was a good thing. When he finally got around to speaking with her again, he'd probably torture the information out of her. Tommy had also been adamant that the handcuffs stayed on.

This had been the worst of it.

I mean, who can settle with their hands cuffed to the railings behind their head?

So, she'd cried and begged for hours for Riddick to take them off, and Riddick had begged her to just let it go, because if Tommy came in and she was free, it'd be dangerous. But she wouldn't have it.

Eventually, Tommy had come during the dead of night. 'Jay, tape her mouth... she's disturbing the kids.'

Riddick doubted hearing her cry was anything to do with the children's anguish; more likely, it was the captivity imposed by Tommy, but he did as the bastard wanted anyway. As Riddick taped her mouth, he whispered to Cecile, 'I'm not who Emma thinks I am any more. She shouldn't have come looking. You shouldn't be here.' However, he then assured her, 'I'll take them off when he's gone back to bed... if you're quiet.'

She nodded, sending tears from her eyes down towards her ears.

Back on the floor, Riddick thought about the chain of events that had brought him to this moment.

During his time working in Bradford, his team had come across Tommy Rose and his empire on more than one occasion. To be honest, Tommy had been on everyone's list for time immemorial, but that was what sometimes happened with these vile beings – they existed on the radar for a ludicrous length of time, and never slipped up. *Ever.* Some officers he'd worked with just blamed luck, but Riddick knew it for what it really was. Determination. Grit. Resilience. If you could find the perfect cocktail of these elements, and then wash it all down with a chaser of immorality, you could just about achieve anything.

Drugs had bothered Riddick, of course. Massively. And yes, Tommy sold drugs. On a massive scale.

But there were plenty of those fish out there, and a limited supply of hooks.

Rumours were that Tommy had gone further. Rumours that had piqued Riddick's interest, because they involved children. But Tommy trafficking children remained just that, a rumour, and so was yet to attract too much attention from an already overworked force.

So, Riddick had followed up independently, and had found some truth.

Tommy was not trafficking children on a mammoth scale in the same way he sold drugs. Human trafficking on that scale was challenging beyond belief. More so than drugs. The manpower required was eye-watering. The more people involved, the more variables. And the more variables, the more chance of it collapsing. So, Tommy, at this stage, was merely dabbling.

He was acquiring immigrant teenage children at the borders, storing them at his different properties in the north, this one included, until he was certain that there was no heat attached to his acquisition. Then, he'd have them transported far off the radar, to someone in the south of England, to begin lives of servitude – which Riddick knew would vary from prostitution, factory work and drug dealing.

Riddick had never pursued it while working in Bradford because the situation involving a young, vulnerable man called Arthur Fields raised its head. Following his young friend's suicide, Riddick spiralled again and fled from his job and his life.

Still, rather than wallow in his own misery, he'd put himself to some use. And when innocent children were involved, he was always available. In this instance, off the books.

Fortunately, he'd made a better job of going undercover than Cecile Metcalf and, fortunately, he'd survived so far, unlike poor Henry Ackroyd.

At three o'clock in the morning, he decided it'd soon be time to act. He peeled off Cecile's tape, who fulfilled her bargain not to shout and cry again. 'Tommy has told me that tomorrow, he'll be away running chores for an hour. He wants me to man the fort while he's gone. We're going to walk out with the children in that other room, and I'm going to make sure that this bastard never does anything like this again.'

She looked at him. Her eyes were raw from tears. 'Is this what it's all been about?'

Riddick nodded. 'I'm sorry you had to get mixed up in this.'

'Why don't you just phone someone? About the children? Get help.'

'I think you misunderstand me, Cecile. When I say never again, I mean never again.'

'You can't...'

He looked away.

'You'll go to jail.'

He shrugged.

'You'll ruin your life.'

Riddick laughed – he couldn't help himself.

* * *

Frustratingly, Tommy didn't go anywhere for the best part of the day. He lingered around downstairs on the sofa, making phone calls.

Riddick still wasn't expected to work. This house wouldn't be back in operation until the children had been moved on.

Having Tommy around all the time made it challenging for Riddick to keep his alcohol levels topped up. The supply in the bathroom cabinet was finished, and, having finished two the previous day, he only had one bottle left, concealed beneath Cecile's bed.

It wasn't enough.

Yet, he wouldn't be able to slip out anytime soon, either.

So, he was forced to ration his intake, which made him feel more on edge and shaky.

At one point, he was checking on Cecile, when he heard Tommy calling down from the third floor, where the children were kept. 'Oi Jay... box of crisps from the kitchen.'

Riddick went down to the kitchen and grabbed a large box loaded with crisps and joined Tommy on the third floor. He stood a metre from the door and called to him.

Tommy emerged and grinned. 'Don't be shy. Come on in and meet the crew.'

Riddick followed the large man into the room.

Riddick's stomach turned as he counted four children. They were a range of ages. One boy couldn't have been older than ten, whereas one girl looked about fifteen. He'd expected them to look a lot more dishevelled, but that didn't help with the nausea. That they weren't battered and bruised brought him relief, though.

'Lithuanian,' Tommy said, ripping open the box and throwing packets at them as if he was feeding the ducks in a river. 'Can't understand a word we say. Or so it seems...' He walked over to the girl who immediately clutched the boy who looked ten – her brother, perhaps? They looked alike. Tommy threw the box down and held out his hand to her. The girl paled, shook her head and gripped the boy tighter.

Tommy looked back at Riddick and smiled.

Riddick clenched his fists.

'But I wonder,' Tommy said, turning back, kneeling. He reached out and placed a hand on the girl's face. She tried to turn from it, but he kept his palm clamped there. 'I wonder if they do *actually* understand everything that I'm saying.'

The girl squeezed her eyes closed, tears springing from the corners.

Gritting his teeth, Riddick edged forward, until he was a metre behind Tommy.

'Because maybe, if they could understand, then they'd be a little more grateful for the life that I'm going to give them.'

Tommy leaned closer, keeping her face clamped in his hands, drawing her nearer. His breath would be on her face. Riddick took another step. The anger surged through him, making his clenched fists tremble at his side.

It'd be so easy to swing right now...

But then what?

The man was a giant and, if he knocked Riddick out of this world, then the children were doomed.

He sucked in a deep breath, willing himself to be calmer.

Then, an idea occurred to him. 'Can I speak with you, Tommy?'

Tommy let his hand slip away and rose. He pointed down at the box. 'Eat as much as you need. I'll fetch another when that's done.'

The girl placed her chin on the young boy's head and hugged him tightly.

'Kids, eh?' Tommy said, heading past Riddick and out into the hall.

Riddick followed him out. Tommy turned and locked the door and thrust the key into the left pocket of his jeans. 'Get to it, Jay... what's up?'

'Just that I think I'm getting somewhere with Pat.'

'How so? She told you why she's here yet?'

'Not exactly, no, but she's vulnerable following the dose she had the other night... she let it slip she's from outside of this area—'

'Which begs the question, how does she know about this place?'

Riddick nodded.

'Go in harder... hurt her.' Tommy hit his arm. 'I know you've got it in you, Jay.'

'I was thinking, I might just dose her again, if that's all right?'

'Good idea. Let me know how it goes.'

'The combination?'

Tommy had changed the safe combination the previous day. 'Not that I don't trust you, Jay, but if we're out of service, then I'd keep it secure from my grandmother until business resumes... I'll get it.'

Downstairs, Tommy opened the safe and handed him a couple of little baggies. 'I need you on the ball, though, Jay. Just her. I've seen how you've developed a taste for it.' He winked down at Riddick.

'Of course,' Riddick said.

'Go and give her some medicine. It's time for my run. One hour.

Got someone pocketing some loose change if you catch my meaning. Time to put a stop to it. I'll grab supplies and some other bits and bobs. You're good to hold the fort? Keep an eye on the third floor?'

'Yes.'

'This will be over tomorrow.' Tommy hit his arm again. Riddick felt anger bubbling inside him. 'And you'll get a good payday.'

After watching Tommy leave the house, Riddick went upstairs and released Cecile.

She perched on the edge of the bed, rubbing her wrists. She wept with relief.

He could feel her staring at him as he readied the syringe.

'Why are you doing that?' she asked.

'Let me concentrate.' He felt agitated by the lack of alcohol and the excess adrenaline in his system.

'But, why—'

'*Please!*' he snapped.

She turned away, shocked.

He felt guilty. 'Sorry... on edge. It's all going to be fine. Just give me a minute.'

After he finished, he flicked the syringe and caught her looking again.

'Whatever it is you're planning to do... you don't have to. We can just get the children and run. That's enough.'

'It isn't,' Riddick said, placing the syringe on the bedside table. 'Whatever we do will never be enough, but I'll at least do what I can while I'm able.' He stood. 'Ready?'

'Yes,' she said, still rubbing her wrists.

'Now listen... As we planned, after I kick the door down upstairs, you grab those children, and you get out of here. Don't look back until you get to your car.'

She'd already explained how she'd left her keys beneath the car behind the front right wheel. 'Imagine if you'd searched me and found the keys to a Lexus?'

'Now if your car is gone,' Riddick said. 'Not outside the realm of possibility.' *Especially with a key hidden behind the wheel.* 'You just keep going. A bus, a taxi, a shop... anything... anyone who can make that phone call. Just don't give anyone this address for two hours. Two hours. Do I have your word?'

She looked away.

'Do I have your word?'

She nodded. 'Yes. Two hours.'

'More than enough,' Riddick said.

'This is stupid.'

'I'll be okay.'

'But if you're not okay, Paul, then what will you be?'

Dead. 'I'm already in for a penny. Just get those kids out, okay, and give me some time? Promise me.'

Cecile nodded. 'I guess you've earned the right to make that decision – I can't think of many people who'd go to these lengths. I promise.'

Riddick helped her up, and she stretched out. He heard her bones cracking.

'I'm sorry for what I did to you,' he said.

She sighed. 'You'd no choice.'

'There's always a choice... don't forgive me that easily,' he said, walking to the bedroom door.

'You chose the children. I can live with that,' Cecile said from behind him.

Riddick placed his hand on the handle.

'I'll ask those children upstairs in a couple of years if they think you made the right choice,' Cecile continued.

Riddick nodded, took a deep breath, and opened the door.

Tommy was standing there.

Riddick's eyes widened. 'Shit—'

A sudden blow to his stomach knocked the wind from him.

He folded forward into the doorframe, so he didn't go to the floor.

Behind him, Cecile was shouting for him to move.

He glanced up and saw the bloody knife in Tommy's hands. A cold sensation spread over his body when he realised that the blood belonged to him.

With no real options, Riddick threw himself forward, wrapping his arms around the large man's stomach, thrusting him against the wall. He rotated slightly as he went, so when they rebounded together, they didn't fly back into the room; instead, the ground disappeared beneath Riddick's feet, and the world started to spin and flash.

Disorientated, it took Riddick a moment to realise that he'd come down the stairs; then, another moment to clock the worsening agony in his stomach.

Tommy, however, hadn't needed a moment. The bastard was already scurrying up onto him.

Tommy rose, shifting his knees to Riddick's arms.

It's over, Riddick thought, expecting to see the knife again that had mangled his insides.

But there was no knife. The fall must have disarmed him.

Tommy threw a punch. Everything turned white. When he opened his eyes, the fist came again. Another flash of white.

'You think I'd be stupid enough to leave you alone?' Tommy snorted. 'You think I don't know you're pissed all the time? Yes... I've had my eye on you since you turned to jelly the other night.' He punched him a third time.

This time, he didn't have the strength to open his eyes. He prepared for another blow, and unconsciousness—

There was a loud smash. Then, the weight seemed to be lifted from Riddick. He opened his eyes. The world spun, but he'd enough sense to see Tommy had hit the floor beside him.

As his vision began to sharpen and the blurry chaos subsided, the figure before him gradually took shape. The hazy outlines solidified, and he could now discern the familiar features of Cecile standing there, holding the jagged remains of a vodka bottle in her hand. 'You okay?'

'No...' He lifted his hand and pointed at the smashed bottle. 'That was my last one.' He spat out blood and rolled on to his side. He groaned. The pain in his stomach was worse than his face.

Cecile knelt and looked at him. 'You need to get to the hospital now.'

'No...' Riddick said. 'We stick to the plan. You get those kids out.'

'He stabbed you Paul, there's blood every—'

Riddick spat out more blood. 'The plan... you promised. You *promised.*'

'What if I can't even kick the door—'

'The left pocket of his jeans,' Riddick hissed.

While Cecile rustled in the bastard's pockets, Riddick looked down at his wound. It was the left side of his stomach. *How long did he have?*

'Got them,' she said, standing up above him.

'Good... first...' He looked up at her. 'Get me the syringe from upstairs.'

She stared down at him.

'Listen, you can't risk him waking up. Think of the children. If I'd the strength to use that broken glass on him, I would, without a moment's hesitation... but I don't.'

She looked at the broken bottle in her hand.

'No...' Riddick said. 'Don't even think about it. This isn't your war. Not yours to live with. Get me the syringe.'

She paled, shaking her head.

'Now.' He coughed. '*Now!*'

She nodded and ran upstairs.

While she was retrieving the syringe, he rolled onto his front, groaning. After getting himself to his knees, he looked down and saw that his front was shimmering with blood. He shook his head, groaning. *And I always thought it'd be the booze.*

Surprisingly, he'd more strength left than he'd realised, and worked his way to his feet. He reached down and, feeling the agony tearing through him, attempted to pull Tommy over the floor by his armpits.

A mistake.

He leaned over, grabbed his knees, and sucked at the air while pain surged through his body.

'I'm here.' Cecile was suddenly there, on the other side of him. She put the syringe on the table and then reached down for his left armpit.

Together, they dragged him to the right side of the sofa. They sat him upright against it. His head slumped forward. 'That'll do. It'll see me off if we try to lift him onto it.' He snatched the syringe from the table. Fortunately, the tube was still there from the other day. He grabbed that, too.

'What're you going to say?' Cecile asked.

Say? Probably nothing, looking at the state of me... 'I'll think of something—'

'What? That he was off his head on drugs and stabbed you?'

Riddick grinned and winced as he took the tube and the syringe from the table. 'Nobody is stabbing anyone on this dose.' He looked down at the blood leaking out onto the floor. 'I'll say that he stabbed me *before...* sat down to watch me die while he enjoyed himself on too much of his own product.'

'Your blood is *everywhere*, though.'

Riddick nodded and knelt. He felt dizzy and knew he needed to get a move on. 'I took pity on him... crawled over to attempt to save him.'

Cecile shook her head. 'Christ... you're a card.'

He tied the tube around Tommy's arm.

'No...' Cecile said.

He looked up at Cecile. 'It's all right. Trust me. It's on me. You were never involved—'

'I just can't watch while—'

'Don't. Get the children.'

Tommy stirred.

Riddick slipped the needle into a vein.

Tommy opened his eyes as Riddick snapped the tube off.

'What're you doing?' Tommy moaned.

'Putting things right,' Riddick said.

Tommy looked down, then up. His eyes widened. 'Shit... no...'

But it was too late.

He shook his head, pushed Riddick away, who slumped back to the floor. 'How much... how much did you give me?' His voice was losing strength.

'How much does it take to kill a child-trafficking monster?' Riddick asked.

'You bastard...' His eyes rolled back. 'No... you bastard.' He reached out.

Riddick slumped back on the floor as Tommy mumbled incomprehensibly.

'Cecile... *please*,' Riddick said. The world was spinning now. 'Go. Get...' He closed his eyes.

He felt a hand on his face and opened them again. Cecile was close to him. 'Keep your eyes open.'

'I will... I promise.'

'Promise?'

'Okay... yes... you keep yours, and I'll keep mine.'

And he kept his promise.

Right until he saw Cecile leading the children out the front door.

Then he closed his eyes and smiled at the thought of his wife and children.

Heart pounding in her chest, hand throbbing from the deep cut, Gardner put a gloved hand on the top of Cecile's Lexus, coughing.

Cecile?

She turned a full circle again, observing the rows of terraces.

Anywhere! She could be bloody anywhere!

She hoisted her phone out and looked down at the picture sent by Cecile several days back of Riddick, sitting on a wall outside a house that looked very similar to many of these others.

Coughing again, she backed away from the car, knowing that she'd have to call it in.

What choice do I have? I can't wander these streets, hoping that this terraced house will just jump out at me.

Never going to happen.

After calling it in, she leaned on the car again, feeling sick to the stomach over what she'd set in motion.

Have I cost Cecile her life?

If she had, there was no coming back from it. She'd demand punishment. With Collette, they'd waved away her cries to be held responsible. This was different. There was no way they could overlook this.

No. She'd pay. She'd have to.

Blinking back tears, she saw a small huddle of people in the distance heading her way. She cleared her vision with her sleeve as they came closer. They were moving at great speed.

She pushed herself back from the car, eyes widening.

No. Her eyes were surely playing tricks on her. *It can't be.*

She moved to meet the group as they came nearer, unbelieving of what she was seeing.

'Cecile?'

'Yes,' Cecile replied, her voice weak and strained, yet filled with relief.

'God... Cecile... thank God. Thank God.' The words tumbled out of her mouth as she darted in and embraced her pale, dishevelled friend. She could feel Cecile trembling in her arms, her body fragile and exhausted. 'What's happened? You look awful—' She broke off to cough, turning her head to one side, her lungs still raw from the smoke.

'So do you,' Cecile said.

'I was caught in a fire. Who are these?' She looked over at the four children, who clung to each other, their eyes wide with fear and confusion.

She looked back at Cecile, who was choking back tears. 'What's happened? Talk to me,' Gardner urged, her brows furrowed with concern.

'I'm sorry, Emma...' Cecile's lips quivered.

'Sorry for what? What's happened?' Gardner's voice grew more insistent.

'You need an ambulance. You *need* an ambulance now. It's Paul.' Cecile's words came out in a rush.

Gardner took a deep breath, her jaw clenching as she fought to maintain her composure. 'What's happened to him? What's he done?'

'I'm sorry, Emma.' Cecile's voice cracked.

'What's the house number?'

'Emma—' Cecile began, but Gardner cut her off.

'*Cecile!*' Gardner's voice rang out, sharp and commanding.

Cecile gave the house number, her hand shaking as she pointed at the children behind her. 'He got these out. He got *me* out. But Emma...'

Gardner thrust her phone into Cecile's hands, shouting the passcode as she did so. 'Call the ambulance.'

Then, without waiting for a response, Gardner turned and ran, her heart pounding in her chest, her mind racing with the possibilities of what she might find. Her feet pounded against the pavement, her breath coming in short, sharp gasps as she pushed her damaged lungs to the limit, desperate to reach Riddick.

Gardner didn't get far.

The smoke inhalation had her.

Leaning against a wall, she coughed her guts up, sucking in deep breaths when she could. Eventually, the attack subsided, and she made it to the house at a more realistic pace. The front door was open. She burst in, shouting for Riddick.

The larger man on the sofa was still and had foam coming out of his mouth.

Her eyes fell to the figure on the floor.

'Paul,' she gasped.

As she moved forward, she slipped. There was a lot of blood on the floor. She was forced to use the wall to steady herself, and then lowered herself down next to Riddick.

His face was pale, and his eyes were closed. She was certain she could see the gentle rise and fall of his chest.

Wishful thinking?

She checked for his pulse.

Weak. But there.

His eyelids lifted slowly. He formed a weak smile. 'Emma.'

She touched his face, forcing back the desperate urge to cough. 'Rest. An ambulance is coming.'

'Did they get out?'

'Yes,' Gardner said. '*You* got them out.'

'Good.' Still smiling, he closed his eyes.

'Open your eyes,' Gardner said. She turned her head to the side to cough. When she'd finished, she looked back and saw that his eyes were open.

'I've missed you... Emma.' Riddick's words were barely a whisper, but they struck Gardner like a physical blow. Her heart clenched, and she felt a wave of emotion wash over her.

'I've missed you, too,' she managed to say, her voice thick with unshed tears. The words felt inadequate, but they were all she could offer in this sea of overwhelming emotions.

This time, when he closed his eyes, she couldn't get him to open them again.

EPILOGUE
CHRISTMAS DAY

Gardner stopped the Christmas playlist.

Along with the mulled wine, it'd served its purpose in steering her through the laborious food preparation, but she'd now reached her limit on these pop classics.

She stood for a moment, enjoying the sound of her children in the other room constructing a train track. She'd invested in wooden toys, rather than plastic this year, and was glad to hear that she'd made the right call.

Then, she moved into the dining room, lit a few candles, so the room was bathed in the flickering lights, and thought of the house fire that had claimed the lives of retired architect, Nigel Beaumont, and James Sykes' murderer, Elizabeth Sykes. Barnett had endured a raw deal with third-degree burns on his legs. Gardner had paid a smaller price with mild smoke inhalation and stitches in her palm.

Gardner sighed. She often thought of Elizabeth's refusal to be saved, and those last words again:

It's inside of me. Of us. Let it burn.

What was she referring to? Evil? Madness? Both, perhaps?

Who could ever know for sure?

One thing was certain, though. Elizabeth's last act in trying to kill her biological daughter was not a sane one. Elizabeth had had her demons. And they'd driven her to the edge.

And yet, even in her insanity, she'd orchestrated the unearthing of the truth so meticulously for the world. But then, didn't they say that sometimes genius and insanity often came hand in hand?

Gardner had kept a keen eye on Jess Beaumont. She'd struggled at first and couldn't make peace with her parents for what they'd done. That they'd *bought* her, or rather *stolen* her, from another was unforgiveable. Imagine discovering that about the people you'd spent your whole life adoring?

Where could you go from there?

However, she'd forgiven Elizabeth for what she'd tried to do.

Gardner had been helping Jess find a new place. Nigel's money would ensure there'd be no problems financially. Emotionally, would be a whole different ballpark. Especially considering she was already vulnerable. Gardner had wanted her to come to Christmas dinner today, but she'd refused. Still, she'd check in on her later all the same.

She took a deep breath and turned to the Christmas table. She moved her eyes over the bronzed turkey at the centrepiece, the plates and the crackers.

Then, one glance at her watch told her that her guest was due any moment.

She moved to the seat her guest would occupy, ensuring that the cutlery was straight.

Gardner was so desperate to make this a day to remember.

Maybe, if she did so, then it'd herald in a brighter year. One marked with less trauma and tragedy.

The doorbell rang.

Excitedly, she ran to get Rose and Ana, who weren't too keen to leave the train set, but did so after a stern motherly stare, and they assembled at the front door.

Gardner opened the door to her younger colleague, who was in a festive red dress and holding tinfoil topped 'O'Brien World Famous Christmas Pudding'. It looked massive!

Her children screeched, 'Merry Christmas, Lucy,' loud enough to wake the dead, leaving O'Brien and Gardner to laugh in a fitting introduction to the day's celebrations.

* * *

Barnett limped around the dinner table to refill his father's mulled wine.

He'd deliberately laid off the painkillers today so he could have a drink himself. With everything that'd happened, it seemed like a long time since he'd last enjoyed himself, and so he wanted to give it a shot today.

Also, it helped with the nerves. There was a special guest arriving shortly.

'Thanks, son,' Richard said, lifting his filled glass.

When he sat down and reached for his glass, he noticed his father still had his glass raised. 'A toast. To my son, the hero.'

Barnett lowered his head.

'That girl is alive because of you.'

Barnett raised his glass but didn't make eye contact. 'Thank you.'

'Do you know how that makes me feel, son? It makes me feel proud.'

Awkward as this made *him* feel, Barnett held back on telling his father to stop. He was glad for his father's happiness.

Richard looked up and raised his glass in that direction. 'And she'll be *so* proud, too.'

Barnett noticed the tears in his father's eyes. He missed her every second of every day.

Later, while watching the King's speech, Richard turned to his son and said, 'She really didn't know about Clarissa.'

'I know, Dad,' Barnett said. 'You don't have to keep telling me that.'

'Even so, I need you to *really* know... I need you to *believe* it. The money they gave her... well... it led her here to me... and to you. If she'd have known, even for a second, that—'

'*Dad*, please, no need! Mum was special. End of.'

'She was that,' insisted Richard. 'She was indeed.'

Barnett stared at a picture of his mother on the mantelpiece and smiled. She was here. With them. And the memories of all their many Christmas Days together were part of this day too. The doorbell rang.

'Come on then,' Barnett said.

His father remained rooted to his chair.

Barnett stood, wincing. He held his hand out to his father.

Richard paled and looked away. 'I don't know if I can.'

'We've talked about—'

'But the shame I feel, son.'

Barnett inwardly sighed. There was no point. They'd been through it countless times. 'Okay Dad. Just wait here.'

Barnett went to the front door and opened it.

Clarissa, his half-sister, stood there, in a Christmas jumper, with a bottle of wine.

Barnett smiled. 'Merry Christmas. It's good to see you again.'

She returned his smile. 'Merry Christmas. I've an hour.' She proffered the wine. 'I thought we could have a glass, but it'll have to stop there as I'm driving.'

They embraced. It was only the third time they'd met, but they felt comfortable with each other.

'You know,' Clarissa had said at the end of their second visit. 'I feel now like I've always known you. Do you know what I mean?'

'I know *exactly* what you mean.'

Now, at the front door, he warned her about Richard. 'My father... he's nervous. I told you he would be.'

Clarissa nodded. 'I'll be gentle. It's not his fault.'

'I know,' Barnett said, 'but the man has a big heart. And his heart is still sore after Mum. And he feels *her* pain now. Feels the pain she'd have felt for letting you down.'

'She didn't let me down.'

'But if she'd known, she'd have felt that way...'

'I can see that,' Clarissa said, nodding.

'Anyway, shall we give it a whirl? We made it this far.' He led her by the hand into the lounge.

His father was already standing. His eyes were red from crying, and Barnett had to swiftly turn away to brush tears from his own eyes. He didn't want this to turn into an emotional outpouring.

'Mr Barnett. Merry Christmas. I'm pleased to meet you,' Clarissa said.

He came forward, slowly, as his hip had been playing up recently, and he took Clarissa's hands. Barnett could tell from the expression on his father's face what was happening.

He was *recognising*.

Clarissa looked like Amina.

'Excuse a foolish old man's tears,' Richard said. 'But you're beautiful, Clarissa. Your mother isn't here today, but I speak for both of us when I say we're very pleased to meet you.'

'Thank you.'

'We're also sorry. So dreadfully sorry—'

'Please...' she said. 'Please don't apologise. There's no need to.'

'Even so. We want to, Clarissa. We really want to. And you'll make us so happy if you let us.'

Clarissa said, her lips curving into a gentle, reassuring smile, 'Of course... I accept your apology.'

'Thank you,' he said, his face softening with relief and gratitude. 'Thank you so much.' He took a deep breath and rocked her hands. 'And now that is out of the way, my dear.' He looked over at the picture of his wife, a wistful expression crossing his features before turning his attention back to Clarissa, his eyes shining with warmth and curiosity. 'Please tell us everything about you. *Everything.* Or at least as much as you can remember. Start with your very first memory... and don't stop until you get to today.'

* * *

Feeling the heat of the prison corridor, Neville Fairweather took off his jacket, brushed snow from it and hooked it over one arm, while the guard unlocked the door.

Fairweather stepped into the room with the guard alongside him.

'Merry Christmas Jack. Nice haircut.'

Jack Moss, dressed in blue overalls, sat on the side of his bunk, looking down at the floor, running his hand over his shaven head.

Fairweather turned to the guard. 'I need ten minutes.'

'I can't leave—'

'I *need* ten minutes,' insisted Fairweather. 'And you *know* that isn't negotiable.'

The guard nodded and walked out. He turned at the door. 'Ten minutes,' he reiterated. 'No longer.'

Fairweather smiled over the guard's desperation to assert himself. Futile. But then, who could blame him? He had some challenging characters in this prison to keep in line.

Once the door was locked, Fairweather sat beside Jack. He started a timer on his watch for ten minutes, and then he joined Jack in regarding the floor. 'Merry Christmas, Jack,' he repeated.

Silence.

Eventually, after a time, Jack said, 'Christmas Day? Really?'

Fairweather looked at his watch. It'd taken him four minutes. Jack had proven himself, many times, to be a sociopath with an art for strategic patience. Four minutes was rather disappointing. He'd expected eight.

Fairweather regarded the bland room. *Must be something to do with the lack of stimulation.*

'Is solitary confinement because of *you*?' Jack asked.

Fairweather took a deep breath. 'You rarely exhibit a tone of voice, Jack. I can tell by your emphasis that you are irritated by this.'

'Christmas Day... protective custody... I wonder what could irritate me?'

'Sorry, have I interrupted your celebrations? Pray tell, what were the festivities you'd lined up?' Fairweather knew this would spark another couple of minutes of silence. He checked his watch. Hopefully, he wasn't cutting it too fine.

Two minutes and twenty-three seconds remained when Jack said, 'So, answer... why protective custody?'

'Well, it's that *or* dead, isn't it?'

'Has something changed?'

'No. Everything is the same. It's just time now. You knew that this day would come.'

Jack lifted his head, stared at the wall for a moment instead, and stood. He put his hands in the pockets of his overalls and strode forward. He turned back, smiling.

Don't pretend to be amused. You don't bother with such feelings. You're merely trying to irritate me because it feels right to do so after I've irritated you.

'Come now, we know each other well, yes?'

Jack raised an eyebrow.

'We're both as black and white as each other.' He looked at his watch. Under two minutes remaining. He stood. 'It's time for your death, *and* I don't want it to happen.'

'Oh,' Jack said, shrugging. 'Use your God-like powers to stop it?'

'Even a god has limits.' Fairweather laughed. 'No, but it's time to act.'

'Maybe you should have thought about that before...' He looked around his cell and held his wrists out together as if bound.

'You act simply by remaining alive.'

'Why are you so bothered about my life?'

'Would you believe me if I said you're like a son to me?'

'No. So tell me why?'

A minute left. 'No time, now. But if you lie down and die, then I can't protect your daughter any more.'

'You've never protected her.'

'Is that what you think? Do you wish to take that gamble?'

Jack edged forward. 'I never bet... How do we stop this supposed assassination attempt? I'm a sitting duck.'

Thirty seconds left. 'We take the target from the crosshairs.'

Jack gestured around him. 'You don't see a problem?'

'Walls are never a problem.'

'They're certainly boring the piss out of me. How then? How do I get out?'

'Your sister.'

Jack shook his head. 'Emma?'

'You have more than one?'

'She would—'

His watch buzzed. 'Oops. Time's up.'

The door swung open, and the guard stood there, looking stern.

'We wouldn't want to upset our host,' Fairweather said, smiling at Jack. 'Merry Christmas.'

'Is that it?' Jack said. 'Anything else?'

'No, not really. Just wanted to give you *fair* warning,' Fairweather said. 'No pun intended.' He gave a swift nod of the head and left with his coat still over his arm.

* * *

Following the Christmas meal, O'Brien remained with the children while Gardner went to the hospital. With a wrapped gift under one arm, a book by James Ellroy, an American crime author, Gardner worked her way through the hospital to her friend's ward.

Some unpleasant news greeted her at the tinsel-decorated reception. 'He's not having a good morning. He's perked up a little, but he's *still* exhausted. That said, you can stay as long as you want if you let him sleep. We try not to refuse company on Christmas Day.'

'I haven't got long, anyway...' Gardner sighed. 'I thought he was on the up.'

'The doctor is about if you'd like a chat?'

'That would be good, yes.'

'You head in, and I'll call him.'

Gardner headed into Riddick's room and stood over him. He looked out for the count. She put a hand on his upper arm, and a weak smile came over his face. 'Father Christmas?' Riddick's eyelids fluttered open. He looked up at Gardner groggily. 'Is it really you?'

'Piss off,' she said, pulling her hand back.

He laughed and opened his eyes fully. Then he winced, and his hand went to his stomach where Tommy Rose had wounded him. 'Why are you here? I told you not to come on Christmas Day. Who's with Rose and Ana?'

'Lucy...'

'Thick as thieves.'

Gardner nodded, avoiding eye contact for a moment. 'How could I leave you with no presents?' She placed the book on the bed beside him and sat.

'Actually, I've presents.' He pointed out some chocolates on the side. 'From Daz, my sponsor.'

'I've met him.'

'Oh, so you have.'

He then pointed out a James Patterson book. 'And that's from Cecile. Now, I know you've met her.' He winked. Riddick looked pale and weak. Until last week, he'd been far on the road to recovery, but a bacterial infection had set him back. One which had led to a nasty bout of myocarditis. The inflammation in his heart muscle had caused genuine problems, and he was still undergoing tests to see how severe the damage was. He was keeping up a brave face, but Gardner could tell that he was struggling. His lips trembled as he spoke, and his voice broke, occasionally.

'Daz will be back later, too.'

Gardner nodded. 'Yes... good, but if it's too much, tell him to go. You need to keep resting.'

'Yes, boss,' Riddick said, grinning.

'I'm not your boss. Been there, done that...'

'Got the blood-stained T-shirt...' Riddick finished.

Gardner smiled. 'Something like that.'

Riddick said, 'Anyway... I've been thinking... you know, about whether you fancy giving it another shot?'

'What exactly?'

'Partners... working together.'

'Partners... is that what we were? Felt like a babysitting gig.'

'Easy tiger.'

'Anyway, it's a bit early to be discussing that, don't you think?'

'Nearly dying gives you some perspective. I need to do something... something *good*.'

'Saving four children from trafficking was good...'

'So, you're condoning my actions?' Riddick asked.

'Not your methods, no. But what you did was special, I can't deny it.'

'Special!' Riddick said. 'I leave a trail of carnage wherever I go. I'm sure you've said that to me before, too.'

'Probably. Cecile claimed you tried to save Tommy's life after he overdosed?'

'Did she?' Riddick asked, looking away. 'She probably remembers more than me. I was out of it.'

'Said he stabbed you, left you for dead and then injected himself. When he convulsed, you crawled over to help him.'

'It's a blur,' Riddick said.

Gardner eyed him up. She knew some suspected this narrative as a falsehood, but with four saved children to his name, it was a hot potato for stringent investigation.

She, herself, couldn't shake off her own suspicions. In the past, Riddick had paid for the murder of his family's killer. Was it outside the realm of possibility that he'd taken the law into his own hands again?

She'd tried to bring it up with Cecile, but she had shut her down with, 'You told me Paul was a good man. Lost, but good. You were right.' That was all she was prepared to say on the matter.

'So, let's see what this is,' Riddick said, reaching over and unwrapping the gift. 'Shit. Used to read this guy all the time. Thanks. I'm sorry I've got nothing for you.'

'Your health will do me.'

'Yeah, about that...' He thought for a moment. 'I think I'm on the mend. And when I'm mended, I want to come back. Have I said that already?'

She snorted. 'Yes, you have.'

Eventually, he grew tired, and his eyes closed. She leaned forward and kissed him on the head. 'I'm letting you rest now.'

'Okay,' he said. 'Thank you for coming.'

'I enjoyed it.'

She reached out and took his hand, and he opened his eyes. They stared at each other for a moment, before his eyes closed again. Once he was asleep, she kissed him on his hand, released it, and then kissed him on the forehead a second time. 'See you tomorrow, mate.'

Outside, Doctor Steepleman was waiting for her.

She'd met him several times before. A rather young doctor with a nervous energy and a jovial demeanour. He led her down a corridor and buzzed around a couple of rooms until he found an empty one for them to sit in.

They began with some pleasantries. It transpired that he was in the first year of his divorce and didn't have the children today for the first time, so he'd volunteered his services.

She'd never have guessed his pain until he said this; he always looked so joyous.

'That's good of you,' Gardner said.

'Distraction,' he said and smiled. 'And I like it here. Did Paul talk to you about his health?'

'Said he was on the mend.'

Steepleman nodded. 'Nothing else?'

'If there's something wrong, you'll have to tell me. He's the most secretive pillock I've ever met.'

Steepleman smiled. Judging by how quickly the smile then fell away, bad news was afoot.

He clasped his hands together and took a deep breath. 'The myocarditis did a lot more damage than we'd expected. The tests have shown it to be rather extensive, in fact. He's faring well, considering. The fever keeps flaring though, and he's having a lot of chest pain.'

Gardner nodded. 'Okay... secretive pillock... like I said. So, what now? Medicine... rest...?'

Doctor Steepleman sat back in his chair and fixed her with a stare.

To Gardner, who was used to reading people daily, this was like a punch in the face.

'Don't...' Gardner said, straightening up. 'Don't you dare... He can't...'

'No, wait,' Steepleman said, holding up his hands. 'I'm sorry. Don't misunderstand me. It's bad, yes, but there's hope... a chance.'

She suddenly felt like she might just throw up.

She squeezed her eyes closed. 'I'm sorry... Please, what's wrong with him?'

'He needs a heart transplant, Emma.' Steepleman reached over and took her hand. 'If we can get him a heart transplant soon... then we—'

But Gardner didn't hear the next words because the world suddenly seemed to collapse around her.

* * *

Gardner looked at herself in the mirror in the hospital bathroom. It was obvious she'd been crying hard, but unless she stayed in here for another hour, she wasn't shaking off the evidence.

She walked straight back to Riddick's room and looked through the window, watching him sleep, before whispering something under her breath and turning away.

All the way down the corridor, out of the hospital, and through the car park, those words she'd said replayed in her mind.

And even when she'd left the car park and had driven right back to her drive, the words remained on a loop.

She lowered her head to the steering wheel.

I love you.

After crying for a while, she lifted her head and took a deep breath. *You'll be fine, Paul.* She caught her bloodshot eyes in the rear-view mirror. *I'll make sure of it.*

ACKNOWLEDGEMENTS

Bringing to life that complex and stormy bond between Gardner and Riddick is not the easiest of challenges. I am indebted, as always, to my wonderful editorial team, Emily Ruston, Candida Bradford, Susan Sugden, for their guidance and faith in my abilities.

To my children, my eternal wellsprings of inspiration and joy, I thank you for the countless smiles you bring to my face. My gratitude extends to the rest of my family, Jo included, for their ceaseless encouragement and understanding of the frustrating daydreamer nestled in the corner.

I also extend my heartfelt appreciation to all bloggers and ARC readers, especially Kath, Donna and Sharon.

So, until our next meeting when Gardner and Riddick's relationship faces its toughest challenge yet, enjoy the stunning North Yorkshire scenery.

ABOUT THE AUTHOR

Wes Markin is the bestselling author of the DCI Yorke crime novels set in Salisbury. His new series for Boldwood stars the pragmatic detective DCI Emma Gardner who will be tackling the criminals of North Yorkshire. Wes lives in Harrogate and the first book in The Yorkshire Murders series was published in November 2022.

Sign up to Wes Markin's mailing list for news, competitions and updates on future books.

Visit Wes Markin's website: <u>wesmarkinauthor.com</u>

Follow Wes on social media:

        x.com/MarkinWes
        facebook.com/WesMarkinAuthor

ALSO BY WES MARKIN

The Yorkshire Murders

The Viaduct Killings

The Lonely Lake Killings

The Crying Cave Killings

The Graveyard Killings

The Winter Killings

DCI Michael Yorke thrillers

One Last Prayer

The Repenting Serpent

The Silence of Severance

Rise of the Rays

Dance with the Reaper

Christmas with the Conduit

Better the Devil

Jake Pettman Thrillers

The Killing Pit

Fire in Bone

Blue Falls

The Rotten Core

Rock and a Hard Place

THE
Murder
LIST

THE MURDER LIST IS A NEWSLETTER DEDICATED TO ALL THINGS CRIME AND THRILLER FICTION!

SIGN UP TO MAKE SURE YOU'RE ON OUR HIT LIST FOR GRIPPING PAGE-TURNERS AND HEARTSTOPPING READS.

SIGN UP TO OUR
NEWSLETTER

BIT.LY/THEMURDERLISTNEWS

Boldwood

Boldwood Books is an award-winning fiction publishing company seeking out the best stories from around the world.

Find out more at www.boldwoodbooks.com

Join our reader community for brilliant books, competitions and offers!

Follow us
@BoldwoodBooks
@TheBoldBookClub

Sign up to our weekly deals newsletter

https://bit.ly/BoldwoodBNewsletter